AN UNEXPECTED ENCOUNTER

"What a delightful day this has become and how terribly misinformed I have been"—the stranger paused and let his eyes rove over her lips—"for there is great sport indeed to be had in the country!"

Kate's brown eyes spit fire but he wasted no time in kissing her quite thoroughly, much to her surprise. Her first inclination, to free herself at all costs, only caused him to tighten his hold on her. And then, her body betraying her, she found her arms suddenly encircling her captor and embracing him as though she had been with him thus many times before. What heaven!

His lips, so rough at first, were now a tender, searching poem and she had the oddest, most urgent desire to remain within the circle of his arms fovever. With a start, she realized that the way she felt, tucked so carefully against him, was the way Lord Ashwell's poetry made her feel. . . .

DISCOVER THE MAGIC
OF ZEBRA'S REGENCY ROMANCES!

THE DUCHESS AND THE DEVIL   (2264, $2.95)
by Sydney Ann Clary

Though forced to wed Deveril St. John, the notorious "Devil Duke," lovely Byrony Balmaine swore never to be mastered by the irrepressible libertine. But she was soon to discover that the human heart — and Satan — move in very mysterious ways!

AN OFFICER'S ALLIANCE   (2239, $3.95)
by Violet Hamilton

Virginal Ariel Frazier's only comfort in marrying Captain Ian Montague was that it put her in a superb position to spy for the British. But the rakish officer was a proven master at melting a woman's reserve and breaking down her every defense!

BLUESTOCKING BRIDE   (2215, $2.95)
by Elizabeth Thornton

In the Marquis of Rutherson's narrow view, a woman's only place was in a man's bed. Well, beautiful Catherine Harland may have been just a sheltered country girl, but the astonished Marquis was about to discover that she was the equal of any man — and could give as good as she got!

BELOVED AVENGER   (2192, $3.95)
by Mary Brendan

Sir Clifford Moore could never forget what Emily's family had done to him. How ironic that the family that had stolen his inheritance now offered him the perfect means to exact his vengeance — by stealing the heart of their beloved daughter!

A NOBLE MISTRESS   (2169, $3.95)
by Janis Laden

When her father lost the family estate in a game of piquet, practical Moriah Lanson did not hesitate to pay a visit to the winner, the notorious Viscount Roane. Struck by her beauty, Roane suggested a scandalous way for Moriah to pay off her father's debt — by becoming the Viscount's mistress!

Available wherever paperbacks are sold, or order direct from the Publisher. Send cover price plus 50¢ per copy for mailing and handling to Zebra Books, Dept. 2625, 475 Park Avenue South, New York, N.Y. 10016. Residents of New York, New Jersey and Pennsylvania must include sales tax. DO NOT SEND CASH.

A Rogue's Masquerade

VALERIE KING

ZEBRA BOOKS
KENSINGTON PUBLISHING CORP.

ZEBRA BOOKS

are published by

Kensington Publishing Corp.
475 Park Avenue South
New York, NY 10016

First printing: April, 1989

Printed in the United States of America

Chapter One

Kate moved slowly along the path, her eyes riveted to the first line of Lord Ashwell's famous poem, *Ode to Morning's Light*. Overhead, the tall, canopied beech trees rustled as a cool breeze shook each leaf. But Kate was unaware of the breeze or the woods, only the poem. She sighed, nearly dropping her favorite fowling piece as she read the line again then closed the book. How easy it was to forget the manor when she read Ashwell's poetry, to forget Jaspar's cutting remarks, to forget his mounting debts.

Pressing the worn volume of poetry to her breast, Kate regretted that her morning solitude was drawing to a close and whistled her dogs in. Three white hounds, tongues lolling from their mouths, broke suddenly through the ivy that filled the forest floor, their eyes sparkling with pleasure. Kate snapped her fingers, bringing them all to heel as she placed her book carefully in an ancient leather satchel that she wore slung across her large blue coat.

A man's coat. How shocked Mary would be if she could see her. But no one would see her. Every morning she rose early to hunt, dressing herself in breeches, top boots, shirt and coat, and a farmer's hat pulled down about her ears, covering her thick auburn hair. But she did not fear discovery, for none of the gentry families in any of the villages surrounding the small market town of Stinchfield ever rose before ten in the morning. And even if she had been caught in her unmaidenly pursuits, most of the matrons of her acquaintance would have

5

merely sighed deeply, as though Kate had been the greatest disappointment in their lives, and let her go on her way. She was Jaspar's daughter, after all, and with Marianne dead in her grave these five years and more, what was to be expected?

Glancing up at the sky that shone in deep blue patches through the thick leaves of the beechwood, Kate could see that the sun had nearly risen over Cowley Hill above Chipping Fosseworth, and she knew that her adventure ought not to last but a few minutes more. She began retracing her steps toward the manor, the dogs in tow, when she realized she had not delivered the few vegetables that she carried in her satchel for Mrs. Coates, who lived in the village of Quening. Mrs. Coates was expecting her eighth baby, and though her husband had steady work on the Earl of Sapperton's tenanted land, the family existed in a tiny cottage and would barely have enough food to eat this winter with the price of wheat soaring since the corn laws were passed the year before.

The fowling piece tucked beneath her arm and a brace of pheasants slung over her shoulder, Kate peered into her satchel, shifting the pheasants slightly and wondering what she should do with the tomatoes. They would not last another day for they were fully ripe, though the carrots and two turnips would keep.

Kate halted in her tracks and muttered a most unladylike sentiment beneath her breath. "Damn and blast!" It was assuredly too late to be traipsing through the open countryside now, dressed as she was. Though she might not give a fig for the neighbours' opinion of her conduct, still, she had rather not set up their backs if she could help it.

The dogs bounded ahead and Kate resumed her steps. She drew the tomatoes from the satchel, suddenly concerned lest they spoil her beloved volume of poetry, and found herself still at a loss as what to do with them. Better give them to the Cook, she decided, and she kicked a rock from the well-travelled path that, though thick with trees, still ran rather close to the lane.

Since she was returning to the manor, the dogs had already disappeared from sight. Kate heard the familiar crunching sound of Lord Sapperton's curricle moving at a spanking pace down the lane and felt a sudden fear that he might see her through the thick trees.

Nearly squashing the tomatoes between her long, fair fingers at the mere thought of the earl, Kate raced for cover, lest Sapperton discover her, and hid behind a thicket. Peering through the dense growth of the holly shrub, dusty from infrequent rains, Kate could not quite make out the crest on the door of the light travelling vehicle.

Her heart began to pound in her ears as a most unconscionable and childish idea suggested itself. Oh, but she could not! But then, Sapperton, who treated his villagers with contempt and strove to keep the cost of wheat high, deserved such ill-treatment.

Dropping the pheasants on the ground along with her fowling piece, Kate stopped breathing for a moment so that she might be able to hear the crunching of the wheels on the rock and so determine how close the carriage had come.

Louder. Louder still. She resumed breathing and placed two tomatoes in her left hand and the third in her right. And in her nervousness it was all Kate could do to keep from squishing the dark red fruit through her fingers. As the crunching of horses' hooves and wheels echoed through the woods, Kate's heart seemed ready to burst from her chest and her liquid brown eyes became focussed quite strangely on the minutest details of the pointed holly leaves in front of her.

The carriage drew close and Kate, feeling the weight of the tomatoes rise and fall in each hand as she handled them with practiced pumping movements, emerged from her hiding place and let them fly. Her aim true, the tomatoes met their mark. But by the time the second mushy orb hit the driver's cheek and trailed down his neckcloth, and just before the third one toppled the tall black hat from the same gentleman's head, Kate knew she had erred.

The man bore no resemblance to Sapperton at all, and the second man in the carriage, who quickly took reins that were shoved so suddenly upon him, was equally unknown to her.

Finding her feet frozen to the forest floor, Kate watched with growing horror as the driver catapulted himself from the gentleman's sporting vehicle, his bottle-green coat dripping

7

with red splotches. He was tall and rather broad-shouldered, and Kate realized that should he catch her, he would not have the least difficulty, even with her own queenly lines, in exacting whatever punishment he wished.

With a strange, mute fascination, Kate observed his approach, her brown eyes wide and unblinking. He was quite handsome in a rugged way, and the nearer he drew Kate realized he was shouting a long string of obscenities that would certainly match any she had on numerous occasions watched roll from her papa's inebriated lips.

But the moment the stranger leaped the low stone wall that separated the road from the woods Katherine's innate sense of survival overtook her sluggardly feet and she turned, sharply, picking up her fowling piece and the pheasants, and raced back down the path that had been her childhood haunt for the better part of her twenty years. If she could but reach the manor, she would be safe!

Encumbered with the long rifle and her bag of shot bouncing against her hip, Kate still felt that she could outrun the man. She was used to a great deal of physical exertion and the back of her horse was as familiar to her as was every room of the manor. But she heard the stranger behind her and realized that he was quite a determined creature.

Suddenly, she felt hunted. Filled with an unbearable panic as though to be caught meant certain death, Kate knew, really for the first time, how desperate the poor fox must feel during a lively hunt. And even though she could reason that, at worst, he would merely thrash her soundly, Kate still felt her heart urge her on.

The obscenities that originally trailed behind her as she passed ferns, bramble, and ivy had long since ceased, only to be replaced by the purposeful footfalls of elegant Hessians on the well-worn path. These dull thuds, along with the heaving breaths of her pursuer, pressed Kate on, her arms flailing in all directions as she struck at low-lying branches and straggling vines. The pheasants slipped from her shoulders, and when a bramble caught her hand, she cried out in pain. Fifty yards in front of her she could see the clearing that meant the home farm. Just a few yards more and he would have to give up chase, for the labourers were in the fields and she could see her maid's brother driving the sheep across the narrow valley to pasture. If only the dogs had remained with her!

And then she felt a pressure at the back of her neck as the stranger caught her, pulling her up short by the coat and flinging her, without any consideration for her person, backward, where she landed with a great thud on her posterior.

Her cry of pain brought the large gentleman around to stand in front of her, his hands on his knees as he bent from the waist to ease his breathing. "And I've not finished with you yet, you impudent whelp!"

His rich voice filled the woods and Kate pressed her hat further down over her auburn curls. Looking him over with great care, she knew instinctively, by his stature, by the firmness to the set of his mouth, and by the sharp anger in his blue eyes, that he meant every word he spoke. But she also knew that whatever he would do to a boy caught in such a prank, he would exact a far more formidible revenge on a female. This thought caused her to feign the country's accent and to lower the timbre of her voice a trifle, "I meant no 'arm, sir. Truly I dinnit. Only a bit of fun!"

"And you've damned near ruined my coat, my neckcloth, and my hat for your little sport!" he shouted, his blue eyes flashing at her.

"But 'twere a mistake only, sir! I thought you was somebody else. I thought you was Lord Sapperton come back from the watering 'ole at Cheltenham!"

The man stared at her in surprise and Kate wondered if she sounded too much like a female. But his response eased her fear. "Sapperton! Do not tell me that scapegrace inhabits these woods?"

Kate smiled. Really, she began to like the gentleman. "Aye, that he does. His lands march along these hills and all about Stinchfield. We call 'im Sapperton of Stenchfield, we do." And she jerked her thumb backward toward Knott Hill.

The gentleman seemed to weigh something in his mind. Straightening his back and pulling a kerchief from the pocket of his green coat, he began wiping the sweat from his brow and the red pulpy stains from his cheek and neckcloth. He laughed,

9

"Since we seem to hold his lordship in some sort of similar dislike, I shall forgive this incident."

Kate felt halfway home now as she released a great sigh. She then made a grand mistake, for she offered up her hand to him by way of asking for his assistance in lifting her to her feet, something a boy would never do.

Eyeing her for only a brief second, he took the hand, pulling her up to stand before him, and with a smile that overspread his features in a truly naughty expression, he cried, "By all that's wonderful! A female!" He laughed aloud, his voice echoing about the woods.

The sun, now overhead, filtered throught the beech trees in sudden brilliant flashes about his tall person, so that he appeared like Zeus who had just captured a wandering wood nymph. "Now, what the deuce are you doing masquerading as some country boy?" And without releasing her hand, he pulled the hat from her head and watched, in quite obvious delight, as her auburn curls tumbled about her shoulders and down her back.

Kate tried to wrench her hand free, but he held her securely and gathered her up in his arms, holding her tightly to his chest. "Faith! 'Tis a beauty beneath that layer of dirt."

"Oh, let me go, do!" Kate cried, trying without any success to wriggle free of his embrace.

"Now, what is this? Your words bespeak a lady of quality, but that is quite impossible! Or is this another masquerade you are foisting on me, for you performed the boy remarkably well. And don't try to humbug me, for I must say that no respectable female would wear a man's clothing, however noble the deed!"

"You are right!" Kate responded in some heat, for she did not like the man's tone as he spoke to her. "I am not in the least respectable. In fact, I am of no importance at all, so now you may release your arms and return to me my liberty."

He looked at her, his blue eyes twinkling. "Not until I have punished you but a little."

Clearly, he thought her nothing less than one of the serving wenches in that seedy tavern beyond Chipping Fosseworth. Indignation rose in her breast and she retorted, quite without thinking how her choice of words, learned most unfortunately at her papa's knee, would affect the gentleman. "Damn you, man, let me be!" Her drawing-room manners completely forgotten, Kate tried to bite his arm and struggled again to free herself.

"A shrew!" he cried, laughing at her. "And how's this? You dress as a boy and curse as well?"

Kate realized that she had just given him every reason to believe that she was of low birth and found she could not answer him.

He continued, "What a delightful day this has become and how terribly misinformed I have been." He paused and let his eyes rove over her lips. And in a low, husky voice, he added, "For there is great sport indeed to be had in the country!"

Kate's nostrils flared and her brown eyes spit fire. "Hell and damnation, man, let me go! I vow I have never been so insulted in my life! You are a boor and a cur, and if you don't release me, I swear I shall tell my papa of your scurvy treatment and see if he does not call you out!"

The gentleman lifted a brow at these words. "I am completely mystified to make you out, my beauty. But I confess I have never heard so many curses spoken so prettily. How do you manage it?"

Kate bit her lip. He apparently knew just what to say to make her laugh, for even though she was furious with his high-handed manner, something in the way he had pursued her through the woods, in his not behaving at all like a gentleman should, and certainly in turning her improper speech off with just such a light remark, pleased her immensely. None of the young bucks of her acquaintance would ever have done so, and she always had the impression that though she had learned to adopt most of society's veneer, they were secretly afraid of her.

The gentleman did not mistake her expression of amusement and cried, "There! I see by the enchantment writ on your fair, perfect features that we shall soon become friends." He then wasted no time in kissing her quite thoroughly, much to Kate's surprise.

Her first inclination, to free herself at all costs, only caused him to tighten his hold on her. This surprised her, too, for she was not a particularly small female, and her own preference for

11

horses, hunting, and any manner of sport added just that strength to her limbs, which would have been a match for any of the gentlemen she knew.

And then, her body betraying her, she found her arms suddenly encircling the stranger and embracing him as though she had been with him thus several times before. What heaven! Kate disappeared into his arms, the closeness of his entire person somehow affecting every sense like some strange opiate. She clung to him and her mind refused to put coherent thoughts together, as though she had fallen under some witch's spell. Sapperton had kissed her once and she had loathed it. Why, then, could she be held by a perfect stranger, a rogue at that, and wish that the forest would close in about them and never let them leave?

His lips, so rough at first, were now a tender, searching poem, and she had the oddest, most urgent desire to remain within the circle of his embrace forever. With a start, Kate realized that the way she felt, tucked so carefully in his arms, was how Lord Ashwell's poetry made her feel.

But when she opened her eyes, the piercing blue ones that met her bemused gaze were laughing at her. Suddenly, the horror of what she had done, the wrongness of it all, seemed to take every precious and newly discovered sensation and cover it with dirt. She pulled away from him abruptly.

"Will you now be shy and maidenly?" he taunted her, his lips now twisted into a careless smile.

Kate knew that she deserved such censure and cried, "I am not, it is not! You are wrong in what you are thinking!"

But he only laughed at her, a sound she found utterly impossible to endure and said, "You are certainly the most despicable man I have ever met."

He advanced on her again, apparently believing that her words were an invitation to accost her a second time, and she kicked his shin with as much force as she could summon. He backed away immediately, and Kate had all the delight of watching him hop about and resume his earlier cursing.

Kate wasted no time in waiting for the stranger to recover, and she quickly picked up her fowling piece, the pheasants, and her hat. Angry that her dogs had abandoned her at so necessary

12

a moment, she offered a curse of her own and tore down the path toward the manor, to Jaspar and to safety.

The moment Kate reached the solitude of her bedchamber, her sides aching from having run the entire distance to the manor, she tore the dark blue coat from her body as though it had been infested with vermin. Her breath came in great gasps as she pulled at her neckcloth, nearly strangling herself in a frantic effort to remove the offending length of white linen. Fear and shame vied for supremacy in her mind—to be caught, to be kissed. How stupid, how foolish, how utterly unmaidenly she felt, and she kicked a footstool out of her path. The tough leather of her scuffed top boots caught the underneath of the stool, and the practiced kick resulted in a hard smash against the panelled wall. And how satisfying to see two most disagreeable watercolors come crashing to the floor.

"Damn and blast!" she cursed at the walls, stamping along the oaken floorboards and working with stumbling success at the buttons of her shirt. She nearly popped them from their moorings on the white linen, her fingers trembling from her recent adventure.

The muffled blast of a fowling piece, fired somewhere on the manor lands, distracted Kate for a moment and she moved to the leaded windows to gaze out at the countryside. How much she loved her Cotswolds—the green hills dotted with sheep, the village that rested in a comfortable nest but half a mile from the manor, the trails through the hills all about Stinchfield that she had traversed since she was able to mount a horse.

Another blast. No doubt Christopher Barnsley had decided to endear himself to some of Chipping Fosseworth's housewives by ridding the valley of a few more rabbits. Not only was a great deal of precious garden fare salvaged, but the extra meat was a welcome addition to any villager's meager table.

Wishing that she were out with Kit as a third shot shook the leaded panes, Kate turned back to the business at hand and, catching sight of herself in the mirror, blushed to the roots of her auburn hair. Unbuttoning the linen cuffs, she took in her reflection. Breeches, boots, shirt. And what was that in her hair? Oh, Lord, tomato seeds! How was it possible she had given in to so childish an impulse, as though with such an effort she

13

could have altered, one whit, Lord Sapperton's miserable treatment of his tenants at Quening. And then to have her prank take so unexpected and scandalous a turn! What would Lady Chalford say if she knew?

When another shot rattled the glass panes, Kate turned abruptly back to the window and realized, with a start, that the repeated shots were coming from the vicinity of the home farm. Barnsley would never hunt rabbits on Jaspar's land and Jaspar, who loved to hunt anything that moved about on a completely optional number of legs, was still in Cheltenham.

She now found herself concerned, for even the gardener, who prided himself so completely on his intricate and noiseless traps, would not be firing the fowling piece. As it was, Kate suddenly had the most clear premonition that something was amiss, and when a scurry of feet down the hall stopped abruptly outside her bedchamber, followed by a sharp rapping on her door, she knew all was not well.

"Miss, miss!" the high, shrill voice of her maid sounded through the thick wood.

Kate called for her to enter, and the maid threw the door open in such a hysterical manner and entered the room in such a wild state that Kate thought Sarah Siddons could not have effected a more dramatic entrance.

Her cheeks red from the exertion of running and her dark hair sticking out in wild tufts from beneath her mobcap, Maggie exclaimed, "Oh, miss, come quickly. Your papa. Do come quickly!"

She then stopped abruptly, her arms, which had been flailing about suddenly falling to her sides as she looked Kate up and down and cried, in a long, drawn-out fashion, "Miss."

"You must forget what you are seeing, Maggie, or I shall certainly whip you at the carttails if I discover otherwise." And after eyeing her maid with a severe expression, Kate scrambled into her faded blue muslin gown.

"Miss," Maggie repeated again, awestruck at having discovered her mistress in so unmaidenly a costume.

"Maggie!" Kate rebuked her sharply.

Maggie dropped a curtsy, her country accent a sweet, familiar sound to Kate's ear, "A pox on me and m'family if ever

14

a word of what I seen crosses m'lips. I always thought p'rhaps ye hunted but I never knew ye dressed as a lad!"

Kate stripped off the stockings and breeches and, ignoring her maid's comments, said, "Now, tell me what has happened. Who is firing the fowling piece? I take it Mr. Barnsley is not about?"

"Mr. Barnsley? Oh, no, miss. 'Tis the squire. He done come home not an hour since, swearing and reeling about like a ship caught in a storm, and Cook done fainted away when he set about firing his piece."

Kate stood staring at her maid for some time. Jaspar was not expected back for two more days. A sick feeling took hold of her stomach as she turned away from Maggie and, in a quiet voice, begged the maid to button her gown.

As Maggie struggled with the eleven cloth-covered buttons, Kate said, "Now, why has Cook fainted? I should think she would be delighted at having fresh rabbit."

"Rabbit?" the maid asked in astonishment. "But ye don't understand, miss. The squire has got into the henhouse. He's been shooting the chickens and Cook says they'll be off laying for a fortnight or more! You must come and make it all right!"

At these words, Kate cried, "He's shooting our hens?"

Maggie nodded and said, "Cook told me to fetch ye!"

Kate looked in the mirror and brushed her untidy hair in quick, jerky strokes that did little more than rearrange her disordered locks, "But I thought you said Cook had fainted?"

"I did, miss, but Cook opened one eye—and a frightful eye it is, if ye take my meaning—and bid me fetch ye!"

Kate choked in spite of her intentions to ignore Maggie's improper speech. And when another blast sounded from the vicinity of the henhouse, Kate felt that the dissarray of her hair had little importance whatsoever compared to the dreadful fate of her laying hens. With Maggie following closely behind, Kate hurried to the home farm.

As they raced for the henhouse, another blast shook the afternoon air, and the desperate screeching and squawking of chickens sent Kate tearing past the succession houses and around the side of the barn to the henhouse, where she threw the gate open and stopped still in her tracks. She felt completely uncertain as to whether she should laugh or cry. The chickens had crowded into one corner of the pen. Blackened holes in the grain barrels smoked from Jaspar's recent assault, and the fence itself was considerably peppered with shot.

But worse than this was the dreadful sight of her father, in his altitudes, reeling about the henhouse with a stupid smile on his face. At the moment, he was attempting to reload the rifle, and Kate now felt a great deal of awe that he had gotten off as many shots as he had given his current state.

But as he prepared to ram the shot down into the wide-lipped bore of his favorite fowling piece, Kate cried, "Jaspar! What are you about? Put that blunderbuss down at once! At once!"

Jaspar Draycott, squire and gentleman, raised bleary eyes and a droopy smile to his daughter and said thickly, "Now, Kate, don't spoil my sport! I've been flushing these pheasants for nigh on an hour."

He then shoved the long rod down into the mouth of the rifle, his every faculty concentrating on this difficult task.

Kate went over to him, gently took the fowling piece out of his unsteady hands, and set it on the gravelly ground. Supporting him with one arm and looking at him in a sorrowful way, she said, "Papa, you are in the henhouse!"

"What? Nay, but you must be mistaken!" He then laughed and fell over on his side, nearly bringing his daughter down with him. His eyes rolled once or twice before they closed, and Kate thought that never had his mouth formed into so silly a grin.

Kate quietly turned back to the maid and bade her return to the house to see if Cook was feeling better. Dropping to her knees, heedless of soiling her serviceable and quite ancient muslin gown that had already seen too many summers, Kate placed a gentle kiss on her father's lined and stubbly cheek. "Oh Jaspar, what am I to do with you?"

He stirred once, opening his eyes to squint at her. How rheumy his eyes looked as his gaze travelled to the chickens that were still huddled in a corner of the pen. When his rather blank stare returned to Kate, his smile disappeared and his bleary eyes suddenly grew quite red.

16

Struggling to a sitting position and pushing away Kate's effort to help him, he bellowed, "Can't a man even enjoy a little sport without a female nagging and pulling at him?"

As Jaspar tottered to his feet, Kate hurried to support his arms, but he shook it off. Brushing at the dust of his burgundy velvet coat, the squire rose to his most stately height and trod unsteadily out of the pen.

Kate's heart sank as she followed in his wake. His demeanor toward her, his bluff, angry words, meant only one thing: He had been gaming again—and all night, by the looks of him— and the hall stood in greater danger than ever of succumbing to an increasing pile of gambling debts. How much more she could bear this battle with creditors and debts, she could not imagine.

Kate caught up with her father and pulled at his arm. "Jaspar," she pleaded.

But he jerked his arm away, stumbling backward. Kate paused at the anger on his face as he spoke. "I'll have none of your lectures, miss." He appeared as though he wished to say more, but looking beyond her, he suddenly swore beneath his breath, "Hell and damnation!" Turning on his heel, he made for the manor as fast as a man might who was in his cups.

Kate wheeled abruptly and saw what her choleric parent had objected to, for there, coming down the lane in a sensible landau and pair, was her dear friend Mary Chalford and her sister, Lydia. Jaspar was not in the least socially inclined, and after a sennight's adventure in Cheltenham, he positively refused to receive callers for another week.

Kate immediately began to walk toward the landau, waving and feeling grateful for their timely arrival. Jaspar was never easy to deal with, but when he was drunk, he was impossible.

The younger of the two pretty Chalford misses fairly bounced in her seat, her sixteen summers evident in her nearly uncontrollable exuberance as she squealed, "Kate! Kate! You will never guess what has happened! Never!"

The landau, driven by a large servant named John, came to a stop as Kate arrived at the lane and greeted her visitors. She smoothed down her hair but had little confidence that she had effected the least improvement. With all the strange events of

17

the morning, she dared not think how oddly put together she would appear and only hoped that Mary and Lydia would ignore her untidy coiffure.

In this she was wrong, for Lydia, a tall, handsome young lady with dark brown hair and sparkling blue eyes, looked her over, gasped, and said, "Good heavens, what has happened to you? I know that in general you do not care for the notice of others, but Kate! You look quite nohow, and what is that in your hair?"

"Lydia!" Mary responded in a clipped voice. "You go too far!"

Kate pulled her long curls forward and saw what Lydia had referred to. Inwardly, she crumbled. More tomato seeds! "I—I daresay when I was in the succession house this morning—"

Mary broke in, "You needn't explain, Kate. We all know how involved you are in the management of your home."

Receiving a jolt to her ribs, Lydia added, "I do beg your pardon. I have been very rude." And then, in her heedless manner, she continued, "And now I have gotten so completely distracted, I almost forgot! We've the most astonishing news! And we've come here directly to tell you!"

Mary pressed her sister's arm, glancing in a meaningful way at John Coachman's broad back, and begged Lydia to be silent. Mary was rather short, kept her light brown hair coiffed in pretty curls about her face, and had eyes that were light blue. She was as unlike Lydia as sisters could be, both girls sharing only one thing—the same engaging smile they had inherited from their papa.

But the younger Miss Chalford, on the far side of the coach, merely shook off Mary's hand and, leaning across her in a confiding way toward Kate, said, "Oh stuff, Mary! As though John Coachman does not know all about it anyway!"

Kate heard the coachman cough in a suspicious manner as Lydia continued, "Guess who arrived in Chipping Fosseworth? Oh, you will never guess, not in a lifetime would you believe who has actually come here!" And in a dramatic manner, her hands folded and pressed to her bosom, she pretended to swoon into her sister's shoulder as she cried, "The poet,

18

Lord Ashwell!"

Kate heard these words as though she had just been kicked in the stomach by a thoroughly spirited horse. "Lord Ashwell?" she queried in a faint voice, looking from one sister to the other.

Mary opened her mouth to speak, but Lydia could not restrain herself, "Oh, Mary, do look! I believe Kate will faint! You must lend her your vinaigrette!" She then chortled in glee as she clapped her gloved hands, "Isn't it the most amazing news imaginable?"

Kate was so astonished that she could only repeat again, "Ashwell? Lord Ashwell, the poet?"

Finally, Mary spoke, her modulated voice at variance with Lydia's intense excitement, "Yes. He and a friend, a Mr. Buckland, have just now arrived at the Swan and Goose." She smiled, her rather close-set blue eyes direct and serene, "I knew you would be pleased. I know how much you have enjoyed his poems."

Kate could scarcely believe her ears and searched both of their faces, wondering if they were hoaxing her. And though she could readily believe that Lydia would be capable of such a deception, Mary would not. Was it possible? Was it truly possible that here, in so deserted a corner of England, in her very own woods and skies, cornfields and hayfields, so perfect, so exciting a poet should suddenly appear? It could not be true! But she read in Mary's face that it was true. Kate felt her soul tear from her body and soar into the air at the very thought of meeting one whose work she worshipped. Her heart flying, her soul wafting along the winds, she saw in her mind's eye Jaspar calling upon the poet at the earliest opportunity, shaking hands with him, conversing with him, inviting him to the manor.

But what was this? Her soul, in mid-flight, plummeted suddenly toward the earth with something Lydia was saying. And when she heard the words "reddish stains on his neckcloth," her soul landed squarely into the middle of a fine cabbage patch.

"What was that, Lydia?" Kate asked weakly, resting a hand on the carriage door to support herself.

19

"I was saying that the reddish stains on his neckcloth and green coat presented the oddest appearance. Did they not, Mary? And I could not but wonder if he had perhaps fought a duel or something that morning, for you must know that he looked just the sort of man, all dark and roguish, who would fight duels."

Kate gulped. Was it possible? In a small voice she asked, "Lord Ashwell had stains upon his neckcloth?"

"Kate, you are not attending to me in the least! Not Ashwell! His companion! That Buckland fellow." Squeezing her sister's arm, Lydia continued, "And wasn't Mr. Buckland wicked, Mary, the way he ogled us then doffed his hat. Oh, it was all so exciting!"

Kate watched a light color invade Mary's cheek as she addressed her sister, "Had you not called out in your most piercing voice, *Oh, do mind our horses, sir, or you shall frighten them,*" I daresay we should easily have gotten beyond the village without attracting his notice. You are such an abominable girl, Lydia. I am quite ashamed to take you about."

Lydia seemed to take her sister's rebuke in stride and merely giggled in response.

Still in a considerable state of shock, Kate invited her friends to stay for a cup of tea but they refused, saying that they had come only to deliver their extraordinary news and that Lady Chalford was expecting them back presently. However, it was agreed that at the earliest opportunity the three young women would assemble to properly dissect the most exciting occurrence to ever overtake the dull villages about Stinchfield.

Several hours later and still dressed in her worn muslin gown, Kate sat before the estate ledgers, staring blankly across her desk at a globe of the world and twisting a long auburn curl about her finger. Wondering precisely how long Ashwell would be staying in Chipping Fosseworth, as well as what brought the famous poet to so obscure a village, Kate let her mind drift for a moment until the sound of Jaspar's voice, as he shouted for a servant to saddle his horse, brought reality sharply back into focus.

Glancing down at the figures she had been scribbling for the better part of an hour, figures that represented her father's most recent sojourn in Cheltenham, Kate rubbed the feather quill several times across her cheek.

Adding the numbers again and again, every futile sum proved the same: She and Jaspar were very nearly ruined, and his latest escapade, a mere sennight's gaming in Cheltenham, would see the last of the tenanted lands mortgaged. And the meagre crops, suffering from a dry summer, meant that the squire could not look to raise the rent on any of his tenanted lands. But what did it matter? The problem was not proper management nor rent increases, but rather Jaspar's gaming. He would gamble the profit away as quickly as the cat could lick her ear.

Setting her pen down carefully, Kate rose to her feet and crossed the small, dimly-lit chamber to stand by the window, where she gazed out upon a vista so beautiful that she felt more tied to her home than ever. Hills climbed toward the sky where the young beechwoods brushed against clouds that lingered just over the rise. She loved the manor and Chipping Fosseworth and never wanted to leave, but at this rate, if she did not do something soon, they would have to quit the hall, probably by the end of the summer. If only one of the younger sons about Stinchfield had ever captured her heart, they could have lived with Jaspar for years to come. But none of the bucks, in all the years she had known them and hunted with them, had caused her heart to leap even the smallest degree.

As she watched a shepherd taking his flock across the pasturelands, she wondered what she could do and why, *why* Jaspar was compelled to gamble. What had happened to him when her mother died? How had he lost all sense of himself?

At one time, they had been so close. He had raised her as he would have raised a son. But it wasn't until her mother's death that Jaspar began treating Kate in a brusque manner that she had never experienced before. In fact, shortly after her mother's death, her father requested that she call him by his first name. Initially, Kate remembered having been flattered, but as the weeks passed, she began to realize that he was

21

putting distance between them. No doubt he feared losing his daughter, as he had lost his wife, and somehow wanted to prevent feeling so devastating a separation again.

Watching the shepherd's best dog keep the sheep in a solid flock, the bleating of the sheep, as the dog nudged them, reaching her ears even from the distance, Kate knew only one thing: She would do everything she could to keep from losing the manor and, at the very least, to secure her own future before she was forced to offer her services as a governess or a paid companion. Kate clasped her hands before her in a tight, painful grip. She could not do either of these things. She had rather marry Sapperton.

Kate watched the last of the sheep trail deeply into the valley as she reckoned with this truly errant thought. Nothing was so bad as marrying such a vile man.

As she scanned the beechwood rising above the manor, Kate remembered the events of the morning and drew in her breath sharply. She had forgotten about Mr. Buckland, and now her cheeks burned with the memory.

And as she thought of Buckland and of Ashwell, her gaze became focused on the windswept grass, primroses, and trailing bramble bushes that flanked the beechwood, and a rather brilliant scheme took shape in her mind. She knew all at once how to solve her difficulties, how to make certain her future was a secure one, how to discharge Jaspar's debts and even, possibly, how she might help the villagers in what looked to be a severe winter.

And her plan was so simple and yet so perfect. She would marry the wealthy Lord Ashwell! Surely, with his sensitivity and foresight, he would be more than willing to fund her various projects.

And then she wondered if she had suddenly crossed from sanity to that nether land of mist called insanity, for how would such a poet be interested in a female who lacked any claim to feminine refinements and whose principal accessory to her wardrobe was a snakeskin riding crop?

Kate folded her arms across her chest, her eyes intent as she regarded the land before her. She would secure her father's land and he would love her again. She would marry Ashwell.

But her mind called up a familiar face, Buckland's handsome, leering face, and with a start, she realized that he could spoil her schemes from the outset and that he would be just the sort of man who would enjoy doing so! Immediately, she reseated herself at her desk and, pulling a sheet of fine Kentish rag in front of her, began penning a brief note to Buckland, begging him to meet her in a discreet place, an abandoned barn and dovecote, on the following morning.

She then set about cleaning her favorite pistol and hoped, for Buckland's sake, that he was not a fool.

Chapter Two

That evening, in the timber-framed inn called The Swan and Goose, the infamous Mr. Buckland stretched his booted legs out before a cozy fire and laughed over a sheet of paper held lazily in his left hand. Occasionally sipping brandy from a glass that he held in his other hand and dangled to the floor, he called over his shoulder to his boon companion of many years, "James, old fellow, do you really think you should compare the lady's eyes to that of a ewe?" And he gestured to the paper before him and swirled the brandy in his glass.

The warmth of the fire and the slow, relaxing effect of the golden brandy caused him to emit a deep sigh as he turned laughing blue eyes to regard his friend.

James, feeling quite defensive at this slur upon his latest effort, responded in a rather curt manner, "I thought the reference to a female sheep carried a certain tenderness."

Buckland laughed again, crossing his legs at the ankles, and said, "Mutton is never tender."

"Bah!" James shifted on the hard ash chair where he was seated at a small writing desk, feathered quill in hand.

Passing the offensive poem back to James, Buckland quipped a poem in response:

> A doe, a turtledove's coo,
> A calf, perhaps! But never a ewe.

James bemoaned his fate. "I shall never be a poet." And

seeing Buckland quite ready to agree, added hastily, "But I shall certainly not give up trying and with this charming masquerade we are presently foisting upon—where the devil are we? Chipping Fossebridge? . . . "

"Worth. Fosseworth."

James continued, "At any rate, I am looking forward to proving to you for the last time that all of this absurd attention you receive from the fair sex has little at all to do with your personal charm and everything to do with your position, your title, and your wealth!"

"Undoubtedly you are right!" Buckland shrugged and tossed off the remainder of his brandy.

James, tilting his chair back slightly and letting the feather tickle his chin, regarded Buckland from a pair of sensitive brown eyes and said quietly, "But why did you agree to this masquerade? I mean, I've known you for some time, George, and you've something going on that I don't know about."

Kicking a white-hot piece of coal that popped out onto the hearth, Buckland responded elusively, "You know of the cloth mill my uncle left me, I simply wanted time to see the mill as it is rather than have my identity affect anyone's performance. Should I have gone as Ashwell, then who would have given me an untarnished answer? No, a mere Mr. Buckland is far better."

"A queer fellow, your uncle. Dicked in the nob, I should think. And you only found out about the mill a fortnight ago?"

"Yes, and the strangest part of it all is that everyone seems to think Sapperton owns the mill. I had that from one of the maids not an hour ago."

James lifted a brow and Buckland responded, "I was not flirting with her. She has a beau that works at the mill."

"I suppose I shall have to be satisfied with that." James smiled, then resumed scribbling with his pen.

"There is something else, however, but it is a frightful bore—a mere request for financial assistance from some poor relations."

"Who?"

"I shan't tell you, for you've just enough of an old woman in you that I cannot trust the least of my secrets to your gar-

25

rulous disposition!"

James wadded up his "ewe" poem and threw it at Buckland, hitting him on the cheek. Buckland happily retrieved the paper and, with a smug expression, tossed it onto the coals, the sheet of thick writing paper wrinkling at first then bursting into flames.

Buckland watched the short life of the poem and said, "And if you hope to pass this masquerade off, I suggest you begin answering to Ashwell."

James frowned, letting the chair fall back to the floor with a loud bang. At that moment, a young lady, one of apparently several females who had been assigned to wait on the needs of the famous Lord Ashwell, flung the door open and, in an excited manner, cried, "Yes, m'lord, did ye be needing some'at?"

Buckland gave a shout of laughter at his friend's surprised expression, and James said politely, "No, I thank you. Just set my chair down. No, nothing at all. You may go." And because the young girl continued to stare at him with a pitifully soulful expression, James waved his hand to dismiss her, a gesture he found necessary to repeat several times before having any effect at all, particularly with Buckland laughing at him the entire time.

When the girl had reluctantly shut the door, he turned to face Buckland and said, in a voice of awe, "Do you know that she is the fourth young lady who has opened that door to wait on us?"

"Oh, your delights are just beginning! Do you remember only this morning the two females in the landau?"

"Pretty things!" James rose from his chair to stand before the fire. Lifting his coattails, a broad smile overspread his features. "I say, this is quite a bit of fun. However, there is one small detail that I have not yet to figure out. If I can scarcely answer creditably to 'Ashwell,' how shall I ever answer to 'George'? Everytime I hear someone call out 'James'—and there is bound to be at least one James among all the gentry families hereabouts—I shall be turning this way and that and answering 'what-what,' like our good deaf king."

"Then James you shall be called, as we shall simply say

that though you were christened George, your mother always called you by your second name."

James nodded, and as the door burst open again with two of the serving girls peeping through the doorway and begging to know if his lordship needed anything, he began to feel a trifle irritated. But more was to follow, for a third face, quite unfamiliar to the men thus far, also peeked around the dark oak door and uttered a long, despairing, "Oh, 'tis Lord Ashwell himself."

A loud thump accompanied these heartfelt words as the newest female slumped to the floor. The gentlemen then heard the other two girls, in disgusted accents, say, "Oh git yourself up, Betsy!" and "Ye look nothin' but a donkey's arse!" the door closing behind them.

"Good God!" James cried.

Buckland poured himself another glass of brandy and raised it to James, "To the enjoyment of our masquerade."

Lord Ashwell, posing as a mere and quite impoverished Mr. Buckland, wondered what the end to this scandalous deception would be. Already he felt wary of the masquerade, a strong instinct telling him to stop the charade while he was able. But how could he and still accomplish both tasks that had drawn him to Stinchfield in the first place? No, better to continue and trust that they did not fall into some curst scrape over their lighthearted escapade. After all, they meant no one any harm and only hoped for a bit of amusement during the dull summer months, after which they would be gone with none the wiser.

Raising his glass to his lips, he stopped suddenly. Except for Sapperton. The earl knew both of them from the recent London season, and not only would he expose their masquerade, but he would use it to his advantage if he could.

He sipped his brandy, his eyes narrowed at the glowing fire. Sapperton. Fate seemed to have directed him here. Too many odd occurrences and old wounds. Perhaps he could at last force the earl to face him.

And what of the wench today, also disenchanted with Sapperton. And what spirit! Biting and kicking, and yet what a puzzle she was. First a boy, then a lady—or so it seemed—and finally a shrew! And why had she seemed so outraged after enjoying a perfectly delightful kiss? Watching the coals grow whiter still, he smiled. The morning's adventure had been worth a stained neckcloth even if his valet did not agree. And how perfect her tall, full body felt, even though she had worn a bulky man's coat. He would enjoy her immensely in the next few weeks.

The door flew open again and this time the eldest of the innkeeper's daughters brought forward a missive that she carried in a reverent manner on a small pewter tray, her freckled face brimming with pride at having such a task to perform.

As the girl advanced into the room she could not keep her eyes from James's face, and at first both men thought that the letter was meant for James. But when he tried to take it, she cried, "Oh, I'll be forgettin' me own name in a minute. No, this be fer t'other gentleman." And she bobbed a curtsy to James, then presented the tray to Buckland.

Taking the missive, Buckland laughed heartily at the maid's clumsy retreat as she stared at James and bumped into chairs and tables, then, finally reaching the door, bobbed another curtsy.

Buckland turned back to the letter and, before he opened it, wafted the missive across his face. He raised a brow. No heavy perfume? How odd.

James cried, "For heaven's sake, man, open the letter! I am all curiosity as to why you have received a particularly intriguing billet while all that I have earned so far is the gawking of several country rustics!"

Buckland broke the seal, and after quickly reading Kate's invitation, left unsigned, he smiled broadly.

James cried, "An assignation! I don't believe it!"

Buckland answered smugly, "It is from my wood-nymph. She is impatient to see me again."

A low mist, white, ethereal, a blanket over the countryside, travelled across the hills, down into the secret places of the hollows, through the dark woods, around tall, stately beech trees to nestle finally beneath the sheltered arbor of forest

28

ferns. Kate's long black cloak, warming her in the early morning mist, brushed the ferns, leaving a trail of dancing fronds and faint swirls of mist all seeming to applaud her mission. Kate hurried down the path that led to the old abandoned flour mill. When she reached the mill, she looked about her to see if anyone was near enough to witness her movements. But no one was about, not even any of the villagers, and she continued down the path beyond the mill, heading for an ancient barn and dovecote that was located at the very outskirts of the manor lands. The air was cooler than she had at first supposed, the veriest hint of autumn in the air, and Kate drew the hood of her cloak more closely about her face.

All morning she had been rehearsing what she was to say to Mr. Buckland and her lips moved silently as she rustled along the path, the damp air pulling at strands of her thick auburn hair and causing them to spring into a riot of curls about her fair forehead and cheeks. What if Buckland tried to kiss her again? A strange, pulling sensation at the pit of her stomach caused her to check yet again the pistol, secreted within the deep pocket of her cloak, which she held tightly against her hip to keep the powder and pistol ball from becoming dislodged from so much movement.

In only a few moments, the stone structure came into view, covered partly with wild bramble vines, the berries beginning to turn from their bright green to a deep red.

The morning light grew stronger, and Kate did not hesitate to approach the open doorway where she remained for a moment, her eyes adjusting to the dim interior. The dampness drew a pleasant smell from the hay in the cold barn, a smallish structure containing a few stalls that were separated by wooden rails attached to massive supporting beams.

"Mr. Buckland?" Kate asked tentatively, for at first glance the barn appeared to be empty.

And then a shadow behind one of the beams became a tall form as Buckland tilted his head to look at her. Kate drew in her breath and hoped that she did not betray the sudden feeling of pleasure she felt at just seeing his face. She had never felt so strong and unexpected a reaction to a perfect stranger, and she

29

closed her fingers more tightly about the pistol.

Fortunately, however, Mr. Buckland was smiling in just such a manner, wearing an expressioin of supreme confidence. Kate found herself irritated by his attitude and quite able to disregard her first response to his flirtatious smile. She waited for him to present himself.

As though suddenly aware of what was expected of him, he moved from behind the beam and bowed to her, a sweeping bow, theatrical, humorous, and very rakish. His voice, deep-timbred and warm, filled the stone room. "Your servant, madame."

Kate moved into the barn, her serviceable half boots a dull sound on the hay. "You were very kind to attend to my request, Mr. Buckland."

He lifted his brow at her proper speech and responded, "Oh, yes, I am at least full of kindness, possessing a considerable tenderness in my heart for damsels who wish to meet me in clandestine locations."

Kate smiled faintly and wished that she might have met him under different circumstances. "I greatly fear that we did not begin our acquaintance properly, sir. I wish to begin again."

"I quite agree and heartily approve your choice of setting." He began advancing on her, his intentions quite clear in both his words and his demeanor.

Kate quickly turned into a stall and he moved to stand within another one, a fence between them. He said, "You are quite beautiful in the morning mist, my cherished wood-nymph."

"Oh, I pray you will not speak drivel, Mr. Buckland. I detest it above all things," Kate responded in a firm voice as she pushed the hood back from her head.

Though he was a little surprised by her words and not entirely displeased, he still continued his attack upon her sensibilities and responded in a low voice, "I never speak drivel."

For a moment, as Kate met his extraordinary eyes, all blue and full of intensity, she felt her stomach take another wretched turn. Fully aware that this man, most certainly a rogue, could not be trusted within a mile of a vulnerable female, Kate squared her shoulders and, taking a deep breath, said, "Our meeting in the beechwood was most unfortunate. And there is truly no excuse for my conduct. I wish to apologize."

The fence between them, he looked down at her and smiled, "I see no need for an apology. In fact, I am fully persuaded that our initial introduction held the most intriguing of prospects. I am certain it did!"

"No, it did not!" Kate responded hotly, and because she was truly a little shocked at his words, she added, "And you, sir, are a rogue!"

He then brought the color to her cheeks by laughing at her and exclaiming, "You are certainly correct in your last statement, but as to the first," he clicked his tongue, "are you a liar as well as a considerable mimic? For yesterday, I had the distinct impression that you enjoyed the kiss I forced upon you."

"And can you think of nothing else beyond the trifling kiss we shared? I have not denied that it was pleasurable, only that such an event was not the best of beginnings."

His expression arrested, he was silent for a pace, something like admiration stealing into his blue eyes, "You intrigue me, madame, most certainly you do. But I am not sure that I can agree with you, for I have often found that one can tell a great deal about another person with a kiss. And I must object to the use of the word *trifling*. I always take my kissing most seriously."

This struck Kate as rather ridiculous and she smiled at him, her tone sarcastic, "I'm certain you do."

"Aha!" he cried, swinging around the beam to face her in her own stall. "I can see you've challenged me to prove my point and I am willing to do so."

"Stand, sir!" Kate cried. She wanted to say more, to implore him not to provoke her, but instead his intention of accosting her was so obvious that she withdrew her pistol quickly and levelled it at him. In a serious voice, she said, "I beg you to stand, Mr. Buckland. In these parts I am considered a fair shot!"

But Mr. Buckland, fully conversant with the truth that no

female could handle a pistol with any degree of accuracy, merely smiled in a perfectly maddening fashion, then advanced on her.

Kate, her hand steady, did not hesitate to fire at him, aiming her pistol at his coat sleeve, her brown eyes intent on the mark. The shot reverberated about the golden stone walls, and Buckland stumbled backward, clutching his arm.

Her eyes wide and dilated, Kate cried, "I warned you!"

Immediately stripping off his dark blue coat, he narrowed his eyes at her and said, "You are mistaken in your abilities. I would hardly call this a good shot!"

"My aim was perfect. A mere scratch above the elbow. Am I correct?"

Examining the burnt tear in his shirt and the small straight line of broken skin on his arm, he nodded at her.

Kate blew on the flash pan of her pistol, cooling it before she dared either set it on the straw or return it to her cloak, and said, "I am sorry that you did not believe that I would fire at you, Mr. Buckland, and I fear that your coat is sadly ruined."

Dropping to the hay-strewn dirt floor, Buckland shook his head while pushing back the sleeve of his shirt to further examine his wound. With a wry twist to his mouth, he said, "I begin to think it is a case with you, some perversity in your nature, that you wish to ruin my clothing. My valet was quite unable to remove the tomato stains from my neckcloth."

Kate sank to her knees in front of him and, clearing the hay from a small space on the dirt floor, set her pistol down.

She astonished Buckland by reaching into the pocket of her cloak and withdrawing a pair of scissors, several bandages of thin muslin, and some sticking plaster.

Buckland fell to laughing, "My dear girl, are you always so prepared to bind the wounds of your victims?"

Dabbing at the wound with a strip of muslin, Kate replied with a smile, "I was nearly certain you would not hesitate in attempting to kiss me again, and the fact is, Mr. Buckland, that I wished to get beyond your kisses. . . . I desperately need your assistance."

He raised his brows in surprise. "You've just shot me, madame, and now you expect me to assist you?"

She spread the sticking plaster over the wound and, when she was done, regarded him in a measuring way, "Though I am not completely aware of precisely what set of codes a rogue has chosen to live by, I suspect quite strongly that you harbor an innate sense of justice. You deserved that I shot you. Admit it to be true?"

He sighed, "I suppose you are right. And now, pray, before my curiosity quite overpowers me, tell me how I may serve you."

She began binding his wound with a bandage made up of the remaining strips of cloth, then responded, "I beg you will not tell Lord Ashwell who I am. That is, I am fairly certain you told him of meeting a deplorable female in the woods, but I beg of you, when we all shall meet in public, that you will not betray my identity to him. I am Katherine Draycott, the squire's daughter here in Chipping Fosseworth." She tied a knot and rolled down his shirtsleeve.

"Draycott?" he asked sharply, his eyes flying to her face.

"Just so. I know you thought I was perhaps . . . oh, I don't know what you thought, only, pray do not betray me to Lord Ashwell!"

He regarded her for a long moment. "That fate should thus our lives entwine . . . " He paused, frowning, then rose from the straw, slapping his breeches. "So you are Katherine Draycott, gentlewoman! I am reminded of another Kate and how she was *froward* as well!"

"I am hardly a shrew!" Kate cried, rising to her feet. Extremely offended that he was referring to the heroine of one of Shakespeare's livelier plays, she added, "Truly, I am not!"

"No?" he laughed, a smile overspreading his face, revealing the most charming dimple imaginable.

Kate lifted her bows in astonishment, staring at cupid's kiss on his left cheek, and exclaimed, "A rogue with a dimple?"

Pulling his coat on carefully over his wounded arm, which stung him a little, he looked at her in a speculative manner and asked, "And why is it so critical that I keep your identity from Ashwell? He is a most broad-minded fellow, I assure you. A handsome devil . . . " He seemed to fall into a strange muse as he began enumerating the poet's many qualities. "I should think you would like him . . . tall"—he stroked his chin thoughtfully —"quite manly, well-respected among the *ton*. Well, at least certain parts of it . . . Quite a favorite with the ladies, too."

"Indeed?" Kate queried, irritated by this recital. "Such a paragon. I begin to fear him."

"You have not answered my question." he teased her.

She regarded him candidly and said, "I mean to marry him, of course."

Buckland's mouth dropped open and cried,"You what?" In all of his schemes in arriving at Chipping Fosseworth under an assumed name, never could he have foreseen that the first female he happened to kiss should also declare her intention of marrying him. How fortuitous, then, that she did not know he was Ashwell, for now he might wreak as much revenge as he desired in retribution for every grasping female who had ever set her cap for the Ashwell fortune and title.

"Oh, do not appear so shocked!" Kate reached down to retrieve her pistol that still felt warm to the touch, and while returning it to the pocket in her cloak, she continued, "You know very well that we females must see to our own futures by way of marriage, or we would be forced to teach young ladies the use of the globe or coddle some elderly female with lavender water at her temples whenever she felt peevish . . . unless, of course, we are well-dowered, which I am not!"

"That is certainly being direct."

"And how would it serve me to be otherwise?"

His face took on an expression of deep disgust as he responded to the point. "I know exceedingly well that you look to the gentlemen of your acquaintance with an eye to their fortunes."

Kate adjusted her cloak and began brushing the dirt and straw from about the hem. "This seems very odd in you to be quibbling over such a matter, because I have been given to understand that you are quite impoverished yourself. In which case I can only conclude that you are hanging out for an heiress, or am I mistaken?"

"You are mistaken," Buckland responded, his face appearing set and immobile. "And how is it that you know of my worth? Ashwell and I only arrived yesterday."

Kate answered succinctly, "From my maid, of course, when she delivered my message to you last night. All of the servants at the Swan and Goose were privy to such helpful knowledge."

"And I suppose by this afternoon every manor house about Stinchfield will know the precise nature of my financial condition."

Kate waved a careless hand. "Of course! I wish it were different, but you must be aware of how intriguing the arrival of two eligible men to our countryside must be." She then reverted to her original subject, as much out of curiosity as out of a hope that he might have some answer she could use in dealing with her own precarious finances, and asked, "Then how do you make your living, sir? Do not tell me that you hang upon Ashwell's coat sleeves, for that I would not believe. You are not at all the type!"

"And I suppose I should thank you for such a compliment."

Kate wondered why he seemed to have been offended by her remarks, but she continued her own line of reasoning, "Do you perhaps sit down to cards and always win? But that won't fadge, for I know most particularly that if ever one needs to win, one cannot." She thought of Jaspar for a moment, biting her lip in an unconscious manner. Her father never won at cards.

He watched her pretty features as they formed into a slight grimace, her large brown eyes frowning, her small, straight teeth biting at lips that were the precise color of ripe cherries and high cheekbones that needed no rouge to accent their exquisite shape. He wondered how it was that such a beautiful young lady, her auburn hair in a delightful mass of curls about her face, had escaped some man's attentions, and then he remembered her costume of yesterday. She was certainly an unusual female and nothing short of a handful, but this scheme of hers to marry "Ashwell" was everything he despised. And, without a moment's hesitation, he determined to fight her every step of the way. But that still did not mean he must sacrifice his own pleasure. And thwarting Katherine Draycott, something of a shrew and yet still quite innocent in a quirky way, might possibly prove the most fun he had

had in years.

In a honeyed voice, as he took a step closer to her, he said, "How I live beforehand with the world is entirely my own affair. And as for this other matter, what do I receive for playing out my role of ignorance?"

Grateful that his features had softened a trifle, Kate regarded him steadily and answered, "A gentleman's reward, the honor of acting chivalrously."

He smiled at this. She answered almost as a young man might—forthright, honest, even blunt. He said, "You amaze me! Are we both now to behave as perfect ladies and gentlemen might? You who traipse the country with fowling piece in hand, dressed as a boy, and I who agree to meet young ladies at ungodly hours of the morning and in the most scandalous of surroundings?"

Kate, unheeding of consequences, lifted a hand and placed it gently on his chest, "I beg of you, Mr. Buckland. I realize I have no right to ask, no claim on your kindness, but I pray that you will do this one favor for me and perhaps, somehow, I can repay you."

The expression on her face, a seriousness that took him aback, caused him to grasp the fair hand on his coat and hold it tightly against his chest. Searching her face, he wondered what it was about her that seemed to catch him off guard continually. And of all the absurdities, he wanted to hold her gently in his arms, this woman who just declared her intentions in the most brazen manner possible. He answered her quietly, "So, you mean to marry Ashwell. I only wish of the moment that I had a fortune so large as his, because I think to be pursued by you would be more than any mortal would deserve."

Kate was not even aware that her hand still remained within the circle of his own. She was thinking of his words, spoken so unaffectedly, and that she believed him. Yet, he was just as Lydia had described him, something of a rogue. Was this how libertines hunted their prey, with blue eyes so intent and sincere that their victims did not even know they were about to be devoured?

In the square of light in which they stood, a small window

36

letting in the early morning eastern sun, Kate felt overcome by his presence, by the breadth of his shoulders, encased as they were, in a well-fitting blue coat that still smelled of gunpowder. How vulnerable she was, and as she met his steady gaze, she realized that he could oh so easily break her untried heart.

Lowering her eyes to his neckcloth, she tried to pull her hand away but he held it in a tight grip. His voice, a mere whisper between them, was suddenly cloaked in anger. "You're not meant for Ashwell, my girl. And, by God, I swear he'll never have you! Look at me."

Kate's gaze flew to his face, and she watched as his fierce expression melted into his habitual, easy smile, though he still held her hand, "I promise you that I will say nothing to his lordship, my wood-nymph, of our first meeting in the woods or of this assignation. But remember, by every fair means of play and foul, I shall thwart this intention of yours. Try if you might to win Lord Ashwell, but I shall be standing by you and I shall do everything in my power to expose your false words and simperings and flirtatious lies."

Kate stepped back from Buckland, rubbing her wrist, her brown eyes wide as she faced him. So be it! She was not afraid of his words, in fact, she understood him and knew that he meant only to protect his friend from what he perceived to be the machinations of a clutching female.

However, she remained steadfast in her schemes, for she was certain that the poet was the sort of man she could love. The way he formed such vivid, brilliant poems . . . She shook her head, as though clearing these thoughts from her mind. And what could Buckland do, anyway, if the poet were to fall in love with her? Nought. A feeling grew within her, as though she smelled the early autumn decay in her nostrils, as though she were seated on the back of her spirited mare racing after the fox, clods of mud flying up from the horses' hooves and the cries of the more determined hunters flowering up about her as she lowered her head and raced headlong behind the hounds.

"As you wish, Mr. Buckland," Kate responded, her wild auburn curls appearing like a flame about her white face.

Preparing to bid the rogue good day, the sound of a horse and rider met her ears and a sense of panic gripped her. She could not be discovered here. As a familiar figure passed the window on horseback, Kate uttered a cry of dismay. Would Sapperton never cease to torment her? How was it possible that he was abroad so early? To what purpose? And as another rider passed the window, Kate felt the color leave her face.

Something in her expression, as well as the faint sounds of riders approaching, must have spoken to Buckland of danger, for he quickly grabbed Kate about the waist and pulled her deep into the hay of one of the stalls.

"Sapperton!" she whispered in an unsteady voice.

Finding herself nearly crushed beneath Buckland's weight, she cried in a hoarse whisper, "If he should discover me here with you . . ."

Voices sounded at the entrance of the barn and Buckland clapped a hand over Kate's mouth. "I am not afraid," he whispered, smiling at her in a reassuring manner.

Kate recognized the second voice as belonging to Lord Sapperton's bailiff.

The earl spoke first. "This shall do nicely, Abbots. A secluded spot, too, and we should be able to store over a hundred sacks of grain here."

"Will Draycott sell?" The high-pitched nervous sound of the bailiff's voice filtered into the stone barn.

No word or sound followed this question, but by the fact that the bailiff answered "Excellent," Kate could well imagine the hideous smirk that Lord Sapperton always wore when he was assured of accomplishing his goal. In her mind's eye, Kate could see his emaciated features drawn up into the veriest pretext of a smile, a nerve in his cheek twitching with satisfaction.

The voice became muffled, moving further away then disappering altogether. Kate stared at Buckland, her own thoughts focused in a fearful manner on Sapperton. "Do you think they have gone?"

"Yes, but I don't think you should fear his lordship."

Kate pushed Buckland aside quite without thought to how roughly she shoved his wounded arm, then apologized when he cried out in pain. "Oh, I do beg your pardon. I am completely lost in my thoughts. Sapperton." She rose to her feet and surprised Buckland by extending a hand down to him.

"Thank you, but no." He laughed at Kate's distracted manner and rose to stand next to her as she brushed hay from her cloak and gown. Pulling some of the straw from her hair, he continued, "Is the earl such a menace hereabouts?"

Kate pulled harshly on her cloak, setting it right and retying the strings, "He is a vile, thoughtless, self-centered scoundrel who is determined to squeeze every tuppence out of his grain at the expense of the villagers. And," she turned to face him, wearing an expression of extreme distaste, "he wishes to marry me! Oh, but I loathe his flea-ridden hide, damned insolent coward!" And she finished tying the strings with a jerk of her fingers.

Buckland was considerably taken aback as he watched her features flame, her cheeks flushed with anger. He frowned slightly. She could marry then, if she wanted, a title and an extremely large fortune, the very title and fortune Amelia had pursued.

Continuing to pluck straw from her curls, he laughed at her and said, "I know for a fact that my good friend at the Swan and Goose would find your picturesque expressions quite unlady-like! For while I find them enchanting"—he caught her chin with his hand and continued—"indeed, beyond enchanting, James—that is, Lord Ashwell— would no doubt censure such conduct."

Kate pushed his hand away, turning to go. "I shall remember myself, Mr. Buckland, thank you very much."

He watched her leave, the long black cloak, obviously worn and still covered with bits of hay, swaying with each of her graceful steps. He wondered just how she might look in London society, begowned and bejewelled. Magnificent, no doubt.

Chapter Three

"Why the devil should I call on Lord Ashwell?" Jaspar bellowed in his thoroughly beefy manner. "Confounded nuisance, these poets. Polluting the woods with love sonnets, of all the balderdash." Warming to his theme, Jaspar sat forward in his favourite winged chair in the drawing room and lifted an affected hand. "They mince around and wave their kerchiefs like simpering females! And just try to shake hands with a poet! All you'll get is a hand as limp as a noodle. Pack of screaming hyacinths, too, every last one of 'em!"

Pretending to be quite shocked at his words, Kate stood near the fireplace, a hand pressed against her bosom, and exclaimed, "Jaspar! You forget that I am a delicately nurtured female!"

The squire leaned back in his chair and ruffled out his newspaper, staring up at her. "No you ain't. Never wanted you to be." As Kate moved from the fireplace and dropped to her knees before him, he cried, "And don't think you can persuade me by batting your lashes or any of that tomfoolery!"

Kate laid her head on his buckskins, which smelled delightfully horsy, and said, "I wouldn't think of trying. But you're wrong about Ashwell. Indeed, you are. I am certain he is not as—as you've described him. How could he be when he speaks of Paphians in his first verses?"

"Now, Kate. Shouldn't be speaking of Paphians. That's man's business," Jaspar responded, clearing his throat.

Kate, plucking at the folds of her blue muslin gown, said, "But you don't understand, precisely. I've every hope of marrying Lord Ashwell, if I can."

"What?" Jaspar threw down his paper and stared hard at his daughter, his eyes bulging. "Why, you've never even met the man! Of all the queer starts! You could no more marry a poet than I could. He's not for you, Kate. You need a strong hand, always said so!"

"Please, Jaspar! I know that Ashwell is not so mealy-mouthed. He couldn't be. Not when he writes of being nearly murdered by a treacherous band of thieves in Portugal!"

Jaspar appeared to ignore her remarks and said, "Always thought you should marry Sapperton. Damme, Kate, but think of the man's fortune. And you'd be a countess, to boot! Though I daresay he's not just in your style, for he ain't a bruising rider, but he's no Bond Street beau like that curst nephew of his."

Kate said quietly, "Please do not speak of the earl. I cannnot marry him." She then reverted to her original request, "But won't you at least call on Ashwell, for my sake? I don't say that I can win such a famous man, but I feel I must try. And everyone will have made his acquaintance, and I deuced well know that if Julia Moreton has her way, she will completely beguile him with her ridiculous affectations." Kate picked up the paper that had fallen across the squire's top boots and slapped it against the scuffed black leather. She looked up at him, her brown eyes beseeching, "You see, I am rather fond of his poetry."

Kate waited, feeling extremely tense, not knowing whether he would yell at her or acquiesce. His moods were always so unpredictable. But in the last few days, following his latest excursion to Cheltenham, he seemed a trifle penitent, and so Kate hoped that he would oblige her.

Jaspar grunted and was silent. And after a moment, as he let his gaze travel beyond Kate to the leaded window that looked out upon the long row of chestnut trees that lined the drive, he said, "Well, if you wish for it, I shall seek him out, m'dear." Kate felt his large hand pat her head, and as she handed the paper back to him, he continued in a gruff voice, "But if I discover the man minces one step, like Rupert Westbourne, I shall not let him cross out threshold. You may be damned certain of that!"

As it happened, Sir William Chalford, particularly nice in his observance of the proprieties, called on the poet long before Jaspar even found it convenient. And when the squire learned that Lady Chalford was giving a soiree in honor of the poet, not five days hence, he disclaimed any necessity whatsoever of paying a call upon Lord Ashwell. As he told Kate, "No doubt he'll be sick to death of meeting a curst lot of strangers I'm certain he had rather not meet at all. And you can have Mary introduce you at Euralia's party." But when Kate opened her mouth to remonstrate with her parent, Jaspar added, in a voice that brooked no argument, "And I'll be damned if I'll make a nuisance of myself. Besides, I saw a particularly large covey of quail just the other side of Brock Farm. Mean to shoot me a brace or two. Care to saddle your mare?"

Kate shook her head at this invitation, too angry to answer with anything bordering on civility, and turned on her heel.

Later that day, Kate was still furious with her father for his complete lack of attention to what she felt was a most critical matter. But her maid soon shed a different light on the subject, pointing out that since Kate was to meet so famous a poet, she ought to wear something a little more fashionable than a nearly threadbare muslin gown, or a stained riding habit, or a white satin gown that looked more the property of a school-room miss than the dress of a young lady well beyond her first come-out ball.

Kate stared at her maid with a horrified expression, realizing the truth to Maggie's observations. Good God, of the moment she felt the most harebrained widgeon. Did she think that her expertise in the hunting field would win a man such as Lord Ashwell? Her wits must have gone gathering and she repaired at once to her bedchamber with Maggie close behind. And as the two young women tore every scrap of clothing from Kate's sparse wardrobe, throwing them haphazardly over the lavender quilt on her bed, they discoverd that there were scarcely enough garments to assemble one decent costume, let alone prepare her to meet a man whom she hoped to dazzle with her beauty and charm.

As she began counting on her fingers the number of gowns, walking dresses, hats, bonnets, carriage dresses, shawls, stockings, gloves, reticules, feathers, ribbons, and capes that ought to form a young lady's proper wardrobe, Kate felt considerably overwhelmed. Years ago, she remembered shopping several times with her mother in Cheltenham, when she had first grown into her young womanhood. But since her mama's death, she had ignored such expeditions as a considerable waste of time—time much better spent traversing the countryside with her fowling piece tucked into Miss Diana's saddle. But now she must go, and how was she to ever pay for such a long list of feminine fripperies? And what would Julia or Kit or Emmet or even Mary say if they were to see her in anything other than her usual riding habit? Well, she would not worry about their opinions, for she had one purpose in mind: to somehow capture Lord Ashwell's admiration.

But all of this would take the most precious of commodities which, at the moment, was exceedingly scarce—ready cash. Bidding her maid to leave her alone for the time being, Kate crossed her arms over her chest and tried not to feel anything. There was only one real solution to this difficulty, and she had for so long been able to avoid taking this drastic measure that she could not help but feel a certain sense of failure at having to take it now. But she could see no other way and wondered what her mother would think if she knew what her daughter was about to do.

Moving to her dressing table, upon which resided her snakeskin riding crop and one empty perfume bottle, Kate pulled out the drawer that contained her lacquered jewel box, a gift from her mama.

She could not hold back the tears that came unbidden to her eyes. So, her affairs had come to this—selling the only remaining part to her once tidy dowry, her mother's jewels. But she could not! And she shoved the box back into the drawer, slamming it shut. Not the jewels. Anything but the jewels.

Sitting in a chair covered in a chintz of trailing pink, lavender, and orange flowers, Kate faced the table of rich cherrywood. Staring at her reflection in the small looking glass, Kate remained as still as sand in the bottom of a time glass. Anything but the jewels. Anything.

But there was nothing else. And there was certainly not a creditor in Cheltenham who would lend her a single shilling for the purchase of perishable gowns. Kate pulled open the drawer again, fingered the jewel box and, with a jerk, pulled it from the drawer.

Running from the room and shouting orders to have the travelling chariot brought round immediately, Kate tied a bonnet over her curls, threw a shawl over her blue muslin gown and, with Maggie scarcely having time to draw a comb through her own untidy hair, found herself moving along at a slapping pace toward Cheltenham, toward her future, toward a life unfilled with creditors and debts.

Buckland wondered if he should be in Cheltenham at all, for the risk of recognition in the large, bustling town that overlooked the Vale of Gloucester was far greater than in Stinchfield or in Chipping Fosseworth. Adjusting his neck-cloth slightly and letting his cane drape over his arm, Buckland quit the inn. He could not be comfortable. After having been shot by Miss Draycott, all he could think about was the coming farce they were both to enact and that for some reason he did not want his summer's pleasure interrupted.

Hurrying toward his bank and settling his hat well forward on his black locks, Buckland breathed a sigh of relief that none of the passersby accosted him as they were wont to do in London, Bath, or Brighton. And if he stayed away from the spas, where any fashionable residents were likely to gather, he could be safe. For a while.

Quickening his steps, Buckland passed a milliner's shop displaying a large plumed pink bonnet, a chandler's shop draped with a vast quantity of candles, and as he neared an open door, the strong smell of tobacco and snuff nearly turned him from his errand with Mr. Rous. But when he cast his glance into the shop and two young bucks noticed him, their eyes lighting with a certain vague recognition, he moved quickly from the door, pulling his black beaver hat even further down his brow.

Crossing the street after a well-laden mail coach rumbled by him, the sound of the coachman's cries bouncing about the cobbled streets, Buckland escaped their dawning awareness of his identity and let his cane tap along the cobbles, sidestepping a larger puddle of recent rainwater.

Finally the bank came into view, and he moved rapidly toward the fine stone building and, a quick manner, jerked the painted door open.

He was about to sigh with relief when a most definite shock assailed him, for there, standing on the other side of the doorway, her auburn hair peeping in a riot of curls from beneath a rather old-fashioned bonnet, and staring at him from startled brown eyes, was the subject of his thoughts. Buckland nearly dropped his cane. "Miss Draycott!" he cried.

"Mr. Buckland," Kate cried, astonished and greatly discomposed.

He removed his hat with a quick jerk of his gloved hands and cried, "How—how do you do? I beg your pardon! I see that I have surprised you." He entered the small antechamber where two clerks, who had been busily scratching into fat ledger books, now regarded them both from behind round spectacles, their bent hands oddly quiet.

Buckland glanced in their direction, and immediately they resumed dipping and scratching in a rather furious manner.

Feeling completely nonplussed at having met Miss Draycott in so abrupt a fashion, he pulled her aside and, in a rushed tone, asked, "Do you know Mr. Rous? Is he . . . I mean, he is my banker, he is not yours as well?"

Kate, taken aback by both his manner and the very strange coincidence of meeting him at her bank—and that after having disposed of her mother's jewels with the intention of purchasing a wardrobe to win Lord Ashwell— turned quite red and replied, "Yes, of course. Yes. For a great many years. I—I must go. Good day."

She tried to move around him but he prevented her by taking her arm. Some of his confidence returned to him as he realized that no one knew the truth, not even Mr. Rous. Drawing her off to the side, he spoke in a quiet voice. "Do you know how pretty you are? What beautiful brown eyes . . . "

She cut him short by jerking her arm away. "Oh, do stop!"

45

She whispered to him, "Making love to me in a bank! Of all the absurdities."

He taunted her, "Were I Ashwell, you would not hesitate!"

She faced him. "And what an unscrupulous thing to say to me."

He bowed, "Of course. I told you how it would be." Then, looking her over ever so carefully, even to the scuffed half boots that she wore, he said, "I sincerely hope that you mean to refurbish your gowns, Miss Draycott. You will hardly catch the eye of so fastidious a man as Lord Ashwell by wearing a muslin gown that, by the absence of ruffles about the hem, must be at least five years old."

"Of course I mean to! I am not such a pea-goose as to think that I could do so otherwise!" Kate responded hotly, then blushed again as Buckland laughed at this perfectly innocent confession.

She moved past him and hissed, "A rogue and a cur!"

Beneath his voice and with a smile to his lips, he whispered back, "Vixen!"

He did not see Kate's half smile as the door closed her out of the bank.

Buckland watched his banker carefully, wondering what Mr. Rous was thinking. He seemed to be in a brown study as he responded politely and methodically to each of Buckland's requests. And when he rose to take his leave, having instructed Mr. Rous to transfer some of his funds to a small bank in Stinchfield, Buckland was surprised when the stately, rather conservative man begged him not to depart just yet.

"This will only take a moment." Mr. Rous smiled in an absent manner as he rose to stand over his desk. Turning to gaze at a lacquered jewel box, inlaid with delicate gilt scrolls, he frowned, running a finger across the top of the box.

Buckland stood before his chair watching Mr. Rous, whose silver head, bent to regard a pretty jewel box case on his desk, shook slightly as though trying to dispel an unwanted thought. He wondered if the banker had discovered his charade, but then why was he so consumed with the box on his desk?

46

Buckland sat down, tapping his cane on the hardwood floor, the sound a gentle rhythm in the small wood-panelled chamber. Trying to keep his voice light, he asked, "Have you discovered some impediment to transferring these funds? Have highwaymen been accosting the mail coaches?"

Mr. Rous lifted his head. "What? Oh, no." He laughed, his light blue eyes crinkling slightly. "Completely reliable. You must forgive me if I seem a bit distracted. You see, I have before me a matter of great delicacy in which I hope you might assist me." He moved to stand before the diamond-paned windows that looked out upon the High Street. Watching the heavy wood signs above the shops swaying in the growing east wind, Mr. Rous wondered how much he should reveal to his customer.

Turning to regard Buckland with a measuring look, his fingers tucked into the small pocket at his waist as he fingered his gold watch beneath his right hand and his ruby-studded snuffbox beneath his left, he asked, "You are from Stowhurst in Kent, are you not?"

Buckland gripped the ivory handle of his cane slightly as he nodded to the banker. He suddenly felt certain that Mr. Rous knew all.

But the banker's next words caught him off guard. "Are you acquainted with a Mr. George Cleeve of Stowhurst?"

Buckland stared hard at the banker, then felt his grip relax from about the handle of his cane, "Cleeve?" he repeated. And when the banker nodded, Buckland responded, "Yes, as it happens, I am."

Mr. Rous withdrew his fingers from his pockets and let out a sigh. "I must confess that I find myself a trifle relieved." He returned to his desk, walking in his usual sedate manner, and reseated himself. As he again ran his finger across the jewel box, he said "Since you are staying in Chipping Fosseworth for the present, I wonder if you are yet acquainted with Squire Draycott or his daughter Katherine?"

How much did Mr. Rous know? Buckland searched the clear blue of the banker's eyes but saw no guile, no attempt at mystery, only concern. Twisting the cane beneath his hand encased in York tan, he answered, "How odd that you should ask, for I became acquainted with Miss Draycott but a few days ago."

Mr. Rous relaxed his shoulders, "A fine, handsome woman, is she not? She will make some young fellow an excellent wife one day. I only wish . . . well, never matter. What I would like to know is if Mr. Cleeve still resides in Stowhurst. You see, as Mr. Draycott's cousin he is heir to the Draycott estate. And Miss Draycott has been attempting to reach Mr. Cleeve for a number of weeks now, but with little success." He waved a hand that sported three gold rings. "Oh, she received some trumpery letter—I think it has been six weeks now—with a vague promise that Mr. Cleeve would visit Chipping Fosseworth, but nothing more. And if you knew the difficulties that young woman has had to bear . . . " He broke off abruptly, his features taking on an angry hue. After a moment he regarded Buckland with a rather intense gaze and, in a pronounced manner, tapped upon the jewel box.

Buckland, a little taken aback by all that Mr. Rous's words intimated, watched this movement and realized that the jewel box belonged to Kate. He lifted his gaze to regard the banker, narrowing his eyes at Mr. Rous in an unspoken question.

Mr. Rous responded in a quiet voice, "Exactly. I will say no more, only I beg you to tell me if you know where I might reach Mr. Cleeve or even if you have the smallest hint as to his whereabouts."

Buckland rose, tucking his cane under his arm, "When I spoke with Mr. Cleeve—who I have found, upon occasion, to be a rather hard-hearted brute—he mentioned that he was going into the country to search for a hunting box he might purchase. It was quite well-known that recently he came into a considerable fortune."

"All the more reason for the man to be tending to his relations." Mr. Rous rose slowly as he spoke.

Buckland bowed to his banker and said, "I am certain he will do so once he learns of the difficulties involved. I will only add that though he seems absorbed in his own concerns, his tenants in Stowhurst have always spoken of him in the highest degree of respect."

Mr. Rous bowed in return, "Then you have given me reason

to hope that he is not beyond compassion in this instance. If you should hear anything regarding Mr. Cleeve's whereabouts, I trust you will inform me. Miss Draycott deserves far more consideration and attention from her cousin."

Buckland moved to the door, where an idea struck him. With one hand on the brass knob, he turned back to Mr. Rous and said, "May I recommend that you withhold the sale of the jewels until Mr. Cleeve can be found? I am fully persuaded he would not have it otherwise."

The banker smiled, "You have confirmed my intended course of action and I rely on your discretion."

As Buckland left the bank and returned to the inn where he had stabled his pair of black geldings and his curricle, he felt a decided pang of conscience that he had so thoroughly deceived Mr. Rous. And as for Kate, though he could never feel kindly toward her schemes to marry a fortune, for the first time he began to wonder what precisely had driven her to sell her jewels. What had happened to bring a once profitable manor to such a pass that the squire's daughter must sell her jewels?

Kate sipped at the glass of ratafia, redolent of peaches, the cold sliced chicken of her nuncheon sitting upon her nervous stomach in lumps. Watching the town coaches and curricles and one absurdly tall high-perch phaeton roll by, she wondered again what she was doing. Not since her mother died had Kate given any attention to her wardrobe, and now she was about to order more gowns than she had owned during her entire existence. Taking a final sip of wine and dabbing at her mouth with the inn's embroidered linen table-napkin, Kate rose upon unsteady feet and quit the establishment. Walking the short distance from the George Inn to Madame Beaumaris's shop, Kate wondered if the clever Frenchwoman would truly be able to create fashions for her that would enchant a most sought-after poet. But her artistry came highly recommended by all the ladies of Stinchfield. Even Mary had her tidy little gowns designed by Madame, and Julia Moreton's flimsy muslin dresses, which she dampened in a most shocking manner, held the light, delicate touch of the Frenchwoman's quick needle.

Kate paused before the door, her hand trembling slightly as she reached for the knob. Surely she was in pursuit of a madcap dream. Her knees feeling made of water, Kate stared at the flagstone beneath her feet, her hand upon the knob, and reminded herself, as she had a hundred times during the past several days, that her purposes were honorable and required only a bit of courage to bring them about. And how was it she could have actually shot a bear, not three years ago, without the slightest quaver in her hands? But in facing an unknown modiste, she thought she might actually faint, so disordered her various senses had become, her heart sitting in her throat.

Becoming quite sickened at her own temerity, Kate finally pulled the door open and took a step that somehow sealed her fate. But just as she crossed the portals, preparing to congratulate herself for having had enough bottom to place one foot before the other, a sight met her eyes that drained the color from her face.

Of all the wretched twists of fate, why must Julia Moreton be in this shop at this precise moment!

Kate stared at the petite, bosomy figure of Julia Moreton, who was the firstborn daughter of the principal family in the village of Ampstone, and thought that never had fate been so cruel. Watching the pert female pirouette in a perfectly enchanting confection of satin and silver lace, her charms thoroughly exposed in a daringly low bodice, Kate felt her hopes plummet. Ashwell had but to receive one bat of Julia's thickly fringed lashes and Katherine Draycott would cease to exist. How she imagined she could ever compete with Miss Moreton's beauty, Kate would never know. Julia's extraordinary blue eyes, dark and as brilliant as sapphires, reigned over the entire community surrounding Stinchfield, and not one of the young gentlemen of her acquaintance had escaped the wounds of her flirtatious lures.

Kate felt suddenly like a fool, a dowdy, stupid female who had concocted a ridiculous, harebrained scheme. And as Julia whirled and dimpled in front of a long gilt mirror, Kate realized how great the odds were against her plans actually succeeding. Her heart failing her completely, she was about to turn and quit the shop when Julia, all wide eyes and sparkling smiles,

50

caught sight of her.

Kate felt rooted to the entranceway, clutching her worn reticule so tight that her nails dug deeply into the palms of her hands.

The beauty just gaped at her, an expression of the strongest incredulity disfiguring her angelic features. Finally, Miss Moreton exclaimed, "Katherine Draycott! Oh, *mon dieu!* I cannot credit my eyes." And then moving toward her with arms outstretched, she ran to Kate and gave her a light kiss on each cheek just as though she did not, in truth, loathe the sight of Chipping Fosseworth's eldest daughter. "Is that really you, *ma chere?*"

This use of her schoolroom French, which Kate had never heard Julia utter in her life, was used undoubtedly to impress Madame Beaumaris. It was all Kate could do to keep from boxing Julia's ears as the beauty led her into the shop. Kate glanced around and had an immediate impression of exquisite taste. The small room was decorated in the lightest blue velvet, with white braiding and tassels. "How pretty!" Kate exclaimed.

Julia twirled again in front of the mirror and said, "Oh, thank you, Katherine." She let out a squeal of delight that raked the nerves along Kate's back, "I knew this gown was perfect. Just look how well it becomes me!"

Kate was bowing to Mrs. Moreton as Julia continued, "You cannot imagine how surprised I was to see you here! You! I nearly laughed, except that I was so completely astonished." She then looked Kate up and down and said, with her most innocent expression, "So you have decided to flirt with Lord Ashwell, too?"

Had Mrs. Moreton not been present, Kate would have delighted in giving Julia a most deserved set-down.

Mrs. Moreton patted her blonde wig and said, in a stern voice, "Julia! You forget yourself! I will not permit you to tease Katherine."

This rather fierce matron, who prided herself for knowing precisely how everyone else should conduct their affairs, took in Kate's serviceable muslin gown and continued, "However, I will say that it is high time you paid more attention to the

51

costumes you sport. How old are you now? Four or five and twenty?" She narrowed her eyes and pursed her lips.

Kate answered quietly, "One and twenty."

Julia, standing behind her mother, pulled a smirking face and disappeared into the nether regions to change her gown.

"Humph! One and twenty indeed! Young girls should be married by the time they are eighteen!" She swelled her ample bosom. "I have told Julia so often and often. And I will say this," she smiled sweetly upon Kate, "that if Lord Ashwell is indeed the reason you have actually forsaken, even for one afternoon, that dreadful mare of yours and all of those quite ridiculous dogs, then I am grateful to him."

Kate, finding that her fears had disappeared in the face of Mrs. Moreton's thoughtless remarks, said with a honeyed smile, "I have always enjoyed Miss Diana and my dogs. They are a great comfort to me. They do not tell me which of my friends I should see or not. No, I could never accuse them of impertinence."

Mrs. Moreton, not mistaking this speech, pinched her lips tightly together and, drawing her green-fringed reticule up before her bosom in a prayerful attitude, responded in a sharp voice, "One can certainly tell that you are Marianne's daughter, over and over!"

And Katherine silenced Mrs. Moreton by saying simply, "Thank you."

Julia emerged wearing a spencer of royal blue which matched her eyes, over a white muslin gown embroidered about the hem in a trail of delicate silver leaves. She was followed close on the heels by a small woman with a pronounced Gallic nose and dark eyes, who wore an expression of keen intelligence.

Madame Beaumaris had heard the brief exchange and felt much as she had when she made the last leg of her journey escaping from France. She knew well the preliminary sounds of an imminent quarrel and immediately intervened. In her most confiding voice, she cried, "But who is this? I do not recognize this young woman, but I surmise that she must come from Stinchfield. *Oui?* But of course! And how delightful."

And Kate watched with great admiration as the vivacious Frenchwoman, who had fled the revolution twenty years earlier, ushered the Moretons from her shop.

Turning to face Kate with a delighted clap of her hands, she said, "*Et maintenant,* the auburn beauty!" She then walked about Kate, one hand pressed thoughtfully against her lips and the other resting lightly upon her waist, where she had secured a tape measure and a number of pins laced through a long red ribbon.

Madame Beaumaris sighed, "Ah, these poets! They drive us mad, do they not? And Ashwell has something!" She kissed her fingers. "But I would love to meet such a man who can write about a storm as though his heart were caught in it!"

Kate remembered the lines of the poem she referred to and saw the scene as a whole—of a ship, of a woman, caught in a fierce storm. Of the man bringing the ship safely through. She loved the man that appeared in his poetry. Ashwell. Somehow she must make him love her, too. To Madame she said, "I have no gowns, nothing with which to capture the attentions of such a man, of any man. I rely on you, Madame."

The Frenchwoman regarded Kate in an appraising manner, taking in the reticule, the worn muslin gown, the scuffed half boots. Patting a straying grey curl back into the knot of curls on top of her head, she spoke quietly. "In the many years I have been in England, I have learned much of people. And that suffering has a way of etching itself upon one's face—" She did not finish her thought but smiled kindly upon Kate and said, "Your coloring! *Jamais, jamais* the pinks or reds. Your beautiful white skin will turn an orange color against such shades. Only blues or the deepest forest-greens, lavender perhaps. *Et blanc, absolument* I forbid it! Insipid, as you English like to say. *Absolument!*"

Ringing for several assistants, who began flowing about Kate in a whirlwind of activity, an hour passed, then another, and the afternoon dwindled rapidly. Exhausted, Kate was about to tell Madame that she most certainly had enough clothes to last a lifetime when the dressmaker brought in a rich blue satin gown, held lovingly across her arms. With a brilliant smile, she begged Kate to don this last, most perfect creation.

Kate regarded her reflection in the long mirror and at first scarcely recognized herself. Madame was right. The deep blue of the gown enhanced her fair skin and auburn hair. The low décolletage exposed her full white breasts, and with a start she realized she could challenge even Julia's beauty, a thought so novel in its formation that she stared at herself in wonder.

Madame did not miss this expression and she sighed. "You are so young, Miss Draycott, are you not? No, no! I do not mean in years!" And she patted her chest. "I refer to the heart."

Kate regarded Madame's face as she continued looking into the mirror, with the dressmaker standing behind her. "I have never been in love, if that is what you mean."

"That, and flirting with men, teasing them. Miss Moreton knows quite well how to flirt with a man, though of love I believe she is an innocent, just as you are."

As she shaped the gown to Kate's tall figure and saw that the young woman's eyes dwelled on her bosom, which seemed to nearly overflow the blue gown, she cried, "Oh, that I had been so! What hearts I could have broken with a mere bending down to pick something up! Men are such idiots! *Vraiment!*"

Kate laughed, her color much heightened by such improper speech. And as she regarded her reflection one last time, she thought of Buckland and knew instantly that he would approve of such a gown. With a wry twist to her mouth, she realized that he would more than approve, the rogue! And she smiled again.

As Kate drew on her faded gown, Madame lectured her severely, "See that you wear your hair in this strict Grecian mode, a ribbon or two, no more, and no feathers! *Jamais!*" And she wagged her finger at Kate. "Keep your jewelery of the simplest, Miss Katherine. Your beauty is made to please the eye of a poet—strength and dignity! Do not let Miss Julia concern you! She might flirt and wave her lashes about like two peacocks, but I see in your brown eyes a challenging quality that a real man cannot resist! *Vraiment!*"

Kate regarded her dubiously and Madame Beaumaris laughed at her. "You must believe what I tell you, for I speak only the truth. And if you find your knees trembling a little, remember that even Lord Ashwell was a baby once! I wish you the best!" Adding up the charges, Madame Beaumaris then had her strong impression of the young Miss Draycott confirmed when she payed her bill immediately. That old hag, Madame Moreton, who wears the wig of the most stupid, still owed her from last summer.

Watching her newest client replace her bonnet and pull on a pair of lavender gloves, Madame Beaumaris winked at Kate and whispered, "I shall see that a terrible fate befalls Miss Julia's gown. It shall arrive the day after the soiree!"

When Kate arrived home that evening, the rushlights blazing in their brass holders by the front door, she entered the ancient stone hall of the manor, only to be confronted with the news that two gentlemen were waiting to see her.

Kate handed her parcels to Violet, the wraithlike maid who served to open the door to the manor's guests. They had not employed a butler for the last three years since old William had passed away. At first Kate had not hired another such servant because she and Jaspar did little entertaining at the manor, save for providing the bucks of her acquaintance with a tankard of home brew after a day's sport in the fields. But when Jaspar's debts began to mount, even had she wanted to, such an expense became an impossibility.

As Violet took the packages, setting them on a round inlaid table in the center of the entrance hall, and helped her employer off with her shawl and bonnet, Kate wondered what Lord Ashwell would think of so dreadful a lapse in proper household management. Every house must have a manservant as butler.

Stripping off her gloves, her shoulders suddenly tense with the knowledge that, by Violet's sniffs and dispproving face, two of Stinchfield's tradesmen sat within her office, Kate walked briskly to the door and flung it open quite without ceremony.

Both men rose, faces flushed, chins set, hats in hand, and Kate waved them back to their leather seats in front of her antique desk of bird's-eye maple.

Without hesitation, she said, "Your receipts, my good men."

Both tradesmen visibly relaxed and, with a shuffling of paperwork, presented her with a number of frivolous purchases made by Jaspar on several occasions in the last six months, for which Kate had never seen bills. She glanced at them and recognized at least one receipt—a dozen whippoints, which she had seen stuck into Jaspar's various coat lapels. The rest she could only assume her father had indeed purchased.

Pursing her lips and settling herself into her own comfortable chair, which was covered in a swirl of wild red roses that Mary had stitched for her two years ago, Kate quickly scanned all of the bills that bore Jaspar's wild signature. Even the way he signed his name seemed to reflect the bluff, bold quality of his personality.

"These seem to be in order," Kate said in her usual authoritative manner. She hesitated for a moment. Her first inclination was to retrieve the large roll of bills from her reticule and pay all of the charges at once. But upon further, very quick consideration, Kate realized that if she did so, the very sight of so many pound notes would send the word flying about Stinchfield—and wherever else Jaspar owed money— that the Draycotts now had ready cash to spare, and she would be inundated with tradesmen.

Kate regarded the men thoughtfully, two honest men who were wearing rather anxious smiles, and wished more than anything that she could pay the receipts at once.

"My good sirs, I beg you to believe that this is the first time I have seen these bills. My dear papa"—here she smiled at them—"is not always faithful to inform me of all of his purchases. I greatly fear that I cannot at this time discharge these debts." And she gestured toward the neat pile that now graced her desk.

Taking a deep breath, Kate watched their faces first take on expressions of disappointment then become decidedly mulish in aspect, much as they had appeared when she had originally entered the room. Folding her hands in front of her on the leather pad that covered the desktop, she continued, "However, if you would but take fifty pounds each upon account, I should be exceedingly grateful. And I think the remainder could be discharged"—here she paused and mentally calculated precisely how many weeks she thought it might take to win a man's heart, then continued—"in let us say, six weeks?"

The tradesmen both let out puffs of air, smiling as they rose to their feet and bowing to her. Their words mixed together, "So good of you." "So kind." "Sorry to be such a damned . . . er . . . deuced . . . sorry to trouble you, Miss Draycott."

After the men took their leave, Kate leaned back into her chair and, lifting her foot, slipped off her half boot. She could not resist spinning the globe at the side of the desk with her toe. She smiled. Even if she had paid only one hundred pounds, to discharge some of Jaspar's mounting debt carried a certain satisfaction.

Kate snapped her fan open with a jerk, then closed it again and felt her stomach lurch within her. The qualms that seemed to fly about her entire person seemed quite similar to the erratic progress of the ancient travelling coach as it bumped along a stretch of rutted road just outside of Chipping Fosseworth. Of the moment she wished she was not going to Lady Chalford's soiree.

Dressed in the royal-blue satin gown sent only that morning from Madame Beaumaris's shop, Kate pulled her mother's fur-lined cape about her shoulders. The cool evening air escaped into the carriage through a hole where a window was missing, and it was for this reason alone that she had delayed their arrival. Ashwell must not see the window. Soon enough he would know of her dowerless, impoverished condition. Certainly there was no need to make this knowledge apparent at the outset.

Glancing up at her father, Kate smiled at his manly appearance. She was always proud of Jaspar's demeanor, his confident ways of charging through the villages about Stinchfield. And though he might irritate many a tenant farmer by taking his pack of dogs across a wheat field, he never failed to send around a brace of pheasant or rabbit, whatever the day's adventure had brought, in penance for his dogs and horse. Kate loved him. She sighed, fingering the fur about her shoulders. If only he did not gamble so very much.

As though aware that his daughter's eyes were upon him, Jaspar turned his head to regard her in the falling summer light and said, "Marianne?"

Kate sank back into the squabs, stunned. And what surprise she felt at seeing the flash of a sudden and very deep pain in his red-rimmed blue eyes. She then heard him laugh and could now release the breath that she was not even aware she had been holding.

Patting Kate's knee with several firm thumps, he said, in his blustery voice, "How you do put me in mind of your mama tonight! Spitting image, you know." And he turned away.

Kate wanted to reach out and slip her hand into his pocket as she had done a thousand times as a child. She longed for the closeness they had had when he was teaching her to ride and hunt. Instead, she let her gaze drift out the window. They were passing through Chipping Fosseworth and the large, heavy sign over the Swan and Goose glowed from the last rays of the sun.

The carriage rattled slowly past the old inn toward Edgecote, a large village but a mile or so beyond Chipping Fosseworth, beyond the ford where the River Wyck entered the Avenlode.

Kate turned to look out Jaspar's window, where the sun caught the tops of the hills all crowded with beech trees, their shining leaves dancing in the wind.

The coach was growing dark inside and Jaspar said, "Where are the diamonds, Kate?"

The fan slipped from between Kate's gloved fingers, sliding down the satin gown and landing noiselessly beside her slippered feet on the floor of the coach.

Shifting her gaze to again look out her window, the cool evening breeze freshening her cheeks, a long row of stone cottages came into view.

The first cottage needed repair to the roof and the second cottage now housed seven children, twins in the spring, and the mother needed nourishment to stay strong—food, wheat, bread. So much work that needed to be done, but Jaspar had used up the funds by gaming in Cheltenham. She answered his question quietly, "Mr. Rous is selling them for me."

Kate could hear that just for a moment Jaspar stopped breathing. And after a few seconds he coughed a rumbling cough and drew his large gold snuffbox from his coat pocket. Taking a hefty pinch of Spanish Bran and sniffing it loudly into his stained nostrils, he said, "I never interfere in the estate. You must do as pleases you."

Kate felt her spine grow rigid with anger and she grabbed the carriage rope tightly in her gloved hand to keep from shouting at him. She must do as she pleased. As she pleased? She pleased to hunt with her dogs, not chase a poet about Edgecote Hall!

It took several minutes to feel the angry warmth recede from her fair skin, and Kate only hoped, as they pulled through the gates to the Hall, that she did not have red splotches over her neck and shoulders. Her fair skin could be quite a nuisance. Why did Jaspar no longer concern himself with what she needed and wanted? Why did he no longer love her?

As Kate had hoped, they were the last to arrive and watched with a feeling of relief as Peter Coachman tooled the dilapidated coach back to Sir William's well-stocked stables. And as they crossed the threshold to Lady Chalford's elegant drawing room, the sonorous tones of a regal butler announcing their names flowed across the large chamber. As if in waves, heads turned in their direction, group by group, and Kate smiled at the realization that her poverty had created a perfect entrance.

All heads snapped toward them and Kate scanned the various groups, her gaze becoming riveted to the spot where Buckland leaned, quite rakishly, over Julia's pretty shoulder. And Julia, all angel's hair and devouring blue eyes, laughed up at him. The only satisfaction Kate could take in this intimate scene was that the gown Miss Moreton wore was an old gown, and she blessed Madame Beaumaris.

But just as the room had fallen silent, Buckland seemed suddenly aware of her arrival, for he lifted his head, his gaze meeting hers and, in an unconscious manner, drew up to his full height. Kate watched him in some trepidation as he scanned her costume from head to toe. And with a nearly imperceptible inclination of his head, she knew that he had approved her.

A surprising wave of pleasure flowed through her and she lifted her fan, wafting it gently across her features. Almost she might enjoy this evening, for whatever else Buckland might be, she knew instinctively that he was a man of excellent taste.

As Lady Chalford moved forward, bidding them a gracious, proper welcome, Kate heard Kit Barnsley exclaim, "By Jove, is that Kate? Why, she looks like a female! Who would've thought!"

Kate glanced over at Kit and shot him a brief, angry glance, which only caused her childhood friend to smile broadly at her.

But she could hardly blame Kit. She knew she was presenting an extremely odd appearance. Neither she nor Jaspar took part in the steady flow of social events that surrounded Stinchfield, and never before had she dressed so fashionably, permitting Maggie to arrange her hair as Madame had suggested, in a simple classical style with a royal blue ribbon wound through her shiny auburn curls. Her gown clung to her womanly form in soft Grecian folds, and a silk shawl, draped elegantly over her arms, completed a portrait worthy of Homer.

"My dear Katherine!" Lady Chalford exclaimed, her kind, sensible face a quieting influence on the butterflies playing havoc in Kate's stomach. "But how charmingly you look. Do ignore Christopher."

Jaspar's voice intruded, his rich baritone bellowing out into the stunned drawing room, "Rigged out to the nines! Slap up to the echo, ain't she? And all for the curst poet fellow." He lifted his quizzing glass and surveyed the assembled company. "Now where is he, Raillie? Don't keep me in suspense. There's been too much bother about the man as it is. Ah, there's a face I don't recognize and there's another. Now which is he?"

Chapter Four

At this loud recital, Kate heard Mrs. Moreton and that odious Mrs. Cricklade snigger at her father's bad manners. Even Lady Chalford seemed angry. Her spine as straight as a beech tree, the baronet's wife smiled thinly at Jaspar and said in a frosty voice, "How strange to hear that silly childish name after so many years. Such a tiresome nickname, Jaspar! But I won't quarrel with you. Please permit me to introduce you to Lord Ashwell."

Kate glanced up at her father's smiling, uncaring face and barely kept a chuckle from escaping her throat. If these poor women only knew that he enjoyed nothing more than goading them in their efforts at extreme gentility. She wished, however, that this evening he might behave himself but a little, then she realized how impossible such a feat would be. And as she stepped forward to meet London's most celebrated poet, her only remaining wish was that Jaspar might not end up in his cups and have to be carted out of the house by Sir William's grooms.

As Kate followed behind Lady Chalford's rigid, proper form, she watched as a tall gentleman, who had been seated near Mary Chalford and the prosaic George Whiteshill, rose to greet them. And in the secret place of her heart, she knew the smallest, most detestable disappointment, which she quickly locked away.

Extending her hand toward Lord Ashwell and feeling it held in a light, gentle clasp, Kate sank into a curtsy and felt her fingers brushed by the touch of the poet's lips. As she rose to the pressure of his fingers, Kate met his gaze, in which lurked the most charming smile, and she felt suddenly quite at home. "I cannot tell you, my lord, how much I have admired your poetry."

Kate waited to hear his voice, wondering if it would be rich like Buckland's, but Jaspar's voice again intruded as he cried, "So you're the damned poet that's got all these silly girls blubbering and bleating like ewes!"

Kate heard a few gasps go up about the assembled company, even Mrs. Cricklade's voice announcing that she might faint, and she thought if ever she had the least hope of charming the poet, she would have to be Juno herself to overcome so bad a beginning.

James, however, was quite astonished that this man could actually be the parent of the goddess before him and, seeing the very faint blush that suffused Miss Draycott's cheeks, was about to speak. However, Buckland's voice, as he circled behind James, reached his ear in a whisper, "Ewes, James!"

Kate watched as the poet turned toward Buckland, wearing at first a startled, then a laughing countenance at something Buckland had said to him.

Lady Chalford, frowning slightly at Lord Ashwell and his friend for having shared some secret, introduced Mr. Buckland.

Jaspar looked him over and said, "Now, you look like a man who knows one end of a horse from another. Clipping rider, no doubt. Hunt the Quorn country? Thought so. Can always tell a hunting man." And looking James over, he said, in quite a serious tone, "Though I daresay you look right enough for a poet! None of the court-card about you!" He turned to scan the assembled company and seeing Rupert, dressed in a white satin coat and breeches, with a deep pink waistcoat and silver buckles on his shoes, lifted his plain quizzing glass toward him and said, "Not like that namby-pamby fellow over there, reading his verses to any whipster that don't give him the go-by. And all with his locks oiled thicker than a coach wheel!"

James bowed and with great good-humor thanked Jaspar.

Patting Kate's shoulder in a jovial manner, Jaspar told her to enjoy her poet, recommended she have "Buckling" instead, then shouted to Sir William that he was parched.

Shortly after Kate seated herself on a sofa of dark tapestry patterns, Buckland moved away to speak with Mr. Cricklade. As the poet seated himself beside her, Kate glanced about the drawing room and realized that the long chamber was bedecked with a great number of flowers from the garden—Mary's handiwork, no doubt.

She was greatly pleased that the poet scarcely regarded anyone else in the room, and Kate had all the delight, for a few minutes at least, of seeing that his gaze did not even wander toward Julia. Mary sat in a chair near the sofa and joined in their conversation. But once Kate had ascertained that Ashwell was enjoying his sojourn in the Cotswolds and that he positively relished the country for gaining all manner of inspiration, dinner intruded on her intentions of charming the poet.

As Lady Chalford began the procession toward the dining room, claiming Lord Ashwell as her own partner, Mary whispered to her, "He is quite handsome, is he not? Only, I'm sorry that dinner ended your conversation so abruptly." Mary squeezed her arm and was gone.

And since Lord Ashwell was seated at the other end of the table, Kate knew for the moment that she must set aside her schemes until after dinner. She regarded the blond beauty, who was every now and again smiling at Kate in a maddening fashion since she had been seated next to the poet, and wondered just how she was to keep from tearing Julia's eyes out. The most provoking cat in the world. Julia Moreton.

Sitting next to Sir William and enduring Kit Barnsley's teasing on her left, Kate at least could relax a trifle, for the baronet was always gracious and Kit had been a favourite of hers since they had made the abandoned mill on the River Chering a secret meeting place. Buckland sat opposite her, and though once or twice she caught his blue eyes laughing at her, she passed through dinner well enough.

At one point, Sir William startled Kate by telling her that she had grown into a beautiful young woman. "And is that a new way you've done your hair?"

Kate nodded, feeling surprised that the usually reserved baronet should comment on her coiffure.

He spoke again, his intense blue eyes seeming to have taken on a faraway look, "You appear remarkably like your mama this evening. Only when I remember Marianne, she was powdering her hair. I hated to see all those red curls covered up."

Extending his hand toward her, he looked as though he was about to touch one of the ringlets that trailed down her back and Kate halted her fork in midair.

Sir William withdrew his hand and, sitting back in his chair, cleared his throat. After taking a sip of Madeira, he asked Kate how Miss Diana fared.

Setting aside her very uncomfortable reaction to Sir William's strange conduct, Kate went over, yet again, the various and most excellent points to her beloved mare.

Christopher joined in, "I knew it was all a hum!" and asked her if she wished to shoot rabbits in the morning, "for the warren south of the Standen beeches has begun overrunning the villagers' garden plots!"

Kate's brown eyes lit up with sudden desire, and then she remembered where she was and how at odds her newly formed schemes were with her former habits. Glancing at Buckland and feeling quite relieved that he seemed fully absorbed in Mrs. Moreton's explanation of how she had cured her husband's gout just before he died, she leaned closer to Christopher and, pinching his arm in a menacing way, whispered in a harsh voice, "If you expose me once, Kit Barnsley, to Ashwell or to Mr. Buckland, I'll have your hide full of buckshot before you can spin around!" And in a normal, rather carrying voice, she continued, "I won't be doing any hunting for some time. I—I must practice with my watercolors tomorrow morning and—and I have a great deal of tatting to finish before Michaelmas."

At least five pairs of eyes looked astonished at this pronouncement and though Kit, thoroughly unafraid of Kate's threats, choked over a slice of ham, no one said a word. Christopher merely leaned over to her, after he had eased his coughing spasms with several healthy draughts from his wineglass, and whispered back, "What a rapper! But I won't

64

say a word. I know what you are about!"

"You do?" Kate asked, startled. Truly she had tried not to appear too obvious in her schemes, but if Kit could see through her motives, then everyone else would as well. For though he was a dear friend and possessed the sweetest of natures, Christopher Barnsley could hardly be termed needle-witted.

But when he spoke, he relieved Kate's mind. Nodding in a self-satisfied fashion, he hiccoughed once and said, "You're just mad as fire that Julia reigns in these woods and you're determined to best her!" He then cast a darkling glance toward Julia.

Kate watched her friend's round, freckled face turn a dark hue, and she realized that she might avert some gossip by making use of the fact that Julia had so recently snubbed the young buck. She had flirted with him for an entire month. But when Emmet Ebring told Julia she was a cattish, frivolous female who was cruel to lead so many ignorant fellows about by the nose, Kit had all the pain of finding that the beauty would no longer have anything to do with him.

Kate often wondered if Emmet were in love with Julia himself, but he seemed so continually at odds with her that she could only suppose he detested her simpering ways as any sensible person would.

Kate said quietly, "You are right, Kit! You know that Julia and I do not get on, and last summer she nearly ruined Miss Diana's mouth by riding her when I wasn't looking! Well! But pray, say nothing about it!"

And since she chanced to reach for her Madeira at this moment, she happened to catch Buckland's critical eye as he shook his head at her. She knew then that he had heard nearly everything she'd said, and by the look on his face, he meant to put into motion some scheme of his own.

With a lift of her chin, she sipped her wine and asked Sir William if his tenant farmers were losing as much of their crops as Jaspar's were.

When the men joined the ladies for tea, and conversation preceded several performances on the pianoforte, Kate found herself sought out by Lord Ashwell.

Praying that she might not offend the poet, she permitted him to lead her to Lady Chalford's most prized settee of rust velvet. When she sat down awkwardly upon one of the pillows that Mary had embroidered for the settee, she giggled, pulling it from beneath her, and when Ashwell was looking in the other direction, Kate dropped the pillow behind the settee.

As the poet sat down, Kate tried to maintain a delicate smile such as she had seen Julia wear times out of mind, and she wafted her painted fan slowly across her face. She hoped that she appeared as Mary always appeared, proper and maidenly.

The tea made graceful rounds, cup and saucer, about the long gold and rust-colored drawing room. Kate sipped her tea and watched Ashwell's almost translucent face, white and lined with intelligent blue veins at his temples, grow flushed with excitement as he began describing in great detail his sojourn in Greece. She soon learned that he had explored this country with Buckland.

Once or twice, Kate put forward a question about current Greek cuisine or anything else of a modern nature, but Ashwell's mind seemed naturally bent, as a poet's would, toward the classical aspects of his stay in Greece—the Parthenon, the Acropolis. Kate watched his brown eyes and thin face and reflected upon his poetry as he spoke, recalling in her mind the flow of the first and second cantos. She frowned, for though Ashwell's poetry was littered with classical allusions, they were generally stuffed between so many adventurous moments that Kate scarcely noticed them. Somehow she expected the man to be more like the exciting details of his verses. How odd.

He was rather handsome, Kate thought, as she watched his pale, interesting countenance, sensitive mouth and large brown eyes. He was a trifle thin and she could not help but wonder if he dined, as Byron did, on vinegar and potatoes. Her glance slid about the room, seeking out Buckland, and quite unconsciously she began comparing the two men. Buckland seemed to command attention, with his rather piercing way of gazing at his fellowmen. He was in no way boorish, she noted, moving easily among Lady Chalford's guests and even flirting with Mrs. Barnsley, Kit's mother, who was a renowned featherhead. He was taller than Ashwell and certainly athletic—a Corinthian, no doubt.

She looked back at Ashwell's brown eyes and thought them kind. How completely different from Buckland's, whose blue eyes were anything but kind—appraising, laughing, leering, but never kind.

Ashwell's voice intruded, "And pray, Miss Draycott, what is your opinion?"

Kate suddenly realized she had not been attending to a single word that the poet had been speaking and stared at him quite blankly. "Of Greece?" she asked lamely.

He chuckled softly, lowering his eyes to gaze at the quizzing glass he held in his white gloved hand. "I thought as much. I greatly fear that I have been boring you."

Kate swallowed hard, her mouth opening slightly as though she should speak. But it was not in her nature to prevaricate, and though she had not been bored precisely, how could she explain what her thoughts had been? And worse, how was she to win the man's love if she could not even attend to his speeches? At the very least, a female ought to listen to what a man said if she wished to fix her interest with him.

"I beg your pardon, Lord Ashwell," she said in a hurried manner, not considering her words too carefully, "but I have the devil of a time—" She broke off abruptly at his lifted brow. Now she had offended him! She covered her mouth with her hand, then said, "Oh, my wretched tongue! I am sorry!"

She watched the poet's gaze turn toward the laughing group by the fire, where five gentlemen had gathered. With their laughter and heated exclamations flowing about the crowded drawing room, they were no doubt comparing, in a rather boisterous fashion, their favorite stories of the hunt. And in the center of the group stood Buckland, completely at ease.

Ashwell lifted his ornate silver quizzing glass, which hung about his neck on a long black silk riband, and levelled it at the group. "Tell me, Miss Draycott. What is it about that man that appeals so strongly to you females?"

"But I—"

He threw up a hand and, in a laughing manner, implored her,

"Do not deny that your gaze wandered to him, nor that you were thinking about him. You would not be the first."

Kate felt the color rising in her cheeks and, in a small voice, said, "I have offended you. Truly there is no excuse for such incivility on my part."

James looked at the extraordinary female next to him and frowned. Buckland had not said one word to her and yet already she had sought out his tall form and appraised him. Looking down at the quizzing glass, suddenly aware that he had gripped it fiercely, James felt betrayed. He was not blind. He had seen an expression of admiration suffuse her lovely face as her gaze drifted over Buckland's entire physique. Damn! He would not let Buckland beat him in this!

Kate felt her heart pounding against her ribs. Ashwell seemed so angry as he stared at his quizzing glass. Almost she could cry for her stupidity! She was about to speak, to try if she might redeem herself, when a commotion among the five gentlemen by the fire soon commanded their attention.

Kit's older brother, Stephen Barnsley, an unthinking hothead, cried, in a carrying voice, "Then you must ask her yourself, Mr. Buckland. She most certainly did shoot the bear!"

And the formidable group of four of the neighbourhood's most eligible bachelors, along with the infamous Buckland, pounced upon Kate in a thoroughly noisy and hurly-burly manner.

"Kate!" Stephen cried, his intense brown eyes full of excitement. "Tell Mr. Buckland how you shot that bear at a mere thirty paces. He will not believe me!" And he folded his arms across his chest.

Roger Whiteshill, Kate's cousin, added his own thoughts, his handsome countenance and blue eyes belying an awkwardness with the fair sex, "Yes, tell him, Kate!" He then addressed Buckland, "Steadiest hands—and not a nerve quivering anywhere! She just lifted her rifle, levelled it at the ugly brown head, and squeezed the trigger. Shot the bear straight through the eye!"

Kate heard Ashwell's voice, a mere whisper. "Good God." Kate wanted to crawl beneath the settee. She had had the bear hide tanned to a soft, supple leather, and on warm summer nights she would open all the windows in her room and lie upon the fur in just her thin muslin nightdress. She regarded the poet and remembered reading his verses there only a month earlier, crying as though her heart would break at the yearnings tucked between every line of his works.

And here he was, seated beside her and sounding shocked. She felt her heart sink.

She watched Emmet Ebring's serious hazel eyes light up with pride. He was also a favorite of Kate's, but at this moment she could have kicked him, for he continued this most dastardly recital of her adventure. "Yes, tell him, Kate!" And again to Buckland, "Came charging out of a thicket of reeds down by Aldgrove Brook. We'd all been hunting stag beyond Waverley Hill, about three years ago, and then this bear appears. We haven't had bear in these woods for a score of years or more. I still think he might've got away from some gypsies." The young men fell to offering each of their opinions as to where the bear had come from, and Kate thought her cup was full until Kit Barnsley answered Buckland's most provoking disbelief by crying, "But she keeps it in her bedchamber!"

Buckland's gaze flew to Kate's face and she hid a deepening blush behind her fan. She wanted to look at something else, anything else other than Buckland's piercing gaze, but she could not. And, damn the rogue, she knew exactly what he was thinking!

Buckland regarded her for a moment as the young bucks about him continued to praise Kate's marksmanship, and he felt a powerful feeling toward her. Good God! A bear skin, one that she had shot and now keeps in her bedchamber! He wanted that skin. He would buy it from her! He would own it, somehow!

Kate watched as a devilish smile overspread his features. The cur, the scoundrel! And why did his smile have to overtake his blue eyes in that perfectly dreadful manner? He bowed to her and said, "So, Miss Draycott, you are considered a fair shot in these parts."

Kate drew in her breath. All of it was too much—his

impudent reference to their earlier meeting, her friends exposing her to the poet, Ashwell's frowns, the falling apart of her clever schemes. Setting her teeth and forgetting about trying to impress Ashwell, she lifted her chin to Buckland and answered him, "I am."

He clicked his tongue, drawing a gold snuffbox from the pocket at his waist. "A mere female? I do not believe it!"

Another cry of protest rose up among the bucks.

He silenced them by saying, "Not that it isn't possible, only I've never heard of such a thing. I should greatly like to see Miss Draycott's skill demonstrated." Flicking his box open, he took a pinch of snuff and smiled.

Kate met his gaze, black look for impudent look, and scarcely withheld grinding her teeth. She responded caustically, "I'm certain you would," her fan moving faster and faster.

"I've just the thing!" Roger cried, his handsome face lighting up. "A shooting match. Kate, remember how we used to shoot the feathers off Sapperton's peacocks?"

Kate heard a choking sound beside her and realized that all of her plans in the last few minutes had been neatly torn to shreds. The poet was beyond disgust at her unmaidenly conduct, hiding his revulsion to her addiction to sport behind his hand that covered his mouth and in the watery look of his brown eyes. Her fan still moving at a maddening pace, Kate thought that it would be quite impossible for such a man, whose ideals were no doubt centered on Olympus, to look upon her as anything other than a mannerless hoyden.

But as Ashwell lowered his hand, Kate discovered, much to her relief, that the poet was actually laughing as he cried, "Sapperton's peacock? Lord, I'd've given a monkey to have seen that!"

Kate relaxed, her fan returning to a slower pace, and as the poet smiled at her, she returned his smile. Hope, so easily shifting about, again brimmed in her breast. Affecting a maidenly voice, she said, "A childish prank. I was quite young."

Kit cried, "What a whisker! It was only two summers ago!"

Kate cast her friend a brief menacing look and Christopher,

70

still smiling, said, "Of course, two years is such an awfully long time."

Ignoring Buckland's burst of laughter at Kit's sarcastic remark, Kate concentrated her efforts on Ashwell. "My papa taught me to shoot. You see, he has no sons of his own, and from the time I could remember, we marched through the beech woods together, fowling pieces in hand."

"But how charming," Ashwell exclaimed as he turned toward her, leaning his arm on the back of the settee and resting his sensitive face lightly in his hand. "And did you really shoot a bear at thirty paces? Why, you might have been killed!"

Kate lifted her brows. Ashwell had at first seemed so disapproving and now . . . why, his voice even held a caress!

Buckland said, "I think a shooting match an excellent idea and I should enjoy taking part in such a contest."

"Here, here!" the bucks exclaimed.

Stephen cried, "We could all have a go at it! Rifles, pistols, I've an old blunderbuss I'd like to try!"

Kate folded her fan on her lap and smoothed the ripples along her blue satin gown. The candlelight from a large branch at the small gilt table beside her danced across the gown and Kate tried again to imitate one of Julia's girlish expressions, "I would not think of such a thing!" she cried. "Truly, it is bad enough that I have admitted to hunting at all, but this! Why, Mrs. Moreton and Mrs. Cricklade would think I had no sense of proper conduct whatsoever!"

"Humbug!" Kit cried.

And Buckland added, "Come, Miss Draycott. Surely you do not fear losing the match. Though if you did not choose to face me, I should certainly comprehend it. No one likes to lose and I am myself considered quite one of the best shots at Manton's!"

Kate squeezed her fan so hard that she nearly cracked the delicate spokes. Picking up the gauntlet, she cried, "I am not afraid of facing you!"

"Then it is agreed?" he asked in a honeyed tone.

Kate glanced at Ashwell and then back to Buckland's provoking face, and she leaned back into the settee. "No. It is not agreed. I will not take part in so outrageous a scheme."

71

Emmet said, with a smile, "But if it were only a very private affair, Kate?"

Kate was doing everything she could to keep from letting her momentary desires outweigh her resolve. And how dismayed she felt when Emmet, who tended to be a trifle more proper than most of the bucks, joined the lists. Already her fingers itched to clean her pistols and begin practicing, and his voice, added to the others, was making it all too difficult to say no.

Emmet added, "And if Squire Draycott approved?"

Kate swallowed, thinking of the manor, of her father's debts, and of Ashwell. She did not know the poet well enough to say yes.

She glanced at him, wondering what he would think of her if she accepted Buckland's challenge. Ashwell seemed to be smiling. And oh, she wanted to face Buckland, but she simply couldn't. Not if it meant jeopardizing her plans.

Kate hesitated, battling within herself until Ashwell took her hand and kissed it in a most charming and gentle fashion. "I would be honored to see you demonstrate your talent, Miss Draycott. Would you consider doing so for me?" He then turned to Buckland and, eyeing him squarely, continued, "If only to see this conceited fellow taken down a peg or two. Somehow I feel certain you are just the one to do it."

Kate was elated at these words. She could polish her fowling piece and choose among her five pistols the best for the match. And oh, what did it mean that the poet had taken her hand and kissed it? Somehow she had secured his interest. Lowering her gaze demurely, she said, "Only if Papa gives his permission. But mind, this is to be strictly a private affair."

Kate then lifted her eyes to regard Buckland's face, feeling a sense of triumph, but what she saw confused her. For he was staring at Ashwell, a rather fierce yet amused expression on his face, and the poet, as she turned to regard Ashwell, seemed quite smug.

When Jaspar was applied to, his response was precisely what Kate had expected. "What? Damned good idea! But you'd better warn Buckland that Kate will beat him all to flinders! Taught her m'self!"

The bucks set about deciding the particulars, Buckland

moved to chat with Mary, and the poet, borne off by Mrs. Moreton to help Julia select some of the music for the evening, left Kate's side with a smile and a bow.

Kate let her gaze travel about the room, her eyes resting for a moment on a large painting composed of a small Cotswold vale where a tidy flock of sheep trailed into the valley, attended by a frisky sheep dog and a tall, thin shepherd. A small river was just visible, and tucked near the hills was an old barn and dovecote. Kate felt the hair upon the back of her neck nearly stand up as she realized that the vale and the barn were the very same ones near the River Chering just beyond Jaspar's manor. Now, why had she never seen it before? Kate studied the painting for a moment, regarding the barn with interest, thinking of Buckland and then of Lord Sapperton. She glanced quickly about the room, searching for the earl, and realized that he had not attended Lady Chalford's soiree. Snubbed her, no doubt. Lady Chalford, much to Kate's delight, paid only the barest civilities to the earl. She had never approved of him and he punished her by refusing her invitations.

Hearing Lydia's boisterous laughter, Kate turned to watch the young schoolgirl, for she was hardly more in all of her playful attitudes. Lydia, who had no musical accomplishments to speak of, was plucking absently at the harp strings and teasing Jeremy Cricklade about something that caused the young buck to turn beet-red. Kate was about to join them to find out what devilment Lydia was up to, when a commotion at the entrance of the drawing room disturbed the gentle flow of conversation about the long chamber.

A young labouring man, who had lost an arm at Waterloo, struggled with the butler and, breaking free of him, rushed into the room, crying, "Miss Draycott! There ye be! Ye must come quickly!" He wadded up his hat beneath his arm and bowed several times to her, his face twisted in concern, "It's me mum!"

Kate looked at the distraught features of Thomas Coates, and without any thought as to where she was, or that she was in a new, exceedingly expensive gown, or that she might offend Lord Ashwell by making a hasty exit, cried, "I'll only be a moment."

Thomas breathed a great sigh and, suddenly aware of the enormous social crime he had just committed, turned a brilliant shade of red.

The entire chamber, full of the very best of Stinchfield society, the squires and ladies and children of all the manor houses surrounding the prosperous market town, fell silent.

The shock of seeing Thomas so unexpectedly now waned, and Kate had time to feel the great surprise and disapproval that seemed to overtake the room.

A footman and the butler hastily accosted the man, but Sir William immediately told them to let him be. He knew what the young man wanted. Lady Chalford had stationed the baronet by the long French windows at the far end of the room in order to keep any recalcitrant young bucks from escaping the forthcoming performances upon the pianoforte and harp. At Thomas's entrance, he moved quickly to join Kate and, in a quiet voice, patted her gently upon the shoulder and said, "It appears you are needed."

Kate looked up at Sir William and felt an inexplicable affection rush over her. Not one word of censure had ever crossed his lips. How different he seemed from everyone else about Stinchfield, as though he understood her. She thanked him and, in quick sure steps, moved from the drawing room, which still remained silent.

She was not aware that she had been followed into the entrance hall until Lady Chalford caught her arm. In a stern, stoic voice, the baronet's wife said, "Isn't it time, Katherine, to be setting aside this foolishness?"

Kate looked at her hostess and said quietly, "It is not foolishness to me nor was it to my mother." She took her cape that a footman had secured for her and flung it about her shoulders.

"But surely there are women in the village who can take care of these delicate matters. Surely!"

Kate regarded her hostess and said, "I'm sorry, Lady Chalford, but I must. Pray, forgive me." Lady Chalford gave her a quick hug and told her to wrap herself up warmly, then disappeared into the drawing room.

Kate requested Jaspar's carriage to be brought around

immediately, then she turned toward Thomas. His dark hair was sweat-stained from having run the two miles between Quening and Edgecote, and Kate asked him about his mother's condition.

Slapping his hat against his breeches, his blue eyes glancing rapidly about the entryway tiled in black and white, he said, "Shouldn't ha' pushed me way in there!" And setting his chin in a mulish fashion as he regarded the cold face of Sir William's butler, Thomas continued, "But tha' man would not ha' give ye me message."

Kate spoke sharply, "It is not of the least significance. All that matters is your mama. And with the squire's coach we shall be there in a trice. Now tell me how she is."

He seemed suddenly embarrassed and looked down at the gleaming floor beneath his dirty boots. "Took to her bed most o' the day. I don't know how she bears it."

"Is anyone with her? Where is the doctor?"

"That old witch, Mrs. Didmar, be with her. The doctor been treating a family with the smallpox, beyond Ampstone. He told me to fetch ye, that he would try to come as soon as he could. I be fear'd for her, Miss Draycott."

As the front door opened and a footman nodded that the carriage had been brought round, Kate glanced toward the drawing room and saw Buckland staring at her. What he was thinking she could not tell, but of the moment his opinion mattered little. But beyond him stood Ashwell, who regarded her with a thoughtful, almost frowning expression. Kate hesitated for a fraction of a second, then passed through the doorway. She would worry about his opinion tomorrow, when Mrs. Coates was safely delivered of her baby.

Buckland took another pinch of snuff and tapped the gold snuffbox. Emmet had told him what Kate was about to do and he could not believe it. It was impossible! No female of his class did such a thing! He turned toward the window, watching the old coach pull away from the steps, the gravel crunching beneath the wheels. The red glow of light from the flamebox blazing by the door did not reflect in the window of the

75

carriage, and Buckland realized with a start that the coach did not have a window.

So that was why the chit was late. She had pride, and yet she would disrupt an entire soiree, bear the censure of her friends and acquaintances, even risk her schemes to win Ashwell, in order to help a woman caught in a difficult birth.

He watched James's quiet face. He, too, must have seen the window.

Flying to Quening, a small village near Lord Sapperton's estate where labourers for the earl's fields and for Postlip Farm resided, the coach pulled before a small stone cottage. After Kate sent Peter Coachman back to Edgecote, for Jaspar's sake, she entered the two-room cottage, pausing for a moment at the entrance to the lower chamber. On the floor of the hovel, earthen and polished with ox blood, lay the sleeping forms of five of the woman's children. Each rested on a pallet of hay, covered with a threadbare blanket, and wore the thin, drawn face of a child who worked alongside his parents, day in and day out, and scarcely had enough to eat. Kate thought of the tomatoes she had thrown at Buckland and she cringed. For a brief moment, she wanted to tear the satin gown that brushed along the floor to shreds.

Thomas seated himself by the fire and Kate immediately ascended the narrow staircase to the second room of the cottage. Here she found Mrs. Coates, her face white and rippled with pain. No sounds escaped her lips, the spasm holding her in its tight grip. Slowly, her face relaxed and she stared at the ceiling, then at Kate.

She looked weary and smiled faintly as Kate ran to her, taking her hand. "Thank ye, Miss Draycott. 'Tis my eighth birthin' and still as hard as the first. Not like other women."

She again screwed up her face, holding back any sounds. Kate understood the woman and knew that, for the children's sake, who must be up early and working in the fields with their papa, she would not even so much as moan. The pain passed.

"I sent Mrs. Didmar home. Couldn't bear her superstitions

76

and chanting. The Lord will bring this baby safely into the world." She looked at Kate's gown and shook her head. "I be sorry, miss."

Feeling the woman grip her hand again and turn away, Kate rubbed her hand and arm and began speaking in a soft voice, telling her to look at the stars outside and to watch the shape of the leaves of the beech tree that brushed lightly against her window—pointed black shadows against the midnight-blue sky. The pain passed.

The woman said, "Yer mama helped me with ta first un. He be Thomas and ta doctor weren't nowhere to be found. Thomas worrits me. No arm, no work." She gasped and turned her head toward the window, squeezing Kate's hand hard. After a moment she took a deep breath and continued, "I ought not to speak, but sommat bad be going about the villages. Men pullin' their ears and wavin' their hands. They be talkin' in whispers. The crops look bad, prices high. The new machines in the mills stealin' work. Miss Kate, I be feared for me family, for Thomas and for Jack, me husband."

As the next wave hit, Kate spoke in low tones, begging her not to distress herself by thinking of these things. The woman lifted her knees, arching her back and writhing, and Kate held her by the shoulders, pressing her down against the bed that smelled musty from years of damp. There was no time for proper airings.

Kate heard voices below and let out a sigh. The doctor had arrived. A feeling of relief swept over her, for if a woman was having difficulty with her eighth, she knew that a doctor's experience was required.

"The doctor is here," Kate said.

"God be praised," the woman said in a whisper, the last pain having drained her. Some were harder than others.

As Kate looked about the room, the whitewashed walls peeling from the damp, the roof having leaked during the winter and most likely for more years than that, she noticed that everything was ready for the baby: the wooden cradle; extremely worn but soft little gowns, some of them smocked and stitched by loving hands; a tall stack of cloth diapers.

The candles smelled from their cheap tallow, having been made from mutton fat, and the yellow flames flickered as good Dr. Adlestrop jerked off his cape and tossed it onto a chair by the door. He was a heavyset man, with large hazel eyes and brown hair touched only lightly with grey for his five and forty years. Kate smiled at his hair, which was receding but kept in tight little curls and pomaded—surely the doctor's only vanity.

He regarded Kate over his spectacles as he examined the mother and, nodding his head, made his pronouncement, "the baby is turned the wrong way. Its face is up, not down as it should be."

Mrs. Coates blinked her eyes and sighed. Her fifth had been turned this way, and the labour was long. She was not like other women who just dropped their babies, one after t'other. She laboured on and on and it just didn't seem fair. But she'd only lost one in her five and thirty years, and she felt blessed.

The hours rolled by, and the silent mother clenched her hands and fixed her eyes on the tall beech tree outside the small window. At one point, she insisted Kate cover her gown with an apron, telling her that she ought to tie it above her neck or the doctor would not be paying proper attention to the baby as he ought.

Kate blushed and the doctor, who had not given her so much as a cursory glance, now looked her up and down as he bathed the woman's head with a cool rag and exclaimed, "By all that's wonderful!" his red-rimmed eyes blinked at Kate. "I've been up for two nights now and can scarcely see in front of me. But, by Jove, you've become a woman!"

As the late night moved to the cool, still early morning hours, Kate sat in a rocking chair and wished for the hundredth time that she could take some of the woman's pain upon herself. But one day perhaps she would have children of her own. A dozen children. She smiled to herself. She had cried so hard when Stephen died. Perhaps as much for Stephen as for her herself. Growing up alone had been just that. Alone.

She, too, watched the beech tree swaying in the breeze. And

78

then the woman said, in a breathy, panicked voice, "I want to push this baby out." And the final rustle of activity brought even Thomas to stand at one of the top steps and wait and watch.

The doctor eased the woman along, "Slowly, slowly. That's it! Well, what do you know! An easy entrance after all!" And the baby, a little girl, slid out as if there had not been hours of agony. And the baby screamed. Screamed with the anger of having had to work so hard, for so long, and everyone cried at the baby's lusty set of lungs.

Even Thomas cried, and Mrs. Coates, her eyes but half open and regarding the baby with tenderness, said, "I will call her Katherine. Katherine Georgina, if ye don't mind, Miss Kate."

Kate wiped her eyes with the soft linen apron and pushed back a few loose strands of hair. Taking the baby in her arms and wrapping it tightly in the warmed towels that Thomas brought from the fireplace below, she whispered to the baby, who was still screaming, "I am honored." Handing the baby to the mother, who immediately loosened the blankets and put the child to her breast, Kate stepped away, feeling overcome by the moment. No, Lady Chalford, I shall never give this up. I shall do as my mother did and her mother before her, and shall teach my daughters to do the same. Never do I want to be so removed from life, caught up in tea and scones and Haydn's sonatas, that I no longer witness the joys of birth, the thrill of hunting, the soil in my hands.

"Thomas," the woman called to her eldest, "fetch yer pa. Tell him it be a girl."

Kate bid Mrs. Coates good-bye, reluctant to leave the miracle that suckled at the woman's breast, and finally, upon the doctor gently pulling at her arm, she left mother and daughter alone.

When Kate reached the bottom of the stairs, she found Thomas waiting for her and was a little surprised at his serious expression. "I'll see ye home, Miss Kate," he said, again slapping his hat against his breeches.

Kate felt a little disappointed, for this time of morning was special to her, the hour before dawn, when the hills lightened from a solemn black to a deep gray and the birds began to chatter quietly. By dawn they would be singing in full force, but now, just before the sun began peeking over Cowley Hill, they would be singing softly, a morning lullaby, a song for baby Katherine. Katherine Georgina.

Stepping outside, Thomas explained that they would need to stop at the Black Bear Inn, where his papa would be waiting. He laughed, "You would think after so many wee uns that he would be accustomed. But he canna bear to see Mama in pain."

Kate looked about the darkened village, a glow from the tavern down the street the only light illumining their path on the hard cobbles.

Kate said, "Thomas, you ought to apply to Lord Sapperton to mend the roof. The damp cannot be healthy for the little ones."

She heard Thomas snort, "His lordship refused." His words were clipped and angry. Kate sighed. Of course Sapperton would no more mend his tenants' roofs than miss sitting in church on Sundays. The hypocrite.

Remembering what Mrs. Coates had said about Thomas, Kate hesitated for only a moment and said, "We've recently lost our stableboy"—she paused, thinking that they had not had one for three years now and Peter Coachman, who was aging and cared for three horses, the stables, and oversaw the work on the home farm, would bless her for this—"and you may have the job if you like."

Thomas paused in his steps and cried, "I don't but know that there ought to be a dozen men in Chipping what would want sech work, but I'll not refuse."

Kate looked at him in a solemn fashion, "I can't pay very much—"

He interrupted her, "Ye canna know wat 'tis been like since I returned from Waterloo." He lifted the stump of his arm, cut off halfway between his elbow and shoulder. "No one hires half a man when they can hire a whole." He was all of seventeen but sounded a score of years older than Stephen Barnsley or even Kit.

As they neared the Black Bear Inn, Kate heard a roar of laughter that sounded oddly familiar to her and she wondered who it might be. She knew only very few of the villagers in Quening, but that voice, deep and resonant . . . She stopped in her tracks. She could not believe her ears, and as they neared the threshold to the inn, she was astonished to find her suspicion confirmed. For there, his head buried in a tankard of beer and sitting vigil with Mr. Coates, was Mr. Buckland.

Chapter Five

Kate smiled. How silly to think of Buckland sitting vigil with an expectant father.

Mr. Coates, catching sight of his son, slammed his tankard down on the table and rose to his feet. He seemed scarcely able to speak as he said, "Thomas?"

"She be a girl, Pa."

Jack Coates, a tall, hulking man and a hard worker, fully able to wrestle any man to the ground in a trice, smiled in a stupid manner and bawled, "She be a girl." With tears splashing down his stubbly cheeks, he picked up his tankard and, lifting it in the air, cried, "To me daughter!"

And Buckland, laughing in an equally stupid manner, rose to his own Corinthian height and clanked his tankard against Jack's. "To your daughter," he slurred, and both men drained their large beer mugs. Wiping their faces and slapping one another upon the back, the two men, completely foxed, turned to face Thomas and Kate.

"Innkeeper!" Buckland bellowed, throwing several shillings upon the table, "Bring my curricle! I must see this enchantressing"—he paused, apparently aware that something in the word he had just stumbled over was not correct and tried again—"this eggsquitish, I mean . . . oh, the devil take it . . . this lady . . . home!" And he waved a very loose arm toward Kate in a wide sweeping motion.

Thomas immediately asked Kate if she wished him to protect her against the drunken gentleman. Kate, looking at Buckland, felt no fear at all and said so.

The rotund innkeeper, one eye on the largess just spilt upon his table and one eye on the tall, generous man who had just overpaid his bill by three shillings, bowed several times, wiping his hands upon his greasy apron, and mumbled, "Of course, of course, at once, good sir! At once."

Jack rose to his feet, put his arm about Buckland's shoulder in a jovial manner, and slurred, "Thank ye, kindly, Mr. Buck. Ye be a man, true and all!"

Buckland then drew his arm about Jack's massive back, and for a moment Kate thought that they might crash into the maze of tables and chairs as they moved toward her, on an impossible course to the door.

But somehow they managed the feat, and the cool night air, as the men brushed past Kate and Thomas, seemed to have a bracing effect on them as they breathed deeply. Jack groaned a little and Thomas quickly moved to support his father. Thanking Buckland, Thomas piloted his father toward their cottage, only to have Jack swing them both around in a precarious manner as he cried, "Thank ye for ta game of cribbage, Buck." And his laughter boomed about the sleeping cottages as he cried to all who would listen that he had won five pounds from Mr. Buck. Five pounds! From the worst cribbage player he'd ever seen!

In a few moments, as Kate and Buckland listened to Jack's erratic progress down the street with his son begging him to be quiet, the innkeeper himself brought the curricle around for the fine, well-breeched gentleman.

Helping Kate to alight, the innkeeper, looking from Kate sitting upright in her seat to Buckland who leaned heavily against the carriage door, wisely handed the reins to Miss Draycott, whom he knew to be a bruising rider, at home to a peg, and able to flick a fly off the leader's ear.

Keeping Ashwell's spirited horses in check was no small task, as Kate soon discovered, and she scarcely noticed that the innkeeper had a difficult time assisting Buckland to climb into the sporting vehicle. As she clicked her tongue to the horses, whose hooves were stamping and whose traces jingled like a row of bells, she heard Buckland's laughter and thought that it was more likely she would be escorting him home rather than the reverse. And had he really been waiting for her, spending the entire night in the company of a common labourer? She had a great deal to learn of Mr. Buckland, a great deal indeed.

Kate thanked the innkeeper for assisting her knight errant into the carriage and smiled as Buckland promptly collapsed against her shoulder. Giving the rein a gentle slap and coaxing the fidgety pair with a few carefully chosen words, she set the curricle in motion.

As the elegant vehicle, which Kate found to be beautifully sprung and a pleasure to drive, passed beyond the cobbles of Quening onto the gravel road, Kate could not resist picking up the whip, stuck neatly into a slot at her right. She hoped Buckland was truly in his cups or he might never forgive her for what she was about to do. Cracking the stiff-handled whip briskly over her head and cutting the thin leather into the cold morning air, Kate felt an exhilaration that took her beyond earthly concerns.

The horses knew the short bark of the whip and responded instantly, lengthening their stride, their nostrils dilating as they moved from a polite trot to a long, easy gallop.

Kate felt her arms relax, and the bulk weighing on her suddenly stiffened and sat bolt upright. "Good God, woman! What are you doing?" he cried, any semblance of an inebriated state completely gone.

But Kate did not care suddenly whether he was back from his communing with Bacchus or not, and she cracked the whip over her head again, the horses picking up speed. What pure and exquisite pleasure! She had never driven such a carriage, the wheels spinning over the rocks as though they were made of the smoothest cobbled stones. The wind tore at the curls and ribbons about her head, the pins slipping into her fur-lined cape and her auburn hair began to fly free in waves behind her.

Buckland was about to grab the reins when he chanced to look at Kate's face, lit with an unholy light of pleasure. Seeing the firm hold of the reins in her gloved hands, he sat back, steadying himself by holding the rail in front of him and watching her profile. She did not even know he existed. What kind of woman was this? he wondered as she gave the horses their head and let them fly. He watched her guide them along the road with the slightest of movements. Any fear he had that she might ruin their mouths vanished and he smiled to himself. And this was the woman who was determined to marry James. She might just succeed.

Kate sighed as the cool wind, now cold as they rushed along, burned her cheeks, and she gently eased back on the reins, pulling the horses to a sedate trot. "What excellent cattle!" she cried. "Such perfect movers! Matched to a hair and so beautifully put together!"

"Thank you!" Buckland cried. "They are nearly perfect, are they not?"

Kate looked at him in surprise and said, "I thought these belonged to Lord Ashwell?"

Buckland cleared his throat, then lied, "I chose them for his lordship personally." It was only half a lie, after all.

"You've an eye to horseflesh, Mr. Buckland. I've never driven so well matched a team in my life, and as for this carriage, why, I feel as though I am floating over these wheels." She stared at him and said, with a smile, "You are not drunk, are you?"

He smiled, "Only half foxed, I daresay." And he took the reins from Kate, who gave them up with a sigh. "And if you don't mind my saying so, you look quite worn out, my dear girl!"

Kate leaned back into the black cushions of the curricle and watched the rims of both Cowley Hill and Birdlip Hill turn a light grey. Birds began chattering in earnest and she wondered if all the chicks had suddenly awakened for breakfast. "I don't feel in the least fatigued, although I am sure I am a dreadful sight!" She felt her hair and realized that Maggie's elegant coiffure had disappeared about a mile past, and she immediately untangled the blue ribbons from her auburn curls.

When Buckland looked her over, she laughed, "I meant to be so proper tonight!"

"You gave us quite a shock. I am still not fully recovered."

"Do you disapprove?" Kate eyed him with a measuring look, wondering what he did think of her.

He frowned. Disapproval had never entered his mind. Only

surprise. "No," he answered after a moment. "No, I think not. Although I must say that you floored me."

As the faint outlines of Chipping Fosseworth emerged just beyond the wooded lane, Buckland said, "Why do you involve yourself in so complete a manner? I mean, do you help the good doctor out of philanthropic belief or is it, as I suspect, a desire to see Mrs. Cricklade faint?"

Kate smiled, "No, of course not. Although I think you've an excellent idea there! Oh, I should not say that I know." She chuckled and continued in a quiet voice, "I had but to witness a birth once, to feel the baby, just born, in my arms. To watch it breathe for the first time, and I swore I would always attend anyone who needed me. Buckland, it is as though God reaches down in a moment of glory and touches our dulled hearts and reminds us that we are alive and that we are not alone."

Buckland slowed the horses to a walk and, staring at the road, thought about London, the last season, and the extreme fuss that had been made over his poems. Women had thrown themselves at him, fainting in his arms, begging that he repair their sandals, sending him secret billets, begging for his kisses. How much a nuisance it had all become. Dulled hearts. He remembered back to a time when he was a young lad and had witnessed the birth of a foal, Jupiter's foal, the stallion he had brought with him, born at night with clouds blowing across the moon. But never would he forget the moment when the newly born foal had risen to his wobbly knees and Belas, his father's head groom, had pronounced him sturdy and well.

"Life from life, like fools we wear it down."

Kate glanced at him sharply and frowned. "Are you a poet as well?"

Buckland laughed, "You cannot help but be around Ashwell and not have some of his nonsense invade your speeches."

"I would never refer to his poetry as nonsense."

"Particularly when you are intent on marrying him."

Kate watched the last of the stars disappear as the sky grew lighter and lighter. She would not rise to his bait and answered succinctly, "You are out there, Mr. Buckland. I have held his poetry in great regard for these six months and more." She paused, adding, "Except perhaps the second canto, where I think he lost his way a bit. But then one can hardly quibble with such genius."

The horses jerked under the odd twist Buckland gave to the reins as he said, "What do you mean the second canto? I . . . that is, I know for a fact that Ashwell spent twice as much time on the second canto as he did on the first!"

Kate shrugged her shoulders. "Well, that explains it then. He dwelled too long upon each word. I think they lost a certain freshness."

Buckland realized that though he might be enjoying his anonymity in many ways, Kate's candid criticism was a result of his masquerade, which he found extremely irritating.

Kate asked, "You did not lose to Mr. Coates, did you?"

He laughed, "No, not precisely."

"Now I find that exceedingly kind in you, particularly when you yourself are no stranger to having to live within straitened means."

Feeling a twinge of conscience, he quickly changed the subject, "Why do you treat the villagers' difficulties as your own?"

"At Quening? Oh, I don't. There is little enough that I am able to do at Chipping Fosseworth."

As the horses kept a steady pace, the steep, pitched roofs of the sleeping cottages came into view around a bend in the road, and Buckland exclaimed, "What a pretty village. We entered it in full daylight and, as you know, I had just had the most unsettling encounter with a sharp-tongued village maiden. But this, with the dawn a cool light over the cottages . . . I can understand some of your intense attachment to the place."

Crossing the ancient three-arched bridge of rough-hewn stone, the clip-clop of the hooves echoing against the stream flowing gently beneath the bridge, Kate smiled and said, "How long ago that seems."

Watching a progressive flickering of lights as the villagers began to stir in their cottages, Kate felt a sudden panic and cried, "Buckland, they must not see us! You know what people are! They will gossip and then Ashwell should begin flirting with Julia Moreton!"

Buckland let out a shout of laughter, which he immediately

apologized for when Kate cracked the hard handle of the whip against his booted leg. Taking the whip from her and letting it fly over the horses' heads, Buckland now gave Kate an excellent opportunity to observe his own skill with the remarkable team. As they flew past St. Andrew's Church, beyond the rectory, beyond the Swan and Goose and finally the cottages, Buckland navigated a steep turn in the road that marked the lane to the manor. The horses moved with such precision, such unity that, as they rounded the corner, Kate could not resist saying, "Damned good cattle!" And she laughed at Buckland's startled expression. "And I don't think anyone saw us!"

"I only hope no one heard you. Hoyden!" he answered back.

Crossing another small stone bridge that traversed the River Chering, Buckland finally brought the horses back to a walk and Kate breathed a sigh of relief. The manor loomed before them, silent golden stone in the dawning light as the sun rose steadily behind Cowley Hill. Soon rays would light the chimney tops, setting the manor aglow, but for now the dawn covered the ancient house.

Pulling beneath a chestnut tree, hiding in the shadows, Buckland set his brake. The horses stamped impatiently at having had their gallop curtailed so abruptly, and Buckland, ignoring their snorts and quivers, turned to Kate and, quite without ceremony, took her into his arms.

Her own heart still beating from the jaunt through the village, Kate fell into his arms as though it were the most natural response in the world. Ignoring any pinches from her conscience, Kate received his lips as a morning breeze washed over them. She could not remember such a feeling of peace and felt that she had come home after some long and wearisome journey.

He grabbed the hair that flowed about her shoulders and, pulling it back, kissed her neck and then her lips again. "Kate," he breathed, and his voice, as it flowed over her, acted like cold water as she suddenly realized what she was doing. Placing her hands between them, she pushed him back.

He still held her in a tight embrace but, seeing the panic on her face, relaxed his hold a little.

She cried, "What have I done? Buckland, you cannot think . . . I am not, I do not . . . I just don't know what I am doing!" She took a deep breath and, steadying her voice, continued, "I suppose I have become slightly disordered, what with having been up the entire night. Pray, forget what has happened." She looked into his blue eyes that appeared a dark grey in the shadow of the chestnut tree. "Why do you affect me this way?" She shook her head, frowning at him, and when he tried to kiss her again, she gave a little cry and pulled away from him, "You damned rascally rogue! Let me be!"

Climbing down from the curricle with Buckland's laughter behind her, she jumped to the ground and turned to bob a curtsy. "And I thank you for bringing me home and—and for waiting for me."

Running for the manor as though her life depended on it, Kate dared not look back at Buckland. For some reason she feared that he had but to open his arms and she would return to him. Holding her cape about her neck, she felt terribly panicked, as she had in the woods when he had pursued her. Only this time he was not physically behind her. But somehow, he had managed to gain a part of her that she did not in the least comprehend, some part of her not given to explanation, some portion of her being that responded quite without thought.

Buckland watched her go, a shimmering blue nymph with her thick auburn curls flowing behind her. Good God, what was he thinking except that she was so very ripe for his kisses? He smiled. What a delightful summer this had become. And in a few weeks he would be gone. The smile dimmed on his face as he set the horses in motion. But leave to return to what? To London? To another round of useless gaiety in the Metropolis?

Kate looked down at the smiling faces of Buckland and Ashwell, and she felt her cheeks grow a fiery red color. How had fate directed these two men, to this very spot, at this very moment? Even five minutes earlier she would not have been several branches high into the oak tree and five minutes later she would have most certainly regained the forest floor. Damn and blast, how Buckland plagued her!

"Hallo," she said in a falsely weak voice, holding her skirts about her legs in great fear that the men could see up her dress to her undergarments. These Madame Beaumaris had sent over with her compliments, and they were the most outrageous delicate things, all lace and ribbons, that she had ever seen!

She could trust Ashwell to ignore them, but Buckland, once he had caught a glimpse of them, would never cease tormenting her. "I am quite stuck, my good sirs," she said, keeping her gaze fixed upon James.

Buckland stood back and shook his head at her while James immediately began to ascend the tree. He cried, "What were you doing? What were you after? Are you hurt?"

She pointed to a nest much higher up in the tree and said simply, "I wished to see the inhabitants. The nest is quite ancient and one never knows from year to year who will be using it."

"You sound as though you visit it regularly? How is it you are stuck?" James mounted nearer to Kate, branch by branch, and by now he was breathing with some effort. He was not the athlete Buckland was.

Kate glanced down at Buckland, who had contented himself by circling under the tree and looking up her skirts. The rascal! Had he no shame at all?

Kate regarded James, a thousand thoughts flying at her at once. He did not appear in the least disapproving, either of finding her in the tree or of her conduct of the evening before. Her heart soared as she spoke in Julia's voice, "I know it must seem quite shocking to you, but I have the greatest fondness for baby birds, and usually Mr. Barnsley climbs with me." She would never tell him that the real reason she climbed was to try and locate a kestrel, which she had seen in the vicinity, in hopes of finding one young enough that she could train to hunt.

He reached her level and, extending a hand, held hers tightly and said, in a low voice, "I feel as though I have discovered a fairy amongst these oak leaves." His expression was so intent that it was all Kate could do to keep from laughing. And she

90

would never describe herself as fairylike.

Her eyes brimming with tears from restrained laughter, she said, in a choked voice, "You are so kind."

Buckland's voice from below intruded, "Ah, the beauty of the forest—the light blue of robins' eggs, the delicacy of the snowdrops in February, and the young fawns that scamper about the forest, all long-legged and graceful."

And Kate could see that he had discovered the ribbons of her pantalettes, as well as her own legs, and that in his own silly way he was describing both to her. She would have his head for this and contented herself by envisioning the needles she would use to stick his hide, blast the man.

But instead of answering him as she wished, she turned to James and said, "Pray, assist me, Lord Ashwell. I feel so very foolish."

And slowly they began to descend the tree, parts of her once exquisitely coiffed hair hanging about her shoulders. Maggie had dressed her in one of her new walking dresses, a charming confection of light blue muslin edged with white lace about the modest neckline, puff sleeves and ruffles that formed several rows and tucks about the hem. Over her head she had placed a straw bonnet, since removed for tree-climbing.

She loved this creation of Madame's, bent up at the sides and worn well forward, with curls and ribbons cascading down the back.

When James reached the ground he picked up her bonnet and handed it to her. She was about to put it on when Buckland halted her efforts. He stood very close to her and insisted on pulling several leaves from her hair. As she watched James's face take on quite an angry hue, Buckland actually began tidying her hair—at least he pulled a few more strands to join those that had fallen and ended by placing the bonnet over her curls.

His lips were but a breath away, and she knew that had they been alone, he would not have hesitated to kiss her again. And she would have let him. Oh, Lord, she thought as she turned to regard his blue eyes so evidently intent upon his task, and she wondered if all the women he knew felt so eager to please him. This must stop, her heart cried, and she lowered her eyes to regard the diamond pin stuck in his cravat. Something about the pin struck Kate as odd. How could Buckland afford such an extravagance? Unless it was an heirloom, which of course it must be.

As Buckland stepped away from her she glanced up in time to see James give his friend quite a darkling look. Kate regarded Buckland's rather masklike features as he in turn looked at his friend. At first she thought that James was jealous of Buckland's attentions to her but, with a sudden insight, realized that more was at play than just two men flirting with a country miss.

Kate smoothed out her dress, feeling a little confused at what had passed between the men and wondering if Buckland had told James the truth. But that wouldn't fadge. In the little time she had been with James, she knew that he was the sort of man who, had he learned such a thing, would be cold—civil but cold. And if Buckland had said nothing, then what was it between the men? Perhaps some age-old striving that kept them slightly at daggers drawn? Not caring too much what afflicted the men, Kate knew that she could use such animosity, mild as it was, distinctly to her advantage. Smiling at them both, she bid her beaux to each pick up a wicker basket, which was full of bramble berries that she had collected throughout the warm afternoon.

She asked them to escort her back to the manor and, with a famous poet on her left hand and handsome Mr. Buckland on her right, all she could think of was, oh vanity of vanities, that she wished Julia could see her now. And Kate released a deep, satisfied sigh.

As they moved toward Chering Brook that cut through Brock Farm, Kate paused and regarded the labourers in the field. Something was wrong. Usually there were a score or more and now she could see only half a dozen.

She stopped in her tracks and scanned all the fields about the brook. Farther up the hill, she could see a shepherd bringing his flock down the long, narrow valley, heading back to the farm. Casting her gaze in the direction of the village, Kate noticed again the absence of the usual number of workers.

James said, "What is it? You look quite pale. What is it?"

Kate began moving toward the village again, concerned that something terrible had happened to pull the labourers away from the fields. She answered the poet, "I am not certain if anything is wrong, but not all the farm workers are where they ought to be. You cannot imagine what it has been like this summer and last! Since the Corn Laws were passed, the villagers have gone hungry and the crops are not producing as we had hoped. A Mr. Hunt came through here last month and stirred the villagers up!"

"That man has done more to harm the countryside—"

At James's words, Kate stopped and stared at him. "Harm?" she asked, her tone angry. "And what has he said that is not true?"

Buckland coughed and Kate wheeled upon him, prepared to do battle, only he was wearing such a smug expression that she realized he had actually given her a warning, that her argumentative tone might not be pleasing to the poet. "Oh!" she cried, and turned back down the path.

With Ashwell at her side, she swallowed hard and said, "I do beg your pardon, my lord! I have the most unforgivable temper at times. But you must understand. I . . . we live in the midst of difficult times here about Stinchfield. And every summer we wait to see if it will be too dry or too wet, for either can mean disaster for the wheat and corn. We live by such things."

"And I had no right to speak so hastily. I only meant that Mr. Hunt, though well-meaning, has hardly been able to offer any workable solution of his own."

"You are in London most of the time, are you not? And did you vote for the Corn Laws as well?"

James glanced at Buckland, who nodded at him, and he answered her question, "Though I know I will gain your displeasure, Miss Draycott, I did indeed and would do so again."

Kate felt her heart sink a little as she stared at the path in front of her. Where were the villagers? Oh, she sighed, if only Ashwell had not voted for the wretched laws that made food a nearly impossible commodity for the labourers to afford throughout the long winter when snow covered the cottages.

Buckland's voice intruded as they continued down the path.

Catching her arm and stopping her progress, he looked at her and said, "If we did not protect the home wheat by high tariffs on the importation of grains, the farmers as well as the landowners would lose more than this country can bear for them to lose."

"That is an argument I have heard over and over, Mr. Buckland, and however much it sounds logical, you have but to live with the villagers for the better part of a winter to see the thin faces of the children, to know that justice has somehow again landed on the glowing hearths of the wealthy."

Ashwell regarded Kate's impassioned face and he said to Buckland, "She does seem to have a point, George." And Kate cast him a grateful glance.

"Then what would you propose, Miss Draycott?" Buckland pressed her, shifting his basket of berries. "Would you propose that no tariffs were imposed at all and that a bulk of the tenant farmers across the country lose everything? For that is precisely what would happen. In one fell swoop, we could wipe out an entire class. Surely your papa earns a great deal from this farm we have just passed."

Kate opened her mouth to speak but could not. She was well acquainted with the yeomanry about Stinchfield and knew, in great detail, their hardships as equally as she knew Mrs. Coates's difficulties. She would not wish their years of toil to end in disaster.

Buckland spoke in a softened voice, "The answer is never simple."

"But why must it affect those who can afford it least? Why is the burden not shared equally?"

"Because that is human nature, human frailty. And it is not true in every village as you may imagine. For example, I know that last year Ashwell here, though he never cares to boast of it, made his corn mill available at a very low cost to all of the villagers in Stowhurst. Am I not correct, James?"

"What?" James looked at Buckland in an astonished manner, then said, "Yes, yes, of course."

Buckland added, "And since he is so good a friend, I will tell you that in addition, because of the high cost of wheat everywhere, he made it possible for those who worked on his

94

tenanted lands to purchase grain at reduced prices."

Kate glanced at the poet and gave him a smile full of affection. "How good you are, my lord! How good and how kind! That everyone had your heart and your sense of justice!"

James did not know what to say. For one thing, she was praising him for something his friend had done, and for another, he had never seen a woman wear so noble and impassioned an expression before. She was beyond beauty, beyond describing in mere mortal terms. She was everything that "woman" ought to be and more. Her voice, as she thanked him, sounded like the voice of an angel, and her face wore a glow that seemed to brighten the countryside. He would write a poem in her honor this very evening. And, given his sudden inspiration, the beautiful fire in her brown eyes, he might just write a poem worthy of Pope or Milton. Unable to speak, he took Kate's hand and, bowing low over it, placed a long, worshipful kiss upon her fingers.

Kate could not mistake James's sudden admiration of her and pressed a hand against her bosom to keep from letting out a great cry of victory. Regarding the head bent low over her hand, she was preparing just such words that would further endear him to her when a shout near the village caused all of them to look toward St. Andrew's Church. And as they saw, in the distance, a crowd of people moving beyond the church, the three turned as one, without hesitation, and began running down the path—the men with berry baskets knocking clumsily against their breeches and Kate with pale blue skirts in hand.

By the time they reached the outskirts of the village, passing the lane that marked the manor's border, a cheering rose up and suddenly all of Kate's fears subsided.

"Oh, no! But how absurd!" she cried. "I had forgotten. It is only a mill!"

The two men looked at one another over Kate's head, both eyes opening wide and taking on the expression of hunters who had just found their quarry, and said in a voice of unison, "A mill?"

And Kate watched in great amusement as they dropped her baskets, a few of the bramble berries spilling onto the cobbles of the street, bowed quickly to her, doffing their hats, and headed in a run toward the rectory. Beyond the parson's house was a stretch of common where a great crowd of all the local inhabitants of Stinchfield, Chipping Fosseworth, and the other villages had congregated. The small road was jammed with travelling vehicles and horses of all kinds. For a moment she deliberated. Had Ashwell not been present she would have enjoyed attending such a spectacle, but given the poet's most recent display of interest in her, she wisely picked up her baskets and turned toward the manor road. And how much fun she would have at the shooting match when she would punish them both for deserting her in so despicable a fashion!

Kate fluttered her fan across her face, the short brim of her poke bonnet trimmed in a spray of pink roses and leaves of the deepest green, framing the fair skin of her face in a charming manner. She pouted but a very little—Julia's pout—as she slapped Lord Ashwell's arm with her fan. "My lord," she complained to him. "There I was, deserted, the object of many desperate glances. . . ." She hid her smile behind her fan, thinking of the grey cat that had eyed her in a perfectly disinterested manner as he lounged beneath one of the manor's chestnut trees, "Oh, how could you abandon me so?"

"I beg your forgiveness," Lord Ashwell exclaimed, raising her hand to his lips. He smiled, knowing that she was teasing him and so delightfully well.

Kate could not resist as she turned toward Mr. Buckland, who was speaking with Mary, and said aloud, "But your friend does not seem in the least penitent."

James smiled, "His manners are boorish, to be sure. I recommend you have nothing to do with him."

Buckland and Mary both turned to regard the pair before them and Buckland said nothing in his defense, merely looking her over quite thoroughly.

Kate had dressed with such care and, oh, Madame Beaumaris was such an *artiste*. Her gown, in the softest cambric print designed with a white background and covered in small lavender flowers, swirled about her in the afternoon breeze at Aldgrove Hall above Stinchfield. Emmet had insisted upon the match being held there because Kate's bear had been shot closer to his village of Lower Aldgrove than any of the other villages.

Kate carried a dainty parasol, which she twirled and poked about like a child. In fact, not since she had been a child of twelve had she owned a parasol. Gazing out at the gathering of the manor families, Kate smiled. The summer day seemed perfect, not terribly hot, with the sky sparkling overhead in the deepest blue. She watched the ladies already knotted in a gossiping group sitting on a rise overlooking the well-groomed lawns in back of the Hall. By a long table, on the lawn and a hundred yards opposite the ladies, the men had gathered to quench their thirst with tankards of beer.

Near the table, Julia, Hope Cerney, and Charity Cricklade teased Roger Whiteshill, and Kate thought Julia, with her piercing laughter rising above even the conversation about her, the most cruel creature on earth. Couldn't she see that Roger had not the least ability to turn off her silly jests? And thinking of Julia, Kate turned toward the poet and realized that he had scarcely paid the least bit of attention to the beauty.

Ever since her arrival, James had attached himself to her side and Kate had enjoyed flirting with him. All of it was so new to her! Once or twice he had complimented her on her manners and she could not help but wonder what he thought of the match. Whenever she brought it up, he seemed to grow unusually silent. She had the impression that he did not approve, yet he had said nothing unkind or demeaning.

They wandered about the yew-hedge maze that Kate had memorized when she was but six years old, which sided the honey-coloured stone hall. Afterward, they watched the servants arranging and rearranging the various targets for the forthcoming match. Every now and again, Kate would let her gaze drift to the targets, and in her mind's eye she could feel the weight of both her fowling piece and her pistols, feel the kick against her shoulder of her rifle and the recoil of the pistols in her hand, and she could scarcely wait to begin the match.

Twice James had called her back from these imaginings and twice she had blamed her absentmindedness on the heat. Would he procure her a glass of lemonade? she asked. Just before he scuttled off to find her a cooling drink, he leaned close to her and said, "I feel it is all my fault that you are now having to take part in this match. It was wrong of me to have encouraged you to do so." His gaze travelled about the assembled company and he continued, "No lady should be asked to expose herself in so wretched a fashion. You must be experiencing the worst sort of mortification. I am sorry."

The words had been spoken and her worst fears, that he was unhappy about her involvement in the shooting match, had now come to pass. What should she do and did he really imagine that she was mortified? Far from it.

Sitting down on a white wrought iron seat, Kate thought that nothing could be further from the truth. The fact was that she felt her stomach churn and her blood rise at the very thought of the upcoming event. Buckland joined them at this moment, just as James was about to proceed on his mission to provide her with a glass of lemonade, and he laughed at her. She was looking at the targets now with Buckland's laughter causing her hand to ball up about the handle on her parasol, but James's words irritated her far worse than any of Buckland's taunting laughter.

"Perhaps you ought to sit in the shade, Miss Draycott. You have been in the sun far longer than any young lady should and I daresay you are suffering from a little sun sickness. Your extreme thirst concerns me."

She hid her face that he might not see the sudden anger she knew burned upon her cheeks. Facing the targets, she replied in a quiet voice, "I will move to stand in the shade when you've returned. I promise." And Katherine Draycott, who had been known to sit astride her horse for hours at a time in all seasons of weather, under a blazing sun or the freezing cold of a January snowstorm, met his concerned gaze and added, "I am certain there is great good sense to what you have said. Thank you, my lord."

At these words he smiled and, bowing over her hand, walked toward the long table where refreshments were being served. She watched his retreating back, digging the tip of her parasol into the sod beneath her feet and sighing. His form was tall, dignified, manly. But oh, he did as he was bid. Lord, she would be bored within a sennight of marriage to her poet. She could even imagine that when he kissed her, his lips would be gentle, not in the least insistent as were . . .

"Now what are you thinking of, I wonder?" Buckland smiled at Kate, his lazy smile that allowed his dimple to show only a very little. He stood a few feet away from her, blocking the bright afternoon sun with his strong shoulders encased in a form-fitting coat of blue superfine. Even in the August heat, his shirt points did not wilt.

Kate felt the color rise on her cheeks again, only this time for a different reason. Letting the parasol sink a little further into the turf as she twisted it this way then that, she patted the white wrought iron seat beside her and said, "You would be very shocked if I told you."

"No, I wouldn't. You were wishing I would kiss you again." And he sat down beside her.

Kate's gaze flew to his face, unable to credit her ears. She would not hedge with Buckland and said simply, "How did you know?"

"Your expression was one of desire."

"Now that sounds like a lot of humbug to me, Mr. Buckland. Something I did not expect from you."

"All right." He took his snuffbox from his pocket, then said, "You were feeling bored with my good friend James and wondering what it would be like to be married to such a fellow. Now, if you were a woman, let us say like Mary Chalford, then I daresay one might describe marriage to James as heavenly. But you, my sweet Kate, *bonny Kate, and sometimes Kate the curst; but Kate, the prettiest Kate in Christendom,* you would likely perish under the man's gentle touch."

Kate lifted her eyes to regard Aldgrove Copse that ran atop Waverley Hill. She sighed. He was right, and already she knew it to be true.

Suddenly, she felt tense. Something had changed. Turning to regard Buckland in the glaring light of the sun, she saw his eyes were clouded with some heavy emotion as he said, "Quit this madness, Kate, now, before we are lost to one another forever. James cannot make you happy and he is just enough of a young fool, with ideals that reach to Olympus, that he will believe you love him."

Taking her hand, he squeezed it hard. Kate, angry at his words, pulled her hand away, saying, "What do you mean, 'before we are lost to one another'? I do not understand. Are you in love with me? Do you wish to marry me?"

Kate watched him recoil at so direct a question, and she pulled at the curls on her forehead, then straightened the bow tied beneath her ear. "I see how it is with you and that James most certainly had the right of it. You are a conceited fellow. Did you expect me to swoon at your feet for speaking such flummery? And you are wrong about one thing: I know that James can make me happy because of how his poetry makes me feel. More resides in his heart than yours could ever hold."

She rose abruptly, unfurling her parasol over her head. She did not wish to create a scene and so remained standing by the bench. She would marry Ashwell. She would lead him as she had seen Julia lead a dozen young men, and she would marry him.

Kate could not suppress the slightest feeling of discontent. If only Buckland were not impoverished, she would try to win him instead. But then, he was the sort of man who never married, who enjoyed sporting with females but who could not quite love a woman, really love a woman.

She looked at the targets, bright red and white canvases in a tidy little row, and wished that the match would begin.

Kate saw James returning with an iced cup of lemonade and, turning to Buckland, smiled sweetly upon him while she dipped a small curtsy. Blast the man for cutting up her peace. She wished that she might jab his ribs with the tip of her parasol, but instead, she moved to stroll toward Ashwell and allowed herself to be led to a quiet, shady spot beneath a large oak tree near the home wood.

Kate levelled her pistol, her favorite pearl-handled one, rifled for accuracy. Through the sight, she could see the center of the target. Her first two shots she allowed to hit to the side of the painted canvas target and she was just beginning to realize how impossible her situation was. She lowered her arm and pretended to check yet again the flintlock mechanism, then glanced at Ashwell. His gaze was sober and she could see in his brown eyes that he disapproved. Resolving not to disappoint him, she raised her weapon and, without so much as a glance down the barrel of the pistol, fired.

She felt the recoil of the pistol and wanted to die. She had not even hit the target, and Kit Barnsley hooted at her. She wanted to tear apart his round, freckled face at his taunting. Even Roger Whiteshill called to her. "Kate, do you intend to shame us all?"

The group of women, still resting on the hill beneath a large beech tree, chattered amongst themselves, the gentle waves of their gossip flitting across the stretch of lawn that separated them from the men. Every once in a while, Kate caught snatches of gossip, of Louisa Moreton's approaching confinement, of favorite recipes for preserving peaches and cherries, of the widow in Edgecote who had been the mill owner's mistress for years, of the mill owner whose recent death had left everyone in a puzzle as to whom the mill belonged. It was rumoured that the cloth mill now belonged to Lord Sapperton, that he had purchased the mill from old Mr. Driffield before he died. Most of these bits of conversation Kate ignored until Mrs. Moreton's voice, carried along by the afternoon breeze, reached her. "I was never more shocked when I discovered that Miss Draycott would be shooting with the young men! Whoever heard of such a thing!"

"Indeed," Mrs. Cricklade responded. "Oh, indeed! Quite dreadful, as I always say!"

Kate wondered if Lord Ashwell had heard Mrs. Moreton, and she set her pistol down upon the table behind her. Buckland increased her discomfort at the entire situation by whispering in her ear, "I knew it to be the grossest falsehood, Miss Draycott. No woman can shoot a firearm with the least precision, and I now count myself fortunate that you did not shoot me dead the other day. A fair shot, indeed!" And he stepped away from her, brandishing his own sleek pistols as though he had been a highwayman.

Kate lifted her gaze to regard Buckland's taunting expression. More than anything, she wished to show him precisely how well she could fire her weapons, but that was impossible. And yet, as she looked at her friends—Stinchfield's hunting-mad bucks Roger, Christopher, Emmet, and Stephen—she began to feel an enormous pressure that she was letting them down. Never could she have anticipated so difficult a task as this—setting aside every normal feeling in order to win a husband. And what of this wretched masquerade that she was imposing upon Ashwell? When she had finally marched him down the aisle, would she then return to her usual pursuits? No, this mask, this pretense of being like Julia or like Mary, would be hers to wear forever.

She turned away from Buckland, regarding the target again as she let out a frustrated sigh. Picking up her second pistol, she loaded it quickly with powder and rammed a pistol ball through the rifled grooves of the barrel, tamping it firmly against the powder as she had done a thousand times before. Approaching her mark, she reminded herself yet again of her future, of Jaspar, of Chipping Fosseworth and how her schemes would make it possible for her to improve the lot of the villagers. She fired, planting the pistol ball into the cork target at the outer rim of the wide red circle. Precisely where she had aimed.

The bucks groaned with disappointment. And when Buckland fired the remaining rounds from his own exquisite duelling pistols engraved in silver scrollwork, the young men applauded his marks, both nearly dead centre. Kate ran to the target, wanting to see these last hits, and then congratulated Buckland on his skill. She began stripping off her gloves, relieved that she could now put all of this behind her, when Emmet startled her by saying. "And now for the second of five volleys." He frowned slightly at Kate.

Kate stared at him and nearly wanted to cry. She could not face so much agitation for an additional four volleys.

Emmet turned to Buckland and said, in his direct manly fashion, "You are certainly the victor of this first volley, but I know that Kate will come about." He then smiled upon Kate and tried to encourage her. "I know it is a trifle warm. Do you care to rest for a few minutes?"

These words were like a bucket of ice water over Kate. How

dare Emmet, even in his sincerity, speak to her as though she were a delicate female who would wilt in the sun if she were not cosseted. How dare he!

She heard Buckland's laughter and, glancing at him, realized that he had seen her expression and was gloating. The cur! And yet she could hardly blame him, for he knew precisely how much her affectations were costing her. And she respected the fact that he gave her no ground, no sympathy.

As he turned to walk back to the table where their firearms were kept, Kate watched him begin reloading his pistol. Stephen Barnsley, who was quite mediocre in his own ability to hit a target, tried to instruct Kate. "I think I know your difficulty. You ought to look down your sight a bit more carefully. And that pistol of yours, do you suppose it throws a bit to the left?"

Kate gasped as she stared at Stephen, and out of the corner of her eye she knew that Kit and Roger were looking anywhere but at her. "What do you mean?" she said in a quiet voice, which caused Emmet to say in a low voice, "Easy, Kate."

Kate ignored Emmet and continued, "You cannot hit the trunk of a fat oak tree at five paces, nonetheless tell me how to fire my pistols. And they do not throw left!"

Stephen's face turned bright red with sudden anger as he answered her back, "Well, you've hardly proven any differently yourself now, have you? And I've only wanted to be kind, particularly after all of us praised you to the skies! You have certainly made us look nohow! Why, Buckland must think we are all mad," he sneered at her, "or liars!"

Kate swallowed hard. She might not like what Stephen said, but all of it was true. She glanced at each of them: Kit and his freckled face that wore an expression of disappointment; Stephen, running hasty fingers through his wavy brown hair, a furrow between his brown eyes; handsome, good-natured Roger, who had always included her in every hunting scheme even when the other young men did not want to; and Emmet. Good, solid Emmet, his wide hazel eyes appealing to her sense of honor as though he considered her—and always would—one of them.

She said, "I'm sorry. But you ought not to care what a man

like Buckland thinks."

The four young men stared at Kate, and Stephen stepped away from her, slapping his breeches in a frustrated manner. Christopher said, in a quiet voice, "I guess we've just never seen this side of you before, Kate. You seem more like Julia today and you're wrong about not caring for that man's opinion. Why, he's worth ten of the poet you're so set on impressing."

Kate dropped her gaze before this censure. A few days ago she had hoped to keep her schemes from all of them, but here even Kit now saw clearly what she was about. She felt an alarming sob rise up in her throat and hoped that she would not add a mountain of tears to her current humiliation. Then they would think she had turned into a watering pot. Did they actually think she was enjoying herself? she wondered. And as for Ashwell . . . oh, hang Ashwell! Biting back her tears, she met her friend's accusing stares and said, "I think I have been behaving a trifle foolishly. I'll do better. Indeed, I promise I shall."

Chapter Six

The bucks, now wearing more hopeful expressions, returned to instructing the servants on setting up the new targets and Kate resumed her place beside Buckland.

He would fire first this round, doing so with amazing accuracy, but Kate knew she could best him. Tossing her gloves onto the table beside the bag of pistol balls, she reloaded both of her firearms and, after one glance at Ashwell, who had become, quite thankfully, engrossed in conversation with Mary Chalford, took her place and levelled her pistol toward the target. Lining up her sights as she had a hundred times, Kate squeezed the trigger and let out her breath at the same time. The pistol ball erupted from the gun with a loud explosion and Kate smiled. What a sweet, sweet sensation. She closed her eyes for a moment and let the smoke from the flashpan burn her nostrils. Hang Ashwell, she loved her pistols.

Down by the targets, a cheering went up and Kate knew the pistol ball had hit its mark. Jaspar came up and slapped her on the shoulder, staggering a little and carrying a tankard of beer. "That's more like you, Kate. Thought you were going to put me to the blush today." He looked over her head at Buckland and, in a slurred voice, continued, "Now we'll see some real shooting, eh Buckling?"

Kate levelled her second pistol and again felt the power of the gun sting the nerves all along her arm as the pistol ball emerged, spinning in an accurate arc toward the target.

Buckland's voice reached her, a low, resonant tone that only she could hear. *"Sweet Kate, bonny Kate, Kate the curst."* And then in earnest, "You are an exceptional markswoman. I bow to your skill."

She inclined her head back and then challenged him, "You cannot best my last two marks." Her large brown eyes lit with a golden fire.

He looked at her in a serious manner and then a smile overspread his features, his dimple playing upon his cheek in a most reprehensible fashion. He lifted his pistol and, closing one eye, looked down the field at Kate's last two hits and planted his own pistol ball firmly between them.

"Good God," she cried. "You've done it! I never would have believed it! Why, none of these men can shoot so well. And James was wrong. There is no way I could possibly take you down a peg or two. You are a nonpareil!" She paused for a moment, then added, "However, I still wish that you had not done quite so well."

He laughed as he turned to pick up his second pistol and said, "Then you should learn never to offer so hearty a challenge. And levelling his pistol at the target, he squeezed the trigger gently and set his second ball a little to the left of the three holes in the center."

Kate, her hands upon her hips, cried, "Oh, that is much better."

He grimaced at her and, with something of a serious expression, said, "Actually, I was a little surprised at that first hit."

"Better and better," Kate said, and she smiled at Buckland, who returned her smile.

Julia Moreton, her parasol twirling happily upon her shoulder, flounced up to them and gushed, "Mr. Buckland! What a fine shot you are! I have never seen anything like it!" she exclaimed, her blue eyes wide and her thick lashes batting in what Kate could only consider the most theatrical manner possible.

Buckland, setting his pistol on the table, answered her in kind, "Why, thank you, Julia. A lovely compliment from a jewel in these rough Cotswold hills."

"Julia?" Kate blinked at Buckland.

Julia looked at Kate, her expression quite innocent, "Oh, Mr. Buckland and I have become the greatest of friends, and he has promised to teach me how to shoot these nasty pistols of his, haven't you?"

Kate regarded Buckland with a satisfied smile and said, "Now, this I should greatly like to see." She turned to Julia and added, "I wish I had known that you had such a great interest in firearms. I could have taught you myself." And she raised a brow at Julia and wondered how the beauty could possibly answer this speech. Surely, she would come off looking foolish.

But Kate was not quite used to matching swords with Julia, who came off the best by saying, "Oh, I would never take instruction from a mere female."

Kate was ready to enter the lists at such an invitation, when the bucks approached her and Buckland, saying that given the evidence of their skill, they felt that their positions ought to be set back an additional ten paces, to lend a little more sport to the proceedings. And after the tables were moved and the firing resumed, the match began in earnest, all thoughts of Julia forgotten, with Kit and Roger each taking turns firing between volleys just for the pleasure of it.

Mary Chalford watched Lord Ashwell's profile as he in turn watched Kate, and she repressed a small sigh. As she let her own gaze drift toward Kate, she noticed that her friend was quite windblown, with some of her auburn curls escaping her poke bonnet and dancing about her shoulders. Tense shoulders, Mary thought, the rifle resting heavily in Kate's arms. The crack of the heavier fowling pieces reverberated about the trees surrounding the green and travelled up the hills above Lower Aldgrove. How could Kate bear to stand in the sun so long and to fire that noisy thing? Mary pressed her kerchief against her temple, closing her eyes for a moment, and she heard Ashwell's voice ask, in a kind manner, "Are you all right, Miss Chalford? You look quite pale."

Mary opened her eyes and gazed into the most sensitive brown eyes she had ever seen. Her heart ached, just as it had that first afternoon when the poet and his friend had entered Chipping Fosseworth and Lydia had behaved so abominably. "No, no. It is nothing, really. Only the headache, a little."

"We are too near this constant firing of weapons. The air positively reeks of gunpowder!"

"You may be right. I think I ought to move."

James, who had forgotten that his goddess was still involved in the match, stood up and looked about him. "There," he said, pointing to a grove of young beech trees that sported a bench and plenty of shade. "The wind will blow across us first and carry the noise of the firearms toward the house. It will be quieter, I think."

Mary looked at Kate and then back at the poet. She knew that her dearest friend was making every effort to win the poet, but her head ached and her heart seemed ready to burst at any moment. So she begged Kate silently to forgive her, then allowed the poet to lift her to her feet and escort her some hundred yards, to the shaded woods.

They sat on the bench, and Mary leaned gratefully back into the slatted seat and said, "How long do you propose to stay here, Lord Ashwell?" And then she regretted her question. It sounded so forward.

But James seemed not in the least aware of anything exceptional about this question and answered quietly, "As long as Ash—er . . . as long as Buckland wishes to stay. I am here on his account, you see."

And Mary understood it all, as though he had just carefully explained the situation to her. From the first, she had thought this sensitive young man quite at odds with his rambunctious poetry, and she could not understand why so wealthy a poet would wear linen that had worn a trifle thin in spots. Oh, no one else would notice, but she was herself so notable a needlewoman and housewife that such small details burnt holes in her imagination. Did the poet pretend to be impoverished, while the impoverished friend pretended to be wealthy? For as worn as James's clothes were, Buckland's were astonishingly new, starched, immaculate, and the man wore diamonds tucked into his shirts!

But what did the two men mean by it? Why would they wish

to take on different identities, except perhaps to find a new way to survive another boring summer? Only one thing confused her and that was James's poetry. She knew from several conversations with him that he was devoted to the muse. She pulled a piece of tatting from her reticule and began working the small silver shuttle. In a quiet voice, as James leaned against the bench and looked up into the trees teeming with sparrows, she said, "I beg you will call me Mary, Lord Ashwell. I am hardly used to anyone calling me by so formal an appellation as Miss Chalford. Indeed, I dislike it immensely."

James smiled down at her, liking her friendly face. "And you must call me James."

She paused in her tatting and could not resist asking, "The title page of your first volume of poetry says that your name is George and I am wondering why you go by James." She watched his gaze shift beneath her own and she turned back to her tatting, satisfied with this unspoken answer.

She smiled at his words as he coughed and said, "Oh, yes, well, it is really quite simple. My—my second name is James and my mother always called me that!"

"Ah," Mary nodded. Still wondering about his poetry, she asked, "And what are you writing at present? Are you writing a third canto to your epic?"

James looked down at her and Mary caught her breath as she gazed into eyes that appeared as though a thousand candles had just been lit in them. "How kind of you to ask, Miss— er . . . Mary. No, I've no intention at present of writing the third canto. I am collecting a group of sonnets on an entirely new theme—on the seasons, the weather—and I most certainly shall write a poem or two or perhaps a hundred to this beautiful Cotswold country."

"Sometime I should greatly like to hear one of your new sonnets, that is, if I am not being too presumptuous."

He smiled in so happy a fashion that Mary blushed a little and concentrated on her tatting.

"On the contrary," he said. "I should be grateful to you for lending an ear."

*   *   *

"You are unconscionable, you know," Kate said in a whisper.

Buckland responded in an equally quiet voice, "Of course, but look at the results. Admit it. Had I not provoked you, you would still be prancing around this estate, your hair as neat as a pin and your spirits in the dust."

As they stood looking over all of the targets, now spread out beneath an elm tree, Kate knew that he spoke the truth. She felt her neck sting and realized that her unprotected skin had become burnt from the afternoon of shooting. Lord, but she felt satisfied, droplets of perspiration tickling the space between her breasts. She removed her bonnet and began wafting it over her flushed features, knowing full well that her hair was straggling about her face and shoulders and that the knot at the top of her head was thoroughly flattened by the bonnet. Oh, but she didn't care! And how content she felt, as though she had been out with Miss Diana all day and had come home weary, with rabbits slung over the pommel of her saddle.

All the bucks went over and over the canvases, and Julia and Charity teased Roger about his curly blond hair. After Kit extolled Kate's performance, he gave her a handkerchief and told her to wipe the dirt from her face. Kate accepted it thankfully and was a little surprised when Buckland took her bonnet out of her hands and began fanning her with it. "Oh, thank you," she cried, noticing that he too looked warm from the exercise.

"Who is the victor?" Mary cried out cheerfully as she and James approached. Kate watched the poet take in her slightly dishevelled appearance and realized what a truly dreadful picture she must present.

James looked at Kate and became aware of how beautiful she was, the exercise of the afternoon adding a glow to her fair skin. And yet she was so untidy! But for some reason he did not care. He looked at the bonnet his friend was wafting over Kate's face and neck, and he felt so intense a streak of anger, of jealousy, course through him that, without any plan for being uncivil, he turned toward Mary and, bowing hastily, said, "Pray forgive me, Mary, but I had forgotten to procure you a glass of lemonade." And with one frowning glance toward

Kate, he fairly marched away.

Kate felt the color rise in her cheeks as she watched him retreat toward the manor, where a servant had just emerged bearing another enormous pitcher of lemonade. The bucks were still busy sorting out the targets and determining who had won the match, so they had not witnessed the poet's sudden anger. Kate looked at Mary, whose gaze was focused on the targets, and then she looked at Buckland, who was staring thoughtfully after James. She had thoroughly disgusted the man she hoped to marry.

Kate pinned as many straggling curls away from her face as she could and reseated her rose-strewn bonnet atop her head. Buckland turned to her and, in a serious voice, said, "I have enjoyed this contest a great deal, Miss Draycott. You are as good a markswoman as your friends have proclaimed." He smiled, his dimple showing. "Except for those first few unlucky shots, which"—he pulled on Kit's coattails—"I beg you will remove from the judging. Consider that canvas our practice target."

The men gave a cheer at this magnanimous gesture, for then they were able to proclaim Kate the winner, since she had neared the centre of each target more often than Buckland. He bowed graciously to her.

Kate curtsied slightly, receiving congratulations from all her friends, a brusque smack on her cheek from Jaspar, a kiss on her hand from Sir William, and stiff nods of acknowledgement from the attending matrons. Julia ignored her, but she cared little for any of it. Only one truth remained: She had offended Lord Ashwell with her unmaidenly conduct.

After she had tidied her hair, Kate made a slow, thoughtful progress back to her friends and neighbours. The contentment she had felt after the match had now become misery of the worst sort. How thoroughly she had exposed herself to Ashwell. And how deeply offended and outraged he must be. She was a hoyden, just as Buckland had said, and what man of Ashwell's sensitivity would ever be willing to take such a female to wife! No man in his senses, surely!

As Kate crossed the lawn to stand beside Mary, she noticed that Julia was wild with excitement. In an undertone, she asked

Mary, "What is it? What has happened?"

"Lord Ashwell has invited us all back to the Swan and Goose for a cold supper of duck and champagne!" Kate regarded her friend for a moment, a little surprised at how pretty and shining her close-set blue eyes had suddenly become. Mary was always the soul of prosaic duty and common sense, and she had never heard her friend so much as evince the smallest interest in any such outing before. Any vague alarm Kate felt she quickly pushed away.

Kate stood at the threshold to the parlour of the Swan and Goose and searched the dim interior crowded with her friends. Her heart skipped a beat when Lord Ashwell moved forward to greet her. He then took her hand and presented her to the assembled company as the day's victor. Kate smiled and bowed to the applause that flowed over her, even receiving a congratulatory nod from Buckland. But how difficult it was to even look at Ashwell, knowing he was angry with her.

Kate waited in silence for the poet to speak. Servants, bearing large trays of local fare, moved in and out of the guests as they wended their way to a long table beneath the leaded windows. And still she waited.

Receiving a glass of iced champagne that Ashwell procured for her, Kate took a sip and, glancing over the rim of her glass, felt several riotous butterflies perform acrobatics in her stomach. Finally, she could bear the strain no longer and cried, "I have offended you, have I not?"

He looked into large fawnlike eyes and felt startled again at Kate's beauty. His brows furrowed, he said, "No, you have not. Whatever do you mean?"

"But I thought, at the shooting match, that you—that I—"

He begged her to be seated and said, "I behaved like a schoolboy. You must forgive me. Only to see you standing with Buckland, I lost my head."

Kate opened her eyes wide. He had been jealous! Ashwell had been angry not with her but with Buckland.

She felt so relieved as she sipped her champagne that she now knew precisely what she should say. For the poet might set

112

all of his feelings down to jealousy, but she knew in her heart that he was still considerably displeased with her own love of sport. In a quiet voice, she said, "And you must forgive me, too, my lord. I should never have taken part in the match today. I suppose Jaspar has not quite known how to raise a young lady. You see, my mother passed away five years ago, and without her guidance, society's shoals have been a considerable mystery to me. Indeed, only recently have I even begun attending the assemblies."

Lord Ashwell, struck by this terrible injustice in Kate's life, smiled kindly upon her. As he guided her toward the table now laden with food, he spoke in a low voice, "Your upbringing has indeed been most unfortunate and, again, I blame myself that you had to submit to the torture of such a public exhibition today. But if you think that I am the least offended by your actions, then you have a great deal to learn about James Montrose."

Becoming a little more accustomed to the poet's aspersions on Jaspar, Kate ignored this portion of his recital and, as she placed a sliver of duck upon her plate, asked, "Montrose? Is that one of your Christian names."

James, who had been taking a sip of champagne, coughed and spilled a little of the bubbling wine on the ancient wood floor. "No . . . that is, yes. George James Montrose Cleeve, Lord Ashwell." And he took a deep breath, turning to see if Buckland had overheard this slip.

Kate pressed his arm. "George Cleeve, and you are from Stowhurst. But you cannot be! I mean, are you my cousin?"

James opened his eyes wide, "What? Your cousin? Good gracious, no! Why, I've never heard of you until a few days ago." This, at least, was true.

Kate seemed so struck by this coincidence that she shook her head as though to clear it. "But do you know of a George Cleeve?"

James looked toward Buckland again and wondered what he should do. He certainly felt that he was about to make a muddle of the whole thing, when a brilliant thought struck him and he smiled. "Of course I know a George Cleeve, of Stowhurst. But, if I may say so without offending you, I don't care for him much above half. A bit too high in the instep for me."

Kate let out her breath that had gotten stuck somewhere in her throat and she laughed, "How stupid of me! Of course you could not be my cousin!" She confided in him. "I know you must think this very odd in me, but I have never met George Cleeve, and since he has had no contact with my father in these many years, though he is heir to the manor, well, you may say as many disparaging things of him as you like."

Kate saw a blur of brown pass by the window, and as her plate was full, she turned to find a seat in the crowded room, only to watch the door fly open and Rupert Westbourne walk in.

Kate smiled at the dandy's entrance, the long lace at his sleeves flapping about as Rupert dabbed at his face with a delicate lace kerchief. "How terribly late I am," he cried, searching the room. Finding Ashwell's face, he minced across the dark wood-panelled chamber, bowed in a fashion more in keeping with the last century than the current one, and exclaimed, "You must, positively you must forgive me, Lord Ashwell! Say you will lest I faint. You see, I had travelled the entire distance to Aldgrove Hall, only to find that everyone had flitted to the Swan and Goose. You can imagine my extreme distress."

Kate shook her head, feeling completely mystified by Rupert, who was also a poet of sorts. She had heard once that in addition to the lengthy sonnets he hoped one day to have published, the dandy also wrote extremely vulgar and satirical verse, fit only for the ears of the cronies who formed his entourage and met almost daily at the Bell Inn on Stinchfield's High Street.

She looked him over, from his curling blond hair to his brown velvet coat and flowered waistcoat, to his fawn-coloured breeches tied at the knees with several absurd bows. Clocks, also from the previous century, adorned his silk stockings, and two enormous shoe buckles decorated his absurdly high-heeled shoes. The bucks could scarcely tolerate him, and Kate thought Rupert a ridiculous macaroni whose poetry was little better than his choice of dress.

Just before she passed beyond the dandy, she noticed that

his brow was quite wet with perspiration, as though he had been running, and that a dark smudge adorned the right leg of his breeches. Since he was usually so impeccable in his dress, Kate could not help but wonder what he could have possibly done to have exerted himself.

The dandy's voice filled half of the room as he exclaimed to anyone who would listen, "I know you must think me quite hen-hearted not to have attended this intriguing shooting match. Who won—Kate? But of course, no one is a match for Katherine Draycott—pistol, fowling piece, or sword. Did they duel with the short sword as well? No? I feel so relieved, positively I do, for you know how I abhor—*abhor!*—violence of any kind." He dabbed at his nose with the kerchief. "Really, I begin to feel faint already!" Then he giggled and approached the sideboard, where Stephen Barnsley, who towered over him by seven inches, could not keep from offering a grunt of disgust over his appearance as well as his speeches and, plate in hand, moved away.

Buckland, heading for the table again, paused before Kate and said, "Are you indeed proficient with swords? Why did I not know of this?"

Kate pursed her lips and said, "You must pay no heed to what Rupert Westbourne says, Mr. Buckland. My father taught me a few tricks only, nothing serious, I assure you." She offered a half smile. "And if you dare to make something of this, to suggest that we have a fencing tournament or some such dreadful thing, then I—I shall never speak to you again."

His blue eyes lit up with laughter as he held a hand against his heart and said, "Then I shall restrain myself, for I should perish if you held a ban of silence against me." And just as he was moving away, he leaned close to her and taunted her with, "Though I doubt that you could refrain from speaking to me, for I know you positively delight in having the very last word, my bonny Kate."

She opened her mouth to retort and he lifted a finger, as though to say, "You see what I mean?" And she closed her mouth again with a smile. She couldn't be angry with him. She was too relieved that Ashwell had not been offended with her to care what teasing Buckland threw at her. And besides, the second glass of champagne seemed to be having a delightfully fuzzy effect on her senses as well as relieving some of the burn from across her back, where the sun had, indeed, left its mark.

After Julia had tried and failed to get Emmet to flirt with her, and after Charity Cricklade and Hope Cerney had cornered Roger Whiteshill for the strict purpose of watching him become tongue-tied in their presence, and after Mrs. Moreton had fallen sound asleep by the fire and had begun snoring—she had imbibed five glasses of champagne—Kate was about to take her leave when a disturbance up the street, near the village shop, grew louder and louder, finally bringing most of the guests out of the inn.

Kate was one of the first to leave the inn, feeling that something terrible must have happened. But she was not prepared for what she heard when the constable, Mr. Compton, ran up to them and cried, "The Luddites have attacked the mill at Todbury! In broad daylight, the scurrilous villains! Smashed the new machines installed on Monday last!"

"Luddites!" Kate cried, feeling the press of bodies behind her as everyone emerged from the Swan and Goose. "But how? Why? I've not heard a whisper of such—" She broke off suddenly and remembered Mrs. Coates's concerns, the men involved in secret meetings, odd hand and face signals. Of course. "Luddism," she said again quietly to herself, her brow furrowed.

She felt Buckland press her elbow and ask, "What is it?" As the constable turned away, heading for Brock farm where Jaspar's tenant, Mr. Fernley, had in former years also served as the constable of Chipping Fosseworth, Kate told Buckland about the mill.

She was a little surprised at his reaction, for he seemed not so much shocked as troubled. And Ashwell's response, as he leaned over Buckland's shoulder, mystified her. "Good God! It is not—?"

Buckland shook his head.

Kate was about to ask what the poet meant when Stephen Barnsley's voice rose above the mutterings of the entire group, "Luddites?" And as they all stood watching the villagers pour from their cottages, shouting and some even cheering at this dreadful news, he exclaimed, "I don't know about the rest of you, but I'm for Stinchfield!" And he raced toward the stables with all the men, save Rupert, streaming behind him.

Kate stood with the young ladies—Mary, Julia, Hope, Cerney, and Charity Cricklade—clenching the soft flowered cambric of her skirts. She did not want to remain behind. She could not kick her heels at the Swan and Goose, not while the men were going to investigate an event of such extreme importance.

As a momentary quiet descended upon the inn while the young men were harnessing their horses and carriages, Kate, still standing on the flagway, could hear Mrs. Moreton's snores drifting from the open windows.

Julia cried, "How wretched that we should be abandoned in this perfectly dreadful manner. And who cares about a stupid mill, anyway!"

Hope Cerney pulling at her blond curls, pouted and repeated her dear friend's words. "Indeed! Who gives a fig about a stupid cloth mill!"

Kate, irritated, said, "I'm certain that the mill owner does as well as the villagers who have their livelihood working for Mr. Bagen."

"Well, of course you would care about such things." Julia lifted her chin and smirked at her. "Any female who would expose herself by firing pistols all day would be more concerned with cloth mills than with getting a husband. How old are you now, Miss Draycott?" She mimicked her mother's words but a sennight earlier. "Three and twenty?" And she turned back into the inn, with Charity and Hope following in her wake.

Kate felt Mary grip her elbow and say into her ear, "Don't go after her, though I know quite well you wish for nothing more than to claw her pretty face!"

Hearing her very proper friend say such an improper thing, Kate smiled at Mary. She was about to apologize for letting Julia send her into the boughs, when Stephen Barnsley came tearing from the rear of the inn on his large white gelding. With one flourish of his black beaver hat, he whisked by the ladies.

Kate found her heart beginning to pulse in heavy thuds against her ribs. Indeed, she could not remain in Chipping Fosseworth to wait for hours before anyone returned with news of what had happened. And besides, men could never be relied on to relay information properly. They would talk about it as though it were their business and the ladies should not bother their heads with such matters.

When Kit flew past on his brown steed, followed closely by Roger, Emmet, and Jeremy, Kate could bear it no longer, determining to run the distance to Stinchfield if she found it necessary. And as Ashwell and Buckland appeared in the poet's sleek black curricle, Kate ran in front of them, in a perfectly hoydenish manner, and shouted for them to stop.

Buckland, who happened to be driving Ashwell's team, pulled sharply on the reins. Ashwell immediately began to remonstrate with her, but Kate grabbed Buckland's arm and cried, "I must go! This is my concern. You do understand that!"

He looked at her intense brown eyes and wondered for the hundredth time how she had come to be filled with such a fire about events that most women would consider, if not a dead bore, then certainly outside of their usual feminine interests. He said nothing, but took her hand and helped her to alight the small sporting vehicle. Scarcely waiting for her to settle herself, he cracked the whip over the horses' heads and the curricle leaped forward, springing down the High Street.

Mary watched them go, her heart sinking. She had no use for this sort of excitement and turned back into the inn where she quietly finished her supper. However, as she listened to Julia's complaints of how their evening had been ruined—and all to the symphony of Mrs. Moreton's snoring—Mary thought perhaps that Kate had chosen the wiser course in joining the men. She was about to become quite blue-devilled herself, but fortunately she carried her tatting with her and was soon engaged in flying the shuttle between her competent fingers. But when Rupert began reading some of his poetry she knew that Kate, at least, would not be bored to tears.

*　　　*　　　*

118

The sun fell behind Waverley Hill across the River Avenlode, just west of Stinchfield, and the mill, but a few hundred yards beyond the small market town, teemed with activity. Some of the surrounding gentry, mill labourers, members of the yeoman class, and all of the scaff and raff of Stinchfield had congregated about the cloth mill, torches blazing in the dusky sky.

Lord Whiteshill, his residence not far from the mill, arrived, and everywhere branches of rushes dipped in tallow were being lit about the mill. The children were nearly wild with excitement, their squeals rising continually above the constant hum of adult voices. Men shouted to give way when Lord Whiteshill, mounted atop one of his splendid hunters, his face pale, edged the solid gelding toward the mill. Kate thought he looked as she had always seen him look—nervous, his cheeks sagging as Jaspar's did, and his decided paunch stretching his coat buttons to popping.

Kate, standing near the entrance to the mill with Buckland and Ashwell, thought that at one and sixty Lord Whiteshill ought to have a little more presence than to walk up to the mill wiping his face with his handkerchief.

The new mill, constructed fifteen years earlier, stood four stories high, with stone-mullioned windows that appeared Gothic and foreboding in the grotesque shadows of the rushlights upon the stone walls of the building. Rough stones barely visible on the wall of the dam and the basement of the mill bespoke an original structure beside the shaded mill pond. Kate slapped her arms as a chill evening breeze wafted across the crowd, the rushlights dancing about and sparks flying into the damp air.

The constable opened the door for Lord Whiteshill and members of the surrounding gentry flowed in behind him, until the constable from Chipping Fosseworth finally cut off the crowd that all wanted to see the interior of the building. Kate saw Mr. Bagen sitting on the floor of his mill, his head bent forward. Several of his new looms were scattered in shreds about him—broken spools and shuttles, wool thread in tangled loops on the floor. Kate glanced at the long chamber, with stairs at the far end heading to the upper levels, and drew

119

in her breath. Four of the fifteen looms had been wrecked by the heavy mallets used by the Luddites.

A silence settled over the crowd, partly in consideration for the mill owner but more out of an astonishment at the wreckage about them. Mr. Bagen, a thin, curly-locked man resembling in a general way Rupert Westbourne, had seen a vision of the future. And at every opportunity he had installed the newest machinery in his mill—the spinning jennies that replaced the tedious spinning wheels, gigs that used teasel heads fastened into metal frames and roughed the wool cloth, and finally, his latest machine, a rotary cutter that sheared the long nap of the cloth. It was these shearing machines that had provoked the recent attack, as he told Lord Whiteshill. "I had received a number of threatening letters, poorly written as ye may imagine, but I thought little enough of it. I'd had similar ones when I brought in the gigs, you know, the machines with drums and teasels." He looked about him, the smashed looms appearing like the broken masts of war-weary sailing vessels. "I never gave a second thought to the letters." He then looked about him and cried, "And they came during the daylight hours, all hooded and waving pistols about." He moved to sit down on a bench by the door as the men in the room shifted uneasily on their feet. He slapped his breeches, and said, "The gigs have been smashed and even the perch-beams have been hammered to splinters."

The door flew open and a woman, clutching a crying baby, pushed past the constable and cried, "And I say 'tis a fine thing they've done, them Luddites! We bein' replaced by all them machines. Me ma taught me 'ow to spin and now I've no work. And me 'usband's a shearin' man. How will we live?" A constable took her elbow and she turned panicked eyes upon him. "I don't want to go to them factories in the north." And she burst into tears but, with just a little gentle encouragement, allowed herself to be led from the room.

Outside Kate could hear the crowd cheering as the woman emerged from the building.

James whispered to Buckland, "Blast that Hunt fellow!"

Kate did not know what to think anymore. As she looked at the broken looms and thought of the new shearing machine

Mr. Bagen had referred to, she could only agree with something Buckland had said a few days ago. There wasn't a simple answer, and all this destruction was no answer at all. The hours saved appealed strongly to her sense of management, yet what about the jobs lost? How would the young family survive?

The constable, clutching his blunderbuss in both hands as though he would be called upon to use it in the next few minutes, addressed Lord Whiteshill. Gesturing politely to the cloth mill owner, he said, "Good Mr. Bagen here was trussed up nigh on two hours with a cloth stuck in his mouth. We want to roust out these varmints wat did this to poor Mr. Bagen and see that justice be done."

Kate glanced toward Stephen and the other bucks, all of whom just an hour earlier had been feasting upon cold duck, partridges, ham, pastries, jellies and cakes, and she could not help but wonder what they thought of all of this. In the many times they had been together, hunting and riding, their conversation had never turned toward local concerns but rather toward how many brace of pheasant each had shot and how many had somehow miraculously escaped their exceptional abilities with a fowling piece.

But the entire room was silent except for the restless shuffling of feet and continual bobbing of heads as each member of the gentry turned to look at the extensive damage. Kate knew what everyone who formed part of the landowning class was thinking—of France and the desperate revolution that had taken place a scant twenty years earlier. And with so much discontent in the land—for everyone knew that there were countless such incidents as this one in the midland counties—some sort of revolution suddenly seemed painfully close to home.

Kate looked about her and felt strangely numb. How many times in the past several years had she felt that something dear to her was being slowly and systematically destroyed? The peaceful life of her childhood had been taken from her bit by bit: Her mother, Stephen, her dowry, even the way Jaspar loved her had changed so much. And Chipping Fosseworth had not gone untouched. Three families had left the village in recent years—one emigrating to the Colonies and the other two heading north to work in the factories. She had heard of the conditions in the midlands—long hours, squalid rows of flats, and the desperate lot of the children who also worked in the factories. But worse. Even if life in the Cotswolds was hard for poor people, at least every cottage had a small plot of land upon which to grow a garden to raise pigs and chickens, and a blue sky overhead that might lend a feeling of well-being. But in the north, no such connection to the earth remained. Here there were only dull grey skies and the children grew up in a tangle of landless brick buildings, breathing air thick with coal dust.

As a child, Kate had visited the weavers' cottages to watch the men fly their shuttles about their looms and create yards of cloth in only one day. But many of them now reported to the cloth mills to work on looms owned by the mill owner. A way of life was disappearing and Kate clung to its remnants. What could ever replace for these people the centuries-old trades that had been passed on from Grandfather's knee to Grandson's eager hands and eyes?

Lord Whiteshill asked the constable if any of the perpetrators of this crime had been found. The constable shook his head, "Nay, not un."

Lord Whiteshill then told two sturdy yeomen to escort good Mr. Bagen back to his house in Stinchfield. At first the slight little man with clear blue eyes stared at Lord Whiteshill, shaking his head in a confused manner. But the baron knew at least how to deal with this and, patting him on the shoulder, coughed and said, "There's a good fellow. Home with you now. Time enough in the morning to sort things out." And the mill owner left without further hesitation.

Stephen Barnsley exclaimed, "Ought to hunt the ruffians down that did this!" And a few others agreed in loud voices.

Lord Whiteshill frowned and, pulling at his ear, said, "Not quite certain what to do."

Stephen said, "I say we should flush each one of these miserable fellows, from wherever they are hiding, and see them all hanged! They can't do this to us!"

He had said it, Kate thought. Us. They were all affected by

the Luddite attack.

Buckland's voice intruded, "I think Bow Street ought to be contacted. What do you think, Lord Whiteshill?"

The baron's eyes, dull and rheumy, lit up at this suggestion. He no more wanted to sanction a group of bloods to pursue some of the villagers, and whoever else was involved, then he wanted to burn his own estate. Lord, he thought, wiping his neck, they would come after him next! "Yes, yes, an excellent idea. I'll see to that m'self! And as for you, Mr. Barnsley, just tend to your lands in Standen and leave this for the law to take care of." He quickly followed Mr. Bagen's exit, telling everyone to return to their various homes, and congratulated himself on thinking that he had brushed through the matter quite well.

As everyone filed out of the mill, Kate remained, moving toward the small leaded window that overlooked the River Avenlode. In the water, Kate could see the reflection of rushlights as a train of villagers made their way back to Stinchfield by way of the footpath along the banks of the river. The sun had set and beyond Waverley Hill, above the black outlines of the beech trees moving in the evening breeze, sparkled a smattering of the first stars. What was happening to her world? Luddites! She had not heard that the movement had progressed beyond the middle counties. Luddites, here, about Stinchfield!

Buckland held back, as the crowd passed through the doorway, for one more glance at the damage. Good God, thousands of pounds of wrecked machinery. By the size of the mill, Buckland thought that Mr. Bagen could no doubt weather this terrible incident. But it was such a blow to a sense of stability. And what would happen to the men who smashed the machines? Death or transportation across the seas, no doubt. His gaze travelled from the smashed looms to spools of thread crisscrossing the planked floor in a mass of thread, and he thought of the new looms and gigs that he was having installed in his own mill near Edgecote. In addition, the new rotary cutter had arrived only the day before. He slapped his beaver hat against his leg. If this was any indication of events to come, he could expect trouble himself. How ironic, he thought as he scanned the long chamber, only one rushlight illuminating the dark room. His sojourn in the pretty county of Gloucestershire was meant to be mostly a pleasure trip and already he had become embroiled in the politics of a region. And not just heated discussions as might occur in Parliament, but actual physical confrontations that might very well result in a loss of life.

As he scanned the room, Buckland had the vague feeling that he was in the midst of the strange twistings of a nightmare.

Beyond the looms that were still intact, he suddenly saw Kate, hidden in the shadows of the dim chamber. Without giving it too much thought, he moved quickly toward her, into the deepening night that encompassed the latter part of the room.

Kate heard his steps and knew without turning around that Buckland was with her. His resonant voice washed over her. "A sad day's work, this. No one has spoken of such activities here about Stinchfield since Ashwell and I arrived. Has there ever been an attack before?"

Kate continued to look out the window, watching the stars, one by one, make their appearance, and said, "There has been scarcely a whisper. But then, Mr. Bagen spoke of many threats. I suppose there would be no reason for the Luddites to threaten Squire Cricklade or Jaspar or Sir William."

Buckland seated himself on a table by the window after brushing off a couple of broken spools, and he looked at her as she stared into the night sky. "Why have you never gone to London, Kate?"

Surprised at this unexpected question, Kate turned toward Buckland and said, "I've never really had a reason to. Everything I want is here." She gestured with an upturned hand and let it drop to her side. The smell of the oiled wool threads and the dusty odor of the recently shattered looms assailed Kate and she covered her mouth with a hand, trying to press back an emotion that threatened to overpower her.

"What is wrong?" Buckland cried, leaning toward her and resting a hand lightly on her arm.

Her eyes brimming with unwanted tears, Kate shook her head. "My world is coming apart at the seams." And then,

124

realizing that she had made a very stupid joke, cried, "The seams, but how absurd!" And her voice broke.

"Kate!" Buckland cried, taking her gently in his arms. "Look at me!" he commanded. And as she lifted her face to him, tears trickled down her cheeks.

She could scarcely discern his features in the failing light, as he said, "Life changes. It is the one certainty we have." He held her chin with his gloved hand and kissed her gently upon the lips. "Perhaps that is why I did not, do not fear my poverty as you seem to fear yours."

The touch of his lips upon her own seemed a compassionate act only, and Kate wondered vaguely why it seemed so reasonable a thing for him to do. But when he spoke of his poverty compared to her own, she pulled away from him, shook her head again, and cried, "But you are a man! It is perfectly within a gentleman's power to do whatever he needs to do in order to secure a livelihood. He might go to India and earn a large fortune there and become a nabob, or he might go to sea and wrest a treasure in prize money after capturing an enemy ship, or he might take holy orders or become a secretary to some diplomat, or— You see how the list goes on and on. But what recourse does a gentlewoman have?"

He seated himself back on the table, folded his arms across his chest, and said quietly, "I have not given it a great deal of thought. Certainly, your paths are more limited. . . ."

She waved a hand about wildly. "Limited? I can think of only three avenues—governess, companion or, had I the talent, which I confess to you now that I do not, I could write charming little novels like Miss Austen. Limited!"

He could see that she would become passionate on the subject and, lifting a hand, cried, "Whoa! I stand corrected, my bonny Kate. The truth is that I cannot imagine what it is like to be a woman or to face a woman's difficulties."

Between crying and then yelling at Buckland, Kate found a most pressing need to wipe her nose, but her reticule sat in a comfortable corner on one of the settles in the Swan and Goose. After she had sniffed twice, Buckland laughed at her and gave her his own handkerchief. "You may keep it, if you so desire. But I hasten to inform you that you now possess an

125

object of great worth. I have it on excellent authority that any number of females in London have tried and failed to secure this significant article."

Kate blew her nose and laughed, "I do like you, Buckland, for all your teasing ways. You are at least able to make me laugh. Now pray, tell me, why would so many females want to possess your handkerchief? Ashwell's I could understand, but why yours?" She continued, "Of course, seeing that you are a conceited man, I suppose my question is silly. And if you wish to provide me with a few more of your handkerchiefs and if you are telling me the truth, then I might just be able to earn a living by selling them. Of course, how much could I earn by selling a few meagre kerchiefs?"

He stood up and drew her arm through his, leading her toward the door. "Oh, not just my kerchiefs, mind, but my quizzing glass, my fobs and seals, a lock of my hair—you may ask Ashwell if it is not so. And now that we have solved all your difficulties, I will gladly relinquish my personal effects to you."

Kate looked up into his teasing blue eyes, his face now glowing from the rushlight near the door, and said, "I should need at least a hundred locks of your hair to make a reasonable profit. Perhaps you ought to go to Cheltenham tomorrow and purchase a wig." At his smiling face, she continued, "However, I think I would prefer to see Mrs. Cricklade's expression should she see you completely bald. Now that would be a treat."

Inadvertently, as they neared the doorway, Kate turned to take one final glance at the mill behind her. The smile she had just given to Buckland began to fade as she wondered what next would happen in their quiet community about Stinchfield.

Chapter Seven

Later that evening, Buckland stood before the long row of windows in the parlour of the Swan and Goose. With the glow from the fireplace behind him, he looked out at the stars above Birdlip Hill and thought about Kate and Mr. Bagen's mill and his own cloth mill.

James's voice intruded, "Well, we certainly shall not lack for conversation tomorrow night at the *musicale*. Let me see, it is being held at Ampstone Court by that extremely irritating Moreton female."

"Julia Moreton?" Buckland asked, looking back at his friend with an apparently disbelieving expression.

"What?" James cried, astonished. "I should hardly describe Miss Moreton as irritating. I refer to her mother. Of course, as I now see by your detestable grin, you knew damn well to whom I referred."

Buckland watched a star shoot across the night sky, then turned away from the window, regarding James with a sober expression. "How do you find Miss Draycott?"

James, who sat before the fire, firmly engaged in mending his pen, looked up at Buckland and said, "You shan't win her, you know. I have every reason to believe that she prefers my company to yours. You did not see how she flirted with me all day at your quite reprehensible shooting match." He then yawned, returning a small knife to his coat pocket.

But Buckland had noticed how much Kate flirted with James, and he wondered what the aspiring poet would think of her if he knew all. Gad, what a coil. Approaching the subject from a different vantage point, he said, "According to Julia, there is a good chance Lord Sapperton will grace tomorrow night's fete. Are you prepared for the abrupt ending of our masquerade?"

James leaned back in his chair and stretched his feet out in front of the fire. Sapperton was such a dog. "We shouldn't be masquerading in the first place, you know. The more I get to know these people the more I like them. Lord, it's as though time stopped here and not one of them has heard of London or Almack's or White's or the Marriage Mart. Take Roger Whiteshill for instance, no Town Bronze, blushes every time a lady so much as glances at him—most of whom he has known since he was a cub—and as honourable a gentleman as you can find. Why, one week in London and he'd be like all the rest of us—callous, indifferent, and complaining continually of *ennui.*"

Buckland sighed, "You are right. Do you recall that village we passed through to get here? It was named Paradise and had an inn called the Adam and Eve?" James nodded and Buckland continued, "Well, I feel as though this place ought to be called Paradise, where extreme innocence abounds. And yet there isn't a village hereabouts that is not rife with every typical country squabble, not to mention the bizarre attack upon the mill yesterday." He seemed to consider all of it for a moment, rocking on his heels a little, and continued, "And who, I wonder, shall be the first to fall from grace?" He laughed as he settled himself before the fire and joined James in a glass of brandy. "Tomorrow night, it may be us." And he lifted his glass to James.

Kate paced the length of the drawing room floor, the numerous tables scattered throughout the long room each bearing a vase and bouquets of summer flowers from the garden just outside the French doors. She awaited the arrival of Jaspar's town coach to take her to Ampstone Court and could not remain seated in any of the chairs or sofas that adorned the chamber. Everything about the room should have calmed her, for it was simple and cheerful, with white walls, colorful chintz curtains, and upholstery fabric to match. Usually this room, which Violet kept in exceptional order—the tables polished regularly with beeswax, the planked ash floor free of dust and lint, the tables laden with flowers, and the embroidery beneath the vases neatly starched—had a calming effect on her. But now, all she could think about was facing Sapperton. Julia had told her at the shooting match that he was to attend. She did not wish to meet him and she did not want him to interfere in her schemes.

She twisted a long strand of pearls about her fingers, then released them. Sapperton. Somehow she had managed to forget him since seeing him in the barn where she had shot Buckland. But now that she would be attending those parties where he was certain to be present, she knew she could no longer avoid meeting him as she had been wont to do for three years and more. And how shocked he would be at her appearance! Kate cringed. He would take great delight in it, and as she glanced down at the flattering neckline of her forest-green silk gown, which seemed to display her bosom to considerable advantage, she felt a nearly uncontrollable desire to fetch a modest fichu and wear it tucked into the bodice of her gown. The earl would torment her, she was certain of it.

Pausing before a table adorned with a vase of roses, Kate took in the rich perfume of the pink and yellow flowers and stared at the portrait of her mother that had hung on the wall in this particular spot for over ten years. She released the pearls that she had kept twisted tightly about her fingers and put her hands on her cheeks. Sir William was right! She looked a great deal like her mother, and she dreaded the remarks Sapperton would make on this point alone. For years he had told her that she had but to dress her hair differently and wear gowns a little more like Julia's and she would look exactly as her mother had looked fifteen years earlier.

The coach rumbled to the front door and the horses stamped their feet, unused to being harnessed quite so frequently to the heavy, ancient coach.

Kate heard the coach and smiled at the portrait. "Wish me well, Mama," she whispered. Her mother's image seemed to smile in return, a wistful expression, as though she wished to be with her daughter. Kate turned away, her thoughts suddenly full of Ashwell.

As the coach progressed beyond Edgecote to the smaller village of Ampstone, Kate could never understand how so beautiful a village, with cottages facing the River Wyck and willows bending their tresses into the slow currents of the river, could be inhabited by so wretched a creature as Julia Moreton. Vain, frivolous, a vixen. She and Julia had been at odds almost from the first.

Ampstone Court, an ancient Tudor manor house, appeared suddenly behind a tall, neatly trimmed yew hedge. Lights from the receiving rooms danced on the gravel drive that fronted the house. Already the rooms milled with Kate's friends and relations, and she was just steeling herself to face the earl, when a yard of tin sounded behind her carriage, and she and Maggie nearly jumped from their skins. She heard her coachman deliver several abbreviated curses and pull the old coach to the side of the drive.

A modern coach, with a crest emblazoned on the side, rushed by them. Sapperton's coach. How like him, Kate thought, retrieving her fan from her new pearl-studded reticule and snapping it open.

Her own string of curses moved silently on her lips as she watched Sapperton's footman jump down from behind the coach, quickly jerk the travelling chariot's door open, and step aside as the earl's tall, emaciated form emerged from the coach.

Peter Coachman put the horses in motion again, and within minutes, Kate was descending the coach, only to find that the earl, upon recognizing the Draycott coach, had waited for her. Damn and blast, but she loathed the man!

As he stepped forward, she watched his small black eyes take in her dark green ball dress, the fur-lined cape, her auburn curls wound throughout with a dozen lily-of-the-valley flowerlets, and the white satin ribbon trimming her gown about the high waist.

"Has Venus come to haunt me in this heavenly shape?" His

eyes travelled again over her costume, coming to rest finally upon her bosom. Maggie sniffed and Kate, her own temper under questionable control, hoped that her anger showed itself in red splotches on the fair skin beneath her pearls.

Kate curtsied, keeping her angry countenance fastened upon the top button of his white waistcoat. "My lord," she said in a cool voice.

"You've become a woman, my dear."

Kate lifted her brows. "If you do not wish me to cause a dreadful scene this evening, Lord Sapperton, I beg two things of you. Pray, do not speak to me in that overly familiar manner and"—she gestured to his coach, which was just pulling away toward the manor stables—"I suggest you speak to your coachman, who has the manners of a highwayman."

Sapperton offered his arm, which Kate felt incumbent to take because of his rank. He then said to her, "But I find your second request both perceptive and yet quite impossible to fulfill. You see, I hired William because he was at one time a highwayman who went by the name of one-eyed Billy, though he has the use of both his eyes, which is a mystery in and of itself. And impossible because, well, one does not instruct a highwayman upon manners of the road." He laughed. "But the beauty does not even smile!"

Kate ignored him, lifting her chin and gazing up into his thin white face. "You are aware that Lord Ashwell is here tonight?" She watched the black eyes glint in the flickering light of the flambeaux as they approached the massive front door.

The earl lifted a brow and said, "How unfortunate. I suppose all of you females will be vying with one another for the man's attention and I will be tossed aside like used clothing." He then looked Kate over and laughed, "So that is it. You've become a woman for the poet. What an absurdity." And as the butler opened the door for them, he leaned close to her and said, "He'll never have you. Ashwell has the most unconscionable reputation in London. Hearts fall upon the flagways behind the man even as he walks, and as for his actually considering a pistol-waving, impoverished country rustic, why, I could laugh at the idea." He then relieved Kate of her long cloak and, after handing his own hat and caped driving coat to the butler, escorted her to the drawing room.

As they stood on the threshold of Mrs. Moreton's gold reception room, several Egyptian-style couches covered in broad gold and white stripes of the finest satin staring at them as they waited for their hostess, Kate wanted to scream with vexation. Somehow Sapperton always managed to make it impossible for her to retort. He knew she could say nothing while they were being announced.

Mrs. Moreton, her blond wig curled in very tight ringlets and crushed beneath a purple satin turban, moved forward in a deprecating fashion. Bouncing several very odd curtsies as she walked, the hem of her pale orange gown, adorned with several rows of purple lace, gave a very odd, vulgar appearance. "My Lord Sapperton," she breathed, her large blue eyes worshipful, "how kind, indeed, how condescending of you to grace my insignificant *musicale*." She tittered behind her fan and sank into a low curtsy.

Kate watched these antics and nearly laughed when the earl found himself required to assist his hostess in rising to her feet.

"Well, there!" Mrs. Moreton exclaimed, her cheeks red from the exertion. "And now, my lord, I have the greatest treat imaginable in store for you." She slapped his arm in a playful manner with her fan. "And no, it is not my dear Julia's harp playing, although you will hear her lovely strains later. No, no, indeed. For you must know"—and here her bosom swelled, straining even Madame Beaumaris's careful needlework as the peach-coloured satin gown threatened to come apart at the seams—"that we have dear Lord Ashwell with us."

To Kate she said, in a curt undervoice, "Do go speak with Mary Chalford, Kate."

Though she detested the earl, she could not but appreciate, as she walked toward Mary, hearing Lord Sapperton ask Mrs. Moreton, in an exceptionally polite manner, precisely why Louisa was not, as mistress of Ampstone Court, acting as hostess. Kate could not resist turning around to see Mrs. Moreton's reactions. But she underestimated the woman's effrontery. "My dear Lord Sapperton, though it is indelicate of me to speak of it, why, I would not think of allowing Louisa to exert herself when she is increasing."

132

She then hooked the earl's arm with her own and led him toward Ashwell.

Parts of the room were still engaged in their own coteries of discussion: The bucks were wagering upon just how soon the Bow Street Runners would arrive to set the cloth mill business straight, Lydia was fully involved tormenting Jeremy Cricklade about something no doubt quite absurd, Julia was flirting with Mr. Buckland, and Mrs. Cricklade, with her daughter Louisa planted firmly by her side, was conferring with Lady Whiteshill over Louisa's confinement. Louisa Cricklade had won her mother's undying love by capturing the rather dull John Moreton and so beautifully aligning the Cricklades with the very best of Stinchfield society. Lady Whiteshill listened kindly to Mrs. Cricklade's prophecies and bemoanments of her daughter's sufferings, and Louisa, who reclined in Grecian pose on a gold-striped chaise, wore an appropriately mournful expression.

Kate moved to a gold-striped couch situated near the fireplace, where Buckland and Julia were conducting their noisy flirtation. Seating herself beside Mary, she wondered just how Buckland and the poet, both of whom professed to loathe the earl, would receive his lordship. Kate glanced at Ashwell, also standing near the fireplace, and thought he looked rather pale.

Mrs. Moreton's voice, bursting with pride, rang throughout the room as she introduced her two most prestigious guests to one another.

Buckland had watched the earl's entrance with the growing sense of anticipation that one always had on the hunting field. The fact was he hated Sapperton, whom he considered to be a thin, greedy, soulless man who was known to cheat at cards. He didn't care in the least whether the earl exposed their masquerade or not, and in some ways he wished for it. How long had it been that he had tried to force the earl to confront him. But the man was slippery as an eel, and even a direct insult did not provoke Sapperton to face him.

As Mrs. Moreton's ridiculously officious introduction came to an end, Buckland glanced at James, who immediately stepped forward and bowed slightly to the earl. James had

133

spoken of nothing else from the moment they left the Swan and Goose, and even now Buckland could see that his cheeks were nearly deathlike in color.

Buckland then regarded Sapperton and was not at all surprised that the earl evinced not the least shock at being presented to James. And except perhaps for a mild lift of his brows, he glanced from one man to the other, smiled faintly, the nerve in the hollow of his left cheek jerking slightly, and addressed Buckland, "Have we met? Ashwell I know quite well, but you, I don't know that I recall your face. You look a trifle familiar. Brook's? No, then White's, of course!"

And with not so much as a flicker of his eye did he ask James, "And how are your scribblings, I wonder? I suppose we may soon expect another lengthy canto or a volume of sonnets, perhaps?"

James, relieved that he had not been exposed, now felt angry at Sapperton's cool, sarcastic voice. Lifting a bored brow of his own, he answered, "Perhaps. I have always had a fondness for that form. But then, everyone begs for the third canto. Really, I have not decided." And catching sight of Kate smiling at him, he bowed to Sapperton and moved away.

James pulled a chair forward, joining the two ladies, and Mary said in a low voice, "Lord Sapperton apparently does not care for poetry in general. He spoke quite coldly to you, I thought."

James shrugged and Kate said in a kind voice, hoping she sounded like Mary, "Do not concern yourself with the earl's opinion. He is a beast." And she cast a darkling glance toward Sapperton, who had been pulled aside by Mrs. Moreton and begged to take the seat of honour for the commencement of her *musicale*.

Her hands folded in front of her in a most theatrical fashion, Mrs. Moreton spent five minutes speaking on the worthy attributes of the famous composers—Bach, Brahms, Haydn, Handel, Mozart . . . ah, Mozart! Kate heard her first three words and then stopped listening. Why the devil had she agreed to attend such a gathering in the first place? The only composer she could tolerate was Vivaldi and no one played his music. He was considered too Italian. Her gaze travelled about the room, taking in the bored faces of the bucks, dwelling upon James's intense interest as he watched Mary play her favorite Bach prelude and fugue, resting upon the matrons who chose seats in the back—nodding to one another and commenting upon and applauding each performance—and finally noticing how all the older gentlemen, including a sleepy-eyed Squire Cricklade, took seats in obscure corners of the room and dipped heavily into gold, silver, and enamelled snuffboxes.

When Julia's harp was brought forward, Kate felt her posterior growing quite numb from sitting so long and thought she'd had less torture when seated for hours upon her horse. The men began to shift in their seats and Kate knew she was not alone. The harp trilled and twanged to Julia's indifferent performance. Only Lydia's quite astonishing and masterful execution of a Mozart sonata caught anyone's attention, and Kate smiled to see that afterward Jeremy applauded louder than most.

As Kate glanced about the chamber, all white woodwork and heavily scrolled plasterwork, she tried desperately to keep from yawning but finally gave in and covered her face with her fan, her eyes watering with her effort at discretion. And as she was blinking away the tears, she chanced to catch Buckland looking at her, his blue eyes twinkling, and knew that her cheeks were turning quite red at having been caught. But his laughing smile only caused her to smile in return. Buckland at least would understand.

Finally, the audience was reprieved for half an hour while refreshments—iced cups of champagne and lemonade—were served, along with a quite ostentatious display of at least twenty desserts—puddings, cakes, chocolate and almond creams, jellies and biscuits of every imaginable shape. Kate did not care for sweets and so, finishing her champagne, moved toward the harp where, through the throng of people in the crowded room, she could just see Ashwell's black coat and brown hair as he bent over the musical instrument. She hoped to advance her schemes and flirt with him, that the evening might not be a completely wasted event, but the poet had become quite involved in trying to repair one of the harp strings. And though Kate watched him labour for a few minutes, by the time she had heard Julia exclaim, "But how clever you are, Lord Ashwell!" for the third time, she quickly sought refuge on the balcony.

The wide veranda overlooked extensive formal gardens, a source of great and rightful pride to Mrs. Moreton, and Kate smiled at the lanterns scattered among the flowers. As dark as it was, the pastel-coloured lamps illumined enough of the geometric flowerbeds to cause even the most disinterested observer to feel that an artist had been at work.

"It is lovely." Buckland's voice intruded on her thoughts.

"Oh, indeed, I was just thinking the very same thing," Kate cried, a little startled at his sudden appearance as she turned to greet him for the first time that evening.

"Quite surprising, actually," he continued, leaning his elbows onto the low stone wall.

Kate looked at Buckland, thinking he was one of the handsomest men of her acquaintance, and asked, "Why?"

He gave her a wry twist of his mouth as though to say, "Think, my dear," then said, "One does not expect a woman who wears a blond wig, like some Abbess at Bartholomew Fair, to have enough taste to arrange a vase of flowers, nonetheless an entire garden. I commend her hidden abilities!"

"Buckland!" Kate cried in a tone of censure. "She is our hostess."

He whispered to her, "She may be our hostess, but she still dresses like an aging Cyprian!"

Kate smothered her laughter behind her gloved hand, then said, "How abominable you are, and you know you should not be saying such a truly unkind thing. And most especially, you should not be speaking to me of Abbesses and Cyprians."

"No?" he queried, his eyes all innocence. "Then I must consider you a great hypocrite. You read Ashwell's poetry. I know you do, for you have thrown it up to me in great heat on more than one occasion!"

Kate lifted her chin and said, "And what is your point, sir?"

"Well," he gestured with a wave of his hand, inching toward her, "I, too, have read his poetry, and he speaks of Cyprians on the third page of his delightful volume of verse. And now I put it to you, why may I not do so if it pleases me?"

Kate could think of a hundred reasons, but the man was standing too close to her for any of them to form on her lips. She gazed into his blue eyes, quite black in the shadows of the darkened balcony, and almost wished they were alone. His flirtations, the rogue, were so practiced that all she could think about was having his lips upon hers again. At this thought, she took a step backward. Lord, but the man was dangerous.

Buckland caught her hand as she moved away from him, and he restrained her from returning to the drawing room. In a whisper, he said, "Don't go. I haven't told you how beautiful you look this evening. I wish I might have you on my arm at Almack's and make every gentleman there press me for your name. And this shade of green"—he fingered the puff sleeve of her gown—"becomes you exceedingly." Kate could bear no more and tried to pull away from him. "Wait!" His voice sounded urgent as he released her hand. In a normal tone of voice, his whispers trailing away on the night breeze, he continued, "I promise to behave myself, only don't go."

When she hesitated, he continued, "It is just that I am so frightfully bored."

Kate responded in a quiet voice, "Buckland, you cannot keep—that is, I am not impervious to your flirtations, but I know as well as you that nothing can come of it! Please."

He regarded her eyes, pleading in the moonlight, and he wondered what he was thinking. Did he want to seduce a young maiden? How easy it would be, for there was more fire to Kate than he had met in any woman. . . . He stopped. In any woman. He had never known a woman like her before. After a moment, he bowed to her and said he would try to do better, then left her alone on the balcony.

Kate turned away from the long doors that led to the drawing room and looked out over the gardens. They had lost a little of their beauty somehow. She was about to return to the drawing room herself when an unwelcome voice intruded.

"But how charming! A tryst on the terrace! And how much the manners and mores of our cloistered gentry have sunk, and that in only three weeks since I left the shelter of these hills for Brighton."

Kate whirled around in a startled fashion, her eyes wide at

137

the sound of Sapperton's voice. Moving backward instinctively, the hard stone of the wall bit into the small of her back. "You make too much of it, my lord."

"Do I?" the earl asked as he lounged toward Kate, his small black eyes glowing as a badger's do in the woods at night.

Kate took a breath and turned slowly around to again face the gardens. She did not wish to look into his eyes. Her heart beating in a painful manner, she tried for a light tone as she said, "I have always found Mrs. Moreton's sculptured gardens to be the loveliest about Stinchfield."

She felt him approach her from behind, the dull scraping of his half boots on the stone of the terrace floor sounding like two pieces of glass being ground together.

Every nerve in her body came suddenly alive with fear as Kate felt his cold fingers touch the backs of her arms.

"Katherine," he whispered, "I have missed you, longed for you. Why won't you end this foolishness, this game you have been playing? Say you will marry me."

Kate resisted the impulse to ram her elbow into his thin, brittle ribs. He was over twice her age! But, oh, the harm he might do if she did hurt him. She felt dizzy at the nearness of his skeletal frame, as well as nauseated. "Do go away, Lord Sapperton. I am feeling quite unwell of the moment."

He grasped both arms, still behind her. "How is this? Then I must escort you home! My carriage and my most faithful one-eyed Billy," he chuckled, "would have you in your nest before that moon rises one degree higher." He forced her head to turn toward the sky, his thin hands like claws as the tips of his fingers pressed into her face. Kate saw the moon and thought that never had the glowing orb appeared so unfriendly.

She wrenched away from him, turning to look into his face. In a low voice, she cried, "And then what, my lord? Would I remain maidenly? No, I think not. I would never return home, would I? Would you marry me then?" She was trembling with anger and moved to rush back to the drawing room. If only he did not stop her.

Sapperton saw her hands shaking in the dim light that fell in dull squares on the terrace stone and he grabbed her, holding her fast in his arms. He wanted her, needed her. His chest began to ache as he said, "You cannot escape me, Katherine. Never for a moment think you can. You will come to me. One day you will come to me and then we shall see. Do you think I am ignorant of your father's debts or that the manor lands are heavily mortgaged?" His voice was low, a menacing breath upon her cheek. "I know every inch of it. Mr. Rous has been exceedingly helpful."

Kate could bear no more and kicked his shin, a movement that surprised him and caused his grip to slacken. Wrenching herself out of his embrace, his breath smelling of wine and onions, she said, in a hoarse, angry whisper, "I despise you, Sapperton. I shall die before ever I become your wife." She could not read his face, though in the dim light it looked the color of the stone, a very dark grey. Wheeling about to stalk away, she was surprised to see Buckland standing in the doorway.

And how frightening an expression he wore on his face! Even in the shadows, Kate could see that he was beyond anger. But he was not looking at her. His eyes, almost glowing in the dim light, were directed over her head at the earl.

She stopped and waited, and could not resist looking back at Sapperton. He, also, was not looking at her but was returning Buckland's stare. Kate shivered, as though both men, their thoughts unspoken, had exchanged some deadly message that passed through her.

Buckland spoke first, his gaze unwavering as he continued to watch the earl. He directed his question to her, "Are you unharmed, Kate? Good. Then I must say I am surprised, for this man would kick a helpless child."

Kate moved to stand near Buckland, unwilling to pass beyond him into the drawing room. She felt paralyzed by fear. If Sapperton, a well-known swordsman, should challenge Buckland . . . she could not have his head on her conscience. Placing a hand upon Buckland's sleeve, she said, "Pray, will you escort me back to the *musicale?* I think Charity Cricklade has begun one of the new waltzes."

Sapperton found his voice. "Oh, do but trail behind Katherine's skirts, *Mr. Buckland.*" He emphasized these words and Buckland knew what he was about, that he referred to his

139

false identity.

Taking his snuffbox out of his coat pocket and helping himself to a generous pinch, Kate's hand still upon his arm, Buckland said, in a calm voice, "Anytime you wish to face me, Sapperton, swords or pistols, you have but to name your seconds." The imperfect rhythms of Charity's waltz drifted out to the terrace.

The earl lifted a brow and began walking toward them. In a voice laden with sarcasm, he said, "I never go out with men who are not of my station."

As the earl brushed past them, just narrowly avoiding Buckland's gold snuffbox, Kate drew in her breath sharply. How could he speak to any man in so degrading a choice of words. *Not of my station.* Even if it were true that a man should only duel with his equals, it had never stopped anyone that she had ever heard of. Kate knew it was an insult.

Gripping Buckland's arm tightly, she whispered, "Do not attend to him, Buckland. He is not worth one cartload of horse dung!"

Buckland, who was preparing to follow Sapperton into Mrs. Moreton's gold drawing room and throw his glove at the earl's feet, after first slapping his ugly smile from his face, could not believe what Kate had just said to him. A bubble of laughter rose up in his chest, completely dispelling his anger. Returning his snuffbox to his pocket, he cried, "Oh, you are impossible, my bonny Kate. A cartload of horse dung, indeed! What am I to do with you?"

Kate relaxed her shoulders and said, "I cannot be responsible for your death. I told you before that Sapperton means to have me and he will do anything he can. He would kill you! I know he would!"

Buckland felt suddenly sobered as he regarded Kate, now standing in the full light of the doorway. A breeze wafted across them both, cooling his temper even further, and he said, "I am not afraid of meeting Sapperton. Indeed, I have long wished for the day."

After Charity had stumbled through her waltz and rose from

the seat of the pianoforte with burning cheeks, Julia again played her harp, with Mary accompanying her on the pianoforte. Mrs. Moreton sat smiling broadly upon Julia and fanning herself with a large, garish fan of ostrich feathers. Taking a seat near Lady Chalford and receiving one scowl from Mrs. Moreton, Kate watched Mary's close-set blue eyes concentrate intensely upon her music. At best, Julia's overly dramatic expression was difficult to follow. Next to her, Kate could hear Lady Chalford's exasperation with Julia's performance in a series of small sighs. At that instant, Kate felt extremely grateful that Jaspar had, in a moment of intoxication, sold their own pianoforte to a band of wandering gypsies.

As the music came to an end, Kate suppressed a yawn, relieved that the long evening was finally drawing to a close. And how little of her plans had been accomplished, for she had barely exchanged half a dozen sentences with Lord Ashwell. And as for Sapperton, she would try very hard not to think of his gaunt features and hungry eyes.

But when she was finally tucked between her sheets, Kate drifted into sleep with the image of a pair of flashing blue eyes fixed firmly in her brain.

As it was, Kate did not sleep well. The moon was full, and though her dreams were unmolested by ghosts or phantoms, they were positively teeming with members of the surrounding gentry. Julia smirked at her, Buckland dogged her heels saying improper things, Kit laughed at her. But the worst was Stephen, who rode about the countryside in full armour, brandishing a huge sword.

When she awoke, her head ached slightly. Perhaps she had imbibed too much champagne. But as she swung her legs over the edge of her tall bed and let her feet dangle, she took in the vision of her green gown, draped over a worn lavender winged chair in the corner of her room, and suddenly she knew the real reason she felt so poorly. Damn, but it was hard wearing the trappings of femininity, listening to hours of the most boring and ill-executed music, speaking in delicate tones, pretending to Lord Ashwell that she was a meek female and that her nearly constant lapses were due to her upbringing. At least last night she had not had any great opportunity to offend Ashwell by expressing her opinions too strongly. Still, she would have much rather risked his censure and furthered her plans a little than to have merely smiled at him in one final parting.

His smile had been quite sweet. Perhaps her schemes were developing as she hoped they were. Rubbing her temples, Kate sighed deeply. How very hard it was for her to be so continually on her guard.

And how she hated so much dissimulation. Only the moments with Buckland, who laughed and jeered at her, kept her sane. He would be quite shocked if he knew that. Or maybe he wouldn't.

Pulling her mobcap from atop her auburn curls, Kate ran both hands through her hair and thought of her dogs sleeping in the barn, of Miss Diana, of her pistols and fowling piece, which she had spent two hours cleaning following the match, and suddenly she leapt from her bed, landing squarely on the planked floor. Without a moment's hesitation, she began pulling on her old riding habit. It was rather threadbare in places but she did not care! Hang Ashwell and all of Stinchfield. She would forget Jaspar's debts today, forget the threat of starvation in the villages, forget the perilous position of those villagers who were involved with the Luddites. She would forget all of it.

Within twenty minutes, she was astride Miss Diana, feeling the cold wetness of the dawn seep into her coat and skirt. And how wonderful the chill felt! The dogs bounded along beside the horse as they travelled directly across the home farm, startling some of the farm labourers already hoeing weeds in Kate's long vegetable patch. They splashed through the River Chering, low from infrequent rains, and then sped across Brock Farm, wending their way deeper into the little valley that rested between Boram and Cowley Hills. She was crossing the old Foss Way, heading toward Fosse Grove, where ancient elm and oak still remained to whisper their secrets to Kate. She loved this old grove, many of the trees pollarded from Queen Elizabeth's day. The forest, in the early dawn, sounded ecstatic from the chatterings of thousands of birds. Birds whose ancestors had claimed the forest as theirs for hundreds of years.

"You do not have to leave!" she shouted to them, letting some of the pain of her life ease from her chest with these words. The dogs began sniffing the ground and moving quickly through travel-worn paths, and every now and again they sent a red squirrel flying up a tree.

"No, stupid dogs, let the squirrels be. Find me something larger, a fox perhaps, who has forgotten to return to his den." Through the forest they pushed on, and Kate let the air have each of her cares as she tossed them from her shoulders one by one. How free she felt, with the rush of wind across her face pulling at the knot of hair atop her head. Mud, from the horse's flying hooves, shot up about her as she raced through the forest, leaping across a small brook that had short yet steep banks, following sharply after the dogs who had caught a scent and were hot upon its trail. The grove ended suddenly and Kate found herself on the other side of the forest, her dogs having discovered the half-eaten carcass of a rabbit.

From the corner of her eye, Kate saw a rustling in the scrubby grassland, fly orchids and woolly thistles growing in purple patches about the green grass that covered the hillside leading up to another beechwood. Immediately, she dropped to the ground, removed her rifle from the holster upon her saddle, and loaded it as quickly as she could. Levelling it at the grass, Kate waited in a frozen posture.

One of the dogs, Hercules, lifted his head and sniffed at the breeze. Kate turned to watch the dog change shape before her eyes as every muscle in its body smelled the creature skulking in the grass. The head lowered, the forepaw raised, the tail pointed, and Kate returned her gaze to the grass.

The other dogs soon joined Hercules and one of them began to whine at having to wait patiently. Kate had trained them as pups. In a moment, the grass split apart as a rabbit leaped from its hiding place, sensing the danger all about him, and raced for the safety of its warren. Kate kept it in her sights, then fired. The rabbit went down easily and Kate sighed with satisfaction. Food for Thomas's family.

The dog brought it to her and she immediately set about reloading the long-barrelled muzzle of her fowling piece, tamping the barrel firmly with powder and ramming the shot

143

carefully on top of the powder.

The dogs had now grown alert and were moving with great stealth and intensity through the grass. Another rabbit bounded from the long blades. Again Kate fired, tense lest the dogs moved within her rifle sight, and the rabbit fell. She repeated her efforts time and again until half a dozen rabbits hung from her pommel. She wished Kit were with her and, sighing again with deep satisfaction, called the dogs in, mounted her horse, and headed back to the grove.

The sun had risen and Kate felt warm from her exertion, the morning air now sitting heavily upon the forest as the breeze disappeared. Kate stopped at the small brook with the steep banks, a rivulet that fed the River Chering, and let her dogs and horse drink while she moved slightly upstream. Taking a handkerchief, she unbuttoned the top button of her riding habit and began wiping her face and neck. As she sat beside the somewhat muddy bank, where a brief rain of the night before had caused the brook to swell for a short time, Kate did not even care that her long skirts were becoming grossly stained.

Kate stared at the sparkling rivulet, reclining on her elbows and digging the heel of her boot into the soft mud, over and over. Since she was a little girl, she and Kit would come here and play, damming up the little stream and then breaking the dam with mud balls. How long ago that seemed. Oh, but life was sweet.

The dogs began to wander through the forest, up the side of the hill, into the dying breeze, following some scent that pleased them. They would scarcely rest, even with their tongues hanging from their mouths and their sides heaving.

Miss Diana snorted as she stepped sideways in a nervous manner, the reins falling to the damp ground. Kate called to her and she settled down. And, just as leaves and twigs crunched behind her, sending a shot of fear along her spine, a familiar voice said, "How pretty you look covered in mud!"

Chapter Eight

Kate heard Buckland's voice, and in the shock of having been addressed unawares, she rose hastily to her feet. But the mud that had collected on her boots proved slippery and she lost her balance, landing solidly on her posterior and sliding down the muddy bank nearly to the water.

To Buckland's laughter, she cried, "You thoughtless, arrogant rogue!" And since she still could not quite gain her footing as she slipped this way then that, seeming to make matters worse each time she moved, she added, "You might at least help me, damned scoundrel."

"Now you sound just like your papa. You are most certainly his daughter," Buckland responded lightly, extending his hands to her.

Kate took his outstretched hands in a tight grasp and pulled herself up the pitched bank, step by step.

He quoted a line from Ashwell's poetry, "'And she, covered in duties, refined and sweet, promised the heavens a soul as meek—'"

"Oh, do stop, Buckland! You needn't throw that line up to me. It is one of Ashwell's poorer ones, after all."

Buckland watched Kate brush some of the mud from her hands and frowned, "What do you mean? I thought it described womanhood quite accurately."

"You mean romantically, don't you? Is that what you want in your wife, duty and meekness? Why, she would be crushed beneath your boots inside of a year! I pity her!"

He felt surprised at this summation of his character, and in lame defense of himself, said, "I would not be so cruel. Indeed, I begin to think you have the most reprehensible opinions of me. I would not be cruel to my wife."

Kate was brushing some of the strands of her hair away from her face and trying to tidy her appearance, but her movements were arrested at his words, "Not cruel? How would you describe, then, every other word that you have spoken to me?"

He smiled, his stupid dimple causing her heart to quicken. Damn the man's smile! He answered her, "I only speak precisely what you deserve, Mistress Kate! If it sounds cruel, then I suppose it is. But you ought not to smile so often at the things I say. Were you to upbraid me, I might learn to sweeten my words a little." He saw her glance at him with considerable misgiving and he continued, "And I think you ought to know that to the world at large, I am generally considered quite a delicate lover."

"Hah! That sounds like nothing less than a great deal of humbug. You, a delicate lover! Why, one might say the same thing of Sapperton!"

He caught her hand as it was about to restore an errant strand of her auburn hair to the unkempt knot on top of her head, and cried, "Don't ever compare me to Lord Sapperton."

The anger that flashed across Buckland's face frightened Kate. She had not meant to provoke him quite so completely. A little, perhaps, but apparently she had touched him on the raw. She wondered what precisely composed his dislike of the earl.

"Pray, Mr. Buckland, I did not mean to offend you. Only to tease you. I am sorry. And"—she paused, feeling that her hand was going numb—"will you please release me?"

He looked at his own hand that held hers in a fierce grip, as though it did not belong to him, and with some difficulty opened his fingers slowly, one by one.

When he had first met Kate and learned that Sapperton lived nearby, he could hardly believe his ears. Why must the earl reside near Stinchfield, of all obscure locales? He had known Sapperton for some ten years now. Ten miserable years, with the earl's thin face seeming to always appear at the same London events he would frequent—whether a ball, the opera,

Almack's, or even a masquerade at Vauxhall. Spring after spring, and never could he force the man to face him in a duel. If he could, just once, he might be satisfied, and some of the pain of that wretched day, ten years ago, might be cleansed from him.

Kate rubbed her wrist, watching Buckland's face in fascination. He has some hurt, she thought, some dreadful secret that forces him through life unable to rest. She knew it as though he had just whispered every detail to her. A woman, perhaps. A scandal, perhaps. She had heard how cruel London could be. And what did Sapperton have to do with it? Sapperton, again. Everything, no doubt.

Kate whistled for her dogs and, telling Buckland that she must return to the manor before the servants began taking naps in the kitchens, was a little surprised when he stopped her from crossing the rivulet to retrieve her horse. With an arm catching her waist as she tried to move past him, he held her tightly and said, "I'm sorry, my bonny Kate! I did not mean to hurt you. I've a curst temper myself."

Kate liked the man so much. Would that he were not as poor as she. And she kissed him quickly on the lips then, pulling sharply away from him and leaping the stream to gather up Miss Diana's reins.

At that moment the dogs, all muddy paws and slobbering mouths, broke through the thick underbrush of the less canopied forest. Shrubs of spindle tree and hazel grew thickly about the ancient grove, along with brambles and wild roses and the poisonous nightshade blooming in purple bell-shaped flowers. And just beginning to show pale mauve flowers, a beautiful meadow saffron suffered a severe curtailment of its summer's bloom as it was trampled beneath the dogs' busy, pounding paws.

Much to Kate's gratification, the hounds immediately set upon Buckland.

Commanding the dogs to cease, his authoritative voice ringing throughout the woods, he might have succeeded in subjugating Kate's dogs, but he lost his footing on the slippery bank and, with a surprised cry, fell on his backside and slid into the water.

The dogs stood at the bank, barking and carrying on as though a bear had just charged through the brush, and Kate dropped to the grassy bank beside Miss Diana, laughing until her sides ached.

Buckland, his blue coat dripping, his posterior covered in mud, emerged from the brook, his buckskins soaked through and his boots filled with water. He bellowed at her, "Cease your infernal laughter at once or I shall pull you in with me!"

But this only made Kate laugh all the more as the man staggered to sit up on the bank. She watched him try to wring out the sleeve of his coat, but he soon gave this up as an effort in futility and instead removed his long top boots. As he poured water from them, Kate began laughing all over again, the sight of Buckland in his stockinged feet more than she could bear.

But Buckland had had enough of Kate's most inconsiderate laughter, and sliding down the bank, his stockings now an interesting shade of brown, he hopped the stream. With Kate screaming in vain and the dogs nipping at his wet breeches, Buckland lifted her into his arms and dropped her into the widest part of the stream, thoroughly drenching the skirts of an already muddy habit.

As her hands sank into the mud at the bottom of the brook, Kate clenched her fists, as she had done a thousand times with Kit, and let the mud fly. Buckland's white neckcloth now sported a great number of brown spots and his expression, one of supreme determination, filled Kate with the worst fear and such exquisite exhilaration that she thought she was in heaven. Just like the time that she and Roger had faced the largest stag they had ever seen and had shot it. And Buckland approached her like a stag.

Kate did not have time to even breathe as Buckland lunged toward her.

In vain, she tried to scoot backward, still sitting in the brook, and Buckland's quick movement sent the dogs into a flurry of excited barking as they danced about the banks of the stream. Buckland then did the only appropriate thing. Grabbing her and pulling her to her feet, he kissed her. Hard.

Perhaps it was the morning's hunt that sent the blood rushing through her veins, her heart pounding with his closeness. Or perhaps it was just Buckland. The rogue. Kate felt his arms slip about her waist, his hands gripping her in a harsh manner, and she felt her knees give way as the stream tried to go beyond their legs.

"Buckland," she whispered as he pressed her hard against him. She felt the length of his body, warm through his wet clothes, his muscles taut, athletic. A Corinthian.

She threw her arms about his neck, and as he kissed her again, she felt him reach up to unbutton her habit further, and she knew the pain of wanting so much for his hands to be on her and at the same time knowing that she could not permit it. Indeed, she could not! What man would ever have her if she continued in this wretched fashion. And Buckland. He would leave her in a moment, as Sapperton had left that poor female in Bath.

She pulled away from him and he jerked her back.

"Don't run from me, Kate!" he whispered into her hair.

She twisted from his grasp and said, "Damn you, Buckland. What would happen to me if—"

And before she could finish the sentence, the muffled blast of a pistol accompanied by a woman's screams tore them both from their private battle.

Kate said, "That is near Brock Farm! Whatever could it mean?" And she hurried toward Miss Diana, leaving Buckland standing in the middle of the stream. As she mounted her horse, she called to him in a pleading tone, "Pray, cease torturing me, Buckland. I cannot bear anymore."

He watched her go, feeling a variety of emotions. He had never enjoyed a quarter of an hour more in his life than this rolling about in a brook with Kate Draycott. And yet, he could not love her. She was nothing compared to what Amelia had been, whose light delicate beauty, whose graceful, elegant manners, *covered in duty refined and sweet,* were all that he had ever wanted. That was Amelia . . . or was it just how he wished to remember her?

James had said she was only playing with him, as a cat does with a mouse, and was merely waiting for her mama to find a title to dangle in front of her. And then Sapperton had entered the lists.

149

He shook himself. Surely all of that was finished. . . . Then he thought of Kate, and suddenly it occurred to him that her hasty run toward the vicinity of the shot might place her in danger. And there he stood, thinking of an old love like any monstruck half-wit. Giving himself a strong shake, Buckland pulled his boots on quickly over his dirty stockings and raced through the grove, down the side of the grassy hill. In the distance, he could see Kate astride her exquisite white mare, speeding across the River Chering toward a group of field labourers that were obviously gathered about the slumped form of a man. He could hear a woman wailing, the sound of her cries bouncing from one side of the small valley to the other.

When Kate drew in her mare, she jumped down from the saddle, unmindful of her appearance, and was only mildly surprised at some of the gasps that accompanied her quite sudden arrival.

As she looked down on the still form of the man who was bleeding from his right shoulder, she felt a shock go through her.

It was Rupert Westbourne.

"Rupert!" Kate cried, immediately kneeling beside the dandy, whose brown velvet coat showed a growing dark stain that did not look red until Kate touched it.

Looking up at the men about her, all standing and gawking, she said, "There, one of you, fetch Dr. Adlestrop. And you there"—she slapped the boot of the man standing behind her—"fetch the cart! We will transport him to the manor."

The labourers, a little in shock themselves, did not move an inch, and Kate cried, "At once!" And the men immediately ran to their respective tasks.

The woman, who was feeling a little lightheaded, sank to the ground and covered her mouth with a small kerchief. "La, Miss Draycott, surely he be dead!"

"No, he is not dead. Nor will he die," she responded, her voice curt as she located the dandy's large white handkerchief and stuffed it between his shirt and his jacket. With both

150

hands, she applied a hard pressure over the wound. The woman started weeping and Kate addressed her, "Were you delivering food to the men?"

She looked at Kate, her large brown eyes staring back in a vacant manner and nodded dumbly.

Kate spoke in a gentler voice, "Pray, will you not see that they receive their bread and ale then? I know it has been nearly six hours since any of them have eaten."

She rose weakly to her feet, nodding again and again. Pricking up a large wicker basket, she stumbled down the path, bursting quite uncontrollably into tears. Kate heard the woman as she wept and prayed, "Lord, deliver we'en from Luddites and murderers!"

Buckland arrived at just about the same time as the cart and, when he looked at Rupert, said, "Is that Mr. Bagen, the clothier?"

Kate said, "No, it is Rupert Westbourne. Mr. Bagen does not dress in brown velvet coats and flowered waistcoats."

"No," Buckland mused as he dropped beside the dandy and began rubbing Rupert's hands. "We've got to get him to the manor. This damp ground won't do at all."

As Buckland gathered three of the men about Rupert's slight form, Kate released the pressure on the wound and the strong labourers lifted the dandy's still body easily into the cart. Kate seated herself beside Rupert and to Buckland said, "I don't like that he is unconscious," as she began to carefully feel around his head. "The wound is little more than a scratch . . . well, a rather deep scratch, I suppose, but, even for Mr. Westbourne's delicate frame, he ought not to have fainted. Ah, there. The knot the size of an egg. He must have struck his head when he fell."

Buckland told the men to resume their work, and Kate kept a constant pressure on the wound as one of the labourers drove the cart back to the manor. Rupert groaned once or twice and Kate let out a sigh of relief. He would be coming around soon.

Buckland led Miss Diana as he walked beside the cart, a frown furrowed between his black brows. The countryside seemed positively full of every sort of intrigue. And who would want to murder Rupert Westbourne? He called to the labourer,

"Did anyone see the man who fired upon Mr. Westbourne?"

The labourer looked down at Buckland and shook his head, "Nay. The shot come from the woods and we was workin' this side of Mr. Westbourne."

"Did anyone go into the woods in pursuit?"

"Nay. I be sorry, Mr. Buckland, but we've no pistols to defend ourselves. Ain't a time to be chasin' strangers through the woods what shoots at unarmed men." And he shoved a thumb back toward Rupert.

Buckland exchanged a glance with Kate. And why was Rupert walking near the River Chering?

An hour later, with Mr. Westbourne reclining on the sofa of bright chintz fabric in the manor's drawing room, his coat and shirt cut away, good Dr. Adlestrop sat on a footstool beside the dandy and dabbed at his wound.

"You were quite fortunate, Mr. Westbourne. A day's rest or so and you should be able to move about as much as you like. A mere scratch, really. I am a great deal more concerned about that bump on your head."

Rupert emitted little cries at each of the doctor's quite gentle dabs upon his shoulder wound, where the pistol ball had little more than grazed the skin. The doctor, who finally had had enough of the dandy's affectations, looked over the rim of his round spectacles and said, "Rupert, if you do not stop squealing like a pig, I shall let Miss Draycott tidy up this business. She is certainly qualified to put sticking plaster on the wound, but I warn you, she would not be in the least as gentle as I am."

Rupert gulped, his face white and contorted in a truly theatrical fashion. "You do not know how I suffer. My constitution is of the most delicate. Not to mention how my sensibilities have been battered in an exceedingly brutal fashion. Lord, I have been shot. But I shall be brave, truly I shall, good doctor."

Kate listened to this recital and found herself quite disgusted at Rupert's performance. Glancing at Buckland, she felt certain that he would join in her censure, but he seemed to be in quite a brown study. Moving near him, as he stood by Jaspar's maroon leather winged chair, she asked, in a quiet voice, "What is it?"

He seemed a little startled at her question, as though he had forgotten she was even in the same room. "What? Oh, I have just been thinking." And he lowered his voice so that only she could hear. "I wonder if that pistol ball was meant for Mr. Bagen and not Mr. Westbourne."

Kate stared at him, her eyes opening wide. "But of course! That would explain everything. You think, then, that the Luddites are involved?" Kate pressed a clenched fist against her stomach. Of course. Luddites.

Jaspar entered the room in his easy, gangly style, his breeches horse-stained from having spent the morning in the saddle. Taking in the very odd assemblage of persons, as well as the muddy appearance of at least two sets of clothing, he poked a finger into Buckland's wet coat, then gestured to Rupert as he said, "The pair of you been duelling over this chit! Hah!" And he roared with laughter. "Imagine Rupert duelling with anyone!"

When neither Kate nor Buckland joined in his laughter, and Rupert winced at the squire's loud voice, Jaspar sniffed his nose. With his large, beefy hands held in a loose clasp behind his back, he rocked on his heels and said, "Ah, well, I see my joke is not as good as I thought." He then moved in three large strides to the bell pull, and after giving it a hardy tug, nearly pulling it from the wall, he slapped his hands together, saying, "I'm parched. What can I get for you, Buckland? Sherry?" Buckland nodded. "And you, Doctor?"

The doctor beamed at Jaspar. He'd been up all night delivering twins in Ampstone. Lord, but every bone in his body ached. He gave the plaster one last smoothing rub, then covered the dandy with a wool blanket.

"If you don't mind, Squire, I think Rupert ought to stay here for the afternoon, just to let the wound rest for a bit. I want to give him a sleeping draught, too."

"Let him stay! Let him stay!" Jaspar's powerful voice boomed through the drawing room. "Stay all night, if he likes."

The doctor glanced toward Kate, coughed, and said, "I don't think that would be at all necessary." He stood up from the stool and stretched a little as he took in Kate's dirty, muddy habit. "Good heavens, Miss Draycott! Did you take a spill from that spirited mare of yours? Anything I should tend to while I'm here?"

Kate flushed scarlet as her gaze flickered toward Buckland's wet coat and breeches, then down at her own wet and dishevelled attire.

"My goodness!" she cried. "I will change immediately." And without answering the doctor's question, she ran from the room, away from Adlestrop's piercing stare and pointed questions.

When news of the attack upon Rupert, which was now quite widely considered to be a case of mistaken identity, became known among the various gentry families, Kate grew disgusted at how many of the females disguised their apparent delight behind any number of shrieks, calls for retaliation, and fainting fits. She thought that she had seen and heard of every absurd feminine display until Julia Moreton informed everyone that she was in the habit of barring her bedchamber door nightly with an ironing board, in the event of a Luddite attack. At that point, Kate stormed through her manor, pacing several of the rooms and shouting to whomever of her staff would listen that everyone about Stinchfield had gone stark, staring mad.

She hoped she was not being insensitive to the plight of those most affected. Indeed, she was deeply concerned for the cloth mill owners, their well-being, and the safety of their mills. But all of this fainting and nonsense made her nearly physically ill with disgust. Had it been in any way genuine, she would not have been angry, but when Hope Cerney fainted into Ashwell's arms merely because he suggested that the Luddites had been known to be quite a serious, dedicated lot, Kate could bear no more. And while taking tea with several of the matrons at Ampstone Court, as well as Mary, Buckland and Ashwell, she caused most of the ladies to shriek when she said, "They are doing nothing more than what we might do if we felt our way of life to be endangered. They are fighting for theirs and I, for one, do not blame them!''

Later, Buckland had laughed at her stupidity for exposing herself to James in this purely offensive manner. Buckland had taken to visiting her in the afternoons. They would stroll through the manor farm as Kate would mentally take notes about what vegetables were ready for preserving for the coming winter months. She explained her actions to him, ''I could not bear to see one more female faint, or squeal, or clutch her bosom. Oddsfish, Buckland, they are enjoying themselves immensely. And how I despise such dissimulation and hypocrisy.''

Buckland stopped her with a hand on her arm and said, ''What?'' in an astonished voice. ''How can you say that when you are acting out this complete masquerade upon Ashwell? You are the hypocrite!''

Much to his surprise, Kate did not fly into a flaming passion at his words. He watched her shoulders sag a little as she sighed deeply, ''You are exactly right, of course! And if you knew how much it goes against the pluck with me—'' She broke off, then continued, ''Sometimes, I wish more than anything that I had not begun this folly.''

He had expected her to rail at him, to defend herself hotly. Instead, she had agreed with him. Why did she always surprise him, and was her case so desperate that she must continue on this course? At least she was honest about it, but then what did that matter? Her motives rankled, and they always would. In essence, even if she regretted her steps, she was still the one taking them. No one was forcing her.

Kate continued, ''I know that you despise me for it, but at least I am not heartless. And should I win your friend, you must believe me that I would do everything in my power to make him happy.'' Not wishing to discuss the matter further, she reverted to her original subject and said, ''But the gentry, the families, our neighbours don't even care that most of the villagers face deprivation and even starvation every winter, and that some of the young men, Thomas Coates for one, have returned from fighting the French only to discover that

155

England no longer needs them."

"London is not very different, my bonny Kate. The streets, though not the ones about Mayfair, teem with the impoverished masses as well as soldiers in tattered uniforms. The Corn Laws, too, for all the good they were meant to do and however much I agree that they were necessary, have worked their mischief, and threats of riot abound." He took a deep breath, "And I came into the country with Ashwell, thinking that I would find life peaceful and quiet here—a summer's idyll."

"I have read of some rioting in the Metropolis. Do you find it amusing or frightening, as our local families do? And what of your friends?"

He looked down at her, at the sun playing upon her red hair knotted atop her head. She twirled her royal blue parasol and met his gaze with a rather challenging look.

He answered her, "No, I will not succumb to your teasing and tell you that everyone I know holds the highest integrity. Though some of my acquaintances find it appalling, and some are amused. But just as Mrs. Cricklade appears to be enjoying the sensation, so do any number of the Beau Monde. They thrive on anything, but most especially, upon shattered lives."

Kate glanced sharply at him, wondering what he meant, "And has your life been shattered?"

Buckland felt a heavy weight on his chest as he thought of Amelia, her death, and the scandal that followed so quickly upon its heels. "No, not my life. I am not such a poor fellow as that. I was referring more to a woman's delicate reputation, to scandal, the veritable meat and drink of the Haut Ton." He kicked a stone out of his path.

Kate pointed her parasol to the field at her left. "Those cabbages must be cut soon. Half of them are eaten through, anyway. We lose a large portion of our crops to birds and insects. Farming is quite a difficult life." She smiled, "But I should like to see Mrs. Moreton in her blond wig, hoeing a row of turnips."

Buckland laughed aloud, his dark mood vanishing. Kate looked up at him, at his clear blue eyes, and said, "So London has misused you, has it?"

He seemed surprised as he looked down at her, her brown

eyes inordinately sympathetic. "What? Did I seem to have fallen into a fit of the dismals?"

"A little, perhaps, but then we all deserve to have something in our history that cuts us up a little."

"And what cuts you up, sweet Kate?"

Kate thought of Jaspar and how she would catch him looking at her as though she were a stranger, sometimes with anger written on his face and at other times a deep pain. She tried for a light tone as she reached down to pick up a small stone. "I can't say, really." And taking aim, she threw the stone at a large blackbird that had settled himself on the wall near the tall, upstanding sheaves of corn. The green tassels, turning gold, shimmered in the summer light. As the blackbird fluttered away, her aim poor, Kate asked, "Are you attending Sapperton's soiree?"

Buckland regarded the dirt path as they strolled along, a frown settling on his strong, handsome features. "Will you be there?" When Kate nodded, he said, "Then of course I shall attend."

Kate felt a warmth overspread her cheeks but quickly turned aside the thoughts that seemed continually to creep into her mind. Buckland. Damn and blast, but she wouldn't think of the possibilities of life with him. It was impossible. How would they exist? And nothing in his demeanor toward her bespoke a man in love. No. She must think of Ashwell and of learning to curb her impetuous tongue.

Thinking of Ashwell and how she had set all the matrons by the ears by speaking so forcefully, she realized that Buckland was right. She had behaved in a perfectly stupid manner while Mrs. Moreton was serving everyone tea in her gold-striped drawing room. For one who meant to attach a rather stuffy poet to her side, she was behaving in a truly bacon-brained, mutton-headed fashion. She would do better. Indeed, she must do better! Ashwell had frowned at her so after her quite improper and impertinent speech!

Lord Sapperton was the only member of the neighbouring families that Jaspar held in awe. The squire might scorn the

Cricklades and their incessant groping after approval of the local gentry, he might treat Sir William with a cool, inexplicable disdain and dismiss with contempt the invitations that were, out of a respect for decorum, sent to the manor on a regular basis, but to Lord Sapperton, Jaspar seemed positively prepared to grovel. Well, it was not grovelling precisely, for a man who talked in bluff, loud tones and thumped people on the shoulder when he approved their sentiments scarcely gave the impression of grovelling. But Kate knew that Jaspar was somehow daunted by the earl's presence.

As Kate and Jaspar crossed the threshold of the entry hall at Leachwood, the earl's estate, Kate felt a coldness wash over her. Lord Sapperton had invited them to form part of his dinner party preceding his soiree. The entire hall was made of marble, save the ceiling, which was decorated in scrolled plasterwork and painted white and gold.

The butler, a faceless, toneless creature who did not look either of them in the eye, bowed in a dignified manner as he offered to relieve Kate of her warm wrap.

Giving up her fur-lined cape quite reluctantly, Kate wished that she might have something to ward off the chill that seemed to emanate from every corner of the room. It was always this way at Leachwood. Harsh, uninviting and, no matter how many fires burned, cold.

Ushered through a small antechamber, which had marble statues set into each of the four walls and a floor peppered in an intricate mosaic design, Kate again felt the cold and hurried with Jaspar to the large reception room where Sapperton waited for them.

The stately butler announced them in formal, decorous tones and the earl rose from his chair, a massive thronelike seat with the arms carved in what appeared to be gargoyles, and greeted them. With his small black eyes glinting in the brightly lit room, which boasted a blazing fire, he extended a hand to each of them, bidding a precise, cold welcome.

Kate saw the fire and felt some relief. The whole house seemed freezing, and touching the tip of her nose she was certain it must now be a pretty shade of blue. At least it would match her gown, and she smiled at the thought. She wore an ice-blue satin gown, embroidered across the entire bodice and throughout the small puff sleeves with hundreds of seed pearls. All of her accessories were in white, and as she watched Sapperton look her over carefully and saw his thin lips form into an approving smile, she realized what a dreadful mistake she had made. Why, he must see her as he sees his statues, since she had dressed in colors of such simplicity. Even the ribbon about her high-waisted gown was white, as were the slippers upon her feet, her stockings, her fan, the pearls about her neck, and the satin ribbon wound through her gleaming auburn curls.

"Katherine," he said in his quiet, silky voice. "But how exquisite. You could not have worn a finer gown to grace my poor chambers." And he bowed to her.

Poor chambers indeed, Katherine thought as she glanced about the reception room. Royal blue, white, and gold. Stripes, which Mrs. Moreton had copied, adorned the Egyptian-style sofas and daybeds. Small gilt tables seemed to abound everywhere, along with mirrors and silver candelabra. A blue flowered wallpaper, *a la chinoise,* swirled about the walls, and at least a dozen large branches of candles lit the long chamber that overlooked a clipped and formal garden. Beauty without beauty, Kate thought. Cold, formal, harsh.

Jaspar stepped forward and grasped Sapperton's out-stretched hand, "Damme, but it's a fine thing to be invited here, my lord. Always thought Leachwood a great house." He glanced at Kate. "A great house indeed."

Kate watched Sapperton's face, seeing the nerve twitch in his cheek that expressed his revulsion of the squire's manners. Slowly, he removed his snuffbox from his coat pocket, an enamelled box—blue, gold, and white—took a pinch, and offered the box to Jaspar.

"Eh? Your snuff is always the best. Thank you, yes." And he took a large pinch, snuffing it loudly through his wide nostrils. Kate watched Sapperton's gaze follow the grains that fell from Jaspar's yellow-stained fingers onto the rich blue Aubusson carpet at the squire's feet.

Kate felt a blush creep up her neck and then she was angry with herself for caring what his lordship thought.

159

A voice behind Kate called to them, "Why, it is my patroness, my rescuer—Katherine Draycott!"

Kate turned, a little startled at being addressed so suddenly by Mr. Westbourne, and smothered a laugh behind her mother-of-pearl fan as she caught sight of the enormous sling, flowing with yards of lace, that the dandy wore. She could not tear her eyes from it, noticing the brooch of emeralds and sapphires that pinned the embroidered cloth together.

"Good God!" Jaspar cried.

Mr. Westbourne merely lifted his brow to the squire, who had fobbed him off onto that very odd young female servant, Violet, as soon as Kate's back had been turned. He minced forward to clasp Kate's hand in a weak, effeminate hold. Raising her gloved hand to kiss it lightly, he said, "Have I told you how grateful I am that you saved my life?" He placed a hand, sporting a large ring on each finger, against his chest and rolled his eyes. "Thank you, thank you. What would have become of me had you not been there?"

Kate could not resist a wry smile and answered him, "I suppose one of the labourers might have carried you to the Swan and Goose."

"Do not speak such heartless words! I cannot abide the thought of one of those cretins touching me, their shirts covered with hay and dust and smelling of stale beer and odours of the most vile! But I bore you. Pray, how thoughtless of me to keep you standing about in this perfectly barbaric fashion." Planting Kate beside him on a settee of blue stripes, he continued, "Do you know that all of us believe Mr. Bagen should have been the victim and not my own dear self? I see I have not surprised you in the least!" He took Kate's hand and patted it over and over. "What a dreadful day that was. And poor Mr. Began, living in fear that at any moment he might be accosted by those miserable ruffians."

Kate thought for a moment, as she regarded his delicate features, that Rupert's eyes, for the briefest second, had appeared quite appraising, as though he wished to know what she thought of the attack.

She regarded him steadily as he continued, "But I think it a perfectly absurd notion that anyone should mistake me for Mr.

Bagen! What an abominable idea!"

After fifteen minutes of the dandy's nearly nonstop monologue, Kate began wishing fervently that some of the other dinner guests would arrive. Surely Lord Sapperton had invited a few others for dinner before the soiree. Surely.

When another fifteen minutes elapsed and they had all been fortified with glasses of sherry, Kate felt a fear growing within her that she and Jaspar and Mr. Westbourne were the only guests. Setting her crystal glass on the gilt table at her elbow, Kate turned to Lord Sapperton, who had reseated himself upon his massive chair, and said, "I begin to think your other guests quite rude to be so late."

Sapperton laughed, "Oh, did I not tell you? I cannot abide a large dinner. I suppose it comes of being a bachelor. You and your dear father, and of course Rupert, are my only guests—for dinner, that is."

Kate felt the colour recede from her face and she turned to Jaspar, saying, "Did you know of this and you permitted it?"

Jaspar coughed and sputtered in his wine and said, "Now, Kate, I thought it was only polite."

"But you know perfectly well the sort of speculation this situation will give rise to!" Turning to face Lord Sapperton, she said, "I do not appreciate this manoeuvre, my lord, and if you think for a moment that it means I will consent to be your wife, you are greatly mistaken."

The earl sipped at his small glass of sherry, letting the bouquet flow through his thin nostrils. Eying Kate with a smile, he said, in his quiet voice, "But then I have not solicited your father for your hand, have I? However, I do apologize, for I can now see that everyone will suppose that I mean for you to marry Rupert." He turned to regard his heir, who was busily inspecting his polished nails through his quizzing glass, then continued, "And that will not do at all."

At this juncture, the tall butler announced dinner as he stared at the Elizabethan windows across the room. The ill-assorted group rose and, in a ridiculously formal manner, walked to the dining room.

Had Kate not been so upset at the lack of guests she might have enjoyed the first course—a clear turtle soup, a basket of

161

pastries, chicken a la tarragon, and cold partridges, along with a variety of side dishes. As it was, everything tasted bitter and the champagne bubbles, served with this course, stung her nose.

To add to her dislike of the dinner, the earl spent the entire first course explaining how each dish was prepared and precisely how long it had taken him to properly instruct his French cook on how to trim a leg of lamb. Kate wondered that the cook ever remained to listen to his employer's officious instructions and was not at all surprised to learn that Lord Sapperton had gone through seven cooks in the last two years.

Jaspar nodded and grunted throughout the entire monologue. Kate thought he had imbibed a little too much champagne, his red-rimmed eyes sparkling in the brightly lit dining room. She was grateful when the second course arrived in great ceremony, with a line of footmen entering the chamber bearing silver trays, for her father's eyes lit up, and in a perfectly delighted manner he clapped his hands together, crying, "Damme, but you serve a fine table, Sapperton! Always said so!" And he promptly filled his plate with a large sampling from dishes of fillets of turbot, carrots and croutons, Rhenish cream, glazed ham, and mutton pie. As long as he dined well, the wine he was consuming would not put him in his cups. At least, not completely.

As she watched Jaspar nearly dive into his new plate of food, Kate covered her mouth with her gloved hand and quickly took another sip of champagne. How she was to endure the remainder of the dinner she did not know. Rupert picked at his food, the earl ate in a meticulous fashion that did not permit the fork to touch his lips, and as for Kate, the room grew quite warm, the glare from the chandelier above her giving her something of a headache.

Sapperton looked toward Jaspar and said, "When I was in Cheltenham recently, since I went there first after my trip to Brighton, I came across a friend of yours. A most particular friend."

Jaspar, his mouth full of food, said, "I have a great number of excellent friends in Cheltenham. Indeed, I have. Well, do not keep me in suspense." He washed down his food with a long draught of champagne. "Who was it?"

Sapperton sipped at the sparkling wine and, after wiping his mouth with a finely embroidered linen towel, said, "Lord Turville."

Jaspar, who had just taken another gulp of champagne, choked at the name the earl just threw at him, "Eh? Turville? Lord Turville? Just so. Good man." He coughed several times, clearing the liquid from his windpipe, and continued, "How—how was his lordship. In good health, I trust?"

Sapperton waved a thin, pale hand, "Oh, I would say that he was in his usual remarkable health. He spoke of you, about some obligation or other, and I told him that since I knew you to be one of the most honourable gentlemen of my acquaintance, he needn't trouble his mind again over the matter."

Kate watched Jaspar's face fall dramatically, and his voracious appetite seemed to dwindle to nothing as he sat back in his chair and just stared at his plate. She wondered how much her father owed to Lord Turville that even she was not aware of.

And as she turned to look at Sapperton, she found his black eyes fixed on her and then she understood. The cur! He was merely flaunting his knowledge of her situation and hoping to force her hand. She lifted her chin slightly and, turning toward Mr. Westbourne, said, "I have been meaning to ask you, Rupert, where you purchased that charming pin and whether you designed it yourself?"

Rupert waved his bejewelled hand about in the air and again rolled his light blue eyes. "At last, a sensible topic of discussion. I abhor this truly ghastly display of culinary delights. Truly, I feel quite ill." And he dabbed his lips with a lace kerchief.

Kate thought that at this moment she and Rupert had more in common than they ever had. Letting her gaze drift over the two dozen dishes sitting on the long table at the side of the room, all she could think was that Mrs. Coates's roof leaked and that if they were lucky, all of their children would survive the winter.

Rupert continued, "But as to the brooch, two days ago I felt

163

well enough to travel, even though I knew I should not. I don't think anyone comprehends the delicacy of my quite fragile constitution! I dread the winter months and all of that wretched snow. I plan to lock myself into my bedchamber and stay there until the snowdrops lift their heads in early February." He then put a hand to his cheek. "Oh, but that is quite a charming sentiment. I do think that I should write a poem, a tribute to the snowdrop. Oh gentle blossom, wild and pure, hanging low—no, that sounds truly wretched! When Ashwell arrives, I shall put it to him. . . ."

And Kate's mind left the table at that moment, with Rupert's chattering having a drugged effect on her as laudanum was wont to do. And with Sapperton staring at Rupert with undisguised contempt and poor Jaspar pushing bits of turbot about on his plate in an absent manner, Kate thought that they were a sorry lot indeed. And Jaspar had never looked older. Ancient, in fact, with a ripple of red veins across his nose and dark spots appearing at his temples where his hairline was receding slightly. Kate could not help but wonder what was to become of them all.

After dinner, as the hour approached eight and the remainder of the guests would soon be arriving, Jaspar pushed Kate to accompany Sapperton, alone, into his conservatory. For a moment, as they crossed the portals of the large, round glassed room, Kate forgot the earl's presence and gave a cry of delight.

The smell of the sweetest jasmine permeated the room. The air felt heavy and wonderful, with a dampness that emanated from growing green things about the tall chamber whose glass windows revealed a lavender sky that resisted the encroaching night. Kate smelled the damp soil at their feet, breathing in the fragrance of rich humus. At last a room with life!

As she turned to face her host, words of praise died on her lips. His eyes blazed, and before she could stop him, he grabbed her and pulled her into his arms, holding her with hands that felt like claws through the thin satin of her light blue gown.

"No," she cried in a low, anguished voice. "No, Lord Sapperton." And tears burnt her eyes. "Let me be, you scoundrel!"

And his thin lips, which she had been trying to avoid, found hers, and his kiss was as vile as she had remembered. His lips were so thin, almost shrunken, and through them she could feel the pressure of his teeth. Crooked teeth.

Pushing with all her might, she wrenched free of his embrace. He stumbled backward and became entangled in several plants—a large palm tree, a fern, the white jasmine—and crushed a growth of beautiful red stock. But before Kate could escape, he rushed to his feet and, with one long leap, grabbed her arm.

Kate cried out in pain, his hand vicelike about her arm. Surely bruises would form there. He cried, "You cannot escape from me." And he began laughing, "Though I love your trying to do so. It will make our final moment so much more—how shall I put it—poignant."

"You are a filthy dog, Sapperton. Why won't you let me be? There must be a hundred females who would leave their reputations in the dust for the mere chance at becoming your countess. Or is that the point? You have yet to marry any whom you have ruined. You are a rogue! I know you are! Will you ruin me as well?"

He raised a hand as though to strike her, his face an ashen hue, his eyes darker than she had ever seen them.

"You dare!" she hissed, her own eyes wide and lit with a terrible fury.

Something in her expression, in her will, forced him to realize what he was about to do and he lowered his hand, releasing the grip on her arm slightly. "One day you will come to me, Katherine, and you will beg. And perhaps I shall have you then or perhaps not. Or perhaps I shall simply take you, as I could now. There are no servants to disturb us here and your father—" he paused and snickered, "your father isn't near enough at hand to make the slightest difference whatever."

"He is not so far that he could not hear my screams, and scream I would!" Kate cried.

165

"Indeed?" the earl raised a brow. "But then that presupposes that your father is in one of the adjoining chambers."

Kate spoke in a sarcastic tone, "Do not tell me that you have ushered him from the house?"

The earl laughed at her, "Do you refer to Jaspar?"

Kate was taken aback by this remark, not quite comprehending what on earth he was about. "Of course I refer to Jaspar."

With a smile he said, "I shall not attempt to kiss you again. I must be getting old, for suddenly I find myself unaccountably fatigued. Now tell me, Katherine, why do you call the squire Jaspar? I find that quite singular."

Kate remembered back to the day, only a sennight following her mother's death, when her father had asked her to call him by his Christian name. At first she had been pleased, crawling into his lap as though she had been a child of six instead of a young woman of sixteen, and then her father had cried and cried. Sobbed. She had tried to comfort him, but Marianne was gone. Gone forever. And afterward he had pushed her physically from him, shouting at her to leave him in peace. No, her mother's death had been the cause of their unhappy separation, as though a wall like Hadrian's in the north had suddenly been built between them.

Kate would not lie, and letting her fingers ripple across the delicate ferns next to her, she said simply, "I do not know."

The earl laughed again. "You are at cross-purposes in every aspect of your life, Kate. I know you better than you know yourself. And I also know the intricate workings of the squire's mind."

"As do I," Kate answered crossly. She did not like speaking of such personal matters to anyone, nonetheless the Earl of Sapperton.

"Oh?" the earl asked politely, his thin black brows raised slightly.

"Yes," Kate said. "He has never recovered from my mother's death."

"Ah."

166

Kate despised the knowing look on his face, and she said, "And I beg to inform you that none of this has anything to do with you, my lord."

He sighed, clasping his hands behind his back, following Kate with his eyes as she moved about the conservatory. He did not like this room, but he had designed it with her in mind. If he could seduce her, it would have to be in a place where the earth was fruitful and rich. That was how he saw Kate—fruitful, laden with life. Life that he did not possess. If he possessed her, somehow he might possess life. Lord, but his loins ached for her and he despised himself for it. He despised her. He wanted to hurt her and he would. A thousand times in his mind he had rehearsed hurting her. Words he would say, harsh physical things he would do and as her husband, no one could complain. As he watched Kate inch toward the door, near the orange tree, knowing that she was attempting to escape from the room, he said, "Ashwell will not have you, Katherine. And truly, you needn't fear. You have my word that I will not attempt to kiss you again."

Kate, who had broken the thick skin of an orange with just the tip of her nail and was smelling the strong citric fragrance as though to cleanse her mind of the earl's presence, glanced sharply at Sapperton and took another small step toward the door.

He continued, "No, you will not win a poet, Katherine, though you might just succeed in marrying a would-be poet. And then how I shall laugh."

Kate scowled at him. How she hated him. "What do you mean? Why do you insist on speaking in such cryptic messages to me? Do you refer to Buckland? Does Buckland write poetry as well?"

"As to that, I suppose the answer is yes. But how good his poetry is I cannot say, for I despise anything that rhymes. It is so . . . I don't know . . . vulgar. But you must ask Buckland about his poetry."

Kate was about to press him further but the butler arrived at the entrance to the conservatory and, after bowing low toward the earl, said, "I beg to inform your lordship that Squire and

167

Mrs. Cricklade have arrived"—he paused for the barest fraction of a second, then continued—"a trifle before the hour." He sniffed, giving expression to his own disapproval of the family who had been in trade before inheriting the manor at Todbury.

Kate released a sigh of relief that now she might return to the drawing room.

Chapter Nine

As the guests filled the large drawing room, the marble entrance hall, and antechambers, Mrs. Moreton cried, "But have you seen Lord Sapperton's conservatory?" Sitting forward in a blue high-backed chair and pressing a lavender lace kerchief against her bosom, she continued, "Oranges, ferns, even the most delightful palms. I should have enjoyed immensely a conservatory at Ampstone Court, but Charles would have none of it. He lacked vision. Truly he did, and now that I am relegated to a mere visitor at Ampstone"—she regarded her daughter-in-law Louisa with great hostility—"well, I need not tell you, Lady Chalford, how little my wishes are attended to."

Louisa, making the most of her delicate condition, much to Mrs. Moreton's extreme irritation, reclined on one of the striped Egyptian chaise longues. To her husband John, who sat close by and wafted a fan over her pale features, Louisa said, "How stuffy the drawing room has suddenly become." And she glared at Mrs. Moreton.

John let out a sigh, something he had been doing a lot in the last year since he had married pretty Louisa Cricklade. Letting the fan stop for a moment as he gazed from his wife to his mother and back again, he heard Louisa moan softly, a most wretched sound, until he resumed fanning her. She was not pretty anymore.

Glancing about the room, he saw Kate and let his eyes rove over her beautiful face and figure. Two years ago, he had thought of marriage to her, but she didn't behave at all as a young lady should and so he had married Louisa. Louisa Cricklade had been modest, well-accomplished, and sneezed whenever she was around horses too much. He had thought her a perfect lady. But as he gazed at Kate, thinking of the hundreds of times he had seen her racing through the countryside, her hair flowing about her face in a truly hoydenish fashion, he now knew that though one might easily subdue such unmaidenly behavior, as Kate seemed to have done, Louisa's greater defects, which resided deep within her character, could not be so quickly remedied—if ever. He thought he might take a mistress in a year or two, if nothing more than to get away from the continual pushing and pulling that went on between his wife and mother.

Buckland, standing beside the fireplace and watching this tender family scene, pressed Kate's arm and said, "What bliss! Why, it almost makes me wish to run to the altar myself."

Kate sighed as she watched John and Louisa. Poor, good John. And as she listened to Buckland's sarcastic tone she realized that she could not fault him. Indeed, she was so relieved that the gentry had begun arriving that she promised herself she would never be angry with any of them again. How cloistered their society was, how small, and yet the distance between Standen and Upper Aldgrove was a full ten miles. As it was, all of the families might as well have resided next door to one another, so intimately were everyone's difficulties known.

Kate refused to rise to Buckland's taunting remark and merely answered back, "I should like to see you run to the altar. What a sight that would be. Given the strong impression I have that more than one female has tried to lead you there, I most likely could make a fortune selling tickets to such an event."

"You are right," he smiled down at her and, lowering his voice, said, "but I think you and I might find some bliss, something a little better than that poor fellow over there. At least, I cannot imagine you being tied to a daybed and requiring that I wave a fan over you for hours at a time."

Kate felt better already, her confrontation with the earl in the conservatory fading as each minute passed. She answered him in a teasing fashion, "You are correct in only one thing, that waving a fan over me would hardly do. The fact is it would hardly be sufficient. I should keep my riding crop at my side continually, and when I needed something I would crack it at your feet. And you would hasten to do my every bidding. Now that is a *vision*, is it not? Mr. Buckland, who I also believe to be a rogue of no mean order, fetching my tea, my slippers, a glass of cordial after dinner, my horse in the morning, waiting upon me hand and foot." She wafted her mother-of-pearl fan over her face and sighed, "You are so right, that would be bliss!"

"I'm sorry, Kate, but I hasten to inform you that I don't think you could ride your horse in the morning. You would be far too exhausted."

Kate did not immediately take his meaning and said, "Indeed? How so if you are waiting on me every second of the day?"

He looked at her and smiled. That wretched, dimpled smile, so completely at odds with his quite rugged face. That despicable smile that had a way of lighting up his ridiculous blue eyes. He said, "I may wait on you during the day, but the night would be mine."

Kate heard his words and felt the shock of it go through her. That is what life with him would be like, and she felt her cheeks grow warm, a feeling that had nothing to do with embarrassment and everything to do with certain very improper visions, which flitted quite suddenly through her head, of marriage to Buckland. She stared at the blue carpet and, in a low voice, said, "But you are absurd!"

"Am I?" He watched her and knew precisely what she was thinking and wished that they were alone. Almost he touched her arm.

Kate wanted to say something witty and clever, to disarm the moment, which had caused a blush to begin creeping up her cheeks, but no such words formed in her brain. It was to Julia that she owed an interruption of this most disturbing tête-à-tête, and it was with mixed sentiments toward the beauty that she heard her address the earl in accents that caused the entire room to turn and listen to each word. "My lord, I have just had the most intriguing notion, but no, I suppose it would be asking too much, but then if one never has the courage to at least ask—?" She paused, waiting for Lord Sapperton to encourage her.

The earl responded in an appropriate fashion, "Pray ask, Miss Moreton. You have but to command."

"Oh," Julia cried. "How truly chivalrous you are. The fact is that I was just thinking"—in truth she had been planning this moment for nigh on three weeks—"how your reception rooms would lend themselves perfectly to a masquerade."

"A masquerade?" The earl withdrew his snuffbox from his coat pocket and appeared as though the idea intrigued him.

Julia cried, "Yes! Wouldn't it be the greatest fun? And think of having so magnificent a ball here at Leachwood! Why, everyone would talk of it for years to come."

Flipping the lid of the enamelled box open, the earl raised a cynical brow and said, "You do very wrong to try to appeal to my vanity. I would not care if anyone spoke of it for longer than a minute."

Julia's face fell and she closed her fan with a snap, her lower lip forming into a pout that caused all the young men in the room to shift on their feet. They all knew that spoiled expression and what it presaged.

But Lord Sapperton had long since left his salad days, as most of these young men had not, and he again lifted Julia's chin, saying, "You look quite ugly when you frown. No, don't eat me, for I mean to let you have your masquerade!"

Julia's angry countenance turned to one of sheer rapture and she cried, "Oh, how good you are!"

Sapperton took a pinch of snuff. "We shall have your masquerade one sennight following your mama's ball at Ampstone Court. And at some convenient moment between times, you must tell me all of your ideas!"

When he saw that she was prepared to do so then and there, he quickly said, "Though not this evening." And in a whisper he asked, "Have you prepared your music, my dear?"

She offered him her very best curtsy and moved to take her

172

seat at the harp.

Kate saw it all and thought they deserved one another.

After Julia had arranged her skirts, the earl announced that in honour of Lord Ashwell's visit, he had prepared a little treat and, snapping his fingers at his heir, called to him, "Rupert, now is your moment of glory. Pray, entertain us." And, he seated himself in his large chair as everyone else, with mixed expressions of pleasure, settled themselves, as a gaggle of geese might, flapping into their nests and fluffing out their feathers.

The bucks, of course, all stood at the back of the room, most of them with folded arms and expressions of disgust twisting their faces. Good Lord! Rupert Westbourne.

The dandy minced forward, scrolls in hand—indeed, yes, his poetry must be written upon scrolls—and took his place of honour, still sporting his fascinating sling. He paused for a moment, waving a hand toward Julia, who began plucking and stroking the strings of her harp. And just as she missed her note, which went quite sharp, the dandy opened his mouth to speak. But this dreadful sound caused him to lift a brow and turn to regard Julia with a scowl. This only caused the bucks to give uncontrolled spurts of laughter, followed by the extremely disapproving glances of Mrs. Moreton and Mrs. Cricklade.

The dandy began, his voice high as he held the scroll in his left hand and gestured with his right, which still rested within the confines of the sling. "Oh lights above and those beneath, dark and dangerous, the roads bequeath; Wander now, oh pagan one, a song to sing, a dog will run."

"A dog will run?" The bucks could scarcely contain themselves. Kate heard the last phrase repeated three times with laughter. Beside her, she watched James staring at the dandy, his expression extremely sober. Even she knew that Rupert's poetry was absurd, and she felt for Ashwell that he had been subjected to this nonsense. Across the room, she saw Buckland watching the earl with a cold expression on his face and wondered what he meant by it. Ordinarily, Buckland would smile in amusement at such absurdity, but this rankled.

173

Of course, the earl was pinching at Buckland's boon companion.

She then caught Mary's face, which surprised her indeed. For her friend's usually prosaic expression was molded into a mask of pain, as Mary's gaze became fixed upon the serious Ashwell. Julia's fingers plinked and plunked and even worse. Laughter boomed from the back of the room, and the dandy paused and begged Julia not to accompany him anymore.

But Julia merely smiled brightly, apologizing for her errors and insisting upon continuing.

"Errant moon and stars that glide; Watch this vagrant pagan ride; O'er the hills and winding vales; Through farms verdure and milching pails." This was too much for the bucks and they broke into a howl of laughter, wiping their eyes and filing from the room.

Julia twanged a note again, and Rupert, looking from the bucks to Julia and then to his uncle, said, "I had intended upon entertaining but not *amusing*." Rolling up his scroll, he approached Ashwell and, bowing low to him, handed him his precious poems. "You, sir, I believe are amply able to appreciate my efforts." And with that he stalked from the room.

James stared at the scrolls, feeling numb. His own work resembled the dandy's vain attempts so much that he felt sick to his stomach. Were they as bad as he thought?

He felt Kate lean toward him and press her hand upon his arm. Her words struck him as though she had slapped him hard across his face. "Never mind, James," she whispered to him. "When you get back to the Swan and Goose, you may throw all of it into the fire."

The Swan and Goose. As he watched Katherine rise from her seat and head for the antechamber where the bucks were taking another round of champagne, he thought, *Buckland is the Swan and I am the Goose.* Was Rupert's poetry really so dreadful?

He lifted his gaze to regard Sapperton, who was smiling brightly upon Julia. "No, no," the earl cried. "You performed perfectly well. Rupert is just overly sensitive. It is the way with poets. They are forever trying to be something other than what they are. And let them hear the least bit of censure and they are in tears. Although I suppose Ashwell is not like that. But then we do not really know him, do we?''

James sat before the fire in his room, leaning against the bed frame, a decanter of brandy and one glass planted beside him. A large pile of white sheets of paper, some blotched with ink, some with lines of verse crossed out and words inserted here and there, and some blank, littered the floor in front of him. Regarding his latest effort, which he held in his hand, he thought of Rupert's "a dog will run" and "milching pails." Inwardly, he cringed and wadded up the page of verse, tossing it hard against the screen that fronted the fire. The crumpled poem bounced off the screen and landed at his feet. In sheer frustration, he stamped the wad of paper flat with the heel of his boot, then sank his head in his hands. Would he ever be a poet?

He lifted yet again Rupert Westbourne's scroll, the words written in a flowery script, and felt that same sinking sensation in the bottom of his stomach. Kate had recommended he burn the dandy's scrolls. But he could not. The rhythm of the words, the choice of words all seemed too familiar to be treated with total contempt. And yet every word was contemptuous, every word a profanity against the written language. He picked up the scroll and crushed it between his hands, tossing it into the fire just as Kate had recommended. And along with it, all of his evening's efforts.

His heart stopped within him as he watched the pages wrinkle and turn brown, then burst into flames. What was his life without poetry? For such a long time, writing verse had been his way of finding some pleasure in life and he had hoped, as Buckland had done, to have his poems printed and in time, perhaps, add a degree of financial comfort to his life that, heretofore, he had not known.

He survived upon what most of his friends would term a mere pittance, though this was not precisely true. He could live upon the very fringes of a gentleman's life, keeping a manservant in his rooms, and a horse and carriage in the mews. But little more. He could not run up tradesmen's bills as his friends were wont to do. He was too damned practical for that. He smiled to himself. Maybe that was why he was not truly a poet at heart. He was too damned practical.

The last of his verse burning in the fireplace turned to a white invisible dust, and with a heavy heart, he opened his sturdy brown leather valise, full of over two hundred pages of scribblings. No, he could not give them all up. Not just yet.

He thought of Buckland and frowned as he poured out a small glass of brandy. And as though he had kept the feeling hidden from himself for years, a strong, bitter anger surfaced in his heart. Why was that damned rogue given so much and he so little? Oh, damn and blast! He did not want to think in such terms, but of the moment, when his future yawned before him in a great nothing, all he could think of was Buckland and his dimpled smile, his title, his fortune, his poems, the women that fawned all over him. Part of him hated Buckland.

He sipped again at the brandy, his face warm from the fire in front of him.

Well, he saw how Buckland looked at Katherine, that he saw her as one he wished to conquer. But he also knew that Katherine was not the least interested in Buckland. No, she made that clear enough whenever they were all together. It was to him, not to Buckland, that she turned to flirt and smile and beg forgiveness for her odd behaviours. James smiled, the brandy easing along his veins. Setting his glass down, he stripped off his coat and sank back against the bed frame. He did not know what her financial status was, but by the look of her wardrobe, she must have a sizeable dowry. Damme, but he wouldn't let Buckland have her! He wouldn't let Buckland's hurtful charm cheat him out of this woman's admiration and perhaps even her love.

Lord, but she was beautiful. A veritable goddess, her lines queenly, her spirit so truly Junoesque. If she spoke with too much force at times, a good husband could gently curb her tongue, and as for hunting, well, that was simply the crude influence of a sporting-mad country squire.

He then fell into a reverie as the fire slowly burned to a white, dying mass of coals. Glass followed glass, as he thought of how his life with Kate would be—in a rose-covered cottage somewhere in the Cotswolds. They would have one or two children, a gaggle of geese, perhaps even some sheep that would scratch themselves against the cottage walls.

Kate smoothed out the letter before her and leaned back into her comfortable chair. In the early afternoon, her office always seemed so pleasant, cool and lit with just the right amount of light as the sun made its progression across the sky. She looked at the missive from her banker and frowned. Mr. Rous had still received no word from George Cleeve.

"A pox on you, Mr. Cleeve, even if you are a distant cousin!"

Sticking out of the drawer in front of her were the ends of several bills that she had shoved into the desk only a day earlier in an attempt to make them disappear. Pressing a hand against her temple, she wished more than ever that Jaspar was bearing these burdens and not herself. Why could she not have had Mary's quiet, wealthy existence? Why must she be forced to endure the day-to-day wearing details of an estate that was going to ruin?

She stopped herself, leaping suddenly from her chair and pacing the room. She could not, she positively could not continue in this maudlin fashion or she would go mad. She must think of her future, of her plans, of Ashwell. At least this part of her schemes appeared to be progressing well. She had not offended him at Sapperton's soiree by saying anything horridly outrageous and had even had a moment to console him when the earl had forced him to endure Rupert's poetry reading.

She slapped her hands against the skirt of her flowered muslin morning gown, a pale green dress adorned with a pattern of bramble berries, leaves, and ivy. About her neck she wore a simple gold locket, with a picture of her mother inside.

Fingering the locket, she popped it open and looked at it. They could be sisters, so similar in appearance, except for the jawline. Marianne's chin was an oval shape, whereas the line of Kate's own chin was extremely well-defined. Kate cupped her face in her hands and wondered whom she resembled in this respect. And for just a moment, she thought that she and Lydia had a similar chin. She smiled. The two of them most certainly held that feature in common—strong chins that quite often grew set, determined, and unquestionably mulish in appearance.

Returning to her desk, Kate folded up Mr. Rous's letter and noticed that an odd piece of paper protruded from beneath the brass candlestick on her desk. A sense of foreboding stole across her heart as she pulled the paper from beneath the candlestick. A bill from Stinchfield. Kate gasped. Three hundred pounds, and that for a saddle she had never seen. Jaspar's signature was scrawled across the bottom. Surely he had not purchased another saddle when they could scarcely afford to pay the chandler's bills. And how many other bills were hidden beneath candlesticks, or in Jaspar's greateoat pockets, or in his own bureau drawers? Had he no consideration for her? Did he not comprehend how hard she was trying to salvage their lives, the manor? Feeling her cheeks burn as she stared at the bill, Kate pressed her hands to her face and tried to calm her temper. But it would not be calmed.

Unable to restrain her emotions any longer, Kate leapt from her chair and quit the room. Muttering in a hoarse whisper, she fairly stomped to the drawing room, where Jaspar was reclining on the sofa of bright purple and red chintz and reading a sporting journal.

"Jaspar," she cried in a furious tone. She watched as her father, startled by her sudden approach and menacing voice, sent the journal flying as he righted himself and sat up on the sofa. He looked so much like a boy caught in mischief, his red-rimmed eyes wide and dilated, that Kate would have laughed had she not been so angry. "What do you mean by this? How can you make such extravagant purchases when you know we are living on the brink of ruin?"

Jaspar took the piece of paper that Kate thrust toward him, and he stared dumbly at it.

As he glanced over the bill, Kate watched his startled expression devolve into a passion nearly as heated as her own, his sallow cheeks beginning to turn a reddish hue. "And I don't think, Miss Draycott, that I need explain this to you at all! Since when does a father render account to his daughter. You may see to the management of this house, but what I do with my fortune is none of your damn business! And in the future, I suggest you address me as becomes a daughter speaking to her father."

Something snapped inside Kate. How many months and years had she born his abusive tongue, his complete lack of cooperation, his evident desire to estrange her? Instead of backing down as she always did, she tore the receipt from his grasp and ripped it up. "There! I shall do as you do! I shall pretend that this bill does not exist, that none of our debts exist. I shall begin gaming myself and watch as the servants must be turned off one by one. And then I shall pretend great shock when the estate is sold out from under us and we are forced to go to debtor's prison! Indeed," she said in a voice of scorn, "why did I not think of this before! We can both bury our heads in the sand." She marched to the small table by the bellpull, where a decanter of sherry rested, poured out a glass, and tossed it off. "I shall take to drink as you have! And all of the families about Stinchfield will point at us and say, 'Like father, like daughter.'"

At these words, Jaspar leaped from his seat, his anger pouring over his body in hot waves as he grabbed her by both arms and said, "Never say that to me! Do you hear? Never say, 'Like father, like daughter.' I'm not—" And before he could say anything else, before he could say words that would shatter Kate, he grabbed her to him, holding her fast, tears beginning to fall across her shoulders as he sobbed, "I'm sorry, I'm sorry! Forgive me, my sweet child!"

Kate could not restrain her own tears and returned his embrace. "What is it, Papa? What have I done to so completely alienate you?"

"Nothing, my pet. Nothing. I swear it. Only, only—"

"What, please tell me."

He pulled away from her, saw her tears, felt the bitter dregs of his soul welling up in the back of his throat. He would tell her. He would be done with it and tell her.

But at that moment the front bell sounded, and both father and daughter began to wipe their eyes in quick, brief strokes.

"Damme, who would be calling on us today? I detest

179

morning visits!"

Kate heard Buckland's voice as she turned away from the door and blew her nose into her kerchief, then quickly turned back to receive her guests.

Jaspar had moved to stand by the window overlooking Kate's meticulous gardens. "Welcome, gentlemen!" he called in his bluff manner, trying to compose himself. "Weather's starting to change. I can always feel it toward the end of August. Sun starts moving away from us, the leaves seem to sparkle more on the beech trees. Don't know what it is."

Kate begged both men to be seated and offered them some refreshment, which they both declined. Her head still reeling from the events of the morning, she sat down on a column-legged chair opposite James and Buckland and smiled politely upon them. How heavy her heart felt and what had Jaspar been about to tell her? Would he still tell her once the men were gone? Kate thought not. The moment had passed.

In a rather blank manner, she watched the play of shadows out in the lane as the sun shone through the chestnut trees. "The weather is starting to change," she said, only vaguely aware that she was repeating what Jaspar had said. "There is always this last minute flurry of blossoms everywhere, and my roses are alive with bees. Isn't it odd"—she shifted her gaze to meet the rather open, concerned expressions on both of her guests' faces—"that during the very height of summer one has a prescience of winter?"

Buckland relaxed and leaned back into the sofa. "I enjoy autumn the most—the rippled leaves turning on the elm trees, the forest lit with bursts of flame."

Jaspar returned to join the others and, sitting down in his favorite maroon chair by the fireplace, said, "Fire won't catch in our forests. It's too damp."

Kate smiled at her father, feeling a tenderness she had not felt for a long time, and said, "Buckland was not speaking literally, Papa. He was referring to the red leaves of the elm tree when autumn approaches."

James said, "Oh," then glanced at Buckland in a startled manner. "Of course." He laughed, "I didn't know what you meant, either."

Kate regarded the poet with a puzzled expression. Of all people, Lord Ashwell should have taken Buckland's meaning instantly, and she shook her head as though trying to clear a distorted vision. She remembered suddenly that Sapperton had told her Buckland also wrote poetry. But this notion she dismissed as absurd. And if he did compose verse, she was certain it was of such a nature that no well-bred female could possibly read it, the rogue.

After a few minutes, Jaspar took Buckland off to the stables to see a new gelding he had recently purchased. Kate could scarcely believe that she would now be alone with Ashwell. In one moment fate seemed her enemy, and in the next, her dearest friend. Hoping to make the very most of this unexpected opportunity, Kate gathered her thoughts. Rising from her chair, she moved to stand near her mother's portrait and said, "How quickly time has passed since you came to Chipping Fosseworth. The summer is nearly over and I shall dearly regret the day when you must leave our society. I hope that will not be very soon?"

"How can I leave Chipping Fosseworth when everything I want is here?" His words startled her as he crossed the room to join her, for his intentions seemed even more serious of the moment than she thought possible. "No, I will not be leaving very soon, if ever. Would that please you?"

Kate drew in her breath. Was he really speaking these words? In a whisper, she said, "Oh, yes, indeed it would."

He smiled and took both of her hands. "I am so glad to hear you say so. Sometimes I have felt that perhaps you favored— that is, I only wish to know if your heart is given elsewhere?"

Kate regarded his dark brown eyes and shook her head.

His eyes fairly glowed. "How happy that makes me."

Kate lifted her face, waiting for him to kiss her. Surely he would want to kiss her, but he seemed content merely to salute her fingers. Pulling her arm through his, he led her out of the drawing room and into the gardens, exclaiming, "We did not come merely to have a cose with you, for Buckland and I wish to invite you on an expedition to Tewkesbury. I have a great desire to see the abbey there."

Kate firmly set aside a most pressing disappointment that he

181

had not kissed her and instead entered into an enthusiastic discussion of his proposed expedition. As they rambled out of the gardens and headed toward the barn to join Jaspar and Buckland, four rambunctious dogs met them, pushing wet muzzles into their hands. And how sweetly James treated them, ruffling their necks and patting their heads.

But when they reached the doorway of the barn, Kate's attention was completely drawn toward Buckland, who stood brushing Miss Diana.

What a fine figure of a man Buckland was. He was always dressed to perfection, and today he looked particularly striking in a blue coat, buckskins, and a snowy neckcloth, the white of his cravat enhancing his blue eyes and black wavy locks.

As Jaspar enumerated the gelding's many fine points, Buckland turned to regard Kate. In an intimate gesture, a mere lifting of his hand and extending it toward her, he seemed to beckon Kate to join him, almost as though they had known one another for years. She left the poet, who was now throwing sticks for the dogs to retrieve, and moved toward Buckland. She smiled at him and he smiled back, and Jaspar's voice became a mere humming sound as Buckland waited for her to reach him. She felt as though she were in some sort of dream. She walked and walked, barely feeling the soft hay beneath her sandals.

And then James's voice called from behind her, "Squire! Your dogs have got into the henhouse!"

Jaspar turned abruptly and said, "Damned dogs. It's that curst gate. And the chickens set up such a squawk!"

James said, "I can mend your gate in a trice if you like, or at least I can make something to hold it so that the dogs can't squeeze themselves through. Do you have any old leather about, harness or something, and a few nails, a hammer?"

"Damme if I don't, I'll dig it up before the cat can lick her ear!" Jaspar called back to him with a cheerful expression. When sober, he considered himself quite clever with his gardener's or coachman's tools. And both men soon left the barn.

Kate, her quite unaccountable dreaminess broken up by the chickens' sudden cries for assistance, reached into a sack of oats. After scooping out as much as she could manage, she held her hand under Miss Diana's wet nose and felt the mare push eagerly into her hand.

"How do you find my father's new horse, Mr. Buckland?"

Letting his gaze rove over the brown gelding once more, he said, "Your father is a considerable judge of horseflesh. And though we both consider him to be a trifle short of bone, he'll do well in the hunting field for many a season."

After a moment, Kate said, "James tells me—"

"James?" Buckland queried, a trifle astonished.

Kate blushed and, feeling defensive, said "Yes, we have been upon such terms for some time. Do you object?"

He caught her arm and, with a lift of his brow, said, "You know quite well that I do. Did he kiss you?"

Kate felt the color rise on her cheeks. "If he did, it is certainly none of your affair."

Buckland released her arm, finding an anger rising to his throat. He could only stare at Kate. James kissing her! Somehow he could not bear that thought, even though on countless other occasions the two men had actually compared the kisses of those flirtatious maidens who gave them freely.

He turned away abruptly. So she would go through with it. Somehow he had never really believed this of her. She would marry him. He felt a very strange chill ripple through his mind, as though this ground were all too familiar. Amelia. And how long it had taken him to realize precisely why she would not marry him. Amelia thought only of her comfort, of her station in life, of being a countess rather than the wife of an impoverished but quite hopeful young gentleman who knew that somehow life would smile upon him.

He moved to a support beam and, leaning a hand against it, felt several leather straps beneath his hand give way. He looked at the straps and realized that it was not harness at all, as he had first supposed, but rather strapping that supported two sword sheaths. Of course. Kate had said she used to fence with her father. Good God! A woman who hunts and fights with swords. He glanced back at her, taking in her pretty costume, a pale green gown dancing with green leaves and berries, her fair, queenly beauty, the surface finery hiding a tempestuous, pistol-bearing hoyden. Even now her appearance was challenging as her eyes followed his movements and seemed to search his face. He knew that she was angry with him for condemning her.

She spoke. "You've no right to judge me, Buckland. No right at all. You've not walked this manor and these villages about Stinchfield for twenty years. You do not know what my life is!"

He loved to watch her eyes grow wide and seem to flame when she was angry. Turning back to the scabbards, he drew a sword out and then another. Moving toward her, he said, "I wish to test your mettle."

"Don't be absurd, Buckland. I will not fence with you."

"No? Then what, pray, have you been doing?" And he dropped her sword at her feet, then prodded her with his own sword, poking her side just beneath her breast.

Kate shoved the sword away with her hand, catching the flat side of the blade just as her father had taught her to do. She hissed, "I will not expose myself again to Lord Ashwell."

He laughed at her, a mocking laugh, as he thrust his sword at her again and she jumped back, landing against Miss Diana and causing her mare to start and dance away from her.

He lunged again, and Kate scrambled for her own sword. Seeing that he was in earnest, she parried his next thrust in a clean, swift swirl of her wrist.

"Very nice," he said, then backed away from her.

Kate felt her heart quicken as she watched Buckland. He was very angry and in a way that she had not seen before, a cold anger that seemed to change even the warm temperature within the barn. Kate let her sword dangle at her side. "Pray, stop this madness at once, Buckland."

He leaped at her and Kate jumped back, refusing to meet his blade. His brows raised, he mocked her, "Buckland? Oh, pray, Miss Draycott, will you not call me George? After all, I have called you Kate for so very long."

"Why are you speaking like this to me?"

"Why?" he said, his voice sarcastic as he approached her. "Because I have just realized that you mean to go through with it. You mean to have the man's title, even though you don't give a straw for him."

She lifted her sword and began sidling away from him, away from the rails of the stall that separated her from Jaspar's new gelding. Her knees feeling a trifle weak at the intensity of his movements, she watched him carefully, never letting her gaze shift from his eyes. She could deal with anything Buckland might say, but somehow she knew that he was beyond himself and that his actions might prove difficult to manage. As he slowly advanced on her, his sword moving in careful menacing circles, Kate's heart began to pound. In a moment of insight, she understood him and, raising her sword high overhead to ward off his attack, cried, "Who is it you are angry with, Buckland? It is not me, is it?" And the blades, as steel met steel, rang through the stone structure, the horses shifting in their stalls and snorting.

Buckland forced her to move quickly in the open space between the stalls, taking small side steps and feinting several times as he said, "Pray, call me George," his voice sickly sweet.

And then all conversation ceased as his attack began in earnest and he forced her to lift her blade, again and again, thrusting as she parried, feinting and twice catching his sword in the skirts of her morning gown. Her heart racing, Kate summoned forth every trick she had learned from her father as she kept her left hand raised in the air to keep her balance neat and light. Her sandals slipped on the hay as she threw off each of his attacks, her breath now ravaging her chest. He was a fine swordsman and she did not know how long she could continue, her sandals slipping again.

Only this time, as she lost her footing, his sword tore the sleeve of her gown at the shoulder, cutting the thin fabric in two. A bright red stain showed suddenly, a rivulet of blood flowing down Kate's arm.

Buckland looked at the arm as Kate sank to the hay-strewn floor, then stared blindly at her face, which was now a chalky color.

Kate put her hand in her mouth and bit hard. She would not scream. She would not. She would not bring Ashwell in to see her like this, the sword now resting on the hay at her side. She looked at Buckland, whose face had also paled, his blue eyes dilated as he gazed at her, unseeing. In a whisper, she said,

"Buckland, put the swords away and take me to the house. I don't want—" But she got no further.

As Buckland dropped to his knees, he interrupted her, "Amelia, why did you not come to me?"

He gathered Kate up in his arms, his vision still blurred, and said, "I tried to warn you, but you wouldn't listen. Why did you not believe me? And why did you not come to me? I would have married you!"

Kate answered in a whisper, "It is a mere scratch, Buckland, indeed it is."

He kissed her in a hungry manner, holding her waist tightly. He did not seem to be aware of her or that she was wounded. But when his lips touched hers, Kate felt the pain in her shoulder disappear. How much she loved the sweetness of his mouth. Tears bit her eyes. She wanted this man so much, this man who had just run his sword across her shoulder, who spoke so very cruelly to her, who thought he was kissing another woman. She felt his lips again and again as he kissed every feature of her face. Sinking back into the hay, he followed with her, murmuring incomprehensible endearments, his warm breath awakening every suppressed dream.

Jaspar's voice, somewhere beyond the barn, reached them, and Buckland pulled away from her, his face wearing a startled expression. "Kate?" he asked gently. "What—what have I done? Kate." He saw the wound and closed his eyes, but as Jaspar's voice called to them, he immediately drew her to her feet.

Both men reached the doorway as Buckland pulled a kerchief from his pocket, ripped the sleeve a little, and pressed her shoulder hard.

Jaspar cried, "Playing with the swords, eh? What's the matter, Kate? Forgot everything I taught you?"

Kate shook her head and started pulling the straw from the back of her hair. "Mr. Buckland fences extremely well and I insisted that we duel, even when I knew that I might get hurt!" She looked at James and said, "I fear I was being quite foolish."

Buckland regarded the squire and said, "She is lying, of course. I was being exceedingly irresponsible. I shall fetch the doctor at once." He stepped away briskly and James, feeling an

186

anger swell within him, stepped into his path. "Irresponsible, indeed!"

Buckland regarded his boon companion with a mixture of feelings—a growing anger that he did not comprehend and an extreme irritation. He did not want Kate or any woman to come between this friendship. He said in a quiet voice, "I'm sorry, James. But let me fetch the doctor."

Kate cried, "There is no need, Buckland. I know what must be done. Do you think this is the first time I've been wounded?"

James stared at Katherine in disbelief. She spoke of her swordplay as if it were a common daily occurrence.

Jaspar cried, "Indeed, Buckland. Why are you kicking up such a dust? I've not raised my daughter to be a simpering ninnyhammer, and as for fetching the doctor, stuff and nonsense." And as he moved to Kate and lifted the kerchief to examine the cut himself, he said, "I can see myself that the bleeding's already stopped. A strip of sticking plaster will make this scratch all right and tight. Never you fear." And he patted Kate heartily upon her other shoulder.

Jaspar turned away from his daughter and gave Buckland a smile. "So, what do you think of my daughter's skill? Surprised you, I'll wager!"

As James moved to Kate and gently insisted that she return to the manor, Buckland felt considerably bemused, as though the past few minutes with Kate had trapped him somewhere in his past.

Answering the squire, he said, "She fences remarkably well."

Though to his own ear his voice sounded quite odd, his response apparently satisfied Jaspar, who immediately launched into a detailed account of his daughter's training with the sword.

Buckland shifted slightly that he might follow Kate and James's progress toward the home farm, and Jaspar's voice became a mere buzzing in his ears. A faint mist swirled at the edges of his vision and Amelia appeared, just as the last sight of bramble berries and ivy, of Kate's floating muslin gown, disappeared from sight.

Amelia. Her delicate beauty took a ghostly form, teasing him from beside an ivy-covered stone fence. He heard her laugh, as in a dream, echoing through time. She wore a mask and a purple domino. A masquerade. How gracefully she moved, whirling and slowing, extending her arms. Then she dropped to the ground, lying still upon a bed of ivy and moss, shrouded in white gauze. She was dead. The scandal, the pain, and all she had wanted was Sapperton's title.

As Kate wanted Ashwell's.

Chapter Ten

Kate slipped another yellow rose into a tall ceramic vase and stepped back to view her creation. Three days had passed since she had duelled with Buckland and for three days her heart had been unsettled beyond reason. And every day James had come to call upon her, asking solicitously about her shoulder and reading Wordsworth to her. Stepping toward the vase, the ruffles about the hem of her lavender muslin gown sweeping the floor as she moved, Kate added a trail of ivy to the roses. An irritation seemed to work its way from her heart to her fingertips, for the flower arrangement grew uncommonly ugly with every twist she gave the flowers.

In the dimmest recess of her mind she knew that she missed Buckland and wanted desperately to speak with him of Amelia. But she had to listen to James's recitation of poetry, instead, which tended to cause her to fall asleep.

Trying one more time to right the wayward flowers, whose buds twirled mischievously at every movement of her fingers, Kate heard a horse in the drive and cringed. Really, listening to poetry for four days in a row would be too much.

But as soon as Violet opened the door to the visitor, all of Kate's irritation vanished, for Lydia's strong, girlish voice echoed into the drawing room.

"Kate! Kate! Where are you? You cannot imagine what has happened!"

When Lydia entered the room, bouncing curls and broad smile, Kate could not resist saying, "What a hoyden, Miss Lydia!"

189

"Fustian!" Lydia cried merrily as she drew off her gloves in short, quick jerks. "But never mind teasing me, for I have such news as will make your head spin."

Kate smiled and turned back to her yellow and lavender roses. "I can well imagine your news, Lydia! Now tell me, has Julia stolen a march on you? Has Jeremy proposed to her?"

"Hah! Much you know of the matter!" Lydia threw her gloves and riding crop onto the table beneath Marianne's portrait, then crossed the room to seat herself in a chair near Kate. "You will never guess in a million years! It is about our Mr. Buckland!"

Kate felt her stomach take an unexpected sharp turn as Lydia adjusted the long skirts of her velvet habit.

Pricking herself on a thorn, Kate gave a cry and sucked the injured finger. Hoping that Lydia did not notice her sudden nervousness, she asked, "What do you mean? What has happened? Is he ill?"

"Ill? No, indeed. But he has saved both Rupert and any number of men from being hanged!"

Kate knew that her mouth had fallen open and that she was staring at Lydia. But nothing her friend was saying made sense.

At the confused expression on Kate's face, Lydia leaned back in her chair and smiled with immense satisfaction. "Now I have got your attention, haven't I? But then, I suppose you are uninterested in the extreme and wish that I would leave!"

Kate tweaked her arm, causing Lydia to give a cry in protest.

"Oh, very well. I see you are not to be teased today. As it happens, last night there was an attack upon the mill above Edgecote, the one we presumed that Lord Sapperton owned. And you will never guess who led the attack!"

A vision of Rupert on the day of the shooting match came suddenly to Kate's mind. She remembered the perspiration on his brow and the dirt on his breeches, so unlike him. Kate shook her head, disbelieving her own conjectures as she whispered, "It could not have been Rupert!"

"None other! And by the time that all our young men arrived, including Buckland and Lord Ashwell, the surrounding yeomanry had the armed men trapped inside the mill. Luddites, again. They smashed the mill to bits just as they had done before, at Todbury. And then, if Kit Barnsley is to be believed, Buckland took matters into his own hands, entered the mill by himself, and within fifteen minutes settled the entire affair, even facing a very nasty Bow Street officer who arrived shortly afterward."

"Was no one arrested?" Kate asked, astonished.

"No! And do you know why? Because Buckland told the officers and the yeomanry that he owned the mill and had hired these men to destroy all of the machinery."

"But that's ridiculous. He doesn't own the mill."

"There you are out!" Lydia cried as she smiled smugly upon her friend. "We were all misled by Sapperton. It is Buckland who inherited the mill from that very odd Mr. Driffield."

Kate felt as though her world had just turned neatly upside down. Rupert a Luddite and Buckland a mill owner! Impossible!

Lydia grew thoughtful and said, "I think we owe a great debt to Mr. Buckland. Even your friend Mr. Coates was involved."

"Oh, no! His wife had told me but I never thought— Oh, Lydia, what is becoming of our little market town? Mr. Coates a Luddite!"

"Well, I don't try to refine too much upon it. But can you imagine Rupert lifting a sledge hammer?" And she fell into a fit of laughing as she mimicked the dandy-poet, *"My word, good gracious, merciful heavens, but what an unbearably heavy implement. I say there, you do the smashing and I shall read you some of my poetry to encourage you in your labours!"*

Kate dipped her fingers into the vase and showered Lydia with a spray of water. Lydia chatted on about the event, relating as many details as she could remember from Kit's recital. Then, recalling that her mother needed her home before noon, she took her leave.

Kate watched Lydia barrel down the avenue of chestnuts, and she reviewed again the astonishing news. Luddites, Rupert, and what of Buckland? A very odd sensation took hold of Kate, as though the attack on the mill had some as yet unexplored significance to her. Sinking into the chintz sofa in front of the windows, she thought of Buckland, of the diamond she had seen flinting in the folds of his neckcloth, of the fine linen of his neckcloth, of his gleaming boots—new boots, Hoby boots, like Kit's and Emmet's. And the cut of his coat. Now what was that tailor's name in London that all of the men raved about? Westmont or something. No, Weston. Assuredly, Weston. Why had she not seen it before? The man wore the finest clothing one could purchase anywhere in England. How blind she had been.

Buckland owned a cloth mill. A smile overspread her face. He was a man of some substance. He was not completely impoverished. The barest, most impossible germ of an idea began to beat in her heart.

The news of Rupert's scandalous involvements in the Luddite risings, which were now expected to disappear entirely thanks to Mr. Buckland's interventions, shocked the various little communities about Stinchfield. And it was considerably ironic to Kate that the source of their astonishment was not that a member of the gentry had been involved but that Rupert had been involved. No one could believe that Mr. Westbourne had done such a thing. Why, he fainted if he sat in the saddle for longer than a half hour, to say nothing of taking a hammer and having to go at looms, teasels, and rotary cutters. And how terribly misdirected he was! Good God, Luddites!

But even more shocking was the news that Mr. Buckland was engaged in trade.

Mary told Kate one afternoon, as they walked about Lady Chalford's gardens, "And to think that Buckland owns Mr. Driffield's mill. We all thought that it belonged to Lord Sapperton. I was never more surprised."

Kate took her friend's arm as they walked along, and said, "Do you know, Mary, I realized only the other day that Buckland's clothing is all of the first quality. How could I have not seen it before? I believed him to be impoverished, but no man who has not two shillings to rub together goes about in boots that, for so sporting a man, cannot be more than two or three months old. They positively gleam."

Mary thought of James's boots which, though highly polished as well, had several scratches and one significant

192

— FREE —

BOOK CERTIFICATE

ZEBRA HOME SUBSCRIPTION SERVICE, INC.

YES! Please start my subscription to Zebra Historical Romances and send me my free Zebra Novel along with my first month's Romances. I understand that I may preview these four new Zebra Historical Romances Free for 10 days. If I'm not satisfied with them I may return the four books within 10 days and owe nothing. Otherwise I will pay just $3.50 each; a total of $14.00 (a $15.80 value—I save $1.80). Then each month I will receive the 4 newest titles as soon as they come off the press for the same 10 day Free preview and low price. I may return any shipment and I may cancel this arrangement at any time. There is no minimum number of books to buy and there are no shipping, handling or postage charges. Regardless of what I do, the FREE book is mine to keep.

Name _____
                         (Please Print)

Address _____ Apt. # _____

City _____ State _____ Zip _____

Telephone (____) _____

Signature _____
                (if under 18, parent or guardian must sign)

Terms and offer subject to change without notice.

4-89

MAIL IN THE COUPON BELOW TODAY

To get your Free **ZEBRA HISTORICAL ROMANCE** fill out the coupon below and send it in today. As soon as we receive the coupon, we'll send your first month's books to preview Free for 10 days along with your **FREE NOVEL.**

GET FREE FREE GIFT

ACCEPT YOUR FREE GIFT
AND EXPERIENCE MORE OF
THE PASSION AND ADVENTURE
YOU LIKE IN A
HISTORICAL ROMANCE

Zebra Romances are the finest novels of their kind and are written with the adult woman in mind. All of our books are written by authors who really know how to weave tales of romantic adventure in the historical settings you love.

Because our readers tell us these books sell out very fast in the stores, Zebra has made arrangements for you to receive at home the four newest titles published each month. You'll never miss a title and home delivery is so convenient. With your first shipment we'll even send you a FREE Zebra Historical Romance as our gift just for trying our home subscription service. No obligation.

BIG SAVINGS
AND FREE HOME DELIVERY

Each month, the Zebra Home Subscription Service will send you the four newest titles as soon as they are published. (We ship these books to our subscribers even before we send them to the stores.) You may preview them *Free for 10 days.* If you like them as much as we think you will, you'll pay just *$3.50 each and save $1.80 each month off the cover price.* AND *you'll also get FREE HOME DELIVERY.* There is never a charge for shipping, handling or postage and there is no minimum you must buy. If you decide not to keep any shipment, simply return it within 10 days, no questions asked, and owe nothing.

gouge on the heel. She looked at Kate's profile and wondered if her friend had noticed James's clothing, and if she did, what she must be thinking. "I have always thought that Mr. Buckland has not represented himself at all clearly to us. What do you think?"

Kate thought about the several kisses she had received, her eyes growing quite fond at the memory of them, and she said, "In some ways, he has represented himself exactly as he is." She would not tell Mary that she thought him a rogue. "But I see what you are at. Who would have thought he had inherited Driffield's mill? Do you suppose he owns his house as well?"

Mary said, "As to that, I understand that Mr. Driffield left the house to a widow by the name of Chedworth."

"Oh, dear. I wonder if Buckland knows. But of course he would. He must have received a copy of the will . . . or perhaps not! Mr. Driffield was quite a strange man. I don't see any of his look in his nephew. I will at least give Buckland that!" And the two girls laughed together, for Mr. Driffield had been quite short and fat, bespectacled and bewigged, most of his life.

Mary said, "But how kind of Mr. Buckland to treat the attack upon his mill in such a gracious fashion! Why, I can scarcely begin to imagine the cost of repairing all of his equipment and he will not press a single charge against the Luddites."

Kate beamed, "Not one!"

Sitting in her office the next day, Kate clenched the arms of her chair, her stomach in absolute chaos. She was waiting for Buckland to arrive. After visiting with Mary the day before, Kate had stopped at the Swan and Goose and asked him to call upon her the next day.

She had thought it all through most carefully and she would ask him, if she could keep her courage going. Yes, she would ask him.

She heard the bell to the front door ring in the nether regions, a clanging sound that caused Kate to jump in her seat. Her heart felt as though it were sitting in her throat and she took a deep breath, leaning back into the cushions of her red chair. Surely the embroidered roses behind her back were full of thorns. She could not relax. He would think she was absurd, or he would be angry, or he might say yes. She would represent to him what a fine housekeeper she was, that she knew how to save a shilling, that she lived daily in the most economic fashion imaginable, that she— Oh, it was Buckland's voice, filling the entrance hall and travelling down the narrow corridor to her office.

She heard the clip-clop of feet as Violet and Buckland approached the door. The door opened and a dizziness threatened to overtake her. Lord, but he was the handsomest creature ever to cross that threshold. And as he bowed to her and the door closed behind him, she moved from behind her desk. She wanted him to see her dark green morning dress of the gauziest muslin. It floated about her ankles when she walked. It was just the sort of gown Julia would have dampened. Kate took his hand and was deeply gratified by the smile and the expression of concern that passed across his features as he lifted her hand to his lips.

He would say yes, she knew it. Certainly they held each other in a degree of affection; they were, after all, somewhat alike. She would tell him that. "How good of you to come, Buckland."

"Will you call me George? I refuse to let James outdo me in this."

Kate begged him to sit down and said, "Very well, George it is, though it seems quite strange." She then looked about her in an anxious manner and said, "Oh, I hope you don't think it too forward of me to be receiving you alone like this?"

He sat down in the chair opposite her desk, flinging back his tails and immediately crossing his legs. What did she want and what was that excited expression she wore? He could not fathom why he had been summoned. He said, "I think that since you once shot me and I ran my sword through you, we ought not to feel it necessary to abide by all the proprieties."

She laughed brightly, feeling quite young and perhaps a little foolish, like the time she had talked Kit into stealing one of Mrs. Kilcott's bramble berry pies off her windowsill. "I suppose it does seem a little silly, doesn't it? Well, I shall come straight to the point." Kate stared at him and felt a blush creep up her cheeks. She then pressed her face with her hands and said, "Would you please not smile at me in that fashion."

"What fashion is that, my bonny Kate?"

She levelled a finger at him. "Like that, and you know very well what I mean." She turned away from him, one hand upon her hip, and began pacing the room from the door to the window and back again. From deep within the valley she could hear the muffled bleats of a flock of sheep. "This will be far more difficult than I imagined."

She reached up to pat a curl in place that was already there. Maggie had taken great pains with her hair, even achieving a little fluff of curls on her forehead, while the rest of her auburn tresses cascaded from a knot at the top of her head. She felt pretty.

"Buckland . . . George . . . I have given all of this a great deal of thought and I have a sort of proposition to put to you." She did not know how else she might go about it so, turning abruptly to face him, her hands slapping her thighs, she asked, "Will you marry me?"

He sat feeling stunned, as though she had punched him in the chest. He then laughed slightly, wondering if she had discovered his real identity.

She spoke quickly, "I can see by your face that you do not like the idea. But you must listen to all that I have to say. Will you do that much?"

He answered quietly, seeing the sincerity on her face, "Of course. Go on." He smiled, "I wish to hear what you have to say very much. I am, if nothing else, fully intrigued."

That was not quite what she wanted to hear, but at least he had not said no. Taking a deep breath, she continued, "Since the other night, when you revealed to us in that perfectly shocking manner that you actually owned the mill near Edgecote, I have had the most wonderful idea and I wished to put it to you. You know something of my circumstances. You know that I am not well-dowered, but I wish to tell you more, that you might understand better what I am asking of you. You see, Jaspar gambles quite a bit and, in fact, his debts have for some time amounted to more than the rents we receive and more than what we are able to get from our own farm crops.

195

He—he has not been the same since Mama died five years ago.

"At any rate, these five years have provided me with tremendous experience in the management of an estate, and so you can see just how perfect our marriage would be."

He frowned at her. Then she knew who he was. She wished to manage his estate. Or did she? "I am a trifle confused. Why do you think that our marriage would be perfect? I don't follow your reasoning precisely. What does your considerable experience as a housekeeper have to do with our marriage?"

Kate felt her heart sink. There was nothing in his expression to cause her to hope. She answered, looking first at the worn carpeting beneath her feet and then at his blue eyes that she felt were masked in some odd manner. No light sparkled from them. She responded, "Because of your mill. I know how to manage things, Buckland, and I know how the mills are operated. Why, I'm certain that between the both of us we might have that mill turning a profit in no time. And think of the families we could help, and then when we had earned a profit, we could begin looking at other mills or properties, perhaps even a corn mill, and we could do so much for so many of the villagers here in Chipping Fosseworth or even in some of the other villages!" Her vision had transported her to another world and she forgot her ladylike demeanor, hopping into the leather chair opposite Buckland, slipping off her sandals and tucking her feet under her in a most unladylike fashion. "And I've been reading about a Mr. Coke of Norfolk—I'm certain you've heard of him—who is continually experimenting with improved methods of farming, and we might do experimenting of our own. I already have done quite a bit of work in our succession houses." She laughed, "Do you remember those tomatoes? I grew them myself. Oh, think of it, George, we could do so much in these valleys to help the farmers. Do you realize that the last three crops have failed—too much water, too little?" And with a blinding smile, she said, "So, tell me what you think. Will you marry me?"

For a moment when she spoke, he had seen a sight in his own mind of fields of wheat flowing in waves of gold from the breezes that seemed to sweep continually over the Cotswolds. But what did he have to do with wheat? And what did he have to do with this female, sitting on her feet like a schoolgirl, her brown eyes lit with excitement as though she had been discussing, as other girls were wont to do, a romantic waltz with a favored beau? Instead, she spoke of corn mills and managing cloth mills and turning a profit.

She was not like other females and yet she was. What was she asking that was not any different from Amelia wanting a title? Kate still wanted him for what he owned, not for himself. He regarded the toe of his boot that he had scraped mounting his horse this morning, "And what of Ashwell? Have you given up on his fortune then?"

Kate, thinking in only the most practical of terms, blurted out, "Only if you refuse me, then I will have to marry him."

He shook his head, forgetting the vision she had so enthusiastically described to him, and felt the blood begin rushing to his face. He despised this part of his class, this hunting out a mate, choosing a spouse based on properties and titles and a matching of dowries and fortunes. "So, it is now my good fortune that you have selected me? Do not tell me it is my excessive charm that made you decide you might abandon your pursuit of my friend?"

Kate saw the change on his face, the anger that was ready to consume him. She leaned back in her chair, feeling her heels press into her posterior. How foolish she had been, and she could not help but wonder why she had thought he would say yes. And because he was angry she felt her own choler rise and she said, in a flat voice, "It certainly wasn't your charm."

He looked at her sharply, his eyes narrowing. "I told you once that I would do everything I could to see that James did not fall into your snare. And now, do you think I will agree to marry you simply because you find it might work out financially? And your various schemes . . ." He waved a hand in the air, his face derisive. "You are not a farmer, nor do I wish to become one."

"And what do you wish to become, Mr. Buckland? Is there some advanced school for rogues where, with subtle instruction, you become a more practiced libertine? What is your life, anyway? At least Ashwell has this for him, that though he has a title and fortune, he still writes poetry."

197

Buckland smiled in a mean fashion and almost told her the truth. But he was too angry to dignify anything she might say. Never would he marry a female who had sized him up, like prime cattle at Tattersalls, and decided he was worth marrying. She stood up, stumbling slightly on her sandals that she had dropped in front of the chair. "You cannot answer me, can you? You merely sit there with that stupid, smug expression on your face and I suppose I am to be cowed by it. Well, I am not nor will I ever be afraid of you or your opinion. What is your opinion to me, Mr. Buckland? Air, a blast of air, nothing more."

He stood up and grabbed her. "What do you know of me? You judge me without knowing anything of me."

"And how can you speak of judgments when from the first I have been condemned? Why? All I have ever done with you is to be honest, to have some integrity. I have never tried to deceive you. Don't you think I could have restrained asking you today and simply begin setting my cap for you?" She was nearly overset, tears threatening to spill onto her cheeks. She was so hurt that she cried, "And if you think I could not win you, I will tell you now that you are wrong. You are far more vulnerable than you know. I would have only to keep you at a distance and to faint a few times and you would be mine."

He was livid and squeezed her shoulders hard. "Damn you, Kate! How dare you speak to me in this fashion! How dare you! And if you think for a moment there is anything you could do to win me, you are wrong. You are not worthy of me. You are like every other female I have known, seeking to marry a man for what he possesses rather than for what he is."

"Did I invent these rules? How do you think I feel being tied to a father who has gambled away my dowry? I could have lived alone the rest of my life on what he lost!" Some of her own pain of the last many years began to flow past her lips. "Do you think I relish the idea of looking at each man that I meet only to wonder how many pounds per year he is worth? I've no other recourse, Buckland, do you understand that?" And her voice broke.

At the sobbing sound she made, he released the tension on her arms, then held her close as she fell against him. "Kate, I'm sorry. I've said many heartless things to you."

"I shouldn't have asked. It was foolish. I only thought that, well . . ." She sobbed again. "Never mind. Pray, forget all of this."

He released her gently to look at her and wiped the tears from her cheeks. "Why didn't I meet you ten years ago?"

"I don't know," she said, then gave a watery laugh. "Although I would only have been eleven at the time."

They both laughed and Buckland grew grave. "I can't marry you Kate, I cannot. Not on such terms or for such reasons. Part of me wants to. I have an affection for you. We are in some ways alike. But the answer must be no."

Buckland rode down the drive, listening to the crunch of hooves upon gravel, his eyes seeing nothing except Amelia's fragile, delicate face. But all life had gone. In its stead was a shell. Cold and white, motionless. He had not cried, even when the unearthly sounds of her mother's hysterical sobbing surrounded the mourners. He had thought himself dead in that moment, staring at her youthful, foolish face lying peacefully beneath a shroud of white gauze. She had played her games with too many men and had torn his own heart from him. How long had his heart been missing? he wondered as the sun beat down on his hat, his shoulders, his thighs.

Amelia had been an unconquerable spirit, willful yet so tantalizing that the gentlemen of her acquaintance found themselves bewitched in her presence. How much of it had been real? And how much of it had been his own infatuation? At first, when she threw out her lures to him, he had merely laughed at her, because he was not one to be entrapped by mere beauty and charm. Or at least he had been conceited enough at three and twenty to have believed himself impervious.

But she was too adorable for words and her lips were as sweet as the first spring rain. How tender they were, a delicate flower you didn't want to bruise. He had believed himself the only one. Maybe he was or could have been, but ten years ago he had had nothing except the barest competence upon which to keep a servant or two, a horse, and a small country property in Kent.

How could he keep the daughter of a viscount, whose father was one of the wealthiest men in the Kingdom, in her extravagant lifestyle? He had once seen her take an extremely expensive bonnet she had grown bored with and toss it into the Serpentine. He could still hear her laughter even now and he could still see the conspiratorial light in her eyes. Lord, but he could not resist her. She had led him everywhere and he had followed blindly. She had kept him on a string. She had kissed him several times—on balconies, in the shrubbery, in darkened hallways.

And all the while she had been baiting Sapperton.

After the front door closed behind Buckland, Kate moved to the drawing room where, with one knee bent on the sofa, she held tightly onto the back of the bright chintz couch as she watched him travel down the drive. A sense of loss weighted her chest as his horse broke into a canter and he disappeared into the lane. Buckland. Ashwell.

Turning slightly and sliding onto the sofa, Kate pressed a small pillow, embroidered in a splash of flowers, against her stomach. As she fingered the feathery stitches of the colourful pansies, Kate stared absently at the ruffles about the hem of her gown. He had not noticed her gown. She smiled to herself. How could he, when she had launched immediately into her ridiculous scheme? She pressed her palm against her forehead, her hand feeling cold against the heat of her skin, a wave of humiliation washing over her. Why had she thought such a man would even wish to marry her? But then she had not known that he would have such strong feelings about marriage. She did not really understand him at all or why, when she had spoken of her situation, he still seemed unable to comprehend her own sense of desperation.

A loud crashing sound, of splintering glass, startled Kate and she headed immediately to the library. As she threw open the double doors on the other side of the entrance hall, she winced at the sight that met her eyes. Jaspar lay on the planked floor and all about him were the remains of a crystal decanter and no doubt a crystal goblet. The fine old room, lined with glass cases full of leather-bound books, reeked of brandy and Kate heard Violet and Maggie rush into the entrance hall. As she stared at her father, unable for a moment to move, she felt the two maids press her arms and shoulder as they peeked inside the library.

Maggie cried, "'Tis the squire!"

Kate shook her head slightly and walked over to her father, where she began picking up bits of glass as did the two maids. When the largest pieces had been disposed of, Kate said, "Violet, please fetch Peter Coachman for me." And after Maggie left to retrieve a broom, Kate examined Jaspar's head for cuts. Looking down into his flaccid face, all sagging cheeks and jowls, her heart rebelled against her father. She couldn't live this way any longer. She could not. Buckland was right in his ideals, but somehow ideals had so little to do with how life landed upon you.

Kate was not different from Mary or Lydia or even Julia, all of whom spoke of wishing that they might fall violently in love and marry. How many times had she read Ashwell's poems and not wished for the same? She might have even loved Buckland. But she would not live out her life in poverty as she had with Jaspar over the past five years. She would marry Lord Ashwell.

Touching her father's cheek, Kate rose from the floor and stepped away from him. She thought of Lord Ashwell. James was so unlike his poetry, yet in some ways more sensitive than his verse. If only he had a little more spirit like Buckland. But she had known enough brilliant romances among their small neighbourhood which, once the knot had been tied, seemed to fall quickly apart. Kate was not naive in that respect. She had only to see Louisa and John Moreton together to know the truth of this. No two people had seemed more in love than they, but a year had seen such a change in John—his eyes pinched, his expression when he thought no one was looking as though he had already died and was simply waiting for nature to claim him.

Looking at Jaspar, who had begun snoring, she knew that she ought to wait for the servants to return but could not. She would let them care for Jaspar this time without her. Walking briskly toward the long French window that overlooked a small topiary garden, Kate left her father behind.

If only she were certain of having a measure of happiness with James. And if she did succeed in charming a proposal of marriage from Ashwell, could she indeed make him happy? On this point she was adamant. It was bad enough that she was involved in this ridiculous masquerade of her own, pretending to be a refined young woman when, at heart, she loved wrestling with Buckland, standing in a stream, with a muddy soaked habit and having his arms wrapped firmly about her. She was worse than a hoyden. She pressed her hands against her cheeks as she walked along the groomed gravelled paths about the topiaried shrubs. She would not think of Buckland. No more. She must instead think of Ashwell, of becoming his wife, of learning how to make him happy.

For every opportunity Kate had during the following sennight to flirt with Lord Ashwell, to try to bring him up to scratch, Buckland was there watching her every move. And yet he had censured her only with his eyes when she was blatantly appealing to the poet's vanity, and in every other respect he seemed to want to keep his distance, almost as though he intended not to interfere in her schemes. She could not make him out. All she knew was that the more he ignored her, the more she felt uncommonly drawn to him, cherishing each word they exchanged as though she were perishing from some unquenchable thirst. Did he know the depth of her attraction for him? She certainly did not comprehend her own feelings and hoped that somehow he did not understand them either.

As for her pursuit of Ashwell, the poet's attentions to her were marked enough to give her the strongest hope that she would soon receive a proposal of marriage. But the more clearly he expressed his interest in her, a feeling grew within Kate that she was now a rabbit caught in a box-trap and unable to escape. And the more she tried to force her mind to envision an enchanting life with Lord Ashwell, the more her rebellious heart would conjure up Buckland's smile and how his lips had felt when he kissed her.

But with every such thought she would remind herself that

with Buckland she had no life. None at all. She had pleased herself in accepting his kisses, and now she must forget them and take the greatest care never to be alone with him again. He was a rogue, a practiced rogue. And she, a very weak female susceptible to his every charm.

As she approached one of several carriages preparing to embark on the excursion to the ancient town of Tewkesbury, Kate noted that the quite large gathering of sightseers most certainly would afford her considerable safety from Buckland. It would also afford her plenty of opportunity to encourage Ashwell to fix his interest on her, and for this she was grateful.

But from the corner of her eye she could see precisely where Buckland was standing and knew that he was watching her. Was it his plan to steal her heart, to make her wish that he might kiss her again so she would forsake her pursuit of Ashwell? If only Buckland had loved her a little . . . But what was she thinking?

With parasol and reticule dangling in her left hand, she greeted Mary, kissing her cheek as both women leaned sideways to avoid catching one another's bonnets together. Her own straw bonnet, made up with a polka-dot ribbon that tied beneath her chin, had a fairly broad brim and Mary laughed as their brims bumped slightly together.

Mary exclaimed, "But how lovely, Kate." And she caught her hands, extending them out that she might look at her friend's pretty gown, "Oh, and the ruffle about your skirt matches your bonnet. How very clever."

Kate linked arms with her friend and, trying to achieve as light a tone as possible, said, "We are both in white and green, and no one will tell us apart." Her eyes drifted to Buckland, who looked tall and handsome against the blue sky.

Mary laughed, "I see you mean to be quite silly today. And we would be twins were I taller, much prettier, had brown eyes and your exquisitely red hair!"

"Nonsense!" Kate returned with a smile as James approached her, wearing a tender expression. He explained their travelling plans carefully, having himself helped Sir William arrange all the carriages.

As the party rustled and exclaimed and clambered aboard

the vehicles, it was with a measure of relief that Kate noted Buckland was in the fifth carriage with Lady Chalford and the vicar. And as the coaches bowled along the lane and travelled at a clipping pace through Stinchfield, she felt her heart grow lighter with every passing mile, Jaspar and his debts quite forgotten. Today she would not think of her difficulties.

Travelling with Mary and James for the first hour or so, Kate did not know how long it had been since she had paid the least attention to their chatter. As for flirting with Ashwell, she smiled at him every now and again and hoped it would suffice. But in the open landau, with the fresh air on her face and a blue, heavenly sky above, even Ashwell could go to the devil for all she cared. And she breathed deeply.

Toward the end of the second hour, the entire party switched carriages, and Buckland, Lydia, and a young woman named Fanny came to travel in the landau as Mary and James moved to sit with Lady Chalford.

Kate refused to look at him but instead busied her hands by twirling her parasol and kept her gaze fixed out the window. And just as she was beginning to relax, listening to Buckland regale the two young ladies with London anecdotes, she saw a young couple embracing in a corn field and felt her cheeks suddenly grow quite warm.

"Don't you agree, Kate?"

Buckland's voice startled her and she jumped a little in her seat, "What? I was not attending."

He pressed a hand against his heart. "You've wounded me! And in front of these two fair damsels. They will know now that you are not the least interested in anything I have to say, and not only will they cease attending to me, but I will gain a most unsavory reputation as . . . a bore!" He shook his head sadly at Lydia and Fanny.

Kate smiled, feeling a little less uncomfortable in his presence. "I apologize, good sir. I was being quite rude."

He lifted a brow. "Perhaps you found the scenery much more to your liking than my paltry attempts at entertainment. Was it a kestrel perhaps, or a turtledove?"

So, he had seen the couple as well. Kate felt the colour rise in her cheeks as she placed both hands atop the handle of her parasol, standing it upright on the carriage floor, "Well, it could have been a bird of prey. In fact, there were two of them, but I could not make out their markings."

"Ah," he said in a knowing fashion. And to the younger ladies he said, while gesturing toward Kate, "And I was given to believe that she was something of an authority in these hills."

Lydia looked from one to the other and blurted out, "What a handsome pair you make. You ought to marry. Indeed, you should."

Kate could not keep from blushing and Fanny wasted no time in shoving her elbow into her unthinking friend's ribs. Fanny was a sweet young lady, whose round, eager face and fawnlike brown eyes made her look more a girl of thirteen than sixteen. She rolled her eyes at Lydia, who cried, "Oh, I'm sorry Kate. You must forgive me, Mr. Buckland. My sister says that I am quite hopeless—and I am—but indeed you look remarkably well together."

Buckland wore a sad face. "Alas, Miss Lydia, Miss Fanny, what can I do? For I have the strongest feeling that Miss Draycott secretly loathes me."

Kate looked up at him and, in the spirit of his teasing expression, replied, "Only a very little, Mr. Buckland. But no more than most married couples dislike one another. I don't think it should stand in the way of our nuptials at all. What do you think, Fanny?" But both girls could only giggle. Kate looked up at his profile as he told Lydia and Fanny to ignore such cynical remarks and launched into another anecdote, and again she could not but wonder what marriage to him would be like. They would hunt a lot and he would kiss her and— She gave herself a shake, directing her gaze back out at the passing hills and woods. Such dangerous, useless thoughts.

As the caravan of barouches and landaus left the Cotswolds behind and descended into the Vale of Gloucester, Kate noticed that clouds had begun piling up in the west over the Welsh mountains and that a light breeze smelling of rain had just begun to cool the early afternoon heat.

In what seemed a short time, the entire party found themselves standing before massive iron gates. Kate had never been to Tewkesbury and regarded the tower of the twelfth-century abbey, which was over one hundred and thirty feet high, with a feeling of awe. It rose majestically before them, cutting into the blue sky.

Sir William moved through the gate and, stamping his cane on the flagway, said, "I shouldn't care to fall off that roof."

Somehow this remark eased the daunting aspect of the abbey, as the party laughed lightly at the baronet's words and moved quickly inside, coattails and pelisses beginning to flap in the growing wind.

As they traversed the various chapels radiating from the choir and admired the vaulted roof, Kate found herself attracted to several of the family monuments, where she stood alone. After a few minutes, she felt a light pressure on her elbow and turned to find Buckland smiling at her.

In a conspiratorial whisper, he said, "Come with me to the tower. I want to share the first sight of the view, which I am told is extraordinary, with you."

Kate, feeling that most of her difficulties were buried somewhere in the Cotswolds, did not hesitate and fell into step beside him. She forgot about James and wanted only to be with Buckland, who took long, quick steps that Kate infinitely preferred to James's slow, meandering walk.

Sir William watched the pair go with a smile, and before his daughter and the poet would notice, he diverted them by insisting they look at the other organs that the abbey possessed.

Nothing prepared Kate for the scenery, in a full circle about them, that met her eyes—the winding Avon lined with trees and grass, the Welsh hills, the Malvern hills, the vales of both Avon and Severn—and she cried, "What exquisite beauty!"

He looked down at her. "Your world has been very confined, has it not?"

Kate brushed a stray wisp of hair from her cheek, the breeze considerably stronger on the tower. "More than I realized. But look at that river. Somewhere in the distance is a great ocean and lands that turn your skin black during a longer summer than I can even imagine, where wild, godless redskins take the lives of colonists, or where ships are being loaded with slaves and smelling of death and everything foul." Aware suddenly of Buckland's intense gaze upon her, she blushed. "I—I'm sorry. I must be shocking you by saying such things. How absurd to be looking at so much beauty and then speaking of slave ships."

His face grew earnest as he said, "I admire your spirit. And I am not shocked. Not in the least." He paused for a moment, thinking of London society, of the simpering females he had danced with at Almack's. He stared at Kate, thinking that at this moment, with his identity so completely hidden from her, he was glad of his masquerade. "Don't ever restrict your speech because of me." He then smiled in a taunting fashion. "You may have to do so for James but not for me."

Kate could not truly be angry with him for this remark, and she merely slapped her parasol against his booted leg and, in a whisper, said, "You blackguard," which endearing term caused him to throw his head back and laugh.

Until this moment, they were not aware that anyone else was present at the top of the tower and Kate was startled when a stranger approached them in a tentative manner, his rather round, boyish face full of freckles, and said, "Ashwell? I say, it is you. How do you do? You may not remember me, but I was introduced to you—let me see—in May, I think, at Lady Symond's quite dreadful soiree. How do you go on?"

Buckland clasped the hand that was thrust at him and said, "I'm sorry, but—but I think you're a trifle confused."

The man said, "You are Lord Ashwell?"

Buckland felt his neckcloth constrict him a little and glanced at Kate. He did not want her to know. Not yet, at least. He then felt a tremendous guilt pour over him, the knowledge that their masquerade would probably ruin her chances at a future. But he would not think of that, only that he could not let this near-stranger end their charade.

He looked directly at the young man and, seeing from the corner of his eye that James and Mary had just reached the roof, was about to set him straight when Kate laughed outright and said, "Sir, you are gravely mistaken." And pointing toward James, she continued, "That is Lord Ashwell."

The young man looked sharply at James and then back at Buckland and said, "But I—that is, yes, of course. One meets so many people during the season. Forgive me." And bowing to Buckland, he turned away to greet James.

Kate looked at Buckland, at his face that now wore quite an irritated expression, and she could not help laughing again. "I'm sorry," she said as she withdrew a kerchief from her reticule and dabbed at her eyes as she giggled some more. "It is just that . . . to think that anyone could mistake you for Lord Ashwell . . . It is quite absurd."

Buckland, annoyed at what he now perceived to be some judgment of his character, said, "And pray, tell me, Miss Draycott, that perhaps I too might share in your amusement, precisely why I may not be Lord Ashwell? Perhaps you are mistaken. Perhaps I am Lord Ashwell and James is a mere Mr. Buckland, and we are just hoaxing you."

For a moment, looking at Buckland's rather angry countenance, she thought he might be speaking the truth. But she knew Buckland. He had a measure of pride that was not at all good for him, and when she looked back at James's sensitive pale face, his slim build, the truly poetic cast to his countenance, she quickly smothered her mouth with her lace handkerchief and laughed until her sides ached. And each time she glanced at him, hoping that she might stop making a spectacle of herself by laughing so hard, she would look him up and down, at his thoroughly Corinthian, loose-limbed appearance, his completely roguish bearing, and she could not stop. Only when Lady Chalford made her appearance on the tower, with the vicar in tow, did she feel she must cool her laughter lest she receive a severe scold. And even then Kate still found herself giggling.

When she finally had laughed enough, Buckland said, "How pleased I am to have afforded you such a hearty laugh."

"Oh, no, please, George, don't look at me as though you are miffed. I cannot bear it, really I can't. My ribs ache dreadfully as it is, and if you fly into the boughs, really, I don't think I could bear it." And she nearly began laughing all over again.

Buckland removed his snuffbox from the pocket of his coat and, taking a pinch of snuff, said in a lighter tone, "I am curious though. You must at least give me that. Why is it impossible for you to picture me as a famous poet?"

Kate looked at him, her laughter having subsided, and with the clouds now overhead and the breeze whipping at her bonnet a little, she thought that he was the sort of man about whom poets wove their magic tales. "You are Olympian, I think," she said, her tone almost flirtatious. "When I first met you"—she paused for a moment as they smiled at each other in silent recognition of the shared memory—"that is the impression I had of you. Zeus. But I suppose you have heard all of this a hundred times." And then, as though the thought were a new one, she said, "Do most women flatter rogues? I mean, do they tell you how handsome you are and that sort of drivel?"

He had never received such a profound compliment in his life and would have answered her, but at that moment James and Mary approached them. James looked at Buckland in a pointed manner and said, "I can't say that I recall that fellow. He said we met at Lady Symond's soiree or some such thing."

Buckland smiled broadly, "One does meet all manner of persons during the season, anyway. But given your fame, I'm certain he was one not of hundreds but of thousands."

James laughed, "Undoubtedly."

Kate wondered what private joke they were sharing when Mary's voice, rather quiet in the growing wind, said, "I do not like to distress you but"—she pressed a trembling hand to her cheek, her face quite pale—"I feel quite unwell. My head—"

And with that she closed her eyes and would have dropped to the hard stone beneath their feet had James not caught her, lifting her easily into his arms. In a rather distraught manner, he said, "I asked if she were ill, for she looked rather sickly all morning and scarcely touched her nuncheon."

"Mary does not have the strongest of constitutions," Kate answered, picking up the reticule that had slid from her friend's limp arm.

Buckland guided James's elbow. "Let's take her belowstairs

at once."

At which words Lady Chalford, suddenly aware of what was going forward, bustled toward the men, exclaiming, "Oh, my poor dear. She has a frightful time with her headaches. William," she cried over her shoulder, "you must send for an apothecary at once! She will need some laudanum." And the entire group followed James down the stairs.

"Kate," Sir William said in a quiet voice. "And you, Mr. Buckland. I have thought it all through most carefully and I fear I must impose upon you both." He was so gleeful at his plan that he had a difficult time keeping a serious expression on his face. "But if you and Buckland wouldn't mind terribly, will you take the younger girls the entire distance to Upper Aldgrove, leave Fanny there, then see Lydia to Edgecote?"

He bowed to Buckland. "I know Lydia's spirits, and she will only distress Mary with her chatter and I dare not let the girls ride with our vicar for the same reason. I fear this outing was a mistake and Lord Ashwell has kindly agreed to travel with good Mr. Brimscombe. I will, of course, be travelling with my poor Mary."

He looked from one to the other and Kate had the oddest feeling that Sir William had some scheme in mind, but what she could not imagine. Kate answered readily, "Whatever we can do, Sir William! Whatever you think best. Is Mary all right?"

Sir William patted her shoulder and said, "Of course she is. Lady Chalford has had a similar difficulty these many years, such dreadful headaches." He glanced at Buckland and said, with a smile, "I'm afraid you're in for quite a journey back to Stinchfield and I only hope you do not call me out when you get there."

Buckland responded warmly, "Nonsense. I shall beat Fanny and Lydia if they dare utter a single sound the entire trip."

Since Lydia and Fanny had just walked up at that moment, with the knowing expressions of those who had already discovered the new seating arrangements, they both giggled at his words. Kate again regarded the twinkle in Sir William's eye and felt a dull blush begin creeping up her cheeks. And as they all proceeded from the abbey, a most disturbing thought assailed Kate: Night would fall long before they reached Edgecote, and by the time both Fanny and Lydia were safely delivered to their front doors, Kate would be spending the remaining journey from Sir William's manor to Chipping Fosseworth in a closed carriage with Buckland!

She paused in her step, a hand flying to her cheek. She could not be alone with him again. Merciful heavens, she couldn't trust him at all. And glancing at his broad back and the way he was smiling down at Lydia and teasing her, she knew the real truth: She could not trust herself with him!

Chapter Eleven

As rain pelted the landau, all of the occupants of Kate's carriage soon grew quite sick of the smell of greasy harness leather. The landau, with its leather calashes folded back, was perfect for travelling in the open air, but when closed it smelled frightfully of blacking and grease. And in the rain the coach became increasingly cold as night descended upon the Cotswolds.

At Winchcombe the entire party stopped at the George Inn, with its galleried coachyard, and enjoyed a delightful dinner. Lady Chalford found Mary a bedchamber to rest in. Kate wanted to see her but the baronet's wife refused, saying, "I'm sorry, Kate, but it will only distress her. She feels she has quite ruined our little party."

James expressed his own distress at the arrangement of carriages but Kate silenced him, quite unexpectedly, when she said, "But I am certain Sir William felt that his own vicar, Mr. Brimscombe, whom I understand to be a scholar of no small repute, would have more in common with you than with Mr. Buckland."

James had looked quite astonished as he said, "Of course! I suppose I had just not thought of it in those terms."

Kate wondered again at Lord Ashwell's seeming disregard for his own status, for his renown as a poet, and responded, "At times, my lord, your humility overwhelms me. Why, one would suppose that you were not Lord Ashwell at all. But then I suppose your fame is of so recent an accomplishment that you still are not used to it."

James blushed a fiery red and moved away to speak with Lady Chalford. Kate was stupefied and could not make him out. She wanted to ask him what she had said to so embarrass him, but just then the coaches arrived and they began making their procession to the waiting carriages.

With a cry of relief, Kate, Fanny, and Lydia discovered that Mr. Buckland had hired them another coach, a roomy, well-sprung town coach that smelled wonderfully of a fragrant potpourri all of them noticed had been scattered on the floor.

To their delighted cries, Buckland, pretending he was Rupert Westbourne, spoke in an affected voice, "I could not, simply I could not bear that terrible odor another mile!"

Lydia cried, "Oh stuff! You did this for us! And what a complete hand you are, for now you sound just like Rupert."

And within a few minutes everyone was settled and bowling out of the inn's courtyard, the three vehicles moving rapidly through the small town.

Sir William had instructed his coachman to return the now-empty landau to Edgecote Hall and the new coachman, his hat dripping with rain, stopped the town coach after they had been travelling for nearly an hour and said, "I be sorry, sir, but I've lost them other coaches. I think I made a wrong turn three miles back at that village wat forked at St. Stephen's Church."

The girls gave little gasps, but Buckland said calmly, "Never mind. Just return us to the proper road."

The coachman, an expression of relief on his face that he was not to receive a severe dressing down, apologized for his stupidity. And after bowing twice and thanking Buckland for his kindness, he had the coach rumbling along in the opposite direction in only a very few minutes.

Kate was worried for a moment that Lydia and Fanny might be upset, but she had all of her fears dispelled on this count, when Lydia cried, "What an adventure! To have actually gotten lost."

Fanny added her mite, "Indeed, yes! And Hope's face will turn positively purple when I tell her so!"

The sky grew increasingly dark as the large travelling coach moved steadily toward the east, the rainclouds blackening what should have been a pretty twilight sky. The coachman returned them to the road that led to Stinchfield, but even after changing the horses and taking the next few miles at a brisk pace, they did not overtake Sir William's old-fashioned barouche or the travelling coach that carried Mr. Brimscombe and Lord Ashwell.

Within, Kate and Fanny sat opposite Lydia and Buckland, and the four scarcely noticed the rain or the cold that seemed to move steadily within, all singing and laughing and listening with great relish to Buckland's recounting of his sojourn in Greece with Lord Ashwell. But as the minutes passed, even Kate could feel the damp air begin biting at her toes.

As cobbled stones marked their arrival at another village and Sir William's coach was still not in sight, Buckland rapped on the roof of the coach and they stopped at an inn. He begged the ladies to wait inside for just a moment and after five minutes, the horses stamping their feet, the traces jingling, the rain beating against the carriage, the door flew open quite suddenly and a fat, smiling man, umbrella overhead, passed from his servant behind him, three hot bricks wrapped in sturdy wool blankets. The ladies all exclaimed their gratitude, which caused the innkeeper to blush rosily, odd shadows from the carriage lamp inside the coach playing upon his face.

Thick carriage rugs were then passed in and the ladies all sighed with pleasure. "Thank you, good sir!" Katherine exclaimed, wondering at such thoughtfulness on the part of the inn's landlord, who answered, "Ye might thank yer brother, my lady!"

At these words, Kate hoped that the man did not notice her red cheeks nor the giggles that erupted from the two young females with her. But the innkeeper was busy about his tasks, and after looking behind him and making an impatient clicking sound with his tongue, another servant appeared. The fat-cheeked man took a large basket from the servant and placed it on Buckland's seat. The smell of fresh hot bread filled the coach and Kate slapped Lydia's hand before she could wreak havoc on the wicker basket. More was to follow, for when he was assured that the basket would not topple from the seat, he handed Kate a large mug and said, "If ye'll each take a sip or two, I'll return this mug to the gentleman wat said if ye dinnit drink he would beat ye with a thin willow whip."

The young girls opened their eyes wide, for the pungent smell of a strong rum punch invaded the roomy coach. Lydia and Fanny giggled and the latter, her voice in an awestruck whisper, said, "I'll not breathe a word of this to no one!" And she took her turn sipping the warm drink, gulping down more than her share of the strong punch. Both young ladies giggled, sipped some more, and felt very worldy-wise. After Kate had drunk a portion of the rum punch, she handed it back to the man, to the protests of Lydia and Kate, and thanked him kindly.

When Buckland entered the carriage, all three ladies showered him with their expressions of gratitude, and all with such fervor that he threw up his arms and cried, "Had I know what a squawk you would make, I would not have done any of it." And he beamed upon them. Never in his wildest dreams would he have found so much pleasure in escorting two school girls anywhere. How far from London he felt.

Kate looked at him, at the expression of pleasure on his face at having delighted them so much, and she thought she had never really known him at all. He was a mystery to her and when, with great drama, he began unfurling the contents of the basket and the girls squealed with delight, Kate found her heart aching a little. In so many ways, he was just the sort of man she had one day hoped to marry, and yet how impossible it was.

As he poured each of them out a very small portion of brandy, Fanny squealed, "Mama would kill me if she knew."

These words did not dismay Buckland in the least, for he responded appropriately, "Then we shall not speak of it, shall we?" And both girls sighed with delight that they were taking part in such a grown-up adventure.

Fanny smiled brightly, and as she sipped the strong brandy and choked once or twice, she said impulsively, "And to think I could not imagine the least bit of fun in travelling to see a fusty old church!" She then turned a bright pink, visible even beneath the coach lamp. In a sheepish voice, she added, "I didn't mean that as it sounded."

Buckland balanced the unwieldy basket on his knees, and as

215

he tore off bits of the hot bread and passed them around, he said, "Nonsense, Miss Fanny! Admit you meant every word of it!" Then the coach pulled out into the dark, rainy night.

But Fanny stuffed a piece of bread in her mouth and refused to answer him. She had grown quite used to his company, but the man was so terribly old—past thirty, in fact—and she simply would not say anything more.

He smiled kindly upon her and finally decided to set the cumbersome basket on the floor, where he began dispersing biscuits and pears and grapes. And when he withdrew a gold-wrapped box of chocolates, all of the girls knew that here was a man who understood how to please a woman.

As the coach rumbled on and every half hour or so the lights and cobbled road of a village would greet them, the sway of the carriage caused both Lydia and Fanny to yawn. And after a third or fourth yawn, with eyelids growing heavy, night having descended upon the Cotswolds, Kate pulled Fanny to rest on her shoulder and Buckland, much to his surprise, in a few minutes felt Lydia curl up into the rugs that draped across his lap. Within minutes she was sleeping deeply.

Kate looked at him and said quietly, "You have done more for their girlish spirits than you will ever know."

"And for you?" he asked with a roguish smile. "Or have I not imbibed you with quite enough wine."

"Your wine has not affected me in the least," she said with a lift of her chin and a smile, "but you've nearly overset me with all of these attentions to our comforts."

Buckland looked out the window, the glow of the coach's lamp near the coachman's seat sparkling in the rain, and wondered why he felt so good, travelling with a schoolgirl nestled beside him and a scheming country miss seated opposite him. He felt more at peace in this moment than he had in the last ten years. What a green young man he had been, his ideals worn so openly on his coatsleeves, his belief in his future more secure than his belief in anything else. And then he had met Amelia—delicate, selfish, wealthy, Amelia. She was as feisty as Kate in some ways but she had no heart. None at all. He frowned at the memory, watching the rain hit the outside lamp and tossing off a shower of wet sparks.

"What are you thinking, George?"

He glanced at Kate and for a moment said nothing. He started to speak, hesitated, and finally said, "I was thinking of a young woman I knew many years ago."

Perhaps it was the wine and the comfortable feeling of all of them snuggled together, of their intimacy, that made her ask what she shouldn't have asked. But she wanted to know. It was important to know. "Did you love her?"

He nodded. How easy that was, to admit it after all these years. He had loved her. "Very much."

Somehow these words struck Kate deeply, yet she did not comprehend why. Turning her head, she tried to look out the window, but because she was sitting forward all she saw was a reflection of Buckland. She could tell he was watching her. She said, "I have never been in love." Fanny stirred against her and she patted her arm. Looking back out the window, she said, "All of my friends and acquaintances would fall violently in and out of love as though it were a contagious fever that they passed around. I used to scorn them for their weakness and now . . . I don't know . . . I suppose I feel as though I have had no girlhood."

Buckland let his arm rest against Lydia, who was now snuggled deeply into the fur rug on his lap, her hands curled up beneath her chin like a kitten. He said, "Your girlhood was lost to you the day Jaspar taught you to shoot."

Kate smiled, "I suppose it was impossible to think that I might have had both. How could I spend my hours pouring over *La Belle Assemble* when I was so busy cleaning my rifle and pistols?" She glanced at him. "Where is your home? Are you from Kent as well? Do you live near Lord Ashwell?" She wondered if it was the wine that made her feel so warm as she talked with him.

He paused for a moment. "Yes, we've known each other since we were able to climb trees."

"Mary and I are friends in that respect—although I could never persuade her to climb trees."

"Yes, you do climb trees, now that I think of it."

His reference to finding her in an oak tree and begging James to help her climb down caused the color to rise on her cheeks.

He said, "And not very well, as I recall. James had to assist you in descending."

"You know very well I needed no assistance."

His smile broadened. "Yes. I know. But I wanted to hear you say it." He then grew quite serious. "You are quite the most beautiful woman I have ever met. How is it your mama let you remain buried here?" He apologized quickly. "I'm sorry. I forgot."

Kate waved a hand, her throat suddenly constricted as she thought of her mother. Her voice cracked a little as she spoke, "How stupid. I mean, I have not shed a tear for years and now, oh, I suppose it was the wine or—" She looked at him and thought that it was his company. He was always pulling things from her, feelings that she had thought long since buried. "Buckland, you are a dangerous man," she said, feeling hurt. "Is this how you get a woman to love you, to need you?" A tear trickled down her cheek. "I'm sorry, I don't know what I'm saying."

But his voice, low and urgent, threatened her countenance further. "If you think for one moment that I speak of such matters with the women who flirt with me, you are greatly mistaken. I do not trade in such emotions, only in the barest of superficial expressions. I did not mean to make you cry, and I am not trying to hurt you or to make you fall in love with me, if that is what you mean."

The tension in the air, no doubt tightening the muscles in their respective arms, caused Fanny to stir and Lydia to raise herself up slightly and say, "What is the matter? Are we at Edgecote yet?"

"No," Buckland spoke gently, pressing her back down into the furs. She gave way beneath his hand and curled her hands back up beneath her chin.

Kate looked at him and mouthed the words, "I'm sorry."

And he did the same.

Afraid to wake the girls again, Kate fell silent, staring pensively out the window and wondering who it was that George Buckland had once loved. What sort of woman had gained his heart? Her leg and back ached from being confined in one position for so long and it was with a measure of gratitude that the coach finally reached the village of Upper Aldgrove.

When Mrs. Cerney took her sleepy-eyed daughter in hand and expressed her relief at her safety, Buckland confessed to the concerned mother, "I must tell you that she had two sips of rum punch and a small glass of brandy. She seemed very concerned that you would not approve of it."

· Mrs. Cerney, the wealthy daughter of a Cit, smiled in an unaffected manner. "I'm sure that you did quite right, Mr. Buckland. Autumn has already nipped at our toes tonight, hasn't it? I do thank you." Buckland thought she was as much unlike Mrs. Cricklade, though they had both been from families of trade, as two women could be. And he had not the least compunction in escorting Gwendolyn Cerney the short distance up the manor steps, though the rain continued unabated. This small attention, as she again thanked Buckland, earned for him that woman's most discerning approval, as she said, "You're a fine gentleman, Mr. Buckland, only isn't it time you gave up this quite reprehensible charade?" And she smiled a dimpling smile that, had she been unattached and a few years younger, might have given his heart a severe turn. So, she knew then.

The remainder of the journey to Edgecote Hall, with Lydia now fully awake and chattering as though she had slept at least ten hours, was quite short. And when Sir William met them at the carriage door, an umbrella overhead, he thanked them profusely, begging to know what had happened. When he had been regaled of the particulars, Sir William thought secretly that he could not have planned anything better for the advancement of his schemes.

With a smile that Kate thought unusually bright, he addressed Buckland, "I know I may rely on you to see our dear Katherine to the safety of her home." And turning to Kate, he said cryptically, "Don't let your stubbornness best you, young lady." And with an admonishing wag of his finger, he shut the carriage door.

Kate felt the emptiness of the large coach acutely, her polka-dot bonnet sitting atop the wicker basket and Buckland sitting opposite her. At least with the girls tucked up about them, he

219

could hardly have accosted her. And what did Sir William mean, anyway? Kate gripped her hands tightly together, keeping her eyes directed away from the tall, silent form in front of her. With so many intimate words exchanged between them during the course of their journey, she felt more vulnerable to his charms than ever and her legs began to tremble.

"You are cold!" he cried and, taking one of the rugs Lydia had used, spread it over her knees. He brushed her hand with his own, then paused near it. He knew he should not touch her. He had the oddest feeling that if he did, he would begin travelling a path he did not wish to travel. Looking at her face, he leaned toward her. Faith, but she was beautiful, for even in the poorly lit interior, the outside carriage lamps their only light, he could see that her brown eyes glinted.

The rain continued, a staccato on the hard roof of the carriage, drumming louder and louder, it seemed to Kate, as the coach slowly pulled away from the safety of Sir William's gates. A sheet of wind and rain slammed against the windows, and Kate jerked away from Buckland and grabbed at the carriage rope. She felt so uneasy, so frightened. Would that Chipping Fosseworth were not so far away. She laughed to herself, a mere two miles and yet so far away.

Buckland watched her grip the rope and for some reason this movement decided his actions. Without hesitation, he joined her on her side of the coach.

"Buckland," she whispered in protest as she extended her hand out to him as though to ward him off. But this was a mistake for, quite without ceremony, he took her hand.

"No," she whispered, pressing back into the squabs and feeling the ribbing of the cushions in rolls across her shoulders. An ache in her throat assailed her as the rain on the coach began sounding like the roar of ocean waves.

Buckland held her hand firmly. Kate tried to withdraw it, but he merely grabbed her wrist and held it in a tight grip. And worse, he did not speak.

Kate felt the coach begin the slow turn in the road that led toward Chipping Fosseworth, and she knew that too many minutes, dangerous and unwelcome, existed before the manor would be reached. She felt his fingers touch the underneath of her wrist, searching for the small pearl button of her glove that kept her hand captive. He found the button and released the small pearl. He then paused, waiting, and Kate knew that she had but to say one word and he would stop. But the terrible pain in her throat, as she leaned her head against the down-filled leather cushions, would not permit her to protest. Though her lips formed the words, she could not speak, and she thought it was terribly ironic that she could curse him verbally, answering his taunts with pointed words of her own, but he had but to touch her and she found herself completely undone.

He said nothing. He did not even gloat but merely slipped the glove from her hand, then lifted her hand to place his lips deep into her palm. And she wanted to cry out, for someone to intervene, to stop this madness. She could not breathe, his lips a torture upon her skin as he held her hand cradled gently between his own hands. He kissed her palm again and again.

She could not bear it and wanted to make him stop, but when she let the carriage rope go, intending to break from him, this most errant hand sought his face, touching his lips with gloved fingers and threatening to ruin her every carefully laid plan.

He kissed these fingers. "Kate," he breathed into the darkness that cloaked them, covering their wrongdoing, protecting their faces from revealing the truth to one another. And then he held both her hands, tightly, painfully so.

His rich, deep-timbred voice filled the carriage. "The light spills across her darkened cheek; My vision clouded fearing lest she speak; And end forbidden night's trespass—" He released her gloved hand, bringing his own to run a finger along her chin, "But I still cannot see you."

Kate closed her eyes. His words reminded her of how Ashwell's poetry made her feel. His words were the rhythm of Ashwell's poetry. She smiled. Twice he had been mistaken for the poet, by the stranger and now by her. The sensation of his warm fingers stroking her cheek washed over her and she whispered, "Buckland," her voice catching again as she felt his hand drift lightly over her shoulder and down her back, coming to rest at her waist.

221

Buckland eased toward her, his muscular leg pressing hard against her own. He wished that he might see her. Damn the coach. Damn the darkness. He wanted to feel her against him fully, like their last meeting at Knott Hill. How long ago it seemed as he pressed her waist, holding her against him.

Kate circled her arm behind his back as she slowly made a long journey away from her every difficulty. The wet smell of his damp clothes still could not obliterate the pungent smell of the soap he used. His hand returned to her face and now she could smell the sweet brandy on his breath as he leaned toward her, his hair brushing her own, his right hand caressing her face, his lips touching the temple of her forehead. And again.

She reached up to touch him, her gloved hand finding the smooth lapel of his coat. And without a moment's hesitation, she pushed it aside to find the thin muslin of his shirt, the warmth of his chest radiating through the gloves covering her fingers.

At her touch, she felt him take a deep breath and slide his hand behind her neck, entwining his fingers into her unloosened auburn curls. His lips travelled gently down her cheek and Kate found herself struggling for breath. She cursed him, "A pox on you, George Buckland!"

And the rogue pressed down hard on her mouth, forcing her back into the cushions, the shirt tearing suddenly beneath Kate's clenched fist.

She could not breathe and she did not care. The feel of his crushing lips, an agony, a pleasure, at cross-purposes to her careful schemes, tore her mind from every sensible mooring. She was free, floating, adrift as his lips became gentle and seductive. Why in his arms must she feel like this, so at peace and secure? Why must his lips feel that she had arrived home after having been lost in the beechwood at Quening?

The coach rumbled to a stop and Buckland pulled away from her. The manor rushlights now washed over the interior of the coach, and the thud of the coachman as he jumped down from the box all meant that the moment was over. The driver could not see them together but still Kate could not release Buckland's torn shirt from about her fingers. She feared letting go of him, of facing the future. If she released him, he

222

would vanish, he would be gone, as his kisses were already gone. She could not bear it, and as the coach door opened, she heard Buckland through a strange buzz in her ears. "Kate," he said as he grabbed her hand and pried her fingers loose.

"Buckland," she whispered. She could do nothing more than just watch the deep frown that overcame his features as he settled his hat securely on his head and descended the coach.

Kate lifted her bonnet from the large basket and put it on slowly as Maggie's worried voice filtered through the rain that still pounded the roof of the coach. "Be that Miss Kate?"

If only the coachman would disappear. Damn Maggie's eyes, anyway. Kate jerked on the glove Buckland had removed and descended from the coach. She looked at him, searching his eyes. The manor rushlights illumined their faces and truth flooded over her—of poverty and debts, of Buckland's scruples, that he would not marry her, how rogues spent their summers seeking pleasure however they might, of the fragile manner in which the precious moments of life always vanished. He stood there in the rain, looking at her as though he was waiting for her to say something. How cold his eyes appeared as rain dripped from the brim of his beaver hat. What did he expect her to say? She looked at the manor beyond him—Maggie huddling close to her, the umbrella overhead, her inane, anxious chatter a humming in her ears—and saw only one thing, Jaspar's bedchamber window glowing dully from the light of a single candle.

Kate stood in the entrance hall of the manor, staring at the floor and watching droplets of water run down her carriage dress onto the stone slab of the ancient manor. Maggie talked in a rapid string of words, expressing her concern for her safety, but Kate did not answer her as she slowly removed her bonnet and gloves. All that she could think of was how cold Buckland's eyes had seemed and yet how warm and comforting his lips were.

Maggie interrupted her thoughts by exclaiming, "I forgot!" Then she dropped a curtsy and backed away from Kate, holding her mistress's bonnet and gloves. Kate wondered at this quite odd behaviour on her maid's part, until a familiar voice intruded.

"Miss Draycott! I have been waiting for hours in anticipation of your return. I am glad to find you in good health."

Kate felt her entire body chill at the low, quiet voice, a cold timbre that stopped her heart, "What—what are you doing here? It is so late. Where is Jaspar?"

Kate did not move from the entrance hall and Sapperton, wearing evening dress, a black coat, and pantaloons, walked slowly toward her. He looked like a thin crow. "Were you alone in the coach with Mr. . . . er . . . Buckland, is it?"

"You know very well what his name is. Where is Jaspar?"

"Now as to that, I suppose he is where I left him. In the library."

Kate turned toward the library but Sapperton stopped her, moving swiftly around her to block her path. "It is unnecessary. He is, I fear, quite dead to the world. Asleep before a cosy fire."

Kate looked at his waistcoat, of the finest black superfine cloth, and said quietly, "He is in his cups, then."

"Such a vulgar expression. I prefer to think that he is sleeping the sleep of Bacchus, god of wine."

Kate moved away from him toward the drawing room and, pulling at the flattened curls on her forehead, damp from the rain, said, "Then you may leave, Lord Sapperton. It would not be seemly for you to remain in this house when my father cannot be present."

Sapperton followed her and, catching her hand, wheeled her around to face him, his grip clawlike. "Unseemly? And how is it you were travelling in a closed carriage with no one to chaperone you with Buckland? Did he kiss you? He is quite well known in London for that art and others, of course. He breaks hearts, you know. He lives for little else."

Kate stared at him, her cheeks a rosy hue, and the earl continued, "So, he has violated your exquisite mouth. And did you enjoy it? Was he tender with you or coarse? I expect he was coarse, for he is a very unrefined, vulgar sort of man."

224

Kate jerked her hand out of his and turned away from him. "I wish you would leave. I am greatly fatigued."

"Does the man's lovemaking fatigue you? But now I am quite curious. Did you prefer his kisses to mine, I wonder? Do you remember the first time I kissed you?"

Kate walked toward the fireplace, picked up a brass-handled poker, and began thrusting it into the white coals. As the sparks flew up about the coals, she said, "Why do you torment me?" She remembered his kiss and where. It was the last time she had bathed in a little stream in Quening Woods. She had been dressed in nothing more than her underclothes, and had been splashing about in the rivulet as a child might and enjoying the chatter of the woodlarks overhead, when she heard the earl's laugh as he stood beside her faded blue muslin gown. She had been a mere fifteen, shortly before her mother's death. He had not seemed so cold then and she had been extremely embarrassed. She had begged him to leave but he would not, telling her he would only leave her alone if she gave him a kiss.

She had heard Kit and Stephen approaching the pool and she emerged quickly, the thin muslin of her undergarments clinging horribly to her womanly form. She had watched his eyes as she ran toward him, how they devoured her, lingering upon her breasts and the fabric clinging to her legs. She grabbed at her gown, which he held in his hands, but he had caught her about the waist and kissed her, a hard, painful kiss on her young lips. His mouth tasted bitter, of snuff, and his breath smelled foul.

She had struggled to free herself and he had planted hard kisses upon her cheek and neck. Then Kit's laughter, still far enough away, filled Kate with a terrible fear of being discovered and she struggled against the earl, her hands scratching at his face and her feet kicking impotently at his booted shins. But it was enough, and she tore from him, grabbing her gown and racing for home, his laughter ringing in her ears.

He was laughing now. "Are you thinking of my kisses then? How beautiful you looked emerging from that pool. Do you still bathe there, I wonder?"

She turned to face him, the poker extended toward him, "You dare to remind me of such an occasion! You are a libertine, Lord Sapperton, a grotesque, shameless monster, and I hate you."

He took his snuffbox from his pocket and, opening it slowly, said in his quiet voice, "But you will have me in the end, nevertheless."

"Never. I shall never marry you."

"So very stubborn and I must say unwise, for I shall not make this easy for you. Already your dear father has confided in me, and I wonder if you might tell me why you no longer wear the jewels your mother left you when she died?" He smiled at her. "You cannot answer me . . . well, I do understand pride. I have a great deal of it myself."

Kate suddenly felt very tired, and she slowly turned around and replaced the poker. In a quiet voice, she said, "Pray, leave me in peace, Sapperton. The day has been long and I want only my bed."

As she turned back to face him, Kate realized she had misjudged Sapperton, for he was upon her, clutching her in his arms and again placing his hard kisses upon her mouth, then her cheeks and neck. "Oh, do stop!" she cried, pushing him away.

Much to her surprise he fell back a little, his arm over his chest as he turned away from her. Maggie appeared in the doorway of the drawing room as the earl said, "Perhaps you are right. The hour is farther advanced than I thought. I will leave you."

Kate watched him go, a little surprised at his quite sudden departure, and Maggie said, "Meaning no disrespect, Miss Kate, I 'ope ye don't mean to marry that stick of a grasshopper!"

Kate sat at her desk, bent over the estate ledgers, trying to find another way of cutting down on expenses. She had just turned the page when the door opened quite suddenly and Jaspar, wearing what appeared to be a new gray drab driving coat of no less than ten capes, entered the room in his brusque manner.

"I'm off, then," he said to her cheerfully. She had scarcely seen him in the last two days.

Sitting bolt upright in her chair, Kate asked, "Where?" A simple question, but she knew immediately that it was a mistake.

"You are my daughter, Kate, not my mother. It is really no concern of yours, but have it as you will. I am off to Cheltenham. Lord Turville has got up a small card party." His chin set in a mulish fashion. "And don't look at me like that."

Kate was not going to say anything, but she had sold her jewels and now he was going to play cards and what would he use as his own stakes?

She could scarcely contain the feeling of rage that rose within her. If he hadn't mortgaged all the lands and gambled away her dowry . . . oh, that it had been properly and legally secured to her. A year after her mother had died, a great-aunt had left a tidy sum of money to Marianne and her children—five thousand pounds. But her will had been so poorly contrived that Marianne's spouse had control over the inheritance, to secure it as he deemed fit. And though Jaspar had faithfully promised to have his solicitors draw up a trust regarding the inheritance, instead he had whittled away at it, usually after each excursion to Cheltenham—two hundred pounds here, fifty there—and, in a mere three years, he had gone through the whole of it.

And now she must pursue Lord Ashwell, a course that daily grew more distasteful to her. "Jaspar, don't go. Please. We are nearly ruined. Don't you understand that? And if you stay"—and she pointed in a wild manner to the ledgers—"perhaps we could find some way of pulling the property together, of trimming our expenses, of—"

He cut her off, his blue eyes bulging with anger, "Do you expect me to stay here? I have no pleasure here. None. And now you want me to look at those absurd books? I don't know why you bother with them. You should have kept the housekeeper and let her manage these things. If you can't keep up with the bills I don't see what I have to do with it!"

"Papa, please. Think of your heir, then. Is this fair to him?"

He looked half crazed at her words. "Don't speak to me of my heir!" he shouted.

Kate took a step back, frightened by his vehemence. She knew very little of her father's past, but her mother had once said that he had been greatly disappointed in love when he was quite young and impressionable, that he and his cousin Jack Cleeve had both wanted the same young woman and that Jaspar had actually been engaged to her, only to have her elope with his cousin. And he had never forgiven them.

He then cried, "You were supposed to be my heir! You, Kate! You should have been my son! You should have been mine! But instead your mother—" He broke off, his expression one of anguish. Kate thought he looked almost crazed as he turned on his heel and quit the room.

Supporting herself with a hand on her desk, Kate sat down, her knees trembling. He was growing worse. He drank more and shouted more and his speech had grown so strange. At times, she was afraid that he would hit her. Why was he so angry with her, his rage seeming to be at a near boil just below the surface of his boisterous, jovial manners?

Maggie peeked her head in and, seeing her mistress's face, said, "The squire left. Will ye be wantin' yer meal at the usual hour? Cook sent me to find out."

Kate stared at her blindly for a moment, then took a deep breath. "No, thank you."

Three days later, Kate glanced up the stairwell of the Cricklades' manor house and met the smiling faces of the younger Miss Cricklades. A pleasant humming of voices issuing from the drawing room did not stop her from taking a few moments to speak to the girls. She approached the stairs with a teasing glint in her eye and said, "I shall tell your mother that you are sitting there."

Grace, who was thirteen, smiled at her words, but the youngest, Arabella, a sweet baby of five years, opened her eyes wide and said, "Oh, no, Miss Kate, you cannot do that. Mama will whip us with her willow whip!" And she rubbed her backside and nodded her head.

228

Kate held out her arms to Arabella, who ceased the imaginary rubbing and scurried down the stairs to throw herself into Kate's arms. "Have you Miss Diana with you?" Bella asked, pulling at Kate's pearl earrings. "It has been such a long time since we shocked everyone by riding your horse through town."

The door opened behind her and James's voice intruded, "You are out there, George. I'll wager you a monkey that old Smythe sold his bay a fortnight before we quit Stowhurst."

Buckland responded, "Done! Hallo. What is this? How charming a greeting!" He regarded the young girls, dressed in white muslin gowns and brightly colored ribbons.

James had moved to peek into the drawing room, but Buckland joined Kate and begged to be introduced. "So you are Miss Arabella. Should I call you Belle?"

Arabella wriggled out of Kate's arms that she might stand on the tiled black and white floor and make her very best curtsy. "If you please, sir!" She then squealed, "Mama is coming!" And before Kate could bid them good-bye, both girls sped up the stairs in a flurry of white ruffles.

Mrs. Cricklade bounded into the entrance hall, calling in a loud voice for her butler, who had taken Kate's wrap into another chamber, vowing to turn the rascal off without a reference, begging them all to join the others, scolding the girls who were well out of sight and all the while curtsying to James. "How do you do, Lord Ashwell? And may I say how delighted I am to have you in our humble abode. I suppose our home is nothing to yours. But we are quite proud of it and may I show you our new gilt mirror, leafed in gold, of course . . . only the finest. But how silly of me! You gentlemen are not in the least interested in such matters."

She took his arm and prattled on, "Have you seen the organ in our little Norman church? You must, you know, for Handel himself played on it. And after you have seen the organ, you must take a peek at our ancestors, all laid out in their cosy little vaults and just sitting there for your inspection and delight."

James looked back at Kate and Buckland, his brows raised and an expression of astonishment on his face.

Kate would have laughed had she not been suddenly

overwhelmed by Buckland's presence. She had not seen him in three days and wished that Mrs. Cricklade had taken him by the arm as well. Instead, Kate found herself alone in the entrance hall with Buckland, and she stood nearly frozen to the floor, her heart sitting in her throat. She tried to think of something to say, but memories of their last meeting seemed to whirl about her—his warm, sweet lips, his soothing hands, and then she would remember his cold gaze.

She felt that he had fallen silent as well and looked up at him.

A deep frown on his face, Buckland spoke first. "I owe you an apology, Kate. My behaviour to you the other night was ungentlemanly. I promise you that I will not importune you again." And he bowed.

Kate knew that they should move into the drawing room before they began giving rise to comment, but when she took his arm, as he presented it to her, she held him back slightly and said, "I am as much to blame. You must think me quite without conduct." And in an impulsive manner she turned to him, her fan clutched tightly in her free hand, and continued, "I do not understand why I let you kiss me, Buckland. Indeed, I do not. And because I can claim no right to your affections, I must apologize to you as well. In any other female, you would suppose that I was flirting with you in the most reprehensible manner possible. But I assure you"—and here she looked at him with such intensity that he took a small step backward—"I don't comprehend your hold over me! And I take it very unkindly in you that you must always appear quite so handsome and—and commanding whenever you enter a room!" And with a great huff of exasperation she dropped his arm and entered the drawing room alone.

Buckland watched her move away, feeling slightly dumbstruck, her auburn hair wound throughout with a blue ribbon and trailing in a riot of curls down her back.

He followed her quickly and barely brushed her elbow with his hand as he caught up with her. He whispered, "A truce, my bonny Kate."

Oh, why did his eyes have to be just that shade of blue? Kate gave him a half smile and said, "All right." And as she glanced about the chamber and saw that they were being watched by several pairs of curious eyes, she said in a normal voice, "What truly delightful September weather we are enjoying."

"Indeed," Buckland followed suit.

"Have you noticed that the evenings are growing colder?"

"No, but then I wear boots, which must account for it."

Kate laughed at him. He was a complete hand, as Lydia had said.

When they had greeted various of their friends and taken a glass of wine from a servant's silver tray, Kate sipped the sweet nut-flavoured sherry and followed Buckland's gaze. He was watching James and laughing.

Kate smiled with him and, in an undertone, said, "The Cricklades were a distant relation from the old gentleman that owned this manor. They were formerly in trade. Poor Mrs. Cricklade, even after ten years, still feels she must try to impress everyone. But I feel very sorry for James that he must endure her raptures."

Buckland looked down at her as he sipped his wine. After a moment, he said, "It will do James a great deal of good to listen to her minute descriptions of the manor's worth. He would never believe me, you know."

Kate looked at him, not quite understanding what he meant. "I'm not certain I take your meaning? I should think James would be quite used to hearing every mushroom imaginable attempt to impress him."

Buckland started. He had forgotten for a moment that he was not Ashwell and, looking at Kate, said, "Of course. I don't know what I was thinking." And as though the thoughts, which had been coming unbidden into his mind since he arrived at the manor, somehow demanded expression, he said, "You've fairly grassed me, you know. I've never had a woman apologize to me for her flirtations. And what do you mean by looking so wonderfully charming when James and I walked through the front door?" He felt bemused both by what he was saying and by the way she looked in the candlelight. "You had that adorable child tucked up in your arms. . . ." He stopped suddenly and looked at Kate, feeling such a warmth flow through him that he could not finish his thought. Instead, he regarded her almost as though he were seeing her for the first time and said, "How pretty you are. Blue becomes you quite well. Your skin, so fair and glowing with light, a radiance, a mystery . . ."

She shook her head at him, the sherry spreading a pleasant ease through her veins, and said, "You must be careful, George. For you are beginning to sound like Lord Ashwell's poetry. Or have you memorized his verses to quote to the women you admire?"

He just stared at her, at the teasing look on her face, the way her brown eyes lit up when she smiled. He still didn't speak, even when Kit came running up to them, dragging her off to settle a dispute between himself and Stephen about the best manner to clean one's pistols. He laughed, thinking that he had spoken to her in his own verse, not anything he had written but just how he had been feeling at the moment. Lord, if he were not careful, he would end up losing his heart to her. But would that be so very bad? He did not know what to think except that she still would not end her pursuit of James. But damme, she had bewitched him!

And in keeping with this truly frightening thought, he immediately sought out Julia Moreton and told her that she cast every other female completely into the shade with her brilliant eyes, perfect little nose, and dewy lips. Julia trilled her laughter, slapped his arm with her fan, and sidled up next to him. When she asked if he intended to seduce her with such flattery and he answered yes, she again let her laughter ripple about the Elizabethan drawing room.

Kate, finding for one of the few times in her life that a discussion of the merit of Manton's pistols was not holding her attention, turned to watch Julia as she flirted with Buckland. And each time the fair-haired beauty laughed, she ground her teeth. Kit also heard Julia's laughter and exclaimed, "Sounds like a screech owl. Oh, she's got Buckland on a string now. Someone ought to warn him."

Stephen said, "Hang Julia and Buckland! What I want to know is how you like your pistols, Kate. Do you ever wish you'd bought something else?"

Kate was not attending precisely and answered, "I think he is quite shameless and flirts with anything in skirts!"

Chapter Twelve

Mary slipped an arm about Kate's waist as they strolled through Mrs. Cricklade's maze of red and gold furniture. In a low voice she confided to her, "I was so mortified at having fallen ill! And then to learn that my father had sent you home alone with Buckland! Of course I did not say anything to him, but Kate, it really was quite scandalous. Did he—I mean, did he behave as a perfect gentleman? I have always thought him the sort of man who might, if given the moment, take advantage of even the most delicately nurtured female. I am a little afraid of him."

Kate looked across the room at Buckland and James, who were both enjoying Julia's charms, and said, "He was as much a gentleman as I a lady." And she sighed. Whenever she saw the two men together, she lost heart in her schemes.

Mary said, "I am so relieved to hear it. Were you not afraid?"

Kate recalled the short trip from Edgecote to Chipping Fosseworth, and the way she had trembled for fear that he would kiss her and then her desperate feelings of loss when she had to part from him, and she answered quietly, lifting her fan to cool her suddenly warm face. "I was afraid at first but then—oh, never mind!" She smiled nervously upon Mary and decided to change the subject. "I'm not certain what I wish to wear to Sapperton's masquerade ball. Lydia told me just a few minutes ago that she had changed her mind and now plans on wearing a shepherdess costume. Now, what was your costume?

233

I know that you spoke of it once already but I have forgotten. What a terrible friend I am!"

Mary looked at James and said, "I was thinking that I might go as some Greek divinity perhaps."

Kate looked at Buckland and said, "A wood-nymph?"

Mary laughed, "Oh, no. Could you imagine me as a spritely wood-nymph? No, I think I require a sturdier guise than that, something more practical." And with a sigh, she added, "Perhaps I should simply borrow our housekeeper's black bombazine and be done with it!"

Kate watched Mrs. Cricklade intrude on James's conversation and she said, "I should like to attend as Queen Anne and see if Mrs. Cricklade defers to me."

Mary let go of her friend's waist and tweaked her arm. "Kate!" she cried. "How can you say such a thing of your hostess?"

Kate hid her face behind her fan and said, "I am feeling quite wicked at the moment. Oh, I know she means little harm but, really, she told Ashwell she had a mirror framed in gilt!"

"No," Mary breathed.

"Indeed, she did. I blushed for her. Well, almost. If only she would give over her airs and just be the rather sweet motherly woman she is. I love her children. When I marry, I shall have a dozen babies." She regarded James and felt her heart sink. She could not picture having his children.

Mary said thoughtfully, her gaze upon James as well, "I should like one or two, I think. I haven't your strength, you see. You could manage a dozen quite easily, but with my headaches—"

She left the remainder of her thoughts unsaid, and Kate tried to console her. "You blame yourself too much, Mary."

"But I ruined a perfectly delightful excursion."

"You did not. If you saw how well George—that is, Mr. Buckland entertained us—Lydia and Fanny were with us as you may recall—you would know that our pleasure was not hindered in the least. In fact, I would not have traded those few hours for anything."

Mary looked shocked. "You are just being kind!"

Kate regarded her with her brows raised. "And when do I say

such things merely to be kind? I am most in earnest."

"Well!" She paused for a moment and, lowering her voice so that no one could hear her, continued, "But I know how you wished to be with Lord Ashwell and I—I felt dreadful about that."

Mary regarded Kate with an anxious look. She had not discussed James with her before, and so many times she had wanted to ask Kate if she suspected that there might be some duplicity involved between the two men.

Kate was about to speak when Mrs. Cricklade ran to the entrance of the room, her red satin gown straining at the seams and rustling at her awkward little steps. Her face glowed with pride as she curtsied to Lord Sapperton and Mr. Westbourne.

Kate had not seen the dandy for some time, and as she watched him mince across the room, she still could not believe that he had been involved with Luddites at all—particularly since he wore a lavender coat over a flowered waiscoat and yellow satin knee breeches. His hair was carefully pomaded and his shoes, studded with pearls, built with a high heel. Had Jaspar not still been in Cheltenham he would have left the room in disgust at such a sight. She then remembered the shock of hearing that Rupert had been involved in the attack upon Buckland's mill. Lydia had said that Rupert's hair was in complete disarray, his affectations had vanished, and he had worn simple country clothing—no dandy there. But here he seemed to have returned completely to his former self. She could not but feel that some great mystery was at work among them all.

She glanced at Lord Sapperton, who spoke with his calm, good manners to Mrs. Cricklade, and then graciously bowed and greeted all of the older women in turn—Lady Chalford, Gwendolyn Cerney, Mrs. Moreton. Each of them seemed genuinely flattered by his attentions, with the exception, of course, of Lady Chalford. Yet never once had Kate heard the baronet's wife utter a disparaging comment upon the earl's character. Was it possible that she was the only one who knew that beneath his polished manners resided a scoundrel? His outer bearing was as much a farce as Rupert's seemed to be.

When Sapperton began speaking with Sir William, Buckland, and James, Kate watched as he bowed slightly to Buckland, then moved to shake hands with Squire Cricklade. Buckland's gaze followed the earl for a moment and Kate was astonished at the hatred she saw gleam in his blue eyes. Someday she would ask Buckland what reason he had to despise the earl. And as she took in Buckland's evening dress she realized, with a start, that his appearance was not one of poverty, nor even the success that might accrue to a cloth mill owner, but rather one of wealth. How had she been so blind in that? After the attack upon his cloth mill, she had been a little aware that his clothing was not completely in keeping with his station in life, but now, looking at the perfect fit to his coat and the diamond gleaming on his hand, she realized that something was amiss with Buckland as well.

A little shock ran through her that maybe he was just like her father and incurred tradesmen's debts without having the least ability to discharge them. But whatever the case, his clothes did not reflect his financial condition, in the same way that Rupert's attire did not reflect his past involvement as a leader of the Luddites.

These thoughts all ended abruptly as Mrs. Cricklade stepped before the pianoforte and presented Rupert as the evening's entertainment.

The young men in the room groaned at Mrs. Cricklade's announcement. For in much the same way as Lord Sapperton had honored Lord Ashwell by having Mr. Westbourne read some of his original work, she had desired to take the earl's lead and do the same. And applauding Mr. Westbourne as he stood up and advanced to stand before the pianoforte, Mrs. Cricklade hurried about the room, pressing everyone, with delicate shoves of her pudgy hands, into quickly arranged chairs.

At James's insistence, Kate sat beside him on a red striped sofa. And though he did not say that he disliked Mrs. Cricklade's schemes, Kate knew by the frown in his eyes that he was unhappy.

In a teasing manner, she whispered behind her fan, "Never mind! The evening cannot last forever." And since James scarcely smiled in answer to this, she added, "Do not distress yourself. If Kit and Stephen have anything to do with it, the recital shall be as short-lived as it was at Leachwood." But glancing back at the young men, Kate saw that this time both Mrs. Moreton and Mrs. Cricklade had stationed themselves about the recalcitrant gentlemen. No reprieve here.

Rupert began his poetry, and the epic poem that had been filling the better part of too many sheets of paper over the summer went on and on, and even Mrs. Cricklade began to yawn. Kate glanced at James once or twice and was impressed with his intense concentration on Rupert's poetry. And when at last the long poem came to an end, Kate thought Lord Ashwell one of the kindest gentlemen of her acquaintance, for he immediately stood up and thanked Rupert. "Your effort is quite obvious. I, too, know what it is to struggle." He sighed, and Kate thought that his brown eyes looked quite sad and very sincere when he added, "Your work is every bit as good as my own and I wish you the very best success with your verses."

Rupert cast an affected hand in a circle and said, "How kind you are, Lord Ashwell. Do you think I might find a bookseller who would take on my work?"

"Most everyone begins by paying for a first volume themselves. If you wish for it and can afford it, there are any number of book publishers in London who would be happy for your patronage." He then bowed and returned to sit beside Kate, his face wearing a stricken look that he tried to hide with a smile. Even his shoulders seemed to sag as he watched Rupert roll up his ridiculous scrolls.

In a low voice, James said, "I shall never write a truly great line of poetry. Not even one."

Kate laid an impulsive hand on his arm and, in a voice of disbelief, said, "You cannot mean that, James. What are you saying? Why, there are times when I read your prose that I hear Milton and Pope applauding in the background. Your words are so full of life. I cannot tell you what your poetry has meant to me."

He regarded her with a deep frown between his eyes and pressed her hand for a moment, fully aware that Mrs. Moreton was watching with baleful blue eyes, then withdrew his hand. He said with a very sad half smile, "I only wish that I were able to live up to such an encomium." She was about to protest again, but he shook off his despondence and said, "Enough, Katherine, of your praise." He stood up and, lifting her to her feet, asked, "Would you care to take a little air on the terrace?"

Kate, having gotten quite involved in defending his work, went with him at once, forgetting Buckland for the first time that evening and feeling a sense of hope that she could love James. She had forgotten, it seemed, that he had written poems that had transformed her soul, making her aware of the beauty of life, of beauty in places and things that she took for granted—in the setting of the sun, the exquisite sight of a field of purple when the pasqueflower bloomed in April, of finer things in existence than just her horse and her pleasures; that though poverty might take its toll, the human spirit could find places of enjoyment that went beyond the harsh edge of life. These were Ashwell's sentiments, James's sentiments. If she could just speak with him, reach that part of him that had already touched her through his poetry, then perhaps she might feel that a life with him could be a wonderful thing.

Buckland had heard every word she had spoken, as well as the urgency in her voice. No female in London had ever said such things to him. Most of the women merely wanted to be seen with him, or wanted to enjoy him in the privacy of his own chambers—that later they might boast of their exploits—or wanted him to grace their ball or fete. He had begun to feel as the preacher felt—*all is vanity*.

Removing his snuffbox from his coat pocket, he watched her go, walking beside James, a light upon her face that meant she hoped to love him, intended to love him. Why did this woman of all women have to be intent on the Ashwell fortune? And then he thought of James, and that his friend might be falling in love with Kate. And what would a marriage be like for them, nearly impoverished as they both were? He knew Kate. If she discovered James's identity after accepting his hand, she would marry him. He frowned as he took a pinch of snuff. She was full of twists and ironies. If only she would give up this ridiculous pursuit, then he might be easy, then he might cease thinking of her day and night.

He heard Julia's voice. "You look quite angry, Mr. Buckland. And I see you are watching your friend and Miss Draycott." He looked down at Julia, feeling only irritation as he regarded her truly exquisite features and her eyes that danced with the excitement of the hunt, for she was hunting him as he had been hunted by a hundred females over the last year. He felt bored by her presence, all the dull sensations from the last season, when he had catapulted into an extraordinary fame with the publication of his first volume of poetry, coming forcibly to mind.

He closed his snuffbox with a snap and said, "You ought to cloak your intentions a little more carefully, Miss Moreton. I know precisely what you are about."

Julia felt a blush creep up her cheeks, and a confusion twisted any words that tried to form in her flirtatious brain.

He laughed at her, "I should not tease you so. And now, how many of these young bucks about Stinchefield have bent their knees to you?"

She dimpled at these words. These were just the sort of sentiments she understood, and she immediately tucked her arm through his and begged him to take her out on the terrace. As they wended their way through the drawing room, Julia said in a whisper, "Will you tell me what you are to wear to Lord Sapperton's masquerade ball? If you do, I will tell you what costume I have chosen."

He said, "I think I might wear the best costume of all and merely come as"—he paused as she opened her eyes wide—"myself."

Julia frowned at him and slapped his arm. "I should have known better than to have expected a truthful answer from you."

Kate cried aloud, "Maggie, you imbecile! You have stuck me again!"

Maggie broke into a hardy laugh and, between chortles, said, "I do be sorry, miss, but I never pretended to be no needlewoman."

"If you stick me again, I shall certainly turn you off." And twisting down to look at Maggie, who was now pinning the hem of the heavy velvet gown, she continued harshly, "Without a reference." She glanced out the window of her bedchamber that overlooked the gravel drive and the line of chestnut trees. Jaspar had been gone for four days and she hoped that he would come home soon.

Kate returned her gaze to the looking glass, regarding herself with a smile as she pressed her hands down her waist and over her hips. The Elizabethan gown, which her mother had worn at a masquerade some ten years earlier and needed a few slight adjustments, was worn over tight corsets that scarcely permitted Kate to breathe. She wondered if James would like her costume, for the close-fitting gown revealed her slim waist considerably more than did the empress gowns that Josephine had made so popular. She debated whether or not to add a lace fichu to the flattened bodice that tended to show a great deal more of her bosom than she thought was acceptable, but the mere thought of seeing Mrs. Moreton's disapproving face decided her against the additional piece of lace.

"I should like a girdle to go about this gown, Maggie. I only wish I had one of gold, but perhaps gold-coloured cord would do as well." The deep green of the velvet set to extreme advantage her fair skin, but in the warmth of the September day the thick, heavy sleeves caused her to perspire. "I hope the evening of the masquerade is cool or I shall never survive."

Maggie leaned back on her heels and stared up at Kate and, with a sweet country smile on her lively face, said, "I think Mr. Buckland will like your costume."

Kate looked at her maid. "What do you mean? What has Mr. Buckland to do with anything?"

Maggie smiled, her dark eyes twinkling.

A coach sounded in the drive, two long blasts from a yard of tin echoing down the long row of chestnut trees and floating up to Kate's window. "Jaspar," she whispered, feeling overcome for a moment with affection. Maybe this time he will not have gambled severely. Maybe he will have won a fortune!

"Maggie, hurry," she cried as she started pulling at her sleeves and trying to clamber out of the gown. But the pins holding the back together stuck her no matter which way she twisted, and Maggie rose to her feet, clicking her tongue and pulling the pins out as quickly as she could.

Kate scrambled into her white flowered morning dress and was just patting a few stray curls into place when the coach pulled to a stop before the door. She looked down at the large, ancient carriage, waiting for Jaspar to emerge, but her heart sank as she watched the coachman jump down from the box and march purposefully to the front door.

"Button me quickly." She could not keep the disappointment from her voice.

When the buttons had been fastened, Kate turned her back on the window and closed her eyes. He must be drunk.

Jaspar leaned against her as she supported him into the drawing room, letting him fall onto the sofa by the front window.

He was laughing and Kate felt a nausea turn her stomach as his breath poured across her face. "You can't pull at me anymore, Kate," he slurred. "There's nothing left now."

Kate took a step backward, the colour draining from her face. He looked up at her, his eyes stained an ugly red colour, his hair unkempt and dirty. "I gambled even the manor lands away." He laughed and immediately grimaced as he put a hand to his head and groaned, "I feel like the devil."

Pressing a hand against her bosom, Kate could feel her heart begin to pound as she swallowed the bile that crept up her throat. He couldn't have! But then he would not be the first man to ruin his family with debts and mortgages.

She backed away from him as he stretched out a hand toward her, begging her to help him . . . he felt so sick. "Fetch Peter Coachman."

But Kate could not hear him. She could hear nothing but the tumult in her brain. She did not even see Jaspar, only the wretched path his weakness was forcing her to take. She felt bludgeoned, her mind reeling, and she stumbled toward the long French doors that led out onto the terrace and down into the garden.

Her feet began moving of their own volition, and she lost first one loosely tied sandal and then another. Rocks bit into her feet as she walked slowly down the gravel path then beyond the formal gardens to a lawn, neatly scythed. The beechwoods loomed above her as she ran through the tall grass beyond the manor lands and up toward the woods, where she might be cool and safe. Her bare feet felt bruised but she continued anyway, lifting her muslin skirts and not caring, when she reached the edge of the woods, that a small branch of holly ripped through her skirts.

Tears unbidden flowed down her cheeks, her heart aching. She had run so far and so hard that she could scarcely breathe. She hated Jaspar. She hated her father.

At the Swan and Goose, Buckland opened the box sent from a tailor in Stinchfield and could not help but smile at the doublet that rested there. Strong colors—black and gold. On a chair beside the table sat a large box in which rested a black velvet hat, with a white ostrich feather curled about the wide brim. Maggie had told him of Kate's costume and he could not resist taunting her with his own choice. If she was to attend the ball as Queen Elizabeth, then he would have to be a courtier.

James sat before the cold, empty grate of the parlour, leaning forward, his hands clasped loosely between his knees. A hundred times Rupert's poetry had gone through his mind, as well as Kate's praise of Ashwell's prose. He shook his head at these thoughts, his gaze fixed on a smudged brass-handled poker by the hearth. He would have given his soul to have received her praise deservedly, her brown eyes lit with such a holy fire. He had been waiting for Katherine to look at him in that manner, and when she did, it had been in praise of his friend's poetical genius.

He turned to regard Buckland, a deep frown in his eyes, his cheeks sagging a little from a sudden dislike of George that welled up within him. What secret did the man keep now as he smiled stupidly over a velvet doublet and ridiculous broad-brimmed hat? Ah, the costume. He supposed Buckland meant to seduce Katherine with such a costume.

He would not let the man hurt her. He knew what George meant to do—to add one more conquest to the ones already cluttered about his calloused heart. Surprising even himself, he said in a tight voice, "I mean to marry Miss Draycott."

Buckland stiffened as he set the hat back into its box. James had said it. James had flung the gauntlet down without knowing that it was a gauntlet. James had cemented the first stone to a wall that would destroy their friendship.

He turned around and asked quietly, "Do you love her?"

A simple question. James answered in a petulant voice, "Of course I love her. I have from first seeing her. She is a goddess!" His anger took hold of his tongue as he stood and cried, "And you are not fit to wipe her boots."

Buckland remembered her boots, caked in mud from the stream near Cowley Hill, and how she felt in his arms. Had James kissed her? Had he come anywhere near her? The thought made his own choler rise as he said, "I won't let you marry Kate. " He shook his head. "Never."

James stood up, squaring his shoulders to Buckland, and responded, "I have never really known you until now. You play the god with all of us, don't you? You are not my friend. Why have I never seen it before? You only want her for yourself because I want her."

"That's not true. But has it ever occurred to you that because you are masquerading as a wealthy man, she might just want you for your fortune? What will happen, I wonder, when she discovers that you are in possession of the barest competence?"

James was beyond anger as he answered coldly, "I know Katherine far better than you. She is not indifferent to me. I know she has an affection for me, just as I know that part of her attraction to me of the moment is that I am wearing your trappings. But I know her heart, her character, as you do not. She will only marry me if she loves me." He raised his voice. "Damn your eyes, George! I love her and will not permit you to break her heart with your careless flirtations." He clenched his fists. "And what do you offer her? You have everything that this world covets. Instead, you make a great game of forcing your way into a person's life and then hurting them." He

243

narrowed his eyes at Buckland. "And don't tell me it is because of Amelia." He laughed scornfully at his friend. "I can see by your face that I have hit the mark. Good God, you wear your one unfortunate cuckolding as though you were the only one to have ever been jilted."

Buckland felt his veins grow hot, a pulsing at his temple and in his neck telling him that if he did not leave, he would crush James's mocking face between his bare hands. Turning on his heel and knocking the box off the table, Buckland left the inn and turned toward the hills above the village. A cool breeze, beckoning autumn to come forth, relieved the burn on his cheeks.

Stephen and Kit, astride their favourite hunters, waved a greeting, and in response he could only find himself able to tip his hat and shove his hands deep into his coat pockets.

A feminine voice called to him, "Mr. Buckland, how do you do?"

Seeing Julia Moreton's pretty face at first eased the knife that James had plunged into his heart and then it irritated him. He bowed to her.

"You were walking in such a hurry that I did not think I could overtake you. My maid is waiting in the shop but I did so wish to speak with you. For I mean to try again to discover what costume you plan to wear to Lord Sapperton's masquerade ball."

He looked down at her, at the pretty flower-strewn poke bonnet trimmed in blue satin that covered her fair curls. She was overdressed for a morning's shopping in the small village of Chipping Fosseworth. Her blue silk pelisse trimmed with white braid certainly set her large blue eyes to advantage, but she would end up quite dirty marching through villages and down country lanes in such a costume. He felt angry toward her for this piece of nonsense and said, "I was going to take a little walk up into the woods. Do you care to come with me?" He smiled in a sardonic way.

She feigned being startled at such a request, one pretty gloved hand flying in horror to her rosy cheek as she replied, in a coy manner, "Without my maid?"

And when he crooked his arm, offering it to her, she quickly wrapped her own silk-clad one about his as he said, "But of course! A maid can be such a nuisance." His voice was low.

He was disappointed but not surprised when she giggled and said, "Well, I suppose I may rely upon you to behave as a gentleman ought."

"There you are out!" he responded in perfect truth as she giggled again.

Julia's chatter, as they climbed the fairly steep hillside up into Quening Woods and across Knott Hill, raked his nerves. But he let her talk and even led her to a little pool he had discovered. How unfriendly the water seemed, still and cold as a cloud obscured the sun and no sparkling shafts of light played upon the surface of the pool. Why did he feel so thoroughly discontent?

Julia said, "I have never been here before and certainly not alone with a man."

Her eyes teased him and he smiled at her. It would feel good to hold a woman in his arms, to let go of some of the pain he felt. He grabbed her in the same manner as he had Kate and kissed her hard, but there was no answering response, only a frightened cry as he released her. Seeing the fearful, hunted look in her eyes, he said gently, "I'm sorry I have hurt you." Perhaps James was right after all. "How old are you?"

Julia had never been kissed in such a fashion before and decided that she did not like it at all. And how many times had Emmet warned her that she ran the risk of being accosted in just this fashion were she not careful. She felt her knees begin to shake. "You—you promised to be a gentleman. You—you hurt me!" And she retrieved a kerchief from her reticule, dabbing at her lips.

Oh, Lord, what was he doing? He lifted her chin, his voice gentle, his eyes concerned. "Julia, I made a grave error, that's all. I did not mean to hurt you." And he put an arm about her as she took a deep breath.

In a small voice she said, "Emmet warned me. A hundred times he warned me. But I never listened to him. And it is as much my fault, only I'd had no idea!"

He began to grow weary of her whiny little voice and said, in a firm tone, "Let's return back to the village and to your maid, that you might be easy again, Miss Moreton. Indeed, I will not force myself upon you if you do not like it."

"If I do not like it!" she cried, unable to restrain giving vent to her feelings. "I detest being mauled in such a fashion!" Oh, but she began to sound like her mother. "And what female, in her right senses, would enjoy being grabbed and kissed as though she were a—a wild horse one wished to tame?"

Buckland thought he knew of at least one female but refrained from answering the beauty. As they left the pool with Julia dabbing again at her eyes and sniffling, he found himself consumed with a desire to turn the wayward country miss over his knee and paddle her.

Kate watched them leave, through the thick leaves of a dogwood shrub. How alone she felt. She had come to the pool, one of her favorite woodland haunts, to clear her thoughts. And what must she find but Julia Moreton snuggled within Buckland's embrace. He was indeed a rogue!

Her heart unable to bear more, she moved away from her concealed spot and headed back to the manor. In some ways, she was glad she had seen Buckland and Julia together. For it confirmed the truth of his nature and the reality of his circumstance. He was the sort of man, after all, that enjoyed as many flirtations as he could manage, even in so small a place as Chipping Fosseworth. She would not blame him but neither would she hold on to him as she seemed to be doing. How much she wished that matters had been different, for Buckland was a strong man, the sort of man that she could turn to in her difficulties, a man of sound thinking and little nonsense. But he was not a man she could set her cap for. And as she descended the hill, Kate knew now that if she were to have a future at all, it must be with Lord Ashwell.

After Buckland escorted the distraught Miss Moreton back to Chipping Fosseworth and to her maid, he returned to the stables of the inn and mounted his black horse. He would not risk encountering any more females today. He let the magnificent stallion lengthen his stride as soon as they left the village heading toward Stinchfield. The wind felt soothing on his face as the horse gathered speed, passing a slow tanner's cart laden with pelts of badger, fox, and squirrel, and Buckland felt some of his anger give way.

Surely he did not intrude into peoples lives and hurt them; surely he was not so callous. Sapperton intruded. He was the sort of man that hurt people. How dare James say that he played the god! He cared about James, about some of his close friends in London, and if the Miss Moretons of this world insisted upon flirting, then how could James call that mean-spirited? Only, James had not referred to Julia; he had been speaking solely of Kate.

Seeing a little-used country lane, Buckland left the main road to follow a dirt path that he soon realized lead him toward Quening, the little village within Sapperton's domain. He considered reversing his course upon the chance that he might meet the earl, but this he dismissed as ridiculous, for Lord Sapperton was not one to traverse the countryside nor to interest himself in the comings and goings of the villagers.

As the lane became quite straight, Buckland regarded the fields about Quening, all separated by hedges. And though the land was wet from the recent rain, the crops showed signs of having suffered severely from a lack of water throughout the summer. This would be a poor harvest, indeed.

He slowed his horse to a walk and looked at the insect-ridden vegetables in one field—the cabbage heads small, beans shriveled on their poles, the turnip leaves worm-eaten. And the fields bearing the country's grains, wheat and barley, showed too many bare patches.

Several labourers, who had harvested half a field of wheat, stood in a group, scythes in hand and talking in earnest tones. At first, Buckland thought they were breaking for a refreshing draught of ale, since one of the village women stood by with a large jug in hand. And though they might have refreshed themselves, he knew that their conversation undoubtedly had taken a more serious turn when, upon seeing Buckland, they turned startled eyes upon him and, in a hasty, nervous manner, returned to their various tasks. The woman walked by him, scowling as he trotted by on his horse. He watched her with raised brow, but her insolent expression never wavered nor did she drop her gaze from his own.

Good God. This village was ripe for rioting of the worst sort. He had seen something similar in Greece when crops failed. But here in England? It seemed impossible.

A scarecrow, sporting nearly a dozen sparrows, told its own story. In Kent, where his country seat was surrounded by hop fields and cherry orchards, the difficulties his tenant farmers faced were of a different nature. But then, he attended to his tenants' needs and the nearby village of Stowhurst was never denied requests for their needy. He saw to his lands as Sapperton did not.

Watching the sun begin to descend behind Waverley Hill, Buckland turned around and headed back toward Chipping Fosseworth. He and James were expected to dine with Lord Whiteshill that evening and he had for the moment forgotten that everyone lived by country hours. It would not do to be late. As he neared the inn, he thought of James and Kate and wished that he had never agreed to a masquerade. Just a mere lark, only now it appeared to be costing him his dearest friendship. And as for Kate, he sighed heavily. She was not indifferent to him, he knew that, but she was determined to marry Ashwell.

Mary's fingers worked quickly and steadily upon her petit point of pink and yellow roses, as Lydia held up Kate's queenly costume to regard herself in the mirror over the mantel. She cried, "I wish I might wear this! How exquisite! Did Madame Beaumaris make this for you?"

Kate answered, "No, it belonged to my mother."

Lydia exclaimed, regarding the bodice, "Mary, look! Kate will be all bosom at the masquerade and none of the bucks will pay the least attention to you or me."

Mary said, "How very vulgar you are today, Lydia. And I must say your remark is extremely coarse."

Lydia draped the costume over Jaspar's favorite chair by the fire and sighed, "Mama has insisted that I wear Mary's old shepherdess costume." She scowled at Mary, then continued, directing her remarks to Kate, "And she will make me wear a lace fichu to cover my bosom. None of the young men will even dance with me."

She picked up a pear from the table near the chair and bit into it. "I think it is most unfair."

"And you have the manners of a savage. Speaking of bosoms!" She clicked her tongue, then quite ruined her effect by saying, "And I wonder what Julia will be wearing, for if ever a young lady has been intent upon displaying nature's bounty, it is Julia Moreton!"

And Kate laughed at her friend, saying, "What a hypocrite you are, Mary. Just because Lydia will speak openly and actually say the word *bosom*, you condemn her."

Mary blushed as she darted her needle through the mesh. "I suppose you are right."

Lydia and Kate laughed at Mary, who wore a sheepish expression, and Kate wondered how it was that two sisters could be so different. Of the three of them, she thought that Lydia looked and behaved more like her sister than Mary's.

A carriage was heard in the drive and Lydia, her heavily ruffled muslin skirts dancing about her ankles, bounded to the window. "Hallo! It is Lord Ashwell. How handsome he is driving his magnificent team. Although I must say he seems to be having a bit of difficulty. The lead horse is lifting its head and trying to strain away from the second horse. One would think he hadn't handled them before."

Kate was on her feet and moved quickly to gather up her costume and spirit it away to her office, then run back to the drawing room. She did not want James to see her costume.

Lydia called out, "He has brought an enormous bouquet of flowers! Why, he must have gone all the way to Stinchfield for them." She turned an awed expression to Kate and said, "Why, whatever does this mean?" And she smiled broadly.

Kate looked at Mary, wondering if her friend would now make some comment, but Mary seemed intent upon her needlework, her fingers flying even faster than before. Perhaps a bit too fast, for she suddenly cried out in pain, "How stupid of me!" And she sucked on her finger, then examined the small piece of embroidery cloth to see if any blood had marred her work.

Kate was about to comment on Mary's carelessness, but the front bell sounded and all three women inadvertently glanced toward the entrance hall and watched as Violet, thin and wraithlike, made her appearance in the hall.

Lydia blurted out, "Oh, to think that you have only a female to open the door upon Lord Ashwell. What must he think?"

Kate said in a low voice, "When I told him that Jaspar did not wish for it and that I had to abide by my father's wishes, he honoured me for my meek, obedient spirit."

Lydia stared at her with disbelief, and just as the poet's voice was heard in the entrance hall, she retorted in a whisper, "Kate, whatever will you do if he should learn of your true nature?"

As James stood in the doorway to the drawing room, his face lit with a tender expression as he gazed upon Kate, he endeared himself to all of them by saying, "And how blessed I am to be greeted by three of the prettiest ladies I have ever known." And he extended the bouquet of flowers toward Kate.

As she received the flowers, Kate noticed that Mary did not even pause in her stitching as Lord Ashwell greeted each of them in turn. How unlike Mary!

Kate thanked him for his offering, and as the rich fragrance of roses filled the room, she asked, "Will you have some tea?" She crossed the room to place the flowers in a vase beneath her mother's portrait and continued, "We were just refreshing ourselves a little and speaking of Sapperton's masquerade."

He accepted a cup of tea and, seating himself in Jaspar's chair that sank a little in the seat, said lightly, "I am looking forward to the masquerade ball with great anticipation." He looked at Kate and said, "I am hoping that his lordship's ball will hold great significance for me."

Lydia said, "What do you mean? Do you hope to win a prize for the best costume?"

Mary looked at her sister and then at Kate and finally at James. "No, Lydia. I think Lord Ashwell refers to something of a more lasting nature."

Lydia seemed thoroughly confused and James, regarding Mary with a warm, serious expression said, "I thought you might understand."

At his words, Kate sank down onto the sofa beside Mary and, from a table at her elbow, retrieved a novel she had been reading. She opened the book in a perfectly blind manner, feeling as though she had just been turned to stone. She could not quite believe what he was saying. She should have been thrown into raptures at his words, or at least have felt a little joy well up within her, but all she felt was a great numbing sensation that deprived her of speech.

Her schemes had actually worked, and under James's intense gaze, she lowered her head to finger the brown velvet ribbon that draped in a curl from beneath her high-waisted flowered gown.

Lydia clapped her hands and exclaimed, "Mary, is it not time for us to be going?"

Kate stood hastily, the worn volume of *Pride and Prejudice* slipping to the floor at her feet. "Don't go," she cried in a nervous manner and met Mary's rather astonished gaze. James rose from his seat as well and bent down to pick up the novel she had dropped. As he stood facing her, a slight frown creasing his brow, Kate said to Mary, in as composed a voice as she could muster, "I'm certain it was not Lord Ashwell's intention to frighten you both from my house."

James seemed embarrassed and immediately bowed to Mary, saying, "No! Certainly not. You must think me quite rude. Pray do not leave." And he reseated himself, still holding the book.

Kate poured herself another cup of tea, her hand trembling slightly. And, as a little of the tea spilled onto the white saucer, she thought that never would she comprehend herself. Her mark had been hit, squarely. Why then could she not step forward and claim the prize? Taking several spoonfuls of sugar, she stirred her tea and stared at Mary's needlework, hearing James riffle the pages of the novel, the room falling to a dreadful silence. What was James thinking at this moment? she wondered. Looking up at him, her cheeks turned bright red at the gentle expression on his face. Stirring in two more teaspoons of sugar in an absent manner, she made a comment on the weather, which each of them expounded upon at length.

And just as she was about to take a sip of her tea, Lydia said, with a teasing smile, "I would not drink that if I were you."

Kate shook her head at Lydia, who was always such a minx, then took her sip. She held the syrupy liquid in her mouth and wanted desperately to spit it out, her eyes watering as she swallowed it down. She dared not glance at Lord Ashwell or Lydia, who emitted reprehensible choking sounds of one who was restraining her laughter. She promptly returned her cup to its saucer, setting both on the table in front of her.

Lydia laughed at Kate. "I told you not to drink it."

James said, "Why ever not, Lydia? I find Katherine's tea exceptional!" And the affectionate smile that he bestowed upon Kate again caused her to blush.

Lydia, fully involved in living out her sixteen summers to their last jolly moment, sat in a chair near Lord Ashwell and, her dark blue eyes bubbling with mischief, said, "The seasons intrigue me greatly. Here the summer is ending, autumn will be shortly upon us, then Christmas and snow and holly wreaths. And then the lambs will be born just before spring begins to break, and then April and May arrive. Don't you enjoy April and May, Lord Ashwell, particularly in the countryside? And you must make an effort to be here during those months, when even the breezes about Chipping Fosseworth will smell of April and May." She sipped her own tea, regarding James over the edge of her teacup, her blue eyes appearing quite wide and innocent and naughty.

Mary muttered, "Abominable."

Kate blushed again and felt a panic begin to rise in her breast.

But James, choking over his tea during this perfectly obvious recital, laughed aloud and said that he always admired young ladies who were full of spirit.

Lydia cried, "Will you dedicate a poem to me?"

A little of the laughter fell from James's eyes as he responded quietly, "I could not do justice to your exuberance, Miss Lydia, with the futile efforts of my poor pen."

Lydia addressed Kate, "See how prettily he speaks. I think you should have him!"

Mary cried, "Lydia, enough. You are embarrassing our dear friend, as well as Lord Ashwell, with your childish comments."

Lydia took this rebuff in her usual manner, for though she stopped chattering, she could not keep from sighing gustily now and then as she sat primly and nibbled on her pear.

Mary began putting away her needlework and said, "We must go."

Kate wanted a little more time to think, to prepare herself for the inevitable, for she greatly feared that were James to ask her just yet, she would say no. Oh, why had he come around so soon?

James said politely, "Pray, do not leave on my account." His words seemed quite sincere, but since he rose to his feet as he spoke, Kate thought that he might as well have thrown both of her friends out the front door.

Mary rose, picking up her reticule and wooden box that contained her precious needles, thread, and embroidery fabrics, then shook hands with James.

Kate stood up as well and Lydia, her teacup clattering down upon her saucer, cried, "We shall expect to receive a visit from you tomorrow, Kate." And she even winked at her.

As the front door closed behind the ladies, who would walk the two miles back to Edgecote, Kate felt her heart beating wildly in her ears. She did not want to hear his proposals—not now.

Chapter Thirteen

James crossed the room and, from the bouquet he had brought Kate, plucked a yellow rose. Returning to stand next to her, he seemed a little uneasy as he pressed the rose into her hand and said, "I realize that this is all quite sudden, but you must know that I am not entirely indifferent to you my dearest, sweetest Katherine."

Kate lifted a hand as though to stop his speeches and, realizing that she could not, held the flower against her lips. She found it impossible to look at him and concentrated instead on the intricate folds of his snowy neckcloth. He was speaking in a low voice and his words scarcely registered in her brain. He spoke of his admiration of her and of his affection. Kate's gaze drifted to the lapel of his coat, and for the first time she noticed that it looked a trifle worn. She wondered why he wore such a coat. His voice urgent, he spoke words that surprised her. "I must know if you feel that love—a strong, mutual love—can overcome any circumstance." He paused for a moment and continued, his voice dropping to a whisper. "For instance, if two people love each other, do you believe, Katherine, that, should they be forced to exist upon a small competence, they could live happily?"

Kate looked up at him, bemused. His pale face seemed even paler still and she felt a sudden affection for him. He was, after all, a poet whose works she admired, a man whose principles always seemed based on an unwavering consideration for others. She did like him as a friend, but what did he mean by such a question?

She let the soft petals move gently over her lips. He was testing her, trying to determine how she might feel if he were perhaps quite impoverished. She almost smiled at this thought, for it was well-known that Lord Ashwell had not only earned a fortune from his latest volume of poetry, but had come into a considerable inheritance through the Ashwell viscountcy a scant two years ago. But prior to that, he must have known something of poverty.

Her thoughts turned all of their own accord to Buckland and his circumstances. And as always when she thought of him, she felt the strongest pulling sensation on her heart. And as though James's question had opened her own heart to examination, she knew a truth so blinding that tears smarted her eyes. Life with Buckland, even in his limited circumstances as the owner of a cloth mill, who would probably not see a profit now for some time to come, would be nothing short of heaven. They would live perhaps in a small cottage somewhere, pink roses trailing about their doors and windows, a small garden that they both might plant and a stream of children running through the woods near the cottage. She sighed, her vision clouded, the reality of her love for Buckland flowing in upon her in great, unstoppable waves. Buckland. Dear, impoverished, teasing Buckland. No, poverty would mean nothing in such a case.

James, forgotten in this reverie, clasped the fingers that she had wrapped about the rose and said quietly, "Dearest, sweetest Katherine, you need say nothing. I can see by the expression on your face how you feel."

Katherine gave a little cry as a thorn stuck her. James apologized, but Kate did not care about her finger, only about refusing the poet. She cried, "But you are mistaken. I mean—" And she got no further, for Jaspar, his countenance quite jovial, his eyes red from drinking and his speech littered with lazy words, blustered into the room. Plopping down on his favourite chair, he demanded to know, "What the devil brings you to our humble abode, Lord Ashwell?"

James was about to speak, his face wreathed in smiles, when a loud hammering sounded on the front door. Kate let out a

255

great sigh of relief. She knew Kit Barnsley's pounding knock, and if she was in the least fortunate, Stephen as well, had just arrived to pay a most timely visit.

Kit, crossing his arms over his chest, sat opposite Kate and said, "We've just been to Julia's. She wouldn't even receive us because of that curst ball of hers!"

Kate watched Mrs. Moreton tug slightly at her blond wig, then twitch at her gown, smoothing out nonexistent wrinkles as her stately majordomo announced the arrival of James and Buckland. Everyone else was forgotten as the plump, full-bosomed female stepped forward, her cheeks wrinkled in smiles as she welcomed them both to her home.

She wore an orange satin gown, her best diamonds, and a white turban and, in a loud voice told them that she expected both of them to dance every dance. Then she brought her daughter forward.

Kate watched Julia greet Buckland with the tiniest reserve, feeling both delighted that her tryst in the woods had not been entirely pleasing to the beauty and at the same time astonished that Julia was not now in love with Buckland, too. What a ninnyhammer!

As she watched Julia present her best curtsy to the poet, she hoped that James would not renew his proposals until after the ball. She had fobbed him off all day with excuses that she was too busy to receive him, but the poet's expression as he met her gaze was so moonstruck that she realized it was but a matter of time before James would offer for her. And how could she face him?

Since the day before, she had searched her mind over and over, part of her knowing that she could never accept his proposals and yet her reason dictating that she had no other course. She felt torn inside, as though her heart and mind had been at war for the last few hours, and she felt tired, even a little bruised as she smiled faintly in return to James's slight bow toward her.

Her gaze drifted beyond the poet to rest upon Buckland's handsome face, and for some strange reason, she felt a great loneliness sweep over her at the mere sight of him. She loved his presence in a room, as though before his arrival the room had been dimly lit and now it glowed. He was dressed to perfection in a white carefully arranged neckcloth, black coat and waistcoat, and black pantaloons. In the candlelight, as he turned to survey the company briefly, she noticed that a diamond glinted from the folds of his neckcloth. On his right hand he wore an emerald. And again she had the most sinking sensation that perhaps Buckland was a gamester like her father.

She frowned at him, then heard Lydia's voice whisper to her, "Has he asked you yet? Who are you staring at? You are not even looking at Lord Ashwell. Kate, you are not in love with Mr. Buckland, are you? You cannot be. He is known to be a libertine. My goodness, you ought not to let Ashwell see you looking at another man in that fashion."

Kate heard all of Lydia's words, but none of them broke through her slightly befuddled mind. She regarded Lydia with a confused expression and asked, "What are you saying?"

And Lydia, her face falling, said in a low voice, her eyes concerned, "You are in love with him, aren't you?"

"With James?" she asked, feeling depressed. "I hold him in affection, indeed, I do."

Mrs. Moreton's well-appointed ballroom, filled with ivy from the surrounding countryside and any late-blooming flowers she could find—white lady tress orchids, roses from her gardens, and purple heartsease that she had nurtured all summer—gave an appearance of spring, the seasons melting into one another as the dancers moved in careful steps to the quadrille and the country dance. The orchestra, made up of not quite fully accomplished players from Stinchfield, though missing a great many notes, kept the rhythms marked and strong. But in two hours, from the time the musicians picked up their instruments and nearly everyone had refreshed themselves with champagne, the music sounded perfect to anyone listening.

Kate danced twice with James, and every time he even approached the subject of his desire to marry her, she brightly changed the direction of their conversation. Kit teased her throughout the next two dances, and when Mary had been relaying to her the dreadful news that in Stinchfield a small group of men had actually threatened the owner of the corn mill near Leachwood, she found herself overwhelmed by Lord Sapperton, who took her hand to join him in dancing a quadrille. She wished she had not been so engrossed in Mary's story or she would have refused the earl.

Fortunately the quadrille, involving three other couples in intricate steps, did not allow for much chatter beyond an occasional commonplace remark, and she was free from his attentions. But afterward, though she protested the entire time in a low string of curses beneath her breath, the earl swept her onto the terrace. Her only other recourse was to cause a scene, which she did not want to do, and since Roger and Emmet were standing nearby and arguing about who owned the better hunter, she felt reasonably safe in Sapperton's company.

But before she knew what he was about, he had taken her hand and placed a kiss upon her palm, his actions concealed to her friends because his back was turned toward them.

Kate pulled her hand away as he laughed at her, and she hissed, "You are despicable, Sapperton." She stepped away from him, intent upon returning to the ballroom, but he said quietly, "I have purchased something in Cheltenham from Lord Turville, which may interest you."

Kate remembered the name, thinking back to the evening of Sapperton's soiree when she and Jaspar had dined with the earl. She paused in her steps and turned toward him as she heard Emmet say to Roger, "I'm thinking of purchasing a new fowling piece this year."

In a low voice, Kate said to Sapperton, "What? What did you purchase?"

Her heart began pounding in her chest and she knew the answer as he just stared at her, his thin lips shaped into an ugly smile. "You bastard," she said in a low, venomous tone as she moved away. He now owned the manor and the lands and could turn them out tomorrow if he liked.

His laughter followed her as she returned to the ballroom.

*　　　*　　　*

Kate entered the Moretons' library and immediately covered her mouth to keep from laughing outright at Stephen. He stood near the fireplace, his dark, wavy hair sticking out in a variety of tufts over his head, his eyes at half-mast. He was looking at Buckland and had obviously consumed enough champagne to make his dancing wholly inadequate.

His speech sounded like a small sailing vessel trying to navigate on a rolling sea. "You are a gentleman, Buckland. A true gentleman. You hunt and shoot and no doubt you box with great science. No mere flourishing." As his speech moved slowly past his teeth, his words falling into one another, Stephen tried to lean his arm on the mantel. And when he missed, he looked at the mantel as though it had just moved away from him. Returning his attention to Buckland, he continued, pointing at Buckland's chest and tapping the top button of his black coat, "You know how to tell one end of a horse from t'other. And James is all right, too," he nodded. "For a poet."

Kit rolled his eyes at his brother and said, "You're completely foxed, Stephen. And you're making a great cake of yourself. Hallo, Kate!" He greeted her as she moved to stand with them. She was escaping James's most dogged attentions.

Stephen slapped his brother's shoulder and laughed. "You feel the same way, though." He acknowledged Kate with a careless wave of his hand and continued, "Tell Buckland what you were saying about poets."

Kit scowled at his brother and shoved his hands deep into his pockets, his cheeks burning slightly.

Stephen did not wait for Kit to speak and said, again tapping Buckland's button, "Poets are generally just like Rupert. All milktoast and dandified, but not James. Though I don't say he's got the seat you've got. Sort of slips around in his saddle if you ask me, but then he's a poet. But nothing like Rupert."

Buckland laughed at Stephen and told Kit he ought to take his brother home and drop him in the duck pond.

"By Jove, what an excellent suggestion." And he grasped Stephen underneath his arm and said, "Come along, old fellow. You've been needing a bath for quite some time."

"Eh? You don't mean to do this. I won't go! I won't—" His

sudden protestations went straight to his head, his eyes rolling backward as he sank to the floor, nearly pulling his brother down with him.

Kit stood over him, his booted leg colliding with the andiron in front of the fireplace, and said, "A trifle too late. Ah, well." He raised laughing eyes to Buckland and said, "Another time I shall certainly take your suggestion."

Kate watched Buckland and Kit lift Stephen to his feet. The latter came around for a moment, smiled at each of them, then promptly fell back into an unconscious state, his head lolling forward.

Kate met Buckland's gaze, his own blue eyes laughing, and she felt such a longing for his company, just to speak with him about the trivial occurrences of each day, that it was all she could do to keep from begging him to return to the library after he had assisted Kit.

Alone for a few minutes, Kate remained in the library, thinking first of Sapperton's ominous news and then wondering for the hundredth time whether she ought to be practical and marry Ashwell just as she had originally intended. But her heart would not let her rest as it brought forth a clear vision of Buckland and the first time she had met him, tomato stains on his face and clothing and what his arms had felt like as he had held her in a constricting embrace. She moved to a window that overlooked a garden lit with small lanterns and pressed aside the velvet draperies, watching night moths dance about the lights. She imagined Buckland now returning to the library in search of her, taking her in his arms, even kissing her. Oh, Buckland. She mouthed his name, leaning her head into the soft gold drapes.

Her thoughts absorbing her completely, Kate did not notice the gentleman in the doorway. And just as he spoke, she saw his reflection in the glass pane of the window.

"What are you thinking, Katherine?" James's voice intruded.

Kate jumped. "Oh, you startled me." And she gripped the velvet in one hand behind her, as though trying to gain support from the drape.

She immediately smiled in a nervous manner and was just

preparing to make her escape when James shocked her by stepping into the room and purposefully closing the door.

Kate felt her heart sink. She did not wish him to ask her to force her to make this terrible decision. Placing a hand on the large Jacobean winged chair, covered in a dark tapestry design that sat near the window, she asked, "What—what are you doing?"

He advanced into the room. "You must know that I have something of a most particular nature to say to you, that I have been trying to speak to you since yesterday. Pray, won't you hear me out?"

Kate swallowed hard, her blue silk gown trimmed in a delicate Brussels lace rustling as she seated herself in the winged chair. She folded her hands on her lap to keep them from shaking, and she could not look at James. Her voice a mere whisper, she said, "Of course. I do not mean to be unkind, only . . . well, never mind." She looked up from staring at her gloved hands and regarded him with a smile. "I want very much to speak with you."

He went to her at once, kneeling before her and, in a rather dramatic manner, which seemed in keeping with his pale skin and large brown eyes, spoke long and fluently about his love for her. He told Kate that though he had at first been a little shocked at some of the things she would say, he had soon grown to realize that she was not entirely to blame. Squire Draycott had quite fallen short of his duty to his daughter. "And not only has your father been careless in your education, but no one in your small community here seems to want to encourage you along different lines, to encourage you to behave as the sort of female I have witnessed in you when we have been together. You are wholly a graceful, submissive female underneath your rough exterior, and I love you deeply."

Kate listened to these words and worked very hard at not letting her anger consume her. As he spoke, she regarded the scuffed tips of her white satin dancing slippers and dared not look at the rather righteous expression on his face. He spoke more about his love for her, how it had grown, occasion upon occasion, as he had come to know her valiant yet sweet spirit, until finally he wished to make her his wife. "Will you do me the great honour of accepting my hand in marriage?"

Kate heard these words and remembered how, several weeks earlier, she had actually planned for him to do so. Her careful schemes had worked. She had succeeded in charming a poet who had had every beautiful female in London running after him, and she alone had captured him.

Looking into his sensitive face that of the moment wore a young mooncalf expression, she suddenly understood everything. She could no more marry Lord Ashwell than she could cease riding Miss Diana or make a vow to never hunt another rabbit again. She did not love him and she would never love him. And what a wretched thing to have done! She pressed a hand against her cheek and gave a little cry as she said, "I'm sorry! Indeed, I am sorry!"

He grasped her hands. "What do you mean?"

"I cannot marry you, my lord." She saw the sudden intense pain flash through his eyes and continued, "I have behaved very badly. I'm sorry, and how stupid such words sound. How can I possibly apologize for my truly wicked behaviour? At one time I wanted more than anything for you to fall in love with me, to wish to marry me. But now I see how foolish I have been. What a wretched, stupid scheme!"

He released her hands and stood up. In a quiet, disbelieving voice, he said, "What scheme?"

Kate covered her face for a moment, feeling thoroughly ashamed of herself. Taking a deep breath, she returned her hands to her lap and continued, "I have led you to believe that your advances would be welcome to me. Forgive me, James, but"—and she looked up at him—"I must refuse you. I do not love you."

James felt the blood rush from his face as he looked into Kate's beautiful eyes. Clear brown honest eyes. Would they but lie to him at this moment, he could be at ease. She did not love him. "But I was so certain that you loved me. I cannot have been so completely mistaken."

She cried, "But I do! I do! But not as a woman loves a man. I love you as I love Kit or Roger or Emmet." Unbidden tears stung her eyes. "Oh, James, I am sorry. I set out to marry not you, but Lord Ashwell. Oh, you know what I mean. I determined when I first knew that you had come to Chipping Fosseworth that I would marry you. I am in the most desperate of circumstances, you see, and to marry the wealthy Lord Ashwell seemed so simple and perfect a solution, particularly since I loved your poetry so very much! I know now how despicable and how impossible such motives are, but you must believe me when I say that I regret my impulses a thousand times! Only do forgive me. Please forgive me." And a tear rolled down her cheek.

James stared at her, not seeing her but hearing Buckland's voice not two days earlier, telling him that it was possible Kate had been pursuing him for his supposed fortune. And he would not believe him. He narrowed his eyes at her and thought back on all the times that he had seen Katherine together with Buckland, and as though he had been denying the truth to himself, he knew now that she was Buckland's wood-nymph! That Buckland had kissed her more than once!

An anger so hot burned through him, of hatred toward his friend, of supreme jealousy, that he reached down and, possessing himself of one of Kate's hands, jerked her to her feet and said, "I will not let Buckland have you. Do you hear me? It is not fair. Not fair to me!" And he pulled her into his arms, bruising her mouth with a very hard, angry kiss.

But no passion flowed from his soul as he held her rather tall, womanly form in his arms. She was too tall, too firm, not soft as Mary was soft, with dimpled arms and smooth, fleshy skin. And he released her, a feeling of surprise replacing his sudden rage.

"Good God," he cried, and a silly smile overtook his features. He shook his head at his ungentlemanly conduct and said, "I am sorry, truly I am."

Kate, too, felt the complete absence of any fine thing between them and suddenly she laughed, saying, "Aren't we a pair? You don't love me either, do you?"

James watched her for a moment, then smiled in return. "I thought I did, but kissing you was rather like kissing one's sister." He eyed her sheepishly and begged her to sit down again. Pulling a footstool up, he seated himself at her knees and

263

said, "I do have an affection for you, though. Perhaps I mistook it for some greater, more perfect emotion, but I think—oh, how I dislike admitting this to anyone—I just couldn't bear to let Buckland number you among his conquests." He propped his chin up on his knees, and staring into the fireplace that had a pile of fresh black coals lying dormant upon the hearth, he continued, "You cannot imagine what it is like to go through life in George's shadow. Not that he makes anything of it, only—" He broke off as he caught the confused expression on Kate's face and said, "But what am I saying? You know yourself how handsome he is, and he has such a way with the feminine heart." He frowned. "I only hope that he has not possessed yours."

Kate regarded him, feeling suddenly quite hopeless.

James frowned at her. "Please say that you have not lost your heart to him." He read the expression on her face and said, "Now I am truly sorry. You deserve better than this."

He rose to his feet and straightened his coat. Looking down at her, he said, "I wish you every happiness. I hope that what I have said about Ash—about Buckland will in some way cause you to look further than his playful flirtations. He is a good sort, truly. Only where you females are concerned, his heart is like steel. I am sorry. I wish that someone might have warned you."

He then bowed to her and, turning to leave the library, paused at the door. Whirling around, his face wearing a naughty gleam on his pale features, he exclaimed, "I have had the most amusing thought. No, but it is too stupid, really. Only—"

Kate rose to her feet and smoothed out her blue silk gown. She was fully intrigued by the expression on his face and cried, "What? You must tell me now or I promise I shall hound you the entire evening."

He went to her and took up both her hands. "There have been times, this I will tell you, that I have had the feeling that Buckland is not as indifferent to you as he seems. Do you remember the sojourn to Tewkesbury? Well, the day afterwards he brooded constantly, kicking at chairs, snapping at the servants, and he would scarcely speak to me. And as I think on it, I wonder"—his eyes shifted away from her, appearing thoughtful—"if he thought he had lost you forever—to me."

Kate recoiled, pulling her hands out of his. "But I could not. I have despised my pursuit of you, pretending to be the sort of lady you would admire. I cannot now deceive Buckland."

"But Kate—I shall call you Kate now—what if a little jealousy were to make the difference to him, I mean, to show him what he is feeling? You don't know what it has been like for him all these years. He's built a fortress about his heart—an impregnable, moated, castellated fortress. What if you could breach the walls by pretending that you were lost to him?"

Kate covered her face with her hands. "Do you know what the past few weeks have been like for me while I set myself in pursuit of you? I hated every false word I spoke."

He looked at Kate and felt such a calm descend over him that he put a gentle arm about her and kissed her forehead. "You must forget all that. In some ways I have been as much to blame."

"You?"

"Yes. For I was only following your lead because I hoped to beat Buckland. I wanted to prove myself to him. What a fool I have been!" He laughed down at the stricken expression on her face and said, "And I cannot tell you how truly grateful I am that you at least had the good sense to say no to my proposals, or we should both now be in the basket!"

Kate nodded, staring at the planked oak floor beneath her feet. "But I cannot do this thing. Thank you for considering my feelings."

"Considering you? Well, to be sure I did say that, didn't I, but really I was thinking how pleasant it would be to watch my friend squirm a little. You see, I don't think he believed that I would ask you to marry me or that you would accept. It would be such a temporary thrill to see him come down off his high horse."

Kate thought his faraway look quite amusing and she laughed.

"Much better," he cried. "Then you shall do it?"

Kate walked away from his light grasp about her shoulder

and opened the door. "Not even to gratify your quite reprehensible desires."

He shrugged, "Oh, well. I suppose it is for the best."

As they approached the ballroom, however, the first sight to meet Kate's gaze, as she scanned the flower-laden room and as a violin let out a particularly screeching tone, was Buckland leaning over Julia's shoulder and saying something to make her laugh.

Kate snapped her fan open. He was such a rogue! She cast flashing brown eyes to meet James's amused face and said, "Do not say a word!"

Taking her arm in his, James said, beneath his breath, "You'll not regret this, I promise you. Oh, but life can be so incredibly sweet." And he sighed with deep satisfaction.

As they walked toward Buckland, James leaned down to whisper in her ear, "A masquerade for two days' time. Then I shall tell Buckland that we were only shamming it to tease him."

As they drew closer to Buckland and Julia, James paused for a moment and, taking both of Kate's hands in his, continued in a whisper, "You must promise, however, to ask Buckland—after we have played out our little game for two days—what his real profession is."

Kate could not imagine what he meant, but since he smiled at her in a tender fashion, for the purpose of taunting Buckland, she played her part to admiration by entwining her arm about his and looking up at him in what she hoped was a lovesick manner.

Buckland looked up from his flirtation with Julia. It had required all of his finesse to restore the beauty's confidence in him, and he had just decided that he was again enjoying his sojourn in the Cotswolds, when he happened to lift his gaze, only to find James and Kate approaching him, both smelling of April and May! Good God! And how oddly numb he felt seeing the expression of sincere affection on Kate's face. And James's happiness—delight even—he could not mistake. Surely they were not engaged to be married!

James, with Kate still on his arm, drew her toward his friend, and for a few minutes the four of them chatted on inconsequential subjects. But when Emmet approached Julia and led her onto the ballroom floor, James turned to Buckland and, in a quiet voice, said, "You must congratulate me, George, for Katherine has accepted my hand in marriage."

Buckland immediately took the hand that James extended toward him and, not mistaking for a moment the happy gleam in their eyes as they gazed at one another, said, "I wish you joy." He shook James's hand and felt as though a mail coach had just struck him down.

"We cannot make our tidings known at present"—James patted Kate's hand and, so as not to raise comment among too many of their friends, released her arm completely—"for Kate wishes to speak with her father."

Buckland bowed coldly and tried to catch Kate's eye, but she appeared to be studying the dancers. She was waving her fan across her features in so unconcerned, almost arrogant a manner that for a moment all he could think about was tearing the fan from her long fingers and snapping it in two.

In a tense undertone, he blurted out, "Have you both gone mad?" And feeling that he might do bodily harm to one or the other, he jammed his hands deep into his pockets. Crossing in front of them and giving Kate a reproachful glance, he fairly marched over to Mary and asked her to dance.

James watched him go, lifting his quizzing glass to observe Buckland's dance with Mary, and said, "Did I detect a note of peevishness in his voice when he said, 'Have you both gone mad?'" And he looked down at Kate and smiled.

But Kate could only give him a faint smile in return. Initially, she had enjoyed seeing Buckland's face turn an interesting pale colour, but then she realized that to play such an ignoble role could only serve to make the next few days quite unbearable. Buckland would not let her rest, and afterward he would never forgive them their hoax.

Later that evening, Kate watched Buckland's approach, her heart beginning to thud in her ears. The hour was well beyond midnight and already half the guests had departed from the Moretons' ballroom. But the orchestra, at Julia's instigation and quite against her mother's wishes, was requested to play a waltz, a dance that had become all the rage in London. Mrs. Moreton strongly felt that so much hugging on the dance floor was just one more example of the dreadful immorality to be found amongst tonnish society. However, she had permitted Julia to have her waltz, when her daughter pointed out that both Lord Ashwell and Lord Sapperton were known to waltz. "And you do not wish to be thought of as a mere country rustic, Mama, do you?" This was entirely unanswerable and Julia got her waltz.

Julia danced with James, Mary danced with Emmet, Lydia had somehow cornered Jeremy, who though rather stiff knew the steps to perfection, and Buckland now lifted Kate to her feet, saying, "I presume you waltz," his voice curt.

"I can follow your lead, if that is what you mean." She spoke in a cold voice matching his, and Buckland regarded her sharply.

As the orchestra began its strains, Buckland held Kate in a tight grip about her waist. A little too tight, Kate thought, feeling that even in this movement his rage was ill-concealed. She felt calm, even a little angry, in the face of his condemnation.

He said, "So, Miss Draycott, you have achieved your end." He looked down at her, his blue eyes a mask of ice. He spoke slowly and deliberately. "I congratulate you!"

Kate said quietly, "Do you mean to squeeze the breath out of me?"

His face taking on a hard, bitter expression, his mouth a compressed line, he responded, "Would that I were able to do so this very instant with impunity."

His words, spoken through gritted teeth, only served to make Kate smile. "Do not let such a consideration weigh with you, Mr. Buckland. I am certain that any court would exonerate you once you explained the intense provocation you have had to endure."

He ignored her. "How could you?" His look was suddenly so intense, so recriminating, that Kate again felt hope spring to life within her. He could not feel so strongly if he were indifferent to her. He continued, "James has been my dearest friend since we marched through the hop fields together about Stowhurst. And you! You will come between us. You will separate us, and for what? But beyond that, you know of James's good heart, his integrity, a character not easily found in this kingdom. You would do this to him? He deserves better. You are a harlot, Miss Draycott. A scheming, vicious harlot."

Kate heard his last words, the venom that so rudely erupted from his tongue, and she grew angry. Even if she had been engaged to James, he had no right to speak to her in this manner. "How easily you condemn me, Mr. Buckland." She spoke formally, an edge to her voice. "But then you have always done so, have you not?" He whirled her a little faster than the music flowed. Then he slowed his pace, trying in a halting manner to regain the rhythms of the music.

Kate said, "Have you forgotten the steps?" And she smiled sweetly at him.

His breathing appeared difficult as he tried to control a mounting anger. "I have been greatly mistaken about you. Somehow I believed that you might be different, that you would at some point think better of your aims, that you would find some other means to end your difficulties." A flush covered his cheeks, and he ground his teeth. Kate thought his blue eyes had turned a trifle red as he continued, "I mean to tell him that you are only after his fortune."

Kate laughed at him. "How stupid you are, Buckland. Do you think I have not already said the very same thing to him? I told you some time ago that I meant to be honest with James." She sighed and glanced at the poet. "He is quite handsome. I did not notice it until he asked for my hand in marriage."

He appeared astonished as he asked, "You told him of your designs?"

"Of course. Did you think I could only be honest with you? But how conceited you are," she responded. "Well, you are wrong about many things. Especially thinking that I do not love your friend. Indeed, I love him very much. More than I knew."

She saw the anger on his face give way to disbelief. "Now you are lying."

Kate relaxed. For some reason, his unconscionable attack no

269

longer mattered, and if she was not telling him the exact truth, she intended to tell the rest of her story with great vigour. "When he proposed to me in the library"—and she let her face take on quite a lovelorn aspect—"all of my feelings became clear to me in that instant." This, at least, was true. She looked back at Buckland, their path about the ballroom becoming slower as he frowned over her words and the expressions on her face. "James is so much what every woman wants. His sensitivity, the poetical quality of his speech, his consideration for one's feelings and sentiments—he is more than I could wish for in a husband. In short, the moment he offered for my hand, I knew that I loved him."

Buckland said, with a deepening scowl, "Did he not mention to you, then, anything of a particular nature about his poetry?"

Kate shook her head and Buckland continued, "Then I do comprehend what you are saying. You have fallen in love with twenty thousand pounds a year."

Kate felt the blood leave her face, and had Buckland not been supporting her, she would have fainted at the vast sum of money that she had just, not an hour since, given up forever. Oh, James. What have I done?

"Why do you look like that? You seem surprised at the amount. Didn't you know? Well, now you may bless yourself all you like."

Kate did not like the cold laughing lines to his face, as though he held some secret that would soon haunt her.

Sir William, watching this interchange with great interest, approached Buckland shortly after this most intriguing waltz had ended and after Kate had moved away to chat with Mary and James. The musicians began packing up their instruments as Mrs. Moreton stood near the entrance to the ballroom and with many a yawn made her desire to see her guests gone more than apparent. Sir William sipped at a glass of champagne and addressed Buckland, "You know, I have often wished that Kate were my daughter. What spirit she has!"

Buckland, who was having great difficulty in speaking

270

properly to anyone, said curtly, "Indeed? Having known Miss Draycott for several weeks now I begin to think you were spared a great deal of trouble."

He was about to brush past Sir William when the baronet stopped him with a pressure on his arm and said, in a teasing manner, "Trouble I should have greatly welcomed. My Lydia and Kate are alike in many respects, and though I love Mary, Lydia seems to speak in the same rhythms that I do." He loved watching the irritation pass across the younger man's face and he could not help taunting him a little. "I had always hoped that a man with a strong hand might come along and take Miss Draycott well in hand. No mealymouthed stripling for her!" He took another sip, his eyes fastened upon the changing expressions on the man's face.

Buckland glanced at Sir William and saw a measuring look in those dark blue eyes. The baronet continued in a low, serious voice, "I hope you will give up all of your masquerades soon, Mr. Buckland. If you do not, knowing Kate as I do, you may lose her forever. She is fearfully stubborn." He paused, looking beyond Buckland. Seeing Kate laugh at something Emmet was saying to her brought a stab of pain to his heart. Marianne's laughter all over again. He finished his thought, "She is too much like her mother."

Bowing to Buckland, he walked toward Lady Chalford, who sat beside Mrs. Cricklade and yawned over something she was saying. He stood nearby, looking down at his prosaic, good wife, who had provided him with several wonderful children and an orderly house, and still the pain did not let up. A little brandy might dull so sudden and sharp a pain, and when they returned to Edgecote Hall, he would avail himself of the decanter in the library. Marianne. And he tossed off the rest of his champagne as his wife rose to join him.

Later that evening at the Swan and Goose, James seated himself in a hard-backed oak chair, placed his hands behind his neck, and stretched his tall, thin body out before the fire. How glad he was that Julia had been flirting with Buckland, for that was the real reason Kate had changed her mind. And what a delight to witness his friend in the absolute throes of anger and confusion. He had not believed that Kate would accept him and, James thought with a laugh, Buckland had been right. But oh, what pleasure it had been to watch his handsome face turn so many interesting colors, twisting in anger, frowning, scowling. He had actually begun to look like a moody poet. And he laughed out loud, crossing his feet at the ankles and swilling another glass of brandy. He was celebrating.

Buckland, standing in the doorway and seeing the triumph on his friend's face, felt his anger begin to consume him again. He had walked the distance from Ampstone to Chipping Fosseworth, over three miles with a three-quarter moon lighting his path, hoping to achieve some measure of peace. He had thought it all settled in his heart, that he would accept the decision made, that he might even help James to increase his own small competence in some manner, but seeing his friend gloat! . . . Well, it was more than he could bear, and he slapped his hat down on the table and said, "So, I suppose you expect me to congratulate you on this latest folly of yours!"

James, a little startled by Buckland's entrance, first frowned at his caustic words, then smiled, pouring out another glass of brandy from the bottle at his elbow. The Swan and Goose had an excellent supply of brandy and James wondered if The Gentlemen were able to send their contraband even along the winding Cotswold roads. To Buckland, he said, "Come! Enough of this ill-humour. Share a drink with me . . . or two, or perhaps we ought to finish the whole bottle in honour of my engagement."

Buckland knew that he must turn James away from this course. For his own good, naturally. Pulling up a chair, he straddled it backward and said, "You must quit this ruinous path. Why, you've hardly enough to keep yourself, nonetheless a wife and children. You know that you must marry a female with at the very least a moderate dowry."

James lifted a brow and regarded Buckland with a sharp look. "You would say this to me. You, George, who are forever complaining about grasping females? I thought you despised such motives."

Buckland leaned back abruptly, as though he had never

heard himself speak before. "Good God, what a hypocrite I have become." He gazed into the fire and said, in a quieter voice, "What do you think will happen when she learns of our deception, when she discovers that you are not wealthy?"

James rose to retrieve another glass for Buckland and, as he returned to his seat, said with a smile, "Something she told me when I proposed to her has led me to believe that such a consideration would never weigh with her."

"You have said nothing to her, then? You asked her to marry you without her knowing the true state of affairs?"

He sat down and again stretched out his slippered feet, then poured Buckland a glass. Handing the snifter to him, he said, with a serious expression, "Yes, and I think it unconscionable. But I did not wish to say anything until I had spoken with you. After all, we are in this terrible thing together."

Buckland inhaled the bouquet of the rich brandy, then sipped the golden liquid. Feeling the slight burn of the cognac as it travelled down his throat and warmed his stomach, he crossed his arms over the back of the chair and said, "I never thought this masquerade would come to anything." And a strange despondence settled over him as he regarded James and pictured him in formal attire, waiting for his bride to make her procession down the aisle. "But then, who would have thought that you would meet and fall in love with a female in so unpromising a place as Chipping Fosseworth?"

James, regarding Buckland's saddened countenance, lifted his glass and said, "To Kate, my future bride."

Buckland lifted his snifter, and glasses clinking together. "To Kate. And, to your happiness." The brandy tasted suddenly bitter in his mouth.

Chapter Fourteen

Kate crossed the meadow behind the manor, which led to the gently rising ground of Knott Hill, her steps light, her walking dress of a fine flowered cambric teasing her ankles. She could not suppress the light feeling that floated about her soul. She was free of her wretched, despicable pursuit of Ashwell. Free! She picked up her skirts and headed up the side of the hill. Her sandals slipping now and then, but she did not care.

Once inside the beechwood, she removed her chip hat, letting it dangle beside her as she held the rose-coloured ribbons. She had not realized until this morning, when she woke up at the unbelievably late hour of ten o'clock, how much of a burden her schemes to win the poet had been upon her. But now, life had lost some of its wretched weight and nothing, indeed nothing, could rob her of her joyous spirit.

As she reached the top of the hill, she began to descend on the other side that opened up toward Quening. Reaching the edge of the wood and plucking a ripened bramble berry from a straggling vine, Kate noticed for the first time the large barren patches among the fields. Labourers moved slowly in waves along the remainder of the field, swinging their scythes, the women following behind and tying up the sheaves in quick, strong movements.

Looking at the berry that was dusty and small, Kate realized what torture the countryside had had to endure this summer, and a little of her joy seeped from her heart.

She heard a rustling sound behind her, and as she turned to

see who had arrived to bear her company, she saw no one, only a kestrel springing from its home high in the woods to begin its hunting flight over the fields. Kate watched it float in the blue sky, its sharp eyes searching for a field mouse or a sparrow; certainly it was a farmer's blessing. The kestrel paused, then descended rapidly upon a small creature hidden in the dry stubble of the harvested portion of the field.

Kate wanted to congratulate the blue-tailed bird on its conquest, and she wished for a moment that she were attired not in her new walking dress but in her riding habit, the train tucked up in her makeshift belt and her fowling piece weighted on her shoulder. With a laugh, Kate suddenly realized that she no longer needed to keep up the pretense of being a refined gentlewoman and, lifting her skirts, dashed around in a mad frenzy of circles.

Kate stopped, gasping for breath as she looked down at the soft fine cambric of her skirts and smoothed her hands along the empress folds of the gown. How velvety the fabric felt and how pretty the gown. With a start, she realized that all she had done in the past few weeks—the creation of an entire wardrobe, her involvement in soirees and balls and alfresco parties—had changed her life forever, had introduced her to some of the real pleasures of womanhood that she had not known before. She remembered a verse of scripture: *And her clothing is fine linen and purple.* Kate again looked over the fields at Quening and her eye drifted beyond the small village, travelling the River Avenlode as it wended its way through Stinchfield and Todbury.

Kate heard another sound behind her and whirled about. "Who is it?" she cried. Someone was there, she was certain of it, and a small gripping fear began growing in the pit of her stomach. She began moving toward Chipping Fosseworth, running down the ivy-covered path at a decided trot, when footfalls behind her sent a shock of fear through her heart. As she spun around to face her pursuer, Lord Sapperton's quiet laughter turned her rising panic to rage as he asked, "Have I frightened the brave, stalwart Miss Draycott?"

Kate was so angry with him that she stopped and cried, "What are you doing here? You never go beyond your lands."

He approached her and said, "How pretty you look among all this forest green."

He looked paler than Kate remembered and she frowned at him as she turned away. "I am going home. It is not seemly that I should be alone with you."

He clicked his tongue and caught up with her, his coat of blue superfine loose upon his thin frame. "You kiss Buckland and seek out as many opportunities as you can to be alone with him, and then you dare to cavil at being alone with me?"

Kate felt her cheeks burn but did not answer him as she hurried down the path. But he moved just as quickly beside her and had no difficulty in matching her pace.

"Ah, I see that I have caused you some mortification. How ungentlemanly of me." And he laughed, catching her arm and forcing her to stop. Pulling her toward him, he said, "I've come to these woods for you, Katherine. I've been waiting for you . . . for days now. I know that you traverse the countryside without your maid." And he laughed at her, his crooked teeth stained. "The woods hide much and no one ventures here; even if they did, my consequence would put them to flight."

Kate looked into Sapperton's small black eyes and saw a film cloud his vision. She did not want to be near him, his absent eyes frightening her more than the grip he had on her arms. As he leaned down to kiss her, Kate strove to free her arms, twisting this way and that and kicking at his shins. But his top boots of fine leather protected his legs and he merely laughed at her, his hands tightening about her arms until she cried out in pain. "What do you want from me?"

"You are speaking absurdities. You know what I want and now I mean to make certain of my ends. What man would have a woman defiled?" He kissed her lightly, his lips cold against her mouth, and continued, "You are mine, Katherine. You've no dowry and I hold the mortgages on the manor lands. But before you regale me with your scheme of winning Lord Ashwell, let me assure you that our famous poet will not have you."

He did not let her speak but pressed his mouth on hers, cold, hard, hurting, and Kate struggled wildly against his viselike grip. But the more she fought him, the more violent his responses were as he pulled on her hair, jerking her head back and kissing her again.

Forcing her against a beech tree, the bark scraping her back through the thin cambric of her flowered gown, Kate felt his bony legs and hips and ribs against the length of her own body. A wave of nausea flowed over her as one hand covered her breast and his intentions became clear.

"Have you found a wood-nymph, Sapperton?"

Kate heard Buckland's voice, full of anger and sarcasm, and she felt dizzy with relief. As the earl jumped away from her, she fell forward slightly and dropped to the leaf-littered path, the strong smell of damp humus cleansing her nostrils from the earl's sickly odor. She looked up at Buckland, who was astride his black stallion and smiled faintly.

"You time your entrances ill."

Buckland laughed, a derisive laugh. "How very like you to remind me of something that I had long forgotten."

As Buckland dismounted, Sapperton stepped back, the heels of his boots colliding with a moss-ridden log, partially concealed by ivy. He stumbled slightly and, regaining his balance, straightened his shoulders. "I doubt that you have forgotten a single detail of that assignation."

Buckland ignored this taunt and said, "I have waited a long time for this moment," he said, his blue eyes fixed upon Sapperton's thin, lined face.

He advanced on the earl and threw him several punches, only to have Sapperton fend each one off and land a fist across his cheek. Kate watched as the two men, now struggling with each other, wrestled with hands and legs entwined in fierce twistings and pullings. Together they fell, rolling over the log, breaking apart and circling one another, their bodies curled like two bristling dogs.

Sapperton caught Buckland behind his leg with his foot and Buckland fell, rolling over to right himself immediately. Kate watched them move, dancing almost among the ivy, and she rose to her feet, moving to stand behind a beech tree. And almost as quickly as she moved, Buckland landed a hard punch to Sapperton's jaw and sent him flying against the tree.

Buckland stood a few feet away, his chest heaving as he bent over to regain his breath.

The earl wiped blood from his mouth and cried out, "You bastard!"

"That was for Amelia." And he pounced on the earl, who again caught his arm and struggled with him, both men trying to force the other back, their faces red and grimacing, each intent on vanquishing the other. Again they fell together, rolling onto the ground, grunting and gasping for air, bits of dead leaves, ivy, and moss clinging to their coats.

Buckland's horse whinnied and shied at the unexplained motion, and twice he sidled a few feet up the path. Kate followed the horse and, catching his bridle, talked in a flow of soothing words to the nervous stallion. Standing apart from the men, holding the bridle and patting the horse's neck, Kate watched the battle that seemed to have more to do with some past affair than with her.

Sapperton appeared to be tiring and Buckland, having pinned him in a wrestling position, released him. The earl rose to his feet and feigned walking away, then turned swiftly to catch Buckland across the side of the head, sending him backward a few steps. His black eyes blazed as though some demon had hold of him, and Kate could not comprehend where, in his thin frame, resided the strength to fight a man as strong as Buckland.

Kate watched in surprise as Sapperton stumbled several times toward her, his maniacal, frenzied prowess ebbing with each step he took. He moved in wayward steps past her, as though not seeing her, holding his arm across his chest, his face red from exertion.

Buckland was about to pounce upon him but Kate cried out, suddenly afraid that he would kill the earl.

As she cried, Sapperton whirled adroitly, letting Buckland's momentum, fatigued as he was, work for him. Catching him in the stomach and knocking the air from him, the earl did not remain to inflict further injury but turned instead immediately up the path toward his estate.

Kate ran to Buckland, who jerked away from her touch as she reached down to caress the bruise forming on his cheek.

"Leave me be!" he gasped, his breath returning to him.

"Buckland," Kate said in a firm tone as she looked down at him. "Don't be foolish. Let me look at your face."

He sat up, taking in a big gulp of air, and said, "I do not need your mercies, Miss Draycott."

Kate sat back on her heels and frowned. "I know you are still quite angry with me, but—" And here she broke off, the shock of what might have befallen her had Buckland not come along now settling in on her. Her voice caught as she pressed her hands against her cheeks that suddenly burned with fear. "What would have become of me had you not happened by?"

"I do not know, nor do I care. But that is a matter, I am certain, that you should undoubtedly discuss with James."

His voice was so cutting as he rose to his feet and touched his cheekbone carefully to see if it was bleeding that Kate remained where she was for a moment, looking blindly at crushed ivy and scattered leaves. She said quietly, "Thank you."

He had walked a few feet away. He meant to leave her but at these words spoken quietly, scarcely audible against the chattering of the birds overhead, he turned around and said sarcastically, "Thank you? Oh, you are most welcome, Miss Draycott. And is there anything else I might do for you? I've already provided you with a husband and now saved your virtue. Perhaps I could give you a decent dowry and build a mill for you at Chipping Fosseworth."

Kate looked back at him, frowning. "Are you all right? I think you've taken to raving! You are mad!"

He shouted at her, "I am mad! Mad! Mad as hellfire, you witch! What have you done, casting a spell over James! And now Sapperton? You are a witch!" He stood before her and grasped her neck with his fingers. "I shall have the villagers try you by ordeal. We shall first throw you into the pond, and if you float, we'll flail you alive! How dare you cast your spell over my friend. My friend! You damnable witch!"

Kate wached him, her eyes wide with fear, his hands gripping her neck. Then he kissed her hard and long. She could not help herself, and she placed her hands on his arms and gripped him fiercely, her nails digging into his coat sleeves. His mouth played with hers, his anger becoming a passion that overtook her senses, drowning her. She would not even float as she succumbed to the ordeal of his lips, the searching, painful movement of his lips against hers.

He pulled away from her abruptly and stared at her first as though he were not seeing her. Then, when his vision cleared, his handsome face grew twisted with anger. His voice was derisive. "And yet you will give your kisses to me? Did you give them to Sapperton as well? Perhaps I should not have prevented his advances!"

Kate could not believe what he was saying. She lifted her arm to strike him across his bruised cheek, but he caught her arm and shoved it back at her. His voice was full of disgust as he said, "No, I've had enough fighting for one morning." And he turned away from her, striding toward his horse. She wanted to tell him the truth, but she was so angry at his cruel words that she kept her silence, hoping he was suffering as she suffered.

But as he mounted his horse and disappeared through the thick trees of Quening Woods, Kate suddenly felt very small and alone.

Having driven over to Stinchfield, Kate left her rather worn whiskey at the George Inn and walked down the High Street, heading toward the draper's shop. As she traversed the flagways, a noisy group of labourers emerged from the ancient Bell Inn and began tottering down the street, all a trifle bosky. Kate picked up her steps to keep out of their path, reaching the shop before she encountered what appeared to be a raucous, discontented group of field workers.

A large woman, wearing a dress of brown drape and a stiff white apron, approached her and said, "How are ye, Miss Draycott? I've not seen ye here in some time."

Kate smiled at the woman and, turning toward the window that overlooked the street, said, "There are so many people about, Mrs. Hobson. How is this? I've never seen Stinchfield so full of labouring men."

Mrs. Hobson nodded, her hands clasped tightly in front of her. "That man Hunt came through yesterday, only fer a short time, but I think some of his own people stayed. They've talked and talked to the rabble—for I'll call them labourers what don't tend to their business nothing short of rabble—and got them all stirred up. Such drinking and shouting, at all hours of the night. I'm feared in me bed."

When the group of men passed by the shop on the other side of the street, Kate turned back to the large kind woman and, taking a deep breath, said, "I feel quite foolish, given the difficulties that many of these unfortunate people are facing, for I have come for a loo-mask, if you've such a thing."

Mrs. Hobson broke into a broad smile. "Miss Moreton and Miss Cerney was in here only an hour since begging for the same thing. Ye'll be 'appy to know that since I heard of the ball, I sent Will, my second son, ye know, to Cheltenham for a supply of them. I've also a nice selection of dominoes, one in a deep violet, wat might become yer fair skin and copper-coloured hair, if ye be needin' sech an item." She paused for a moment and, hoping to persuade Kate, added, "Miss Moreton purchased one—a rose domino."

Kate pursed her lips and said curtly, "I shall need a mask only, thank you. A simple black mask of silk."

Mrs. Hobson opened a box of masks, some embroidered with flowers or sewn with pearls and paste diamonds. The shopkeeper tried a different tack. "Of course I was a little surprised when Miss Moreton purchased a plain black mask as well."

Kate glanced sharply at the woman, who stared back at her with seemingly innocent eyes. And after shaking her head at Mrs. Hobson, she selected a very simple black mask.

Mrs. Hobson sighed. She would have to beat William for choosing so many extravagant masks. Just then the door opened and Mrs. Cricklade entered the shop with Charity in tow.

Kate, looking at the variety of rather gaudy masks, said quietly, "All is not lost, Mrs. Hobson, for I know that Mrs. Cricklade has a penchant for diamonds—paste or otherwise."

Mrs. Hobson smiled and shook her head. Miss Draycott was always a young miss what was fly to the time of day. Chuckling

281

softly to herself, she wrapped up the ordinary mask and gave it to Miss Draycott.

After greeting Mrs. Cricklade and her daughter, Kate received the parcel wrapped in brown paper and was about to quit the shop when shouting erupted across the street. Moving to the window, Kate pushed back a fall of window lace to better see what was transpiring, and Mrs. Cricklade took up a prominent position next to her. "Oh, my word, my heavens, what is going forward? What are those vulgar, brutish men about?"

Charity cried, "Do move aside, Mama. I can see nothing."

Mrs. Cricklade, her nose nearly pressed against a window-pane, said sweetly, "Charity, my pet, you should not speak to me in such a disrespectful manner, and quit pushing. For heaven's sake, child, find your own window."

Kate said, "Those servants—the two that the others seem to be harassing—work at Leachwood."

Mrs. Cricklade cried, "Leachwood? Those are Lord Sapperton's servants? Impossible! Merciful heavens, what has this town come to when a nobleman's servants are accosted in the streets?"

Feeling her chest tighten, Kate held her package to her breast and said, in a stifled voice, "He mistreats his people."

Charity, her voice breaking, said, "It is just like the revolution in France. The whole countryside will break into riots. I do hope they will not set up a guillotine!"

Mrs. Cricklade thumped her shoulder. "Stupid girl. Who ever heard of such a thing!" She ruined this attempt at consoling her daughter by turning to Kate, her hazel eyes enormous with fear. "Oh, do you think they would, Katherine?" She fingered her bright red hair. "And I've just had my new French maid touch up these—oh, I mean, I would not care at all to die in such a truly vulgar fashion!"

Kate looked at her, at the wrinkles about her eyes, at the powder flaked on her cheeks, and she could not help smiling. "I daresay it will not come to that."

Mrs. Cricklade dabbed at her eyes with a wisp of a lace handkerchief. "I only hope you may be right."

The shouting grew louder and the labourers began pushing

the earl's servants. Mrs. Hobson said, "I suppose you know that his lordship ha' closed the flour mill."

All three women stared at her in astonishment, and even Charity, whose understanding of the world was not profound, said, "But how will the poor people make their bread? Most of them have only the gleanings after a crop is harvested and they rely upon the miller's kindness to grind their flour. Why, they cannot afford to buy bread from the baker. Already the cost of bread has nearly doubled!"

Kate knew that Sapperton had closed the mill for a purpose, and she clutched the brown parcel to her chest. Staring at the men as they continued shouting at the earl's servants, she felt unable to move. He had done this thing to torment her, to try to force her hand. She knew how his mind worked and that she had but to agree to marry him and he would reopen the mill. For though Buckland had interrupted his schemes in Quening Woods, Sapperton would not let that stop him.

As a variety of curious people began emerging from the nearby shops, traffic slowing on the High Street, a constable astride a large brown horse galloped toward the men, waving a long stick and striking them across their backs. One of the labourers, completely foxed, grabbed the stick and was about to pull the constable from his seat when Roger and Emmet weaved through a growing bottleneck of vehicles, calling to the men to disband at once. Seeing that one of Lord Whiteshill's sons had arrived, most of the men backed away as the earl's servants picked themselves up from the flagway and brushed off their breeches. But one of the labourers still held onto the constable's stick and stumbled about, holding on fast, as though he had a large trout at the end of the pole.

Kate heard Emmet cry, "You there, let go at once!"

The man was not able to comprehend much in his inebriated state. He only knew that he was holding onto a stick of some sort and that if he let go, he would fall on his arse. Kate put a hand to her mouth, trying not to laugh. She hoped that no one would get hurt. Fortunately, the man's friends came to his assistance and unwrapped his hands from the constable's makeshift lance.

But he did not welcome their help with gratitude as he shook them off and stared wildly at the earl's servants. He walked several feet away from all of them and turned to shout, "Ye be no friends of mine. Ye sleep wi ta devil Sapperton!"

But his friends were indeed loyal to him and, ignoring his curses, dragged him bodily away from the constable and the crowd that had begun to gather about them. In less than two minutes, all signs of a disturbance on the street had disappeared. The carriages began moving up and down the High Street and everyone returned to their respective shops.

Roger and Emmet continued up the street, Charity argued with her mother over whether to purchase the pearl-laden mask or the one embroidered with flowers, and Mrs. Hobson, pleased with their delight over the loo-masks, decided to give her darling Will a shilling for having had such remarkable foresight. Only Kate remained at the window, her package still at her breast.

In a moment, she shook off the despondency that seemed to strangle her chest and she left the shop without bidding her friends good-bye. Slowly, she returned to The George, clutching her reticule and brown package against her stomach as she retraced her steps along the flagways. She tried to keep a growing fear from rising to her throat and escaping her in a loud cry. What now was she to do? James and Buckland would soon leave Chipping Fosseworth forever. And where would Sapperton stop in his pursuit of her?

But more than this, she would never know Buckland's love. He had loved once. He had loved a heartless female whose name she despised—Amelia. And somehow Sapperton had known her, too. Suddenly she blamed Amelia, for though she did not know the details, she could still imagine from the little James had told her that Buckland had been hurt deeply by an insensitive grasping woman who played upon hearts as Julia did. Perhaps that was why Buckland had seemed so angry with her own pursuit of James. She turned into the George and realized she had not said her farewells to Mrs. Cricklade and Charity. They would think her quite uncivil.

As she waited for her light whiskey to be brought around, Kate still clutched her reticule and brown-wrapped package as though they kept her from falling to pieces. She looked out the window and saw a fiery black horse pass by, Buckland's tall, manly figure astride. What a feeling of desperation overtook her and tears smarted her eyes. "Buckland," she whispered beneath her breath. How she loved him! She wanted to race from the inn and call after him, but what would she say? And she did not want to look into his accusing eyes. Would that she had never set her cap for James.

One of the labourers entered The George and she watched him, the corners of his mouth worn into a perpetual frown—a frown of fighting poverty every day—as he disappeared into the tavern. She had little more than that man now. And she had given up twenty thousand pounds a year because she was deeply and irrevocably in love with a rogue.

Kate entered the ballroom at Leachwood, her brown eyes sparkling behind her loo-mask that covered her nose. She released Jaspar's arm when he shook it slightly. His words did not surprise her as he reached up to take off his own mask. "Confounded nuisance! Don't know why you drug me here! Where's that damned servant with the champagne?" And he left her to go in search of anyone who might wish to get up a game of cards.

She watched him walk through the dimly lit ballroom, and she could not resist smiling as he hitched up his Roman toga, exposing his top boots below the white and gold linen robe.

Tonight she would enjoy herself. Tonight James promised to tell Buckland the truth. And tonight she intended to do everything she could to win Buckland.

The room buzzed with chatter as everyone present tried to determine who was who. There wasn't a person there who was not dressed in an elaborate costume except for an easily recognizable Stephen Barnsley, who wore only the hip boots and cape of a French Musketeer. He wore the boots over his buckskin breeches, and his cape looked quite at odds with a loosely tied belcher kerchief. He had not even bothered with a broad plumed hat. So like Stephen, who hated such events.

As she stepped into the room, James, sporting the Elizabethan clothing and pointed beard of The Bard himself, greeted her by taking both hands in his and raising her ungloved fingers to his lips. In a whisper, he said, "Hallo, dearest Kate."

"Am I so easily recognized, then?" she cried, finding it a little difficult to turn her head because of the frilled and starched white ruff about her neck.

He smiled at her. How full of life his smile appeared to Kate. He seemed free and joyful somehow as he tucked her arm in his and said, "I fear it is your auburn hair. And yet, had you worn a wig, I still would have known you, for only Kate Draycott enters a room"—and he paused, his brown eyes twinkling—"with such majesty."

Kate slapped his arm with a fan, the heavy velvet of her costume a weight on her arms. She was perspiring already, the late summer's evening quite warm, and she began fanning herself as she said, "I don't know that I've ever heard you joke before, Lord Ashwell."

Some of the light fell from James's eyes as he responded, "I wish you wouldn't call me Lord Ashwell, and I wasn't joking entirely." And taking her arm, he began propelling her about the room. As they walked by Lord Sapperton, whose height and thinness were accentuated by his costume of knightly mail, the small metal links shimmering in the soft candlelight, James continued, "For I have always thought that you have a certain commanding presence, no doubt learned from so many hours in the saddle, that is only heightened by your queenly costume."

Kate had never thought of herself in those terms. She felt generally quite inadequate in social settings and responded lightly, "You are in your altitudes."

And then James laughed, a loud, happy sound that came from deep within his chest, and Kate looked at him as though she did not know him. "I cannot credit my ears, Lord Ashwell—"

He interrupted her, "Please do not call me that ever again. My name is James."

"James, I've never heard you laugh before. Not like this. What has happened?"

But she soon realized that James was not attending to her.

His eyes were intent upon the figure of a rather short female, whose brown hair was gathered into an unusual halo of curls, sitting in ringlets upon her shoulders and cascading down her back. The sprightly costume was a veritable flight of thin triangles of an extremely delicate muslin, shaping an outfit that appeared to float when she walked or moved.

Kate did not at first recognize who on earth had worn so exquisite a disguise. She thought that were the hair not light brown, so pretty a picture would most certainly be Julia. And then with a start, the water-nymph—for she wore a seashell on a strand of pearls about her neck—turned to face them, and Kate saw at once that Mary inhabited the nymph's gossamer costume.

"Oh, how lovely!" Kate cried. "It is Mary!" And as they approached her, Kate glanced up at James and saw a momentary expression fleet across his pale features, a certain affection softening his eyes, even though they were nearly hidden behind a mask, that gave her pause. James and Mary.

Mary greeted them both and looked up at James with so sweet a smile that Kate took a startled step backward. What a fool she had been! Mary loved James and she remembered, as though her mind had hidden each moment until now, all of Mary's quiet, furtive motions in the last few weeks that had said she loved him.

Kate glanced up at the poet, who was exclaiming his praise of Mary's costume, and she saw love reflected in his smile as well. For a moment she felt faint with the knowledge that her own selfish stupidity might have separated her dearest friend from an only love forever. She knew Mary. Mary would never have spoken a word.

Buckland scanned the ballroom, alive with unusual colours and shapes from the various costumes, as some fifteen couples started a sedate country dance. Taking a pinch of snuff, he felt a little warm in his long boots, short black wig, and plumed hat, and the black and gold velvet doublet made him sweat. He had travelled to Leachwood in a hired coach separately from James and had even toyed with the idea of going on to Cheltenham.

But as he neared Quening, he had thought of Kate and wanted to see her once more. He had already told James that business would take him shortly back to London for a month or two. A lie, of course, but for some reason he could not bear the thought of watching the happy couple smile into each other's eyes for weeks on end.

As his gaze drifted over the long chamber bedecked with palms and ferns, he saw James, dressed as Shakespeare, laughing at something a female dressed as a nymph was saying to him. Most likely Julia, as he scanned the delicate costume. And next to James, her regal profile also regarding the nymph, was Kate. He knew her immediately because of Maggie's pointed description of her costume. But even if he had been ignorant of the details, he would have known Kate anywhere, for the queenly appearance of a long, slender waist and the carriage of a noblewoman had always belonged to her, even if she rode a horse like a bedlamite or spent her mornings hunting. He watched James talking with her and the nymph. He watched Kate smile at his friend, a laughing, tender smile, and suddenly his eyes were opened and he understood himself. He loved Kate! He loved the damned, scheming wench! And nothing she could do, however ignoble, would ever change that.

He stood as if in a trance, watching her, letting his eyes rove over her dark green costume that hugged her breasts and small waist and cascaded from her hips. And he would never know her, never again feel his arms about her, about that waist, nor feel the soft round curves of her breasts beneath his hands, nor rest his head on her breasts and let her life restore his own.

He moved to circle the three of them, watching Kate all the while. He could not believe what he was feeling. He wanted to remove the ruff from about her slender neck and kiss her there and tell her that he loved her, the he wanted her. How long had it been since he had felt anything for a woman beyond a mere fleeting passion? Not since Amelia had his heart been so full of an intense desire to possess a woman, as she had possessed his heart.

But Kate belonged to James.

A voice drifted to him, coming from behind. A low, quiet

voice, a man's voice, hollow and cruel. "So, *Mr. Buckland*, you enjoy a good masquerade, I see. And what will she say, I wonder, to your masquerade?" He laughed and moved on, brushing Buckland's shoulder in a taunting fashion as he passed by him.

Buckland held his rising anger in check. He would not let Sapperton goad him, and if the earl should choose to reveal their terrible duplicity, then so be it. He looked back at Kate and found her eyes fixed on him, her beautiful liquid brown eyes that glinted behind her mask. How easy it would be to make the woman his mistress. Except that he loved James as a dear brother and he would never cause his friend to be cuckolded.

Kate met Buckland's flashing gaze, his blue eyes sparkling behind his black silk mask. How handsome he was tonight and how well the costume became him. Even wearing the wig and hat draped with a white ostrich feather, he looked not in the least a dandy, as Rupert did wearing a lavender doublet. Instead, power seemed to emanate from every aspect of Buckland's frame, the cape, tied over one shoulder and slung down about his waist, giving an impression of movement, as a man fleeing on horseback. And his hip boots, with a thick band as they folded over, reaching down to the tops of his knees, seemed only to emphasize his powerful thighs and made Kate long for things she dared not even form into coherent thoughts. How she loved him and how much she had missed his company as on the trip to Tewkesbury, and his teasing, and his enjoyment of the very things she enjoyed. But he was a rogue, after all, and all that he had to his name was a mill in desperate need of repair.

For a moment, as she regarded him, she wondered if she could be his mistress. His gaze finally released her as he turned abruptly and made his way to a group of young bucks gathered about a bowl of rum punch—Sapperton's well-received gentlemanly contribution to his masquerade. Could she set aside every convention, every right mode of behaviour that, though she flaunted some of society's conventions, still comprised her set of values? . . . And to live with a man in an unwedded state was a terrible thing. Only the most wanton of females did so.

She could not tear her gaze from him as he drank down a hurried glass of punch, meeting her eyes every now and then with no smile to warm her heart. What if, when he knew of her false engagement, he asked her to become his mistress?

The country dance ended and the earl's voice, as it silenced the chatter that flew about the ballroom, drew her attention away from Buckland. Sapperton announced that the unmasking would take place at midnight and that a prize would be awarded to the person who had carried off his costume to such effect that no one guessed his identity. With an odd, knowing smile, he said that he already knew who the winner was! Everyone talked in a swell of wonderment that subsided when he continued, "You will all be so surprised that I am sorely tempted to unveil the person now. . . ." And he let his eyes rove over the assembled guests.

Kate could feel the excitement about her and frowned as she glanced at the assembled guests, for she knew who everyone was. There was no one whom she did not recognize. Not believing herself to possess a truly extraordinary intelligence, she addressed Mary, "Who can it be, do you think?"

Mary glanced at James and then at her, stumbling over her words, "Oh, I don't—that is, I haven't the least notion."

Aware that Mary knew something that she did not, Kate tweaked her arm gently and cried, "Oh, do tell me, Mary. Who can it be, for I have studied all of these costumes and there isn't one that I do not recognize."

Mary blushed and again stammered, "Oh, Kate! You've—you've mistaken me! I have no idea who the winner could possibly be!" And she again glanced nervously at James.

Kate cried, "What a rapper!"

James narrowed his eyes at Mary and said, "I do think that you and I should dance the next dance. Would you do me the honour?"

Even in the dimly lit room, Kate could not mistake her friend's reaction. At first an expression of alarm overtook Mary's close-set blue eyes, and then a wave of pleasure flowed over her countenance that made her positively glow. She answered the poet, "As you wish, James."

The orchestra, brought all the way from Cheltenham, picked up their instruments and, after a few moments tuning, struck up a wonderful waltz that set the entire younger portion of the dancers to squealing and exclaiming with delight. Sapperton's masquerade would no doubt be talked of for years to come.

Kate felt a hand on her shoulder as James moved away with Mary, and she whirled about to stare into Buckland's face. He said, "I am surprised that James has deserted you for the nymph. You ought to be offended."

Kate, her heart suddenly sitting in her throat, could scarcely make herself heard and said, "Do you mean Mary? I should never be offended that James should dance with my dearest friend."

And without as much as a by-your-leave, he led her onto the ballroom floor. Kate glided into his arms as easily as if she had tumbled from her bed. She loved him, loved his strong arm about her back and the way he led her about the floor, whirling to the music, his hand guiding her through the firmest pressure, his steps sure, his manner all that she could ever want.

Time stopped as the violins and bass viols, the flutes and oboes, played their clear, marked rhythms and the dancers in the half-light, hiding behind their masks, smiled and laughed and did not care for a few moments if every word spoken was entirely proper. And if a kiss or two was stolen on the terrace, this was, after all, a masquerade. Kate felt caught, too, gazing into eyes that seemed dark pools in which most assuredly she would drown were she to once let herself step into them. Buckland. Why did life have to be so unfair?

When the dance ended and he bowed to her, Kate thought that he opened his mouth to say something, his eyes intent, but Kit Barnsley, having imbibed a little too much of the punch, caught her about the waist and marched her back onto the floor as a country dance took up where the waltz had left off. And afterward Stephen danced with her, also a little bosky, then Emmet, James, and even Sir William, saying that he had always wanted to dance with Queen Elizabeth, made up part of a quadrille with her.

The hours floated one into the other until the clock chimed a quarter hour to midnight and James claimed her for a second dance, saying that he thought midnight might be an appropriate time for revealing to Buckland that they had been taking part in their own little masquerade.

Kate said, with a sudden urgency, as she saw Buckland leave the ballroom floor having danced with Julia, "Pray, James, let us tell him now. I—I can't bear this deception any longer. I despise deception. You don't know how terrible I felt all those weeks when I had set my cap for you." As they moved toward Buckland, she stopped him for a moment, her hand lightly on his sleeve and said, "You've been a true friend to me, Lord Ashwell, and I shall never forget how easily you forgave me for my imperfect motives."

Kate watched as James's face took on something of a reddish hue, and because part of his face was concealed by his mask, for a moment she thought he was angry with her. But when he coughed and said hastily, as Buckland approached them, "Remember to ask George how he earns his living, for it is most important," she realized he was embarrassed.

Kate suddenly had the feeling that something was very wrong. She wanted to ask James what he meant but Buckland was upon them, and Mary also, at that moment, walked up.

James said simply, "George, Kate and I have decided to unmask now. We are not at all engaged but only pretended to be, so that I might have the pleasure of besting you just once."

Kate watched Buckland pale. She had never seen him pale and the most unusual light brightened his blue eyes as he took off his mask, staring at her as though he had never seen her before. An almost overwhelming feeling of hope surged up within Kate's breast. Did he love her? Was this the expression of a man in love? He was about to speak when the clock began chiming the hour and the entire ballroom became a rush of noise as the orchestra played unison notes in time with the great oak clock, and the midnight hour burst upon the assembled company. A cry went up and everyone began removing their masks. And Kate, her gaze fixed on Buckland's face, slowly untied the strings of her mask, her heart aching unbearably. Was it truly possible? Did he love her?

Buckland stretched out his arm toward Kate but James caught it and, addressing his friend, said, "You are not angry with me?" his voice nearly shouting in the general commotion of the excited ballroom.

Buckland laughed and shook his head. "Angry? No, how could I be angry when you have just given me back my life." He then searched James's eyes and said, "I would not have known otherwise."

James replied, "I thought not, but my motives were not so kind." He laughed, "I only wanted to see you squirm."

Buckland again reached toward Kate but a strange silence had suddenly descended upon the crowd. Kate turned to see that a path had formed in a direct line from the earl to Buckland and James. As she looked about her, she noticed that everyone seemed bewildered at what Sapperton was doing.

She, too, felt considerably bemused when the earl, bearing a large basket of flowers, breads, spices, and coffees, walked toward Buckland and said, "Yes, for the very best masquerade, though I find the costume rather indifferent, actually, I hereby award the prize to Lord Ashwell!"

Kate was mystified as to what Sapperton was about. Why was he presenting the basket to Buckland, and why did James step away from Buckland as though he were bowing out gracefully from some contest?

Chapter Fifteen

James and Buckland exchanged a glance of resignation and Kate heard Jaspar cry, "Confound it! I know who Ashwell is supposed to be. That playwright. Oh, blast, what is his name? Wrote *Hamlet* and all that other nonsense."

A general cry rose up about Sapperton as complaints rolled in from every quarter. Why was the earl giving the basket to Mr. Buckland, and what did he mean by Ashwell's costume being indifferent? And as for the masquerade not being recognizable, why, it was quite obvious to everyone that Lord Ashwell had come as Shakespeare, pointed beard and all!

Kate felt Mary's hand grasp her own, and when she looked down at her friend, she saw such pity in Mary's eyes that she knew again a very odd sensation that something was terribly wrong. She shook her head, feeling very confused.

As Kate glanced at Buckland, then at James and again at Mary, suddenly everything began happening in a slow marked time, as though regular time had ceased and what remained was the frightening quality of a nightmare that one could not escape.

Again she felt Mary grip her hand hard as the earl pressed the basket, not upon James but upon Buckland. The room was a fog of muffled noise, and the air grew so stifling that Kate thought she might faint, her heavy velvet gown a dull weight to her ankles.

Buckland's smile disturbed her as he took the basket and bowed to the earl. What was it that Sapperton was saying, and

294

why did he turn to look at her with so smug an expression? "I present the real Lord Ashwell. The best masquerade, lasting longer than six weeks and taking place among all our fair little villages and manors and estates. All under our noses. And I would not have guessed myself, save that my acquaintance with Ashwell has been one of long-standing." He bowed in a sardonic fashion to Buckland and added, "Ten years, in fact."

Kate made out only snatches of words—masquerade, noses, acquaintance, Ashwell."

She looked at Buckland, the sound of the crowd gasping in disbelief. He caught her eyes and smiled in a perfectly rueful manner, mouthing the words, "I'm sorry."

Mary's hand hurt her, and as she looked down at her friend she also knew that Mary had known for quite some time this unbearable truth. She looked at James, who wore a sheepish expression. She could hear his words, "Forgive me, Kate."

Kate shook her head in mute disbelief. It could not be true. It could not! George was an impoverished rogue, a cloth mill-owning rascal who had kissed her and flirted with her and cut her with his sword and swore that she would never marry Ashwell. Her thoughts stopped as though a brick had just split open her head. He . . . was . . . Ashwell!

The beginnings of applause mixed with laughter flowed throughout the ballroom, along with exclamations that all of it had been a great joke. Who, then, was James? James Montrose, friend and aspiring poet? Who would have guessed? Everyone crowded around Buckland, for which Kate felt an immense gratitude. She did not wish to speak with him and he had twice reached for her. She had heard him call to her, the usual rich timbre of his voice sounding strained and panicked through the thick haze of her reeling emotions. She would not speak to him! The scoundrel!

And the crowd all made noises that they had known, of course, it was true. All along this one or that one had guessed the truth, and Kate felt sickened by it.

Mary, still holding her hand, said, "I only wish that I had said something. I am sorry, Kate."

Kate looked down at her, feeling stricken to her core that life had just dealt her some great final blow, some terrible ironic twist that would leave her scarred forever. "What does it matter?" And she withdrew her hand from Mary's, looking at the crowd forming about Buckland and James, all of whom were demanding to be told the entire truth.

Kate heard Mrs. Cricklade say to Mrs. Moreton, "I always knew that such a man, with such a fine leg, could not be an ordinary sort of person. No, indeed. I always thought he must be the poet, the real poet. Only look at him, so handsome, his blue eyes so sensitive, and he is worth twenty thousand a year! Only I do hope he rids himself of that wretched mill! It is not at all seemly for a man of his station to actually own a mill!"

Kate told a servant to call for her carriage and, in a dazed manner, followed Jaspar into the card room. When he became aware of her presence, he said, "So that is the end of your scheming."

Sir William, following closely behind, entered the card room in time to hear these words, and he knew a desire to call Jaspar out. He looked at Kate, at the stricken pale cast to her face, and wanted to console her, to advise her. Instead, Jaspar continued, his head unclear from having drunk two bottles of port, "You must find someone else then, Kate. That man will never have you."

Kate, embarrassed that her father would speak to her in such a manner in front of Sir William, tried for a light note, saying, "How absurd you are, Papa. I've only come to tell you that I have called for the carriage and will be going home now. I—I have the headache. I'll send Peter Coachman back for you."

"Now, Kate, don't fret yourself," he answered her with a twisted, laughing smile. "Some likely fellow, maybe a musical composer, will come to Chipping Fosseworth tomorrow and you may set your cap for him!" He laughed heartily at his joke.

Had Kate not been so thoroughly sick at heart she would have burned with shame at her father's coarse humour, which made her look so small in the eyes of Sir William. But she was numb and merely bent down to peck a kiss on Jaspar's cheek and quit the room.

Sir William stared down at the man who had married his beloved Marianne and knew so intense a hatred for him that it was all he could do to keep from smashing his face with both fists. "How could you, Jaspar? Can't you see the chit is in love with Ashwell?"

Jaspar's face, his vision a little blurred, turned a fiery, angry hue as he retorted, "You bastard! What right have you to interfere with my daughter!" His eyes blazed as he dared Sir William to answer him.

The baronet checked his anger. "Will you not forget what happened some twenty years ago? And will you continue to punish Kate for it? I beg for your forgiveness, Jaspar. I can do no more. I would have that day undone a hundred times, except for Kate." And he turned on his heel, leaving Jaspar's mouth agape with astonishment.

The two men had never spoken of the matter before.

Ashwell had seen the look on Kate's face, her fair skin taking on a deathly hue. He had hurt her. Terribly. And now he only wanted to speak with her before she left, to tell her that he loved her, that he wished to take on the burdens that had robbed her of her girlhood, that he wished to take her to Italy, to Greece, to the Levant if she wished.

He had seen her enter the card room, and as she came out, he rudely left Mrs. Cricklade in the midst of a speech about how one in his position had a responsibility to throw off his connections with trade forever, then cut Kate off before she could reach the entrance hall.

No one was in the antechamber that connected the drawing room to the hall, and only Jeremy Cricklade and Lydia were in the drawing room, seated at the pianoforte and smiling at each other in a sweet manner.

Ashwell called to Kate and caught her arm, pulling her up short as he forced her back into the wall that separated the antechamber from the entrance hall. "You must hear me out! I never meant for this to go so far. I never meant to hurt you!"

Kate, still numb, stared at Buckland with unseeing eyes. She remembered his cool stance in the barn when she had said that she meant to marry Lord Ashwell. And *he* was Lord Ashwell. How he must have been laughing, amusing himself daily at her expense.

"You are the foulest dungcock that ever walked this earth. My thumb to you!" And she bit her thumb.

He felt as though she had just kicked him hard in the stomach; her words were so vile, so full of hate. "Kate, you can't mean what you say, and where did you ever learn such filth?"

"Will you now," she said, staring with brown eyes ablaze, "correct my manners or my tongue? You who live without a conscience, without a sense of right or wrong? You who live only for your pleasure, for your amusement? And did you find the summer a great amusement? I wonder."

"But—but I wish to marry you," he blurted out, certain that if she knew his intentions now, she would realize he was sorry for not telling her who he was.

Kate laughed at him, her arms folded over her chest. She felt so cold like the statues surrounding them in Sapperton's marbled antechamber, even though the velvet gown had earlier caused her to perspire. "Is that to make everything right? Do you always offer marriage as an ablution for your wrongdoing? Am I now to seize your offer with gratitude? How stupid you are! I refused James when I thought he was Lord Ashwell, so you see your title, your fortune means nothing to me."

"I am not offering my title or my fortune. I am offering myself." Lord Ashwell felt these words some of the finest he had spoken and he waited for his love to fall into his arms. Only she did not appear to be so inclined, her face a hard mask of hatred.

Kate felt an anger blaze in her. Only it was not hot. It was a cold blaze, like a fire built on a ledge of ice that burned but heated nothing around it. "Of all the absurdities," she cried. "that is the best! Your title and fortune, as empty as they are, still I think count for more than *yourself*."

The butler appeared in the doorway and at first backed away, seeing that the couple was in the midst of an indiscreet and extremely heated tête-à-tête, but Kate cried out, "Wait! Is my carriage brought around?"

The answering nod gave Kate reason to push Ashwell away and to follow the servant. Ignoring the viscount's plea for her to remain, to speak with him, to hate him if she liked but to at least listen to all that he wished to say to her, Kate entered her carriage and bid Peter Coachman to set the coach in motion at once. Settling into the squabs, the coach rocking as Peter mounted up into the box, Kate thought of her mother. How much she wished that she were here to advise her, to tell her what to do, to tell her that she would be all right, that in a few months time Buckland—Lord Ashwell—would be but a silly memory and that, together, mother and daughter would laugh heartily over it.

As she glanced back at the colonnade entrance of Leachwood, she saw Sir William standing in the doorway, the light from the entrance hall glowing behind him, a beacon in the dark night yet obscuring the baronet's face. She wondered why Sir William had come to watch her leave.

Kate stood before the long gilt mirror in her bedchamber. She had sent Maggie to bed. She wanted no one with her at this moment. "Fool," she said aloud, the single word echoing about her chamber, her mind hearing a ghostly echo of fool, fool, fool, from the old lavender chair, from her bed, from the prints on the wall, from the bearskin rug on the planked floor.

"But I loved him," she said to the image in the mirror as she placed her hands on the cool glass, seeing the cold image touch her fingers in response. She lifted up each finger in turn, setting it down deliberately again onto the mirror, "But . . . I . . . loved . . . him!"

Pressing her forehead against the mirror, the cold glass biting her heated skin, she closed her eyes and held back a deep, shuddering sob, her throat constricting and causing her such pain that she gasped for breath and swallowed hard. Her fingers balled up into two fists and she beat at the mirror in a short yet harmless rhythm. "I hate him. I hate him."

She saw it all now. Even from the first, in the barn, *Our lives thus entwined*. The poet. She hated him. How could he have done this great evil to her?

She pushed herself away from the heavy mirror and turned to face her bed, her eye catching on the book nearby. His poetry. Ashwell's—Buckland's—poetry. She crossed the room to pick it up and again her throat pulled tightly in on itself. She clutched the book to her bosom, which overflowed the tight lacing of her corset. Ashwell's poetry, his words that had filled her heart and mind for months on end. Buckland, Ashwell. And Sapperton had told her that Buckland wrote poetry.

In a towering passion, she threw the thin volume of verse across the room and it crashed against the mirror, splitting the glass into two jagged parts. Two parts. Ashwell and Buckland.

As she regarded her reflection, she saw a stranger, a woman, a beautiful woman split into two parts. She was truly refined now. She could speak as Julia or Mary spoke. She could walk with grace and speak of other things beside pistols and horses. She could dance and feel almost at ease in society. And where had this part of her lead her but into a terrible morass that she could blame on no one but herself. She had pursued Ashwell. She and she alone would suffer.

Finding it difficult to breathe in the restrictive costume, Kate pulled hard on each sleeve, wrenching the gown from her shoulders. But the buttons were fastened through the narrowest of slits and she could not reach the back of her velvet gown. Crying out in impotence and rage, she tore at the fabric, at the shoulders, and felt the first button give way and then the second and a few more, but not enough for the dress to slip from her arms.

If she could but get the gown off her, she would not hurt so badly, and she began struggling with the heavy dress made up of nine yards of fabric. Twisting about the room in wild, frenzied movements, Kate bumped into her cherrywood dressing table, knocking the empty perfume bottle over, her snakeskin crop rolling onto the floor. But the dress had been stitched by careful fingers and the remaining buttons would not give way, nor would any of the seams. Kate stumbled over a footstool, tumbling to the floor and bruising her knee and her shoulder. How stupid she felt, and being close to the bearskin rug at the end of her bed, she crawled toward it, laughing at her stupidity. And as she reached the rug, she found she could not stop laughing as she recalled every incident where Ashwell had played her for the fool. But the laughter that overtook her somehow opened up a floodgate within her and the tears that she had been fighting the entire evening began flowing quite suddenly. She could not stop them, and the more they poured from her eyes as she buried her face in the thick, coarse fur, the more they came. She pounded her fist against the fur over and over as she cried, and her arm began to ache. She hated Ashwell for doing this to her, and worse! She hated him because she had fallen in love with him.

Awakening the next morning to the throbbing sensation of a world gone awry, Kate did not at first know where she was until she looked at her arm, still half covered with the green velvet gown. She struggled for a moment to sit up, then lowered herself back to the floor. Somehow she had managed to fall asleep, not on the rug but on the hard oak floor. How cool the wood felt against her cheek, but oh, how her head throbbed. From some muffled distance, she heard the strange sound of a cow lowing.

As the long bawling, unhappy sounds of the milch cow kept pulsing into her open window, Kate finally righted herself and, before standing, tried again to remove the gown. As the dress slipped easily from her arms, the buttons scattering across the wood floor, Kate smiled weakly. After all her struggles, she did not even know she had achieved her end.

Standing up, Kate let the gown drop to the floor and untied her strangling corsets.

A series of soft taps sounded on her door and Maggie entered without Kate having given her permission to do so. She bore a tray of food and did not even lift a brow when she saw her mistress standing on the bearskin rug in her undergarments.

Maggie, her dark eyes smiling, said, "Ye look like ye've been caught in one of them fulling machines what hammer at the mills day and night."

"Thank you," Kate answered, her eyes burning and swollen from having cried the night before. She smiled at Maggie as she stepped out of the circle of her stays and the deep green velvet gown piled about her feet.

Setting down the tray of food that she had brought for Kate, the smell of coffee permeating the room as well as fresh-baked bread, Maggie soon had the gown hung up in the wardrobe and the corset tucked away in a dresser drawer.

She then bade her mistress sit before her mirror and began unpinning her dishevelled hair, brushing it in long, slow movements.

Kate closed her eyes, wincing slightly at the first strokes that pulled through the tangles of her auburn hair. But as she grew accustomed to Maggie's hand, she relaxed and thought that with each pull, life began to ebb back into her numbed spirit.

The cow continued to low, and as Kate sat in her chair and sipped her coffee, she asked, "Where is Peter, that our cow must bawl outside the window?"

"He's a fever this morning."

"And why hasn't one of the servants—Thomas, someone—tended to the poor beast?"

Maggie did not meet her gaze in the mirror as she answered airily, "Cook drank too much last night, since you and squire was at Leachwood, and Thomas has the day off. There's just Violet and me. The rest of the labourers are in the middle of the harvest."

"Get help from the village then. One of the women."

Maggie looked shamefaced. "I tried, miss. Truly, but most of the labourers are harvesting the grain, and what two or three remained gave me such grievous answers that I ran from the Swan and Goose. I don't like it, miss. There's something fierce happening hereabouts."

"You mean you could find no one to milk our cow?" Kate asked as she took another sip of the steaming black coffee.

"No one, miss." Maggie pinned up Kate's hair into a tidy knot and, while her mistress began eating a slice of bread and butter, knelt down on her hands and knees and began collecting the green cloth-covered buttons that were still scattered about the floor.

"Then you'll have to milk the cow, or Cook or Violet."

Maggie, who had reached under a small table to retrieve a button, came up so quickly at these words that she knocked her head against the hard oak. Emerging from underneath the table and holding her head with her hand, she cried, "Oh, no, miss. I canna do it. Cows frighten me. I had wanted to work in a dairy once, but I could not get near them fearsome creatures. And—and Violet said she would rather leave this house than milk a cow. And Cook, though I did not want to tell you this, done passed out on the kitchen floor!"

Kate, biting into the fresh bread, stared at it suddenly and said, "Where did you get this, then?" And she lifted the warm bread dripping with butter.

Maggie, still on her hands and knees, said, "What? Oh, that! From the inn."

The cow lowed again, a pitiful crying sound, and Kate set her bread down with a sigh. "Get my muslin gown. What a set of useless females I am surrounded with! And don't think I am not aware what you are about. You know very well that I learned to milk cows when I was a little girl. What a stupid childhood I had, after all. And I used to think it full of many fine things."

Kate leaned her head against the cow's warm side as she pulled in steady rhythms on the soft teats, the milk hitting the side of the wooden pail and streaming into an ever-growing pool of milk. She wondered how it was that she had come to this. She laughed. Last night Queen Elizabeth and this morning a milkmaid. But she couldn't bear to hear the cow suffer, and who would be about this morning to witness her in so ill-bred an activity anyway?

The coarse cow hair tickled her face as she talked softly to the large animal, its tail swishing in response. The day had dawned warm and still, and the men in the fields would be drinking a great deal of weak beer. Her eyes still felt swollen from the night before, and she wondered if Peter had caught anything particularly dangerous, like a dreaded well-fever from bad water. He had three babies at home and such a fever might rob him of his wee 'uns.

She would not think of that but would concentrate instead on the cow's contented breathing, the sides swelling and receding against Kate's puffy face. She smiled suddenly, for she was quite adept at milking, and should she need to seek employment she could always work as a milkmaid. She closed her eyes, the sounds of the farm, of animals chewing their food and rustling their hooves in their stalls, of Miss Diana's whinnies, of birds nesting in one of the windows high above the loft, of the sounds of sheep bleating in the distance, all worked a magic on the raw edge of her emotions. She would melt into these lands. She would become a common labourer and would tend to the animals, muck the stalls, milk the cow, groom the horses and ride them through the fields, into the hills, and the cool wind would soothe her burning face. She had cried too much last night. And her skin burned.

Something didn't feel right, something in the air; something had changed and she snapped her eyes open to stare down at a man's polished, exquisite top boots. They were so shiny, the gleam peaking through just a small amount of dust, that Kate wondered if the gentleman used champagne, as Rupert did, in his blacking. Her thoughts rambled, a strange numbness still keeping her mind from operating clearly.

Ashwell's voice reached her from his tall height as he stood over her. "Where are your servants that you have been forced to milk a cow?"

Kate sighed, answering in a voice that sounded worn-out even to her own ears, "Peter has the fever, Cook has a fuzzy mouth, Maggie would die rather than touch one of these beasts, Thomas has the day off, and Violet considers it beneath her dignity." She looked up at him and, seeing the frown on his face, continued, "And none of the villagers would come. Maggie seems to feel that some mischief is brewing, a riot perhaps."

She leaned her head against the cow, feeling very weary as she continued pulling on the teats. "They ought to riot. They have every reason. There will be very little flour for them to buy, and now that Sapperton has closed the mill near Stinchfield, I don't doubt that many people will face starvation this winter."

When Ashwell entered the barn, Maggie had already told him that Kate was milking a cow. And though he was prepared to see her engaged in this activity, he was a little surprised at the force of his reaction when he walked into the stone barn and saw her seated on a stool and leaning against the brown and white cow. How he loved her! Hay was strewn about her feet and clutching at the hem of her blue gown, sunlight from a high window danced on her auburn hair, and her milk-white skin appeared even paler than the night before. She looked heavy-lidded, as though she had not slept well, and yet her expression was one of mystery, a faraway look. He loved her. And who but Kate Draycott would actually milk a cow? Amelia would have starved first. He loved that Kate did what was necessary, that she shirked no responsibility, that she considered such tasks as her own. He knew in that moment how much he hated London, its insipidities, its concern for gossip and tittle-tattle, for dancing and gaming, for nothing that meant really living. Kate lived. She had tremendous burdens, but not once had she asked for his help or for anyone else's help for that matter. Her only sin—and one for which he had punished her cruelly—was in setting her cap for a man she didn't love.

He looked down at the knot of curls atop her head, also sporting a few wisps of straw, and smiled. And after all was said and done, she still could not go through with her schemes.

James had told him everything. At first he had been piqued that his friend should have used him in such a wretched manner, pretending an engagement, but then he realized that however wrong it was of them both, he had deserved nothing less. He had hounded Kate from the beginning, punished her for Amelia's wrongdoings, not her own, and had even set out to break her heart if he could. And how ironic that in so doing he had been the one caught. Caught in so firm a trap by this female who sat on a stool, smiling into the flank of a cow and pulling firmly on the cow's teats, that he would never be free of his love for her. Faith, but he loved every inch of her.

And he wanted more than anything to take her away from the manor, to take her to Paris, to travel all over Europe—to Italy, to Greece—to share with her every spot of beauty that would please her own poetic soul. A soul he loved as if it were his own. And it was like his own—passionate, alive, strong.

But how was he to tell her all of these things so that she

would listen? Loving her as much as he did somehow made it impossible to use the right words. What a gapeseed he was to approach her and say, of all the stupid things, *Where are your servants?*

Lord, but he was a complete moonling himself, and every bit of his considerable experience in the art of wooing a female failed him at this moment.

The pail was full and the cow satisfied. Kate rose from her labours, her back aching a little at the confined position, and walked past the poet as though he did not exist.

"Kate!" he called to her. "Please stay. I must speak with you."

She turned back to him, cradling the bucket of milk in her arms, her lips compressed tightly together. "What is it, Lord Ashwell? I certainly hope you have something of interest to say to me, for I am rather busy this morning as you can see."

He gestured in a hopeless manner, "I—I thought the night would have given you counsel. After all, we did not part on the best of terms."

Kate, her heart feeling like a stone weight within her chest, replied, "You are right in one thing. We parted. Have done with it, Ashwell. You have had your summer's idyll, you have been amused. And now you may leave Chipping Fosseworth." She had meant for this to be the end of her speech, but she could not keep from adding, "And I do not comprehend in the least why you have been so easily forgiven by the surrounding gentry for this despicable masquerade, except that several are known to be some of the greatest toadeaters alive! But I do not forgive you, Lord Ashwell, if that is what you have come to discover. No. I do not forgive you." She thought back to the many occasions when he had condemned her for pursuing Ashwell and all the while he had been involved in a despicable scheme of his own, "For you are less than a man. You are a lying, cheating rogue. A scoundrel. A cur. And I despise you!"

"Kate, you cannot speak such things to me. Not now." He felt a measure of panic overtake him. What if she could not forgive him? "I love you, for God's sake. What I did was unconscionable, yes, I admit it. Only, what was I to do that early morning in the barn when you had so declared your intentions upon my fortune?"

"In all of this, though I have behaved badly toward your good friend James, I have been completely honest with you. What could you have done? The truth would have been the only remedy and now the truth is too late. And pray," she said, her voice sounding slightly hysterical, "is there anything else about you that I should know? After all, you hid your ownership of the cloth mill and fooled everyone about your identity as London's most famous poet. Are you perhaps the Prince Regent in disguise as well? Or mayhap King George! Oh, do leave me in peace, Lord Ashwell." She turned away from him. "Leave me in peace." Kate walked toward the barn doors, the milk sloshing in the bucket at her jerky movements.

He ran up behind her and stopped her again, pulling gently on her arm. "Don't leave me like this, Kate. Don't let only your pride separate us. I know you love me—that is, I think you love me."

Kate looked up at him, her affections for him buried so deeply that all she felt was a great black pain. "Pride is nearly the only thing I have left, besides a quite useless wardrobe."

He watched her go, uncertain what to do. He could not leave matters as they were and, heedless of how wretched his words would sound, all of his tact and famous abilities for charming the female sex abandoning him at this most necessary of moments, blurted out, "What prospects have you, then? You must marry me, Kate. You've nothing else you can do."

Kate whirled on him, her anger surfacing in a great wave of heat. "Do you think that if I rejected 'Lord Ashwell' once regardless of my prospects, I would not do so again? You are a conceited fool. Do you expect me to fall at your feet because now I know who you are? What do you think my refusal of James was about, anyway? I refused him because I did not love him and I refuse you because you are a man I cannot love."

Her words stabbed him. But he could not be angry with her and, in his desperation, committed a second grave error by trying to take a woman—a furious woman who was also holding a bucket of milk—into his arms. She tore away from

307

him and, with one deft movement as she stepped backward and swung the bucket over him, promptly emptied the pail of milk over his entire person. Giving a nod of satisfaction at his drenched clothes as well as at the look of horror on his face, Kate set the pail on the ground and walked in a stately manner from the barn.

Ashwell, stunned and feeling the complete idiot, began laughing as he took his half-soaked kerchief from his pocket and wiped his face, his hair, his coat. On his lips he could taste the sweet, buttery milk. The animals, at so much combativeness, moved restlessly in their stalls, and as Ashwell gazed at them, he saw many a brown eye that seemed to be laughing at him as well.

He walked out of the barn and watched Kate make her dignified progress toward the manor. As he wiped at his coat sleeves, he felt unsure of himself, worried lest love, having alighted upon his shoulder for the second time in his life, would not fly away and leave him destitute once again. For this time he had created the difficulty, by his subterfuge, by his pride, by his wretched boredom that caused him to seek amusement at her expense, by wishing to hurt her because she had been blatantly honest about wanting the Ashwell fortune.

And what had she wanted it for but to help those that she loved and to secure her own future. Amelia would have spent thousands of pounds on finery alone, on every piece of trumpery that might catch her eye, for she had never known poverty as he had; she had never known a time when her smallest whim had not been indulged. And every indulgence had cost her, ultimately, her life. For when Sapperton had taken advantage of her in a clandestine meeting, Ashwell had discovered them both, pistol in hand. He knew Sapperton, if Amelia did not. He had tried to force the earl to face him then, but Sapperton had merely laughed at him. But worse, Amelia had laughed, too, and told Ashwell not to be such a simpleton. He remembered how coyly Amelia had looked at that moment, glancing back at the earl with a flirtatious smile.

He had tried to reason with her, to convince her that Sapperton meant nothing by his promises and kisses and groping hands. And three weeks later, when Lord Sapperton left on a trip to the West Indies, Amelia had killed herself—an overdose of laudanum. Beautiful, thoughtless, heedless Amelia.

When Kate entered the manor, the long walk back to the house had done her a great deal of good. She felt a little lighter in spirit, having been able to vent some of her feelings upon the one person who deserved to receive her anger. As she passed through the kitchen, she heard a slight groan coming from the buttery and, peeking into the small chamber, found Cook sitting on a tall ash stool and holding her head in her hands.

Kate, irritated by the servant's condition, said brightly, "And how are you, Cook? My, but I am feeling particularly well! And how hungry I am this morning! So much dancing last night at Leachwood—not to mention milking the cow this morning!" She watched Cook wince at her loud words as the older, stout female lifted her head and tried to tuck a grey curl back beneath her untidy mobcap.

"Hallo, miss. I—I'm not feeling too spry." But so much talking was a little more than she could manage and she dropped her head back down into her hands.

With a wonderfully malicious feeling, Kate said, "Pray, take your time. I am not in any great hurry, only when you are feeling a little better, I would like some ham, a little bacon, eggs, bread, and coffee."

As she turned away from the buttery, heading toward the kitchen, she heard Cook groan and felt that she had more than accomplished her mission.

Violet met her in the hall looking quite frantic, her blue eyes wide and appealing. "I dinnit know wat to do. He's here, in the library."

"Who?" Kate asked, feeling a little alarmed and patting her hair in an absent manner.

"The earl! Lord Sapperton!" the maid breathed, awestruck by their noble visitor.

Kate gripped the railing of the backstairs and said, "You must tell his lordship that I will be a few minutes more." And she turned up the stairs. She would not face the earl in all her dirt. When she reached the first landing, she turned back to the maid and asked, "Where is my father? Is he with Lord Sapperton?"

The maid nodded, and Kate's footsteps became quite slow, plodding almost, as she considered what a visit might mean.

Kate stood at the threshold of the library, the long, narrow room lit brightly by the midday sun. The leaded glass doors of the bookcases reflected the images of two men. One, seated in a low slung winged chair by the fire, slumped forward, his hands clasped loosely between his knees. How old Jaspar looked, Kate thought as she regarded her father. Even his cheeks sagged and the withdrawn expression in his eyes gave him a look of despairing age.

Lord Sapperton greeted her cheerfully, his tall image reflected in the glass and appearing broken by the leaded strips. He was as broken a man as Jaspar was, having no thoughts in his head but possession and dispossession.

Kate, still holding the door handle, finally released it, then closed the double doors quietly behind her. She was dressed in a dove-grey morning gown of twilled muslin. Maggie had coiffed her hair in a severe style, pulling it back away from her face, save for a few curls on her forehead, and twisting her long auburn locks into a knot at the back of her head. She wanted Lord Sapperton to find her unattractive.

But his expression, as it rested on her, was far from one of revulsion as he came forward to greet her, extending his hand, which she promptly ignored. She walked by him to stand next to Jaspar and, placing her hand on her father's shoulder, said, "Did you wish to speak with me, Lord Sapperton?"

Jaspar patted her hand with his own yet said nothing.

Lord Sapperton, not the least discomposed at having his greeting so summarily set aside, withdrew his snuffbox from his pocket and slowly took a pinch. Moving to a sofa table that backed the olive-green couch situated across from the fireplace, he quickly drew the snuff into his thin nostrils. After pressing each side of his nose gently and taking a deep breath, he said, "I've something here that might interest you. Indeed,

I am certain of it."

As he returned the white enamelled snuffbox to his pocket, he gestured, with a hand clad in York tan, to a rolled piece of parchment tied with a crimson ribbon.

He picked it up from the sofa table and tossed it at Jaspar's feet, his thin face a mask of derision.

Jaspar looked up at him, then grabbed the scrolled piece of paper, which was quite yellow with age, and handed it over his shoulder to Kate.

Kate knew, without even looking at it, that she held in her hand the deed to the manor. She glanced at Sapperton and her expression of anger caused him to say, as he held a thin hand to his heart, "Do not accuse me of any wrongdoing, Katherine. I am concerned only for your welfare."

"How could you do this and then pretend that you are concerned about anything, save your own vile schemes?"

He rounded the sofa table and seated himself at the end of the faded green velvet sofa, crossing his long, thin legs that looked like great sticks with boots attached, and said, "Someone would have purchased the estate and Lord Turville gave me quite excellent terms. I could not refuse, really, besides thinking that such an expenditure of my funds would return the investment a hundredfold."

"What do you mean?"

"I intend to turn all of this land along the River Chering into a sheep walk, of course."

Kate cried, "But what of the field labourers? They are none of them shepherds. They will have no work to do!"

Stretching his hands out in a beseeching fashion, Lord Sapperton said, "Now, that is hardly a concern of mine, is it? However, I know that you have many strong, though ill-guided feelings upon this subject, and if you wished for it—"

He let the words hang as he propped his head up, by one bony hand, upon the arm of the sofa.

Kate unrolled the parchment and looked at the title deed to the manor. The property was entailed, of course, providing that the owner did not find it necessary to sell. And Jaspar had found it necessary. They had nothing and she had nothing. Nothing, that is, save a pretty wardrobe of completely useless gowns.

She walked between Jaspar's chair and the sofa, crossing the room to stare out at Birdlip Hill topped by another fine beechwood, Much like Quening Woods, her haunt from childhood, and yet had any of it truly been hers? She seemed to realize for the first time that she did not belong here. The manor was entailed upon male heirs and was never meant to belong in any form to the daughters of the house. Out of the earnings of an estate, a good owner could set money aside as a dowry for his daughters or a daughter might have her mother's inheritance as her dowry, but not the estate, lands, property, household property, money invested in the funds—nothing. And yet she had given her soul to the manor. She glanced back at Jaspar and realized that she had given her soul, hoping he might love her as he had once loved her.

Jaspar met her gaze and said, "I'm sorry, Kate." And he shook his head as though he did not even realize where he was.

Kate said, "Did you not even contact your heir? Surely Mr. Cleeve should know something of what has transpired. You owe him that."

Jaspar's face hardened. He was a stubborn man. "I owe him nothing."

Lord Sapperton stood and joined Kate at the window. He said airily, "Oh, do I hear sheep in the distance? But of course, the farmer over at Brock keeps a few sheep, doesn't he? Well, then he shall be delighted to hear that I, as his new landholder, will be permitting him to increase his flock. Ah, how I shall enjoy seeing this land farmed properly. None of this ridiculous wheat. We shall raise sheep and return this economy to wool. But how delightful."

Kate asked quietly, "I understand you have closed the flour mill in Stinchfield."

"Yes. And I am always amazed at how quickly news travels among these little hills and vales. I should think the price of wheat would double, mayhap treble, with only one mill above Todbury running. Squire Cricklade was most agreeable to my making this move and sharing the profits, of course."

Kate eyed Sapperton with such contempt that he laughed at her, running his finger alongside her cheek and saying, "You are overly scrupulous. And you should have seen the gleam in his eye. For all of Mrs. Cricklade's complaining of her regretful past life, Mr. Cricklade was delighted at the opportunity of squeezing another groat or two out of the villagers and the inhabitants of Stinchfield. Once in trade, always in trade."

"You are despicable," she whispered, and nearly crushed the yellowed parchment between clenched fingers.

"Then we understand one another and I've only come to ask what day you wish to be wed, for I suppose I will have to post the banns, for there is not a bishop nearby from whom I can obtain a special licence." He stepped closer to her and Kate smelled the rather sharp fragrance of his cologne, nearly choking on its bitter quality. He continued, "I suppose I could travel to Cheltenham, but I do not wish to leave your side for a single moment."

He then took the parchment out of her hands and said, "If you say the word, I shall do right by you. No sheep, if that is truly what you wish, and I suppose I would have to disappoint Cricklade and"—he slapped the paper against his gloved palm—"I shall tear this up instantly."

Chapter Sixteen

Kate looked back at her father, who wore an almost hopeful expression on his face, and she said quietly, "Will you leave us for a few moments, Jaspar. I wish to speak with Lord Sapperton"—she paused and gave the earl a measuring glance—"alone."

Sapperton seemed pleased and Jaspar rose to his feet, smiling in a stiff manner and saying in his gruffest voice, "Of course. Of course. As it should be. You've a lot to say to each other." And taking the narrow chamber in a few long strides, he shut the door noisily behind him.

Sapperton took one of Kate's hands and pressed his thin lips against her own ungloved fingers, "Dearest Katherine," he began.

But Kate withdrew her hand in a pointed fashion, her expression cold. He laughed at her, "Do not be missish with me. Remember that I know you are not as innocent as you pretend."

Kate turned her back on him and, in a quiet voice, said, "Then I wonder that you want me still. After all, I'm not certain that I could guarantee our first child would be yours."

He seemed stunned at her words, his face becoming a mask of stone.

She directed a harsh, uncompromising gaze at him, closing her arms across her chest. "You are a loathsome, vile creature, Sapperton. Would you not have me were I found to be less than virtuous in truth? Ah, I see by your face that I've the right of it. In fact, you may have your way with whatever female you choose, but I, being a female of gentle birth, must remain virtuous."

"I withdraw all my offers if you speak the truth."

She moved to sit in the chair Jasper had quit and said, "I sincerely doubt that you would have kept them, anyway. But I confess that I have lied to you, if only to see your eyes shift about in so interesting and reptilian a manner."

His face, once the shade of white marble, now turned an angry hue as he moved to stand over her. "Don't trifle with me, Katherine. You will only come off the worse for it." And he pulled her up by the elbow, grabbing her skin hard and forcing her to look at him.

He pinched her, twisting her fair skin until she wanted to scream, but Kate would not cry out. She would not give him the satisfaction. She hated the man and knew that life with him would be just this way, his cruel nature forever surfacing.

He released her suddenly, letting her fall back into the chair. "I look forward to our nuptials. I thought we might travel first to London, for I intend—even if only a few of England's nobler residents have their town houses opened—to display my hard-won prize." He turned toward her. "Do you know how much I am worth on the 'change? No, I shall tell you—half a million. Surprised? I have a town house in Grosvenor Square and a hunting box in the Quorn country, a mansion in Scotland and another town house in Brighton." He smiled at her. "You should want for nothing, and your dear father—though I would have to find some way of restricting his play—could remain here until he passed on to be with his tankard-draining forebears."

Kate wondered if she had suddenly grown quite, quite insane to refuse his offer, for not only would she be a peeress of the realm, but all of her wildest dreams would come true. Was she merely being foolish that she would now refuse the man? For a moment she had another vision of what she might accomplish with so much wealth, but then she felt the tender spot on her arm where he had hurt her.

Kate watched him, his face shadowed with the early afternoon light behind his head as it streamed through the windows. She said, "I have never understood why you wished to marry me."

She thought his expression was one of surprise, and he said succinctly, "Because your mother refused me, of course, or did you not know that?"

"My mother?" Kate asked, astonished that she did not know this portion of her mother's history. "But how is this? I mean, how could you have even thought she would? The age that separated you alone would have been a great hindrance."

He shook his head at her, "She was only two years my senior."

"Then I shall follow my mother's example and refuse you as well. Did you suppose that I would marry you now? Did you really think for one moment that I would give in to your dismal threats of flour mills and deeds and my father's future? You've never known me or understood me."

His face took on the aspect of a dying fish, his mouth opening and closing in strange spasms, his face a remarkable grey color.

Kate rose to her feet and waved a careless hand toward him. "I had rather starve with the villagers than . . . oh, how shall I put this, take my meat at your table?"

Kate watched as Lord Sapperton raised both fists in an impotent gesture, his arms trembling from suppressed rage. "You fool!" he cried. "You stupid, ignorant female! Who will have you, I wonder? Or do you not yet know that Ashwell has been amusing himself with you? And do you think that I will permit you to remain here? Besides," he said, his expression changing to one of such intensity that Kate took a step backward, her leg bumping into the chair as he continued, "you have no connection to this place, to Chipping Fosseworth, at all. You are more nearly connected to Edgeworth, and you can even call Mary, who I know to be your dearest friend, you can even call her 'sister.' Yes, now you stare, now I have your attention. Now you will listen to me. Why do you think that you've no siblings and that the only one Jaspar could produce died at birth? Or do you not know about breeding stock, about matching strong blood with strong blood, about strong offspring and weak offspring? Why do you

316

think the squire is but a brittle shell now where once he was a fairly vital man? Because she told him. Marianne told him. Yes, your mother. I asked for your hand when she was dying and she refused, and I told her that I would tell Jaspar what I knew if she did not give you to me. But the fool told her husband, and see what a pleasant life you've lived since."

Kate felt the room grow warm and yet suddenly fill with a very dense fog. "What do you mean?" she asked in a faint voice, struggling to find the arm of the chair behind her. "You speak in riddles. What are you saying?"

"Why do you call him Jaspar, then? Tell me that? Why do you not call him father? Because he won't have it, will he? And why won't he have it, stupid girl? Think. He won't have it because he is not your father."

Kate stared at him, the fog closing in about her, the room growing to an intense heat. He spit at her, "Sir William Chalford is your father."

And he turned on his heel and was gone.

Kate opened her eyes slowly. The ceiling had stopped whirling around and around, and now she could sit up. She had come so close to fainting and for a moment she could not remember why. And then the earl's words began flowing over her in an echoing rhythm that made her head throb—Sir William.

What irony! Life seemed to hold so many twists and turns for her. Ashwell, Buckland, Ashwell, and now this! Sir William. Her eyes began following the intricate plasterwork, shaped into trails of ivy and flowers. Around the ceiling they trailed, twisting and turning, her heart twisting and turning. Ashwell, Buckland, Jaspar, Sir William.

And she knew it all to be true. Sapperton had spoken the truth. Truth. How sweetly truth should glow from the tongue, healing and balming the soul. But this truth and Ashwell's truth hurt her. No wonder Sir William had looked at her so many times as though she had somehow made his life complete. She had even wondered if he had had a *tendre* for her, but now his sincere affection was fully explained. He had loved her mother. This was truth. He had loved her mother, for whenever he spoke of her his blue eyes burnt with a warm flame, spilling from his eyes. How many times had she wished that she were his daughter, especially in the last five years—only in the last five years.

She thought of Jasper and suddenly knew all that he had suffered and forgave him. She wanted to stand, to go to him, but her knees buckled slightly as she tried to gain her feet and she fell back into the chair.

The door opened and Jaspar peeked his head in, a frown on his face. Kate burst into tears. "Papa," she cried. "Papa."

He went to her, his frown turning into an expression of such anguish that she opened her arms and he immediately fell into them, burying his head on her chest as she sat on the sagging old winged chair.

Kate cried, "Why did you not tell me the truth? Have you been punishing me all these years, these last five years, because of someone else's wrongdoing?" A sob shook his frame as she continued, "I love you. I still love you. You are my father. You always were my father. Jaspar, Jaspar! Why did you let this awful truth come between us? I would not have cared!"

He began crying in earnest, and Kate thought her heart would break as deep sobs poured through his body. He pressed his head against her and, in a desperate voice, cried, "I couldn't forgive her. I couldn't forgive her. She had taken Stephen from me and then she took you. I had no bairns to call my own. And why did she have to die? How could I live without my Marianne, and then to know the truth? I couldn't look at you without thinking that she had lain with William. I hated her for that and, God forgive me," he looked up into Kate's face and said, "I began hating you. Kate, Kate, I loved you so much. I still do!"

He buried his head in her lap, his tears drenching the front of her dove-grey gown. And as he let his grief, which for years had been pent up within his stubborn heart, finally give way, Kate ran her fingers through his hair again and again. It was a long time before his tears subsided, and when he had been quiet for some time, Kate said, "Papa, pray get up, or Maggie will think I've taken to dampening my muslin."

Jaspar rose unsteadily to his feet, chuckling at her words. Removing a wrinkled handkerchief from his coat pocket, he wiped his eyes and blew his nose soundly. His gaze fixed on the bookshelves behind Kate, he shook his head absently and said, "I've been a donkey's arse."

Turning to his daughter, he frowned at her and said, "I've hated hearing you call me Jaspar. How could I have done that to you?" And he extended his arm down to her and she took it, rising to her feet. He folded his arms about her in just the sort of hug he used to give her as a little girl.

They swept down the narrow valley rimmed on one side by Quening Woods and the other by Standen Beeches. Following the ancient Fosse Way, their horses galloped in ever lengthening strides as father and daughter took one last hearty ride through fields of grain, crossing the low stone bridges of the River Chering as the stream wound through the valley. Kate followed behind her papa, and the wind seemed to drag some of her despair through her auburn tresses that flowed behind her, letting it dissipate in the warm late summer's air.

She loved him so. Had he only spoken of his pain earlier, they would not have lost so much—the manor, her small fortune, and five years of living separate, anxious lives beneath the same roof.

He pulled in his reins slightly, allowing her to come abreast, and they both slowed their mounts to a walk. His face seemed younger, even in the full light of day, than she had seen it in years, and he said, "We'll make a new life for ourselves, Kate," his gruff voice enthusiastic. "I've always wanted to go to the Colonies. Fortunes can be made there with a bit of hard work and luck."

Kate smiled at Jaspar, feeling such a rush of affection for him that she readily agreed, "Yes, oh yes. Do let us go. I have longed to travel my entire life."

He looked at her with a surprised expression. "You've never said nought, my girl!" He then shook his head a bit sadly and said, "Save when you were younger. Lord, but I've been the biggest sapskull that ever walked the earth. If you never forgave me, I'd understand."

Kate slapped her reins, unwilling to let him see the tears forming in her eyes. As she moved ahead of him, she called back over her shoulder, "I'll beat you to the ridge of Boram Hill."

Over the doorway of the Swan and Goose hung the large wooden sign, creaking in a slight afternoon breeze, which seemed at any moment ready to fall upon one of the passersby. James looked up at it and said, "Good God! How does that cumbersome thing remain when the east winds blow through here?"

Lord Ashwell, drawing on his gloves of soft York tan, looked at the sign that wound together, quite strangely, the necks of the two rather unlikely waterfowls, and said, "No doubt so that the villagers would have something upon which to wager."

In front of the inn, Ashwell's curricle, cleaned and polished by one of the stableboys, stood waiting, the black geldings stamping their feet and snorting, twisting in their harness and ready for a strong, difficult journey through the Cotswolds. The stableboy held the horses' heads as best he could and cried out, "Fresh as bedamned!" with such a smile that Ashwell smiled in return. Fine bits of flesh and bone, he thought as his eyes gazed fondly at the matched team that James, through sheer cowhandedness—for he was a mere whipster—nearly ruined. Another near-misfortune of their wretched masquerade.

This thought caused him to think of Kate and the scheme he had just concocted in hopes of undoing the wrong he had created. But Lord, if this went awry, she really would slip through his fingers. As he mounted the sleek gentleman's curricle, he also knew that nothing else would bring her about. She was as stubborn and unforgiving a shrew as he had ever known. And he loved her now to the point of distraction.

Taking the reins in hand, he was about to dismiss the stableboy when a disturbance within the inn caught his attention and he cried, "Hold, there. One moment," to the startled groom.

James, Ashwell, and the boy all turned to look at the inn's doorway, and the viscount thought he had never seen a more surly lot in his life than the villagers who emerged from the inn's tavern and began pouring out onto the flagway. "Keep them steady, lad," he called to the groom, who spoke in low tones to the beasts he had become attached to in the past six weeks.

A group of labourers, some sauntering, some staggering, swelled behind the curricle, several actually going so far as to thump the wheels as they moved around the light vehicle and then taunted the horses, who began rearing slightly, the sudden shouts a cacophony on their sensitive ears.

Ashwell called to his horses, "Gently, gently."

The men moved on, and James stepped near to the carriage and said, "I didn't know what to do. One of these fellows actually jostled me."

The innkeeper came out, rubbing his hands in a nervous manner on his apron, and said, "I be sorry for their rude manners. Are ye all right?"

James asked, "What's amiss?"

"That ye might not know. 'Tis the flour mill at Quening wat's got them all worked up, and there's a rumour that the earl means to buy up all the wheat hereabouts and ship it to London. Their families will starve."

"He wouldn't be such a brute!"

"He'd do that and more if he thought he could squeeze one more tuppence off the backs of every poor man about Stinchfield. He lives in a grand style, that he does, and the poor folks die early. If ye're both all right, I'll return to me labours. I'll not have it said that John Beverstone treats his guests shabbily."

The short, broad-bellied innkeeper returned to his duties, and when the viscount gave the stableboy the order to release his horses, the groom held fast and, in a quiet, earnest voice, said, "Please, yer lordship, a word! Them fellows, they be talkin' queer. I be worrited about Miss Draycott an' others."

James exchanged a glance with Ashwell and said to the

servant, "How's this? Have they talked of riots?"

"Aye and worse. Of takin' Leachwood." He paused for a moment and said, "I thought ye ought to know. Miss Kate been kind to me family, but if matters came to a riot, I dinnit think she would be safe."

James whistled long and low, and the viscount, still keeping his horses in a strong grip, cried, "Good God!"

When the erratic progression of the villagers no longer resounded down the street, the horses grew quiet and Ashwell continued, "Have they spoken of times or dates?"

"No, only soon. Most o' ta wheat has been harvested."

The viscount looked down at James and said, "I'll be back in two days time. If anything should transpire, will you see that Kate and the squire are safe? You know what a mob is. They'll not care who you are nor how sympathetic you are to their cause, only that you belong to the landed class."

James nodded and said, "Don't worry. I'll see that no one harms Kate. I—I'm certain nothing untoward will happen."

But since the expression on his face was one of twisted anxiety, Ashwell laughed at him and said, "Yes, I can see that you are perfectly at ease. Well, never mind. Two days."

James had nearly forgotten Ashwell's purpose in travelling to Cheltenham and said, with another frown, "Do you think your plan a good one?"

"My dear fellow, I love the termagant and comprehend her inner workings far better than you. And I have a milk-stained coat, a red stained neckcloth, a blue coat destroyed by a pistol ball, as well as a torn muslin shirt, all to prove my point. Yes, my scheme is perfection itself and the only proper method I know of by which I can make her my wife!"

And with that, he bade the groom step aside and, with a slap of his reins and a cry to his best horses, departed.

James moved away from the curricle, shaking his head at his dearest friend and wondering what would be the end of this latest masquerade.

He walked back into the inn, gathering up his hat and gloves, and headed back to the stables. Mounting his own hack, a neatish bay that Ashwell had once referred to, most unkindly, as the showiest, most worthless piece of horseflesh he had ever seen, James trotted out of the cobbled stableyard and headed toward Edgecote. Mary had invited him for tea and had promised to have her special macaroons on the tray. Damme, but he liked her twinkling blue eyes, even if they were a trifle close-set, and her sweet smile was enough to set him to thinking of his future. Mary's smile was like Kate's in a way. But that often happened with friends. The longer they were together the more they began taking on the same manner of speech, the same laughter. Of course, beyond a similar smile, he could think that Mary and Kate truly had nothing else in common.

As he entered the High Street from the stableyard, James wondered if he and Ashwell resembled each other in the least. And he laughed, for not once had he seen any of the young gentry ladies look at him with that appraising, rather hungry look that they sported when scanning the poet from head to foot. No, he and the viscount resembled each other as much as—he again regarded the sign above the inn—as much as a swan and a goose. Now which was which, remained to be seen.

Mary received her guest with only the undermaid in attendance, for Lydia was visiting Fanny Cerney and Lady Chalford had taken the younger children to visit the Cricklades. The truth was, Mary had told her parents that she had fallen very deeply in love with Mr. Montrose, a fact that, because his portion was quite modest, could scarcely please them. Mary was a considerable heiress, having received an enormous portion of her great aunt's wealth, as did each of Sir William's children. But whether James was aware of her dowry Mary was not certain, nor was her distressed father.

Sir William could not like the match. His Mary was not a beauty, she was like her mother. But she did have thirty thousand pounds, and to let her wed a man she had known for only six weeks, and who had shown himself only a sennight earlier to be quite violently in love with Kate, was not his idea of a brilliant connection. But setting aside Mary's fortune and James's lack of one, Sir William knew only too well what it was to love, for he had known Marianne Whiteshill for only two days and had fallen head over heels in love with her. And his feelings for her, even after her death, had remained strong and unwavering. Over the last few weeks he had watched his daughter actually bloom. Prosaic little Mary, busy with her stitchery and helping her mother in every household chore, walking about the manor with a smile on her face, her laughter echoing through the rooms. Mary had never laughed like that before. And the glow that had formed upon her cheeks, even her entire person, since she and James had become friends, seemed to transform the stoic, rather plain-faced female who was his daughter into a charming, pretty young woman.

He had hesitated, telling Mary that he did not know James well enough, that he could not be certain Mr. Montrose was not pursuing her for her fortune! But these were the wrong words to say, for Mary, who never displayed the least emotion, had dropped her head in her hands and sobbed. Mary! Faith, but she had nearly broken his own heart in that moment and after taking her gently in his arms, he told her that his little lamb could have whatever she desired, adding that of all his daughters Mary, with her steadiness of character, deserved to have her fondest wishes realized.

Mary smiled at James, who was seated across the tea table from her, and remembered her father's soothing words. She handed James a cup of tea and, out of the corner of her eye could see the undermaid sitting at the far end of the drawing room, staring out the window in a bored fashion and kicking her feet. She would have to reprimand the servant for her unseemly behaviour.

To James she said, "I'm sorry that my family was not here to attend you."

James looked about him, at the empty gold and rust chairs, and for the first time realized that they were virtually alone. Noticing a slight blush to Mary's cheeks, he understood that she had wished to receive him alone and he smiled. Somehow his future had just been decided as Mary handed him a cup of tea. He gently caught her wrist and said quietly, "I'm glad they are not here. For as fond as I am of your family, I am grateful to have these few moments with you." And he pressed her wrist, then released it.

Mary's blush deepened and she tried to speak of other things, but every time she looked up and saw his sensitive brown eyes smiling at her she lost all train of thought. With great presence, she asked, "Would you like a macaroon?" And she handed him the sugar bowl.

James laughed, "I have looked forward to your biscuits more than you can know, but I don't think this is quite what I had in mind."

Mary looked at the sugar bowl, gave a little cry, and then offered him the plate of macaroons. "How stupid of me."

But this presented him with a difficulty, for in his right hand he held his tea cup and in his left the bowl of sugar. And somehow Mary's confusion brought his every emotion into sharp focus and he knew that he loved her.

Mary realized what she had done and took a deep breath. Setting the plate down on the table and retrieving the sugar from James, she said, "I'm sorry. I don't know what has come over me today. You must think me a complete idiot."

"I think nothing of the sort." And he surprised her by rising to his feet and moving to sit, quite cosily, beside her. "Dearest Mary," he whispered and, taking her in his arms, kissed her gently upon the lips.

Mary thought that if that stupid servant now raised up a squawk, she would ring a peal so loud over the girl's head that she would not be able to hear for a week. But the maid apparently was not attending to the interesting couple on the sofa and Mary gave herself over to the extremely pleasing sensation of James's lovely mouth pressed so sweetly upon hers.

Releasing her, he asked, "Will you do me the honour of becoming my wife?"

Mary, her blue eyes wide and her heart pounding furiously in her ears, answered in a constricted voice, "If you like it, James, yes, indeed, I will!"

When James heard precisely how much Mary's fortune was, as Sir William stared hard at him over his spectacles—used exclusively for reading and for intimidating suitors—he thought that the room shifted beneath his feet a little.

Sir William's stern expression melted into a smile. "So, you did not know. Pray, be seated, lest you faint! You are looking oddly white about the gills."

James sat down, falling back into the tall chair by the fireplace, and accepted rather blindly a glass of sherry that Sir William shoved into his hand.

Looking into the brown liquid, the rather pungent bouquet striking his face, James shook his head numbly, saying, "I didn't know. I'd no idea." He then tossed off the glass, choking a little as he did so, and said, "I've a small competence and an even smaller property in Stowhurst. I want you to know that. But I'm no fortune hunter. That is surely the farthest thing from my mind. I hope you believe me."

Sir William, sipping at his sherry with one hand behind his back, rocked on his heels a little and stared out at the formal gardens where Mary could be seen smiling to herself and cutting roses. "I don't think it would matter in the least if you were."

"How's this?"

"She loves you, James, and I can see that you're an honest gentleman. You and Mary have every chance at a contented life together." He gestured toward the window, where Mary was engaged in speaking with one of the gardeners. "She's a housewife, born and raised, and your estate and your children will have everything they'll need. No waste, no neglect."

Both men stared at Mary, who raised her voice slightly to the servant and watched as the gardener bowed three times to her and scurried away. Sir William laughed, "Neither of them, my wife nor Mary, can abide the barest hint of slothfulness." And turning to James as he drained his own glass, he said, "Let that be a warning to you."

James did not know Sir William quite well enough to laugh, but he did smile and thanked him for the sherry. The baronet pushed his future son-in-law through the long doors that opened onto the garden and told him not to make a cake of himself, but to lose himself in the shrubbery if he were so inclined.

James let the fragrance of the late summer blooms and the warmth of the sun flow over him as he approached his beloved. He felt like a swan now and not quite the idiot as when he had

326

asked Kate to marry him. He wondered how Ashwell had fared in Cheltenham.

Two days later, the sound of feet dancing about the gravel walk, accompanied by Mary's unusual squeals of laughter and Kate's cries of, "Do give it back or I shall never speak to you again," filled the rose garden behind the manor. Mary and James had ridden over on the following day to tell Kate their news, and just after she had congratulated them both, a special messenger from Mr. Rous's bank in Cheltenham had arrived with a letter from, of all the unexpected people, George Cleeve, Jaspar's heir.

Kate grabbed at the letter, which James kept just out of reach, and Mary, held securely about the waist by James's free arm, found herself whirled around as she also tried to reach for the missive.

"James," Mary cried, then squealed again with laughter as he tickled her ribs. "Pray, give Kate her letter and stop funning!"

"Oh, no!" he cried. "Not until I have read every sentence aloud and made my own pithy observations upon the quality of the author." His brown eyes scanned the next line and he said, "Good God, listen to this!"

Kate gave up trying to reach the missive and returned to fetch her basket, which had been overturned in their scuffling. She knelt down to retrieve the two dozen flowers, rich in fragrance, leaving pink, yellow, and red petals upon the gravel walk as James read aloud, "'And so, having enumerated my excellent qualities—including my extreme wealth, which, given your own unhappy circumstances, must all join to promote my pursuit of your fair hand—I live in a suspended state awaiting your prompt acceptance of my proposals. I do trust that my observation upon your *fair* hand is an accurate one—I hope I have not been misled in this, for I have the greatest repugnance of truly ugly females—for I do have something of a poetic soul and find that beauty eases the daily troubles of life. But of your beauty, my source cannot be questioned, for—dare I boast!—no less a personage than Lord

Ashwell has been the very one to list your features in minute detail.'"

James interjected, "I did not know that George knew your Mr. Cleeve. How fascinating!"

Mary cried, "Kate, what sort of man would speak in such absurd language? And though I do not wish to sway you, I doubt very much that you would get on with Mr. Cleeve. He sounds very pompous."

Kate placed the last flower in her basket and rose to her feet. "It hardly matters. I shall not accept his proposals. My only reason to accept his hand would be to remain here, and I do not wish for it. Not in the least!"

James and Mary were silent and watched Kate for a moment. She felt their eyes upon her and asked, "Why do you stare at me? Do you think I am sad to be leaving Chipping Fosseworth? Not a bit."

She looked about her, about the rose bushes, half of which she had grown from cuttings brought round by the villagers, and beyond the garden to the manor and to the woods standing tall against the skyline. Her gaze swept the hills, passing on to the narrow valley where, but a few weeks ago, a man named Buckland had found her and kissed her. "You are much mistaken. I shall miss none of it!"

She continued down the path beyond them, snipping another bud and placing it slowly in her basket. Mr. Buckland no longer existed.

James's voice interrupted these thoughts as he continued reading, "'I beg you therefore, dearest cousin, to accept my proposals, for your own sake, as I know fully the extent to which you have become impoverished. Your father's debts in Cheltenham—'" James paused and said to Kate, "Perhaps I ought not to read this section."

"James!" Kate cried. "Will you now return the letter to me?" And she laughed at him. What did it signify who knew of her difficulties?

He answered solemnly, "These are personal matters. I should not have teased you so."

Kate turned to look at James and Mary and said, "You are two of my dearest friends and I wish you to know everything.

Pray continue, James." And they walked about the garden as James scanned the letter. "Ah, yes, here it is. 'Your father's debts in Cheltenham I have discharged. I owe your father that, for I have a strong feeling of filial duty, even though I cannot approve his gamester ways.'"

Kate cried, "Hah! What a noddlecock! I detest him quite thoroughly already!"

Mary frowned and said, "Do not judge him too harshly, Kate. Perhaps you could meet with him once or twice and see if he is more acceptable in person."

She glanced up at James, her eyes twinkling. Kate saw the sparkle in Mary's eye, as though she shared some secret with her betrothed. To be in love in so sweet a fashion!

Kate answered quietly, cutting another bloom a little too savagely, "I have heard enough to have formed the opinion that Mr. Cleeve is a complete bottlehead and I want nothing to do with him. Any man who would insult a woman at the same time he is telling her that he means to love her is hardly the sort of man destined to charm my heart."

James, still holding Mary fast, turned the letter over and read, "'I am at present negotiating with Lord Sapperton—'" Stopping their progress past the dogwood tree and yew hedge, James cried, "The earl owns this manor? How is this?"

Kate shaded her eyes from the glaring sun as she looked up at James. "My father lost everything to Lord Turville, one of his boon companions in Cheltenham, and Sapperton, ever so kindly, purchased the mortgages from Turville."

James whistled. "Good God!" Setting them all in motion again, he continued reading, "'Sapperton—negotiating over the property—so there is no need for you to rush from the house, although when my housekeeper arrives to set everything in order, I hope that you will give up your keys immediately. She is very competent and I am certain will be able to set everything to rights.'"

Kate cried, "Set everything to rights! How very insulting! And he even speaks as if my father is dead! The presumption! The insolence!"

James, trying to keep the laughter from bubbling up in his throat, said, "But his last portion is particularly endearing.

"'In short, you must accept my offer, as it is the only means by which you will have any claim to gentility in this life—even Lord Ashwell agrees with me on this point. And though I am certain that no angel could equal your own quiet disposition and yielding feminine temperament, without a dowry what can your future hold but misery of the very meanest sort?'"

Kate had heard enough and, dropping the poor basket, attacked James again. When she had secured the letter she tore it into shreds, then showered it over the lovers. "There! You have had your laugh and now the pair of you may leave, for I have boxes to pack, lists to compile, and a bottle of wine to consume with my nuncheon."

After picking up the basket, her head held high, Kate stalked away from her very good friends. James and Mary watched her go, their eyes shining. And how, they mused, would Ashwell resolve so ticklish a muddle?

Kate found Maggie sitting on the back stairs and crying into a frayed piece of linen. "Good heavens! What is the matter?"

Pulling the linen, which happened to be a well-worn pillowcase embroidered with blue forget-me-nots, gently away from her maid's face, Kate looked into Maggie's swollen eyes and asked, "Come, what is it?"

"I know I ought to 'ave more gumption, Miss Kate, but I been hearin' things wat have me frightful scared. And I love 'im, I do, an I doan want 'im hurt!"

Kate released the linen and Maggie buried her face in it. "Who?" she asked in a quiet voice.

"Thomas," she cried, her voice muffled behind the pillowcase. "And I doan care that he's missin' an arm. I don't care a bit. He's the manner of a gentleman and I want to marry him, only how can I if he gets himself killed by taking part in ta riot."

For the first time in this conversation, Kate found something to disturb her and, taking one of her maid's hands, gripped it tightly and said, "What riot?"

Maggie, her face streaked with tears, her hair sticking out in all directions beneath her mobcap, said, "It's Sapperton's fault, miss. In the next few days, he means to ship all of ta grain from hereabouts out of Stinchfield and ta villagers in Quening mean to riot. He never repaired their roofs, nor did anything he promised, and Thomas says that ta earl has hired some waggons from Cheltenham to come and fetch the grain away. The harvest has been poor and them folks don't know what they'll feed their babies this winter. Nor ta folks here in Chipping, since he owns the manor now. He means to take all this wheat as well!"

Kate released the trembling hand and sat down on the stairs beside her maid. She looked down at the roses in the basket, already wilting, and wondered what to do. Did Sapperton think that she would now relent?

"Ye know the earl. Isn't there somethin' ye could do?"

Kate placed her hand on the back of Maggie's neck and, looking at the tears trailing down her face, said, "What can I do? He once told me that if I married him, he would make amends, but"—and here she looked into Maggie's dark eyes, her own vision clouded slightly—"he is the sort of man that has no soul, no conscience. He would not keep his promises. He has already proven that. He is like an icicle that has slowly been melting in the heat of a late winter sun—cold, without real substance, and one day he will be gone. He cannot live forever."

"But how will everyone eat 'til then?"

"I don't know, Maggie. I'm not even certain how I will live."

Chapter Seventeen

Kate took a dusty bottle of claret from the buttery, and as she passed through the kitchen she begged Cook to send her nuncheon to the library, where she intended to begin packing her mother's books. She swung the basket of flowers in one hand and was nearly out of the room when Cook stopped her progress by calling out, "Ye'll be needin' a glass, miss, and why don't I open that fer ye?"

Kate, completely distracted, her mind reeling from the suddenness of receiving a letter from Mr. Cleeve, said, "What? Oh, I daresay I don't know what I'm doing today. I keep walking in circles. I shall leave this wine with you then. Please send along a glass." And she set the basket of flowers on the long wood table that sat in the center of the large old-fashioned kitchen.

Staring absently at the stone floor, the bottle of claret still held securely in her left hand, Kate said, "A few slices of cold chicken, perhaps a little bread and butter. Nothing more, Cook, thank you." And she moved from the kitchen, the flowers left on the table and the wine still in her hand.

Cook shook her head at the basket of flowers sitting on her clean table and let out an oath as several tiny bugs from the roses crawled out onto the clean, polished surface. Slamming her large hand down hard on the bugs, she cried, "An' I hope ye've learned a lesson from that!"

*   *   *

Kate set the bottle of bordeaux wine on the sofa table, only vaguely aware that Cook had told her to leave it in the kitchen. She regarded the two empty trunks gaping at her from the floor and sighed deeply. So, Mr. Cleeve had kindly given his permission for Jaspar and herself to remain at the manor. And all she must do is hand over her keys!

Angry at Mr. Cleeve's chilling presumption, Kate put her hands on her hips and crumpled her ice-blue morning gown beneath her restless fingers. Moving to the bookcases and pursing her lips, she began removing her mother's books from several of the shelves and putting them gently into the leather-strapped trunks. Most of the books in the library would remain intact as property of the house, but during her lifetime, Marianne had amassed a fine collection of novels, historical works, and several volumes of poetry—Milton, Dryden, Pope, even a thin volume of Byron's famous epic, *Childe Harold's Pilgrimage*. These had been left to Kate as a part of her dowry. Her dowry. Kate slammed a book down at this thought, kneeling beside the trunk and sitting back against her heels. A few calfskin-bound books were all that remained of her dowry. She had even sold her jewels for her useless pursuit of Ashwell. This thought caused her to wonder again about Mr. Cleeve. His letter had seemed so absurd, and yet surely marriage to him would be better than the uncertainty that now awaited her.

Kate regarded the book she had just treated quite roughly, a novel entitled *Waverley*, and noticed that a small square of paper had slid from between the thin pages. Kate retrieved the note and read her mother's flowery script, "My dearest William." And she felt as though she had slipped through some window of time and could hear her mother's laughter, could feel a younger Sir William breeze across the room in pursuit, and could hear their laughter as down a long corridor, and then silence.

The library door opened and Cook entered, carrying a tray and a glass and a wine-bottle opener.

Kate let the second glass of wine dull her senses, and after her meal she curled up into the low-slung maroon leather chair and dozed. Half asleep, half awake, she thought she heard her mother calling her and awoke, startled. She saw that the sun was low over the hills, the room falling into dusky shadows. A voice, rich in timbre, flowed from the chair opposite her own on the other side of the fireplace, "How pretty you look in this red glow."

Kate regarded him from sleepy eyes. She must have consumed a little more wine than she had thought, and for just a moment she forgot how much she despised the rogue and smiled. "Hallo, Buckland," she said, her heart beating with a sudden joy at having him so near.

Lord Ashwell nearly forgot every resolve as he saw the look on Kate's face. He loved her desperately and strained every muscle to keep from taking her in his arms. But he knew that she was still in a dream state, no matter what had disturbed her sleep, and he knew equally well that if he were to touch her now, she would fight him like a baited bear.

Instead of kissing her, as he wished to do, he examined his nails, the play of the last rays of light upon her auburn hair more than he could observe with indifference. He spoke in a light tone, "Have you forgotten so soon? Mr. Buckland no longer exists. Only Ashwell." He glanced at her and watched as a rigidity overcame her entire form.

"And who, pray tell, permitted you to come in here?" She eyed him with astonishment. "Do not say that you have been watching me sleep the entire afternoon."

"Oh, no. An hour or so, that is all," he said with a careless toss of his hand as he rose to his feet.

Kate watched him walk to the sofa table and cried, "An hour! You've been here for an hour? What will the servants say? Does Jaspar know you are here? And do not think for a moment that because you have placed me in an awkward situation I will now agree to marry you in order to preserve my reputation. For I will not!"

He ignored everything she had just said and asked, "May I have a glass of this fine claret? I've done nothing more than sniff its bouquet and then count the minutes until you should awaken." He cast her a disarming smile, his dimple showing in what Kate felt was a truly treacherous manner. He continued,

"After all, though I did steal in through the garden doors with none the wiser—for Maggie is quite determined that you should wed me—a fellow ought not to drink wine, under such circumstances, without permission."

Kate looked away from him, her chin raised slightly as she uncurled her feet from beneath her and stretched them out to the footstool in front of the chair. "I wonder that you bother asking at all." She regarded him with an accusing expression, a frown between her brows, and said, "And I also wonder that you did not take any liberties with me."

He laughed, "Oh, I did not come here to make violent love to you, if that is what you mean. Ah, I see that you are disappointed! Well, my dear Kate, my bonny Kate—"

"Disappointed!" Kate cried, her choler rising, particularly as she watched Ashwell pour himself out a glass of wine. She had not given him her permission at all. "And you may not drink that!" she added, pointing a finger at the innocent glass of claret.

"Are you as selfish as you are stubborn? Or have you taken to drink?" He poured a glass of wine and brought it to her, his expression softening. "There, have done for a moment, Kate. I did not come here to torture you."

Kate took the glass, and because his words were spoken in a sweet voice, she said. "You are incorrigible! First you make me want to scream with vexation and then your words positively drip honey. Stop staring at me and drink your glass of claret!" Taking a hearty drink from her own glass, she added, "And then you may leave me in peace. As you can see," she gestured to the trunks at her feet, "I am making preparations to quit the manor." She stared moodily into the empty fireplace, the shadows deepening all about them, and took several gulps of wine. A depression began settling upon her and Ashwell appeared beside her, the wine bottle in hand, and refilled her glass. He remained standing over her, a thoughtful expression on his face.

Kate leaned back into the leather chair, her feet resting comfortably on the footstool. She did not speak for a long time as the rich claret began easing its way throughout her body. She drank a little more, her eyelids growing heavy again as they had earlier in the afternoon. She said, "Papa and I—"

"Papa?" Ashwell asked quickly as he again refilled her glass, then moved to reseat himself opposite her. "I've never heard you call him anything but Jaspar."

Kate smiled and wanted to tell him what had happened, to regale him with all of the particulars, when she realized with a start that Lord Ashwell was quite the cleverest man she had ever known, for he could twist her so quickly that, were she not careful, she would fall under his spell again. In a flat voice she said, "I discovered that Sir William is my real father."

Ashwell was about to take a drink of the claret but paused at her words and remarked,"Do you know that I have often thought Lydia was a great deal like you. So Mary and Lydia are your sisters." He fell into something of a muse as he continued, "Life is full of so many ironies. Like you, for instance. You are a great poetic irony in my life. I came here to look at this property—" He stopped, suddenly aware that he had almost ruined his own careful schemes. He had almost told her his last wretched truth. In what he hoped was a smooth manner, he corrected himself, nearly certain that Kate had drunk just enough wine to ignore what he had said. "Er, for a little summer's amusement, to escape the pressing admiration of the ton, and then I met you." He gestured toward the window through which the beech trees could be seen sparkling in the sunset, the shadows long, the sky a dark grey behind them. In a quiet voice he said, "We met in those woods for the first time. I came for amusement and instead I found love.."

Turning his gaze from the window, Ashwell regarded Kate with an urgent expression that startled her as he leaned forward in his seat. "I wish that I could do it all over again, my bonny Kate. I would have told you the truth and then let you try to win me! You would have, you know. You did." He knew he should not press her but he could not help himself. "Please marry me. You have become my life, the reason that I arise in the morning, the hope for my dreary future."

Kate's nostrils flared as she rose and walked toward the window. "Your dreary future," she said in a hard voice. "Your dreary future. I laugh at such a phrase. Lord Ashwell." She looked back at him. "You came for amusement, and despite all

336

your efforts, you fell in love with me. And then despite the fact that you have some of the finest connections in the land, as well as a truly decadent fortune, you must say, in a remarkably pathetic voice, 'my dreary future.'" She walked to his chair and stood over him as she said, "I'll tell you what is dreary, my lord. Dreary is watching every bushel of grain being moved from this countryside and knowing that the village children will sleep upon vermin-infested pallets of hay, their stomachs empty. Dreary is feeling life in your stomach, the unborn infant kicking, and wondering, because you've not eaten well for nine months, whether the baby will be strong enough or whether you'll be healthy enough to make it through one more winter. Dreary, Lord Ashwell"—and she peered into his blue eyes—"is what I feel when I think of how you have misused a society that opened their homes to you so freely and with so hearty a welcome."

He leaned his head back and let out a satisfied sigh. Almost, he had expected her to fall into his arms at his declaration of love. Lord, but he'd grown conceited in the past few years, James was right in that, and she was the first woman to ever take him to task over an expression designed to cast her into raptures.

He said simply, "I am a reprobate and need your firm hand to guide me."

Kate looked down at his smiling face, feeling a little dizzy from the wine and laughed in an exasperated manner. "You are hopeless!"

As she turned away from him, folding her arms across her chest and staring out at the beechwoods, he set his glass down quickly on the table to his right and immediately came up behind her, saying, "You are right! Have it as you will! I am hopeless." He was near enough to her to smell the scent of roses that clung to her muslin gown. He wanted to touch her arms but again restrained himself. "Don't desert me, Kate. Not now. Give me another chance to prove that in my character resides a grain, a glimmer of goodness, rightness. Please, Kate."

Kate wished for the hundredth time that his voice was anything but that rich sound that seemed to resonate through her body and pull her heart along with each word he spoke. "I did not mean to be so unkind," she answered in a quiet voice. "I know that you are not hopeless. And you have a good quality to you, only"—she bit her lip—"how could you have used me so ill?"

He knew that this was the moment to set his plan firmly in motion, and he said in a sad voice, "I understand. What I did has put me beyond the pale. I have used you and everyone else in these surrounding woods abominably." He moved to his chair and, picking up his glass of wine again, said, "I am also extremely selfish, for I have brought such news from Cheltenham that can only affect your future in the most positive way, and all that I have spoken to you has been about me and what I want from you. How right you are to have nothing to do with me. I am unconscionable, a brute"—he paused for a moment as he turned bodily away from Kate, facing the fireplace—"not at all like Mr. Cleeve. Now, there is a true gentleman. He required only my assurances of your character to decide his intentions toward you while I . . . well, we do not need to discuss how I have treated you. He has told me to act as his agent and to try to persuade you to accept his proposals."

Kate wheeled around to regard Ashwell's back and wished for the hundredth time that he were not built along such Corinthian lines. She cried, "Mr. Cleeve has spoken to you of his desire to marry me?"

Ashwell turned back to her, his blue eyes wide. "Of course! I discovered him in Mr. Rous's office and, naturally given the circumstances of our having grown up together—"

"What?" Kate cried, then frowned. "Do you mean that you reside in the same village?"

"Oh, no. But we are near-neighbours and I could not help but express my interest in your welfare." He looked down into his wine and affected a sad expression. "I think, though I am not certain, that he ascertained the depth of my regard for you. I suppose I knew it when he patted me on the shoulder and said, 'There, there.'" Ashwell took a sip of wine and said, in a flatter voice, "A most soliticitous fellow. Charming. And I understand he is worth ten thousand a year. Not as much as I

338

am—" He let these words hang and Kate, casting him a frosty glance, returned to her own chair. Picking up her wineglass, she finished the claret and thought Ashwell was being exceedingly polite to retrieve the bottle and again refill her glass.

He said, "A bit pompous, though, if you don't mind my making a trifle criticism of his character."

Kate sniffed and was about to answer that at least good Mr. Cleeve had not deceived her as one unnamed despicable person had, when a scratching on the door prevented her from delivering this quite pointed observation.

Maggie entered with two branches of candles and said, "I knew it would be dark soon." And in a nervous manner, as she cast an encouraging smile to the viscount, she scurried from the room.

Lord Ashwell walked to the table by the door and, with tinderbox in hand, had all the candles lit within a matter of minutes. Kate finished her wine and watched as the viscount moved in seemingly slow steps to place a branch of candles on the desk by the door and the other on the mantel. How cosy the room seemed, and warm suddenly, as she pressed a hand to her flushed cheeks.

He said, "Since you have refused my proposals, Kate, I hope you don't mean to marry Mr. Cleeve. I know you. You could never make him happy. You are too volatile for his gentle spirit."

These words rankled with Kate and she answered sharply, "I thought you meant to act in his stead! You are not fulfilling your obligation very well. And I am not in the least volatile!" He poured her another glass of wine, and she smiled stupidly upon him. "I shall thank you not to offer your opinion as to what I should or should not do. If I choose to marry my distant cousin, that is my business and not yours." And for no reason at all, she giggled.

"A set-down," he bowed to her. "Deservedly so. Still, I don't think you should marry him. He is not at all like me and, in truth, I think you are fond of me. You would not like Mr. Cleeve."

Kate answered succinctly, twirling the glass between her

fingers and nearly spilling the wine over the maroon leather chair, "I like Mr. Cleeve well enough. Besides, he does offer the one thing you cannot."

Ashwell sneered at her, "Of course. He offers Chipping Fosseworth! Still, I don't think you should marry him. He is a meek sort of person and you would henpeck him before the honeymoon was a sennight spent."

"I would not," Kate answered, offended by such an aspersion on her character. When she tossed off the remainder of her wine, he emptied the rest of the claret into her glass. How convenient the wine had been. Kate was not used to drinking quite so much, for even at dinner he had never seen her consume more than two glasses, and in her present state he was certain he could provoke her sufficiently to achieve his end.

He crowed with laughter, "Ho! And now you will tell me that the moon just set behind those hills"—he gestured toward Knott Hill— "and that the sun is rising in the night sky."

Kate was on her feet in an instant, wobbling and swaying as she gained her balance and cried, "Are you saying that I would not know how to conduct myself as a wife? You make it sound as though I would not treat him with the respect due to my husband." She shook her head, wondering why her speech sounded so strange and slurred to her own ears.

"Your ungovernable tongue is incapable of such a feat!"

"You are insufferable!"

"And you, my bonny Kate, are a shrew! You might as well admit the truth. You've not the stuff to make dear Mr. Cleeve a proper, biddable wife."

Kate felt a little fuzzy at the outer edges of her mind, the wine nibbling at her brain. "There you are out! I would make any man a most admirable wife. I can be kind," and she added with an expression of triumph, "—when the gentleman deserves kindness. Which, I am certain, is the case with Mr. Cleeve. His letter was most agreeable."

She tried to lean her hand on the arm of the chair for support, but she found it drifting away from her in a most inexplicable manner.

Lord Ashwell said, "You've not enough bottom to marry good Mr. Cleeve! You talk and talk and never do anything!"

'I do too have enough bottom!" And in a most unladylike manner, she patted her posterior and dropped her wineglass. "Hell and damnation!" she cried and dropped to her knees to retrieve the glass. When she stood up, she nearly toppled over but held firmly onto the chair until she had gained her footing.

"You haven't the bottom nor the good sense!" he said in a taunting voice as he inched toward her and looked down into her face with a challenge in his blue eyes.

As befuddled as her mind had most strangely become, she blinked at him and knew by the fierce expression on his face that he had thrown down the gauntlet. With a triumphant voice, she said, "You have always been wrong about me, Lord Buckland . . . I mean Mr. Ashwell! For I intend to marry Mr. Cleeve. I always intended to marry him, for then I would be able to remain here in Fossing Chipworth . . . in Chopping Fissworth . . . in Chipping Fissing." She broke off. "You know what I mean."

"Indeed I do. But I don't think you will go through with it. You are merely making a show of bravado for my benefit. You mean to hurt me as deeply as you can."

"Yes! No, of course not. I am not so base." Kate moved to set her glass down carefully upon the mantel near the candles. Pleased with so much control when a fog had begun to descend upon her, her legs feeling quite weak, she felt for the back of the tall winged chair and, inching her hands along it, was able to seat herself.

Lord Ashwell said, "I don't believe you for a moment."

"No," she said with some satisfaction. "Well, I have said that I will marry Mr. Cleeve, and I will."

"In the morning you will change your mind. You are fickle, like all females."

"I will not change my mind!"

Kate saw a blur and realized that Ashwell had disappeared. She caught the briefest glimpse of his broad back passing through the doorway leading to the hall. Her vision began to swim and she pressed her hand to her forehead. The sun had disappeared completely, and when she opened her eyes she saw Buckland again and said, "Hallo, George. What a handsome devil you are?" She then shook her head and focused on his face. "Oh, it is you."

"You must write Mr. Cleeve now, Kate, or else I shall know that tomorrow you will change your mind."

Kate, angry with the realization that she had let her guard slip for a moment, took the paper that was shoved at her and, after creasing it several times because she could not hold onto it, finally set it upon a tray that appeared magically on her lap. Looking up at the poet, she asked, "What am I to do with this?"

Ashwell smiled at her, "Write a brief message to Mr. Cleeve and I shall deliver it to him in the morning."

Kate lifted a brow and smiled in a smug fashion upon her enemy. Dipping carefully into a brass inkwell that the viscount held for her, she penned a short missive accepting Mr. Cleeve's proposals.

Ashwell took the letter, covered liberally with inkspots, threw sand over Kate's untidy script, sealed it with a wafer, and tucked it into his coat pocket.

Kate said proudly, "There! You were quite mistaken, were you not?"

Ashwell removed the lap tray from Kate and, taking her hand, lifted her to her feet and held her in a tight embrace. Kate could not have moved if she wanted to, for besides her spinning head and his firm hold on her, something always happened to her when she was in his arms. Damme, but Ashwell was all that she wanted in a man and she received his lips as one who had hungered for them for years. She flung her arms about his neck, returning his kiss with every ounce of her strength. Somewhere in her mind she knew she should not be kissing the poet, but for the life of her she could not remember why.

He felt her response and knew that, given her present inebriated condition, he could do anything he desired to do. And oh, he wanted to remain with her so much, his lips finding every feature of her face and placing gentle kisses upon them. "Kate," he whispered to her. Every second that passed made parting more and more difficult for him, and when her feverish, searching lips reached a most devastating place just beneath his ear, he pulled away from her. Only a few days, he told himself, as he looked down into her hungry eyes. He set her firmly away from him and, bowing in a formal manner, said, "I shall never kiss you again, Kate. I should not have done so now."

She threw herself at him, her lids half closed, and cried, "Why ever not?"

He gripped her arms and laughed at her, "Because, my dear, silly goose, you have just accepted Mr. Cleeve's proposals."

Kate felt as though he had just thrown a glass of extremely cold water over her and she stepped away from him. "Oh, I had forgotten."

Staring at him in a dazed fashion as he bowed again and moved toward the door, Kate sank down into the olive-green sofa, her feet curled up beneath her. Even in her foggy state she could not resist asking, "George, what does he look like?"

Ashwell turned to regard her, his heart begging him to stay. Steeling himself against such a path, he answered, "Respectable. Rather short and squat, but his features are nice."

Kate echoed weakly, "Short and squat?"

Ashwell nodded. "And quite bald."

The viscount's laughter reached her as the rich timbre of his voice filled the hall. "Bald," Kate said to herself. She rested her head on the back of the sofa. Yes, life held its little ironies. She could have married a famous, wealthy poet, a peer of the realm and one of the handsomest men of her acquaintance. Instead, she had agreed to marry a squat, bald, pompous idiot.

Kate buttered her bread for the third time. After sipping at her coffee, she nibbled on the slice of bread and, scarcely able to swallow, set the remainder of it back on her plate. Good heavens! What had she done? To marry Mr. Cleeve!

Jaspar, regarding Kate from over his copy of *The Morning Post,* said, "You'll grow a fine layer of mold atop that piece of bread."

Kate regarded her father and said, "What?" And, looking at the bread on her plate, she said, "I suppose I shall. Papa," she regarded him, her head still aching a little and her mouth now as fuzzy as her mind had been the evening before, "I think I have decided to marry Mr. Cleeve." And she frowned at the slice of bread as though it were to rise up at any moment and bite her.

Sitting in the dining room, a small, cosy chamber sporting bright chintz curtains over diamond-paned windows, Kate sighed. How she wished she had not let Ashwell fill her glass so many times.

Jaspar set his paper down on top of his teacup, the cup and saucer clattering as he cried, "What? But I thought you were in love with that damned poet!"

Kate picked up the bread again and wished that her father would not talk so loud. "Love should never be a consideration in marriage. One should contract a sensible alliance or—or take one's parent's advice. Yes, arranged marriages. That is how it should be done. Don't you agree?"

Jaspar looked at his daughter, noticing the circles under her eyes and the way she winced every time he spoke, and said, "Damme, but you were in your altitudes last night! I tell you plain, Kate. Only one thing does any good at all the next day and that's a large tankard of home-brewed."

As he rose from the table, heading toward the bellpull, Kate cried, "No, Papa! I daresay you are quite used to such a remedy but—but I find the suggestion particularly nauseating."

Jaspar paused in his steps and returned to the table. "As you wish. So, you have decided to marry Mr. Cleeve. Does he look at all like Ashwell? I mean, you seemed so taken with that man."

Kate, still holding her bread in one hand, smoothed out her long-sleeved morning gown of lavender muslin with the other. And in a voice full of disappointment, she said, "Your cousin, Papa, has no hair, no height, and Ashwell says he is squat."

"Squat?"

Kate nodded. "And besides that, he is pompous and full of flowery, ridiculous absurdities."

Jaspar reached a hand toward Kate and wrapped his bearlike paw about her own, "I suggest you forget about Mr. Cleeve. You cannot love him and, frankly, I don't care to have such a son-in-law. There is no love lost between me and the Cleeve family. You know that."

Kate said, "It is too late. I have written to him accepting

his proposals."

Jaspar asked, "Did you perform this feat last night, after you found yourself in your cups?"

Kate nodded again.

"Take my advice, daughter. End your engagement with good Mr. Cleeve. And if he has any wisdom at all, he will bow out gracefully."

Kate took a bite of the bread and felt her stomach rise. She chewed slowly and carefully, trying not to think about how the bread seemed to cleave to the roof of her mouth. "No, I must marry him. Ashwell expects it."

Jaspar looked as though he would say something, then he closed his mouth as he flipped the newspaper back into position. After a moment, he said, "Well, if Ashwell expects it and you are determined, then I suppose nothing more need be said."

Kate took a second bite of bread, chewing slowly and swallowing hard. "Of course, if you forbade me—" she offered, with a rather sickly twist to her mouth.

Jaspar did not look at Kate, lifting the paper so as to obscure his vision of her, and said, "No, no. Don't believe in interfering. I trust you to make a mull of it all on your own."

Kate looked about the manor and realized that with her engagement to Mr. Cleeve she did not have to complete the packing of the barrels and trunks that were scattered about the drawing room. She should have felt quite relieved, but instead she felt such a depression descend upon her that when she gazed at the woods atop Knott Hill, she felt as though she were regarding a most formidable enemy. Suddenly, they seemed a great trap to her—iron bars, large keys grating in the lock, gaol. She did not wish to marry Mr. Cleeve, she did not wish to marry anyone. Yet she had given that stupid letter to Ashwell and he, no doubt anxious to see her made miserable, had already delivered it to her—dare she even think the word?—fiancé.

Kate pressed her hand to her forehead. Of all the scatterbrained schemes she had perpetrated, actually rising to

Ashwell's bait and insisting upon marrying the doltish Mr. Cleeve, this was perhaps her worst. Faith, the man was bald, short, and a complete sapskull. She tried to console herself with the notion that now she was free from worry forever—no debts, she could now purchase all of the gowns she could ever wish for, she would have a house in town . . . everything, in fact, that Lord Sapperton had offered her, save a title. Kate smiled at this absurd thought, which streaked so suddenly across her brain. Mr. Cleeve was untitled. Of course! And she laughed in a purely mad fashion. She ought to refuse her cousin because he lacked a title. Why did she not think of it before?

In keeping with the overwhelming sensation that raced across her mind, that she had just escaped from Bedlam, Kate raised her arm and, pointing toward the beechwood, cried, "Absolutely not! It is quite impossible. I cannot marry you."

"How relieved I am," a male voice intruded on her performance. "For the fact is that I am already married."

"Sir William!" Kate cried as she whirled about to face the baronet. And before she could catch her breath at his sudden and unexplained appearance, she flushed a dark red to the very roots of her hair as she remembered that before her stood the man who had loved her mother—her own natural parent, in fact. "Please, sit down." She moved to walk quickly toward the entrance hall and said, "I shall fetch Papa for you."

Sir William caught her arm as she moved near him and said quietly, "I wish to speak with you, not Jaspar."

Kate stopped in her tracks and regarded the hand that held her arm so tightly. She felt frozen to the floor and scarcely able to breathe.

His hat still in hand, Sir William released Kate's arm and turned his hat, inch by inch, beneath his fingers.

Finally gathering courage to look at him, Kate lifted her eyes and saw such anxiety within Sir William's kindly gaze that she let out her breath. "Of course."

Sir William said, "Violet showed me to this room. I'm sorry to intrude, only—" he broke off and said in a harsh voice, "someone has told you the truth. That is why you look so frightened."

346

Kate closed her eyes, her head still aching a trifle, though her stomach had finally settled down. She brushed a hand across her forehead and felt his hand again grasp her arm as he led her to a chair. "I must speak with you. It is most important." She sat down on the tall column-legged chair and found that though she never sat with her hands folded tightly together, of the moment, she could not pry them apart. "Yes," she answered him in a quiet voice, staring at her folded hands. "Papa—that is, Jaspar told me only a few days ago."

Sir William seated himself on the sofa opposite her, perching himself only on the edge of the cushions and setting his hat, brim up, on the table. Stripping off his gloves of York tan and tossing them into the hat, he said, "I'm glad you know." And with these words, he leaned back into the sofa and continued, "In fact, in some ways, it will make what I have to say to you a great deal more meaningful." He looked at her with a steadfast gaze. "For I have come to try, if I may, to persuade you to marry Lord Ashwell."

Chapter Eighteen

"How do you know that he wishes to marry me?" Kate asked, stunned by his pronouncement.

Sir William shook his head, narrowing his blue eyes. "He wears all the appearance of being violently in love with you. His eyes follow you about in every room I have ever shared with him, and since the masquerade, when his quite ridiculous disguise was exposed, he has made it common knowledge that he intends to marry you." He smiled in a conspiratorial fashion. "I had all of this directly from Mrs. Cricklade."

Kate began loosening her fingers one by one. "And Mrs Cricklade is nothing short of an addle-brained, gossiping mushroom."

Sir William lifted his quizzing glass and, crossing one leg over another, began inspecting his highly polished black boots and said, "Had I known you would bite my head off this morning, I should not have ventured out-of-doors."

Kate leaned forward slightly and said, "I am sorry, only I detest tittle-tattle, particularly when I am the subject."

Sir William dropped his quizzing glass and, regarding her with his open blue eyes, said, "Then you should not have made the man fall head over heels in love with you."

"I didn't! He doesn't love me, not really. He is simply angry that I won't have him. He has a monstrous pride and cannot believe that I do not love him."

"You are in a fit of bad temper, are you not? For now you are telling whiskers as well."

Kate rose in a swift, jerky motion, unwilling to meet his penetrating gaze, and moved to stand by the window to the side of the sofa. She watched the chestnut trees being tossed about by a stiff morning breeze.

"Look me in the eye, Katherine, and tell me again that you do not love Lord Ashwell."

Kate looked at him and, feeling trapped, said, "He is insufferable and—even if I do have a certain misguided affection for him, and it is only because—because, oh, I should rather speak of a hundred other things than Lord Ashwell."

Knowing that her mother would not have approved in the least her sitting on the back of the sofa, Kate did so anyway. Sir William turned to regard her, his arm resting on the back of the sofa, and said, "You are grown into the image of your mama. Do you know how difficult it has been for me to see you through every round of seasons that compose your one and twenty years and not be able to ask you all those silly things I ask Mary and Lydia? Like what colour you favour the most and where you hide your love billets."

Kate cried, "Surely you have not asked them where they secrete their letters. Surely not!"

He laughed, "Mary blushed when I asked her, but Lydia showed me."

Kate laughed, "Of course Lydia would."

"You are much alike, you and Lydia." He shook his head slightly, as though trying to clear a vision, and fell silent.

Kate watched him as memories flickered across his features, wrinkles just beginning to etch themselves about his eyes, his brown hair now streaked with silver.

The clock on the mantel ticked quietly in the chamber filled only with Sir William's silent thoughts. Kate sighed, wondering how her mother had committed so grievous an indiscretion, and because Sir William was so easy to talk with, she asked, "Why? Why did you—I mean, how is it that you and my mother—?"

Sir William, his face taking on a pinched aspect, said, "I was in love with Marianne and she with me, long before Jaspar made his intentions known. She was a minx, your mama." His eyes took on the appearance of sparkling blue skies just following a rain. "I loved her so much. I had loved her for years. But she was impulsive and terribly headstrong. She wanted a season in London, though I begged her to marry me when she was just eighteen. And she had her season, then wanted another. In some ways she never seemed satisfied, as though my love for her was not enough. I don't know. I still don't think I really understood her. But finally, as though she had been running for a long time and wished for quieter pastures, she agreed to marry me."

Kate was surprised. Her mother had never said anything to her of Sir William.

"So, she did not tell you. I often wondered if she had told you anything." He paused for a moment, regarding his neatly pared nails, and said, "But we argued, about something stupid. About whether to honeymoon first in Paris or in Florence. She was so shrewish at times! I shall never forget that day! She hefted a number of expensive vases at me. I even bear a scar—a cut across my brow." He fingered the faint indentation and Kate felt a slight flush creep up her cheeks as she remembered shooting Ashwell.

Sir William's voice grew quieter as he said, "And then she eloped with Jaspar. They ran to Gretna Green and for three years I saw nothing of her. I removed to London, where I eventually met Euralia. She was kind and prosaic and I knew that she would make an admirable wife. And she has a sort of quirky sense of humour, though she rarely permits anyone to see it. That delighted me. I toyed with the idea of marrying her. And I spent several months at Edgecote Hall, making my decision. How odd to think that Marianne would make the decision for me."

His voice dropped lower still, and Kate prayed that he would not stop his recital now, that he would not omit what had happened to have actually brought her into the world.

He continued, "I came back to see her, for the first time in years. It was snowing and Jaspar had gone to Cheltenham. . . ." He stopped and said, "I should not be telling you this!"

Kate reached over, tears smarting her eyes, and touched his hand with her own. "Pray, continue. I wish to know."

Sir William looked at her for a moment, his expression solemn, and said, "It had been snowing and for a brief moment the storm cleared; for an hour the sky showed spots of blue. She wanted to go for a walk. She was more lovely than ever, though a little sad that she'd not had any children in three years. She said she loved Jaspar and though he enjoyed gaming a bit more than he ought, still they had a comfortable life together. She seemed happy! Truly! She seemed not to regret her marriage at all. On that point, I wish to be firm. It was only that . . . well, at any rate, we walked along the River Chering, for it was a first snow and the river had not frozen. We threw snow into the swift water, watching it disappear, and then we threw snow at each other, as children might. We continued walking, even though a breeze had come up, blowing hard and steady.

"We had not gone far, or so it seemed, the blue sky having long since disappeared and the snow starting to fall again. Not in gentle flakes, but in sheets as the temperature dropped suddenly. I suppose we had time to return to the manor, but Marianne urged me to take shelter in an old barn past the mill."

Kate stared at him. She had shot Ashwell in that barn.

"I can say no more except that we were alone for too long—old interests surfaced, old loves, old dreams. We did not return to the manor until the next day." He gripped Kate's arm, "But I swear to you that it never happened again. I never meant for it to happen, nor did your mother. I regret it, infinitely." He paused, his own blue eyes swimming a little. "Save for you, my dearest Kate, I wish heartily that the deed had never been done."

Kate dabbed at her own tears, the sadness on his face, of a love that had somehow slipped away from him, bringing her own pain to the surface.

"And when I heard she was increasing, I returned to London that winter and married Euralia. You and Mary were born six months of each other. And you've no idea how grateful I was that Mary was a girl. I could not have borne having you grow up in our cloistered society and not having had a daughter of my own to pet and pamper." He laughed, "Though you and Mary haven't a thing in common. I'd say Lydia has more your temperament."

He slapped Kate's hand, which surprised her, and said, "And that is what I wished to tell you. You've a stubbornness in you, Kate, that I fear you inherited from both of us. Maybe your mother knew that we would always quarrel. I don't know. Perhaps I was too stubborn about Paris. It seemed such a stupid thing to be arguing about and neither of us were willing to give way. And here you are, steeped with such breeding—Lord, heaven help you, you've inherited your stubbornness from us both. Don't let it destroy your happiness forever. Ashwell loves you, and though what he did was quite unconscionable, still he has since heartily regretted all of it."

"But Sir William," Kate cried, "he deceived all of us—me! He made such a fool of me, you've no idea. It was cruel, from the beginning. You cannot know the half of it!"

"Kate," Sir William beseeched her, "pray, hear the words of a man who wishes he had been around to see you take your first steps, to hear your first words, to comfort you in your tumbles and spills. In a few years, what will his silly masquerade seem to you then but just that—a ridiculous schoolboy's prank that was unfitting for a man of his station? And that is all.

"But if you reject him now, I know his character. He'll never return for you. And what will you have then? No, I do not refer to your circumstances; I am speaking of your heart. What will you have then but your pride? And through how many winters' nights will your stubbornness and your pride and your unforgiving spirit keep you warm?"

Kate, feeling extremely uncomfortable with all of Sir William's sound reasoning, blurted out, "But I saw him kissing Julia Moreton in Quening Woods!"

Sir William rose to his feet at these words, picking up his gloves and carefully stretching his fingers into each one. He laughed at her. "And what blue-blooded Englishman who calls himself a man has not tried to kiss Julia?"

Kate knew that her mouth had fallen open in a most unbecoming fashion.

"Think on what I've said, Kate. He loves you and though he

352

did behave as a perfect idiot, his character is quite one of the finest I've known. Don't let stubbornness rule your heart."

Kate moved among the chestnut trees in the drive, the breeze freshening a little as she pressed her bonnet more firmly about her ears and retied the ribbon. After advancing a few more steps toward the lane that ran to Chipping Fosseworth, Kate saw the figure of a woman in the distance—a tall thin woman carrying a bundle in her arms.

With a start, Kate realized that the woman was Thomas's mother. Giving a cry of delight, Kate picked up her lavender muslin skirts and ran to the woman who was carrying the infant Katherine in her arms. The baby, but a few weeks old, slept soundly, her eyes closed in a deep slumber that the mother's steady pace, walking as she had from Quening, seemed to have occasioned.

Kate whispered, "How glad I am to see you and the baby. How is she? I hope she has been well."

"Ay, that she has, Miss Kate. Strong little girl, suckling as she ought. She'll see a great many days, this one."

Kate let out a sigh as she watched little Katherine squirm slightly, appearing unhappy about the lack of motion. Mrs. Coates handed the baby to Kate, who took her in her arms and held her close, rocking her in a steady rhythm as she swayed from side to side. "I hope one day I have such a precious one. How fortunate you are."

"Ay, I am an' that! A quiver full, ye might say." She regarded Kate with a steadfast eye and appeared to weigh something in her mind.

Kate cocked her head. "What is it? I know you've not come all this way just to let me hold Katherine." And remembering suddenly what Maggie had told her the other day, Kate cried, "Oh, no! Tell me at once."

Mrs. Coates folded her arms across her chest and frowned. Her words were quipped and hard. "Thomas be with thirty other men in Stinchfield. They've been drinkin' all day and they be fixin' to burn the waggons wat Sapperton hired to

353

transport his crops." She laid an impulsive hand on Kate's arm, the baby stirring slightly as Mrs. Coates inadvertently pressed against the infant. "Ye've got to do something, miss. Me own Jack has taken up his scythe, as though it were some sword. I be feared o' what will come o' this night's work." Tears brimmed in her brown eyes. "I can't lose me husband, Miss Kate. What would me and the little ones do? Life be hard as it is." She grasped the edge of her shawl and quickly dabbed at her tears as she said, "And wat would I do without Jack? I love him, I do!" And a sob rent her thin frame as the baby wriggled slightly in Kate's arms.

Kate looked down into the peaceful face, content even in the midst of chaos when cared for by loving hands and satisfied at her mother's breast. Regarding the baby with a sudden intense sadness, Kate handed her back to Mrs. Coates. She asked, "But what would you have me do?"

Mrs. Coates wiped the last of her tears and said, "Won't ye talk to his lordship, Miss Kate?"

Kate looked beyond the woman, her gaze fixed on Standen Beeches in the distance. "He won't listen to me, Mrs. Coates. I have tried to talk with him before, but he has no conscience, no soul."

Mrs. Coates looked down at her baby and another tear dropped onto the worn wool blanket that swaddled the infant. To Kate she said, "I oughtn't to have bothered ye." And dropping a small curtsy, she turned on her heel.

Kate watched her go again, feeling an odd sadness attach itself to her heart. She envied the woman her family—that she loved her husband and had so many wonderful children. She thought of the earl, of his desolate, useless life, of his thin white face, of the way he would sneer and speak in caustic tones. He was beyond cruelty now, loading his waggons with grain so that many of the villagers about Stinchfield would barely make it through the winter. He was a monster.

As Mrs. Coates disappeared into the lane, Kate strode toward the stables and had Miss Diana saddled. Surely there was a part of the earl that would listen to reason. Surely! Surely he held within his emaciated ribs some vestige of human compassion. At least Kate felt she must try. While Peter

Coachman, still a little pale from his recent bout with the fever, prepared Miss Diana, Kate returned to the house to don her riding habit. Her thoughts turned again to Sapperton and how strangely he had been behaving of late. Even his attack upon her in Quening Woods was not in keeping with his habitually controlled demeanour. And how many times had he seemed to experience a great pain in his chest.

As she rode out of the drive, she looked back at the manor and felt for just a moment that she ought to take Maggie with her. But the earl would hardly dare to hurt her in the glaring light of day and especially not with a complete staff inhabiting Leachwood, including a very prudish housekeeper. Yes, she would ask first to see the housekeeper.

The days had begun to shorten considerably, and at five in the early evening the sun seemed to tarry upon the countryside in a purely impatient manner, the shadows long and thin and the cooling air a prescience of autumn. Candles lit the parlour of the Swan and Goose, and Lord Ashwell dabbed at his mouth with a starched linen napkin.

James was at Edgecote and the viscount dined alone, now setting the napkin on his lap and drinking a rich port wine when a tapping sounded on the door. He tensed instantly, afraid that yet another unknown female would enter to serve him some other forgotten dish hidden on a shelf in the kitchen. Since having been revealed as the true poet, his masquerade had given him an even more romantic aspect than usual, and he had been inundated with every form of feminine advance.

But before the door opened, an altercation appeared to be transpiring in the hall and a female voice cried, "I'll speak wi' his lordship meself," followed by a clattering of metal on the wood floor and the shrieks of one of the serving maids.

Maggie burst in upon him and Ashwell was on his feet at once, seeing the intense panicked expression on her face. The maid presented an odd figure, her black hair flying from beneath a straw bonnet and her cheeks red as though she had run the entire distance from the manor. She cried, "M'lord, 'tis Miss Kate! I dinnit know wat to do!" And she promptly burst into tears.

Ashwell nearly overset his chair as he shoved it backward and reached the girl in three quick strides. "What is it? What has happened?"

Maggie took a handkerchief that he thrust toward her and blew her nose. "She took Miss Diana out in the late morning and no one has seen her since."

Ashwell glanced at the clock, which promptly began tolling the hour of five, and exclaimed, "Good God." Gripping her shoulders, he forced her to look at him. "Now you must tell me where she is. Did she take a lunch or take her fowling piece? Perhaps she has gone hunting and has forgotten the lateness of the hour."

Maggie shook her head, "Nay. She took nought with her, which made me think she meant to visit one of her friends. And she never visits the villagers without takin' along a basket filled wi' jellies and bread and—tomatoes!"

She burst into tears again and Ashwell reached absently up to his own cheek, the memory of his first day in Chipping Fosseworth speeding back to him.

"Maggie," he cried. "You must help me a little. Please!"

Maggie shook her head. "I doan know. Violet said she was speakin' with a woman from Quening in the drive but a few minutes afore she left."

"Quening," Ashwell mused. "She wouldn't have gone to Leachwood." From the corner of his eye, he noticed an odd movement. And, glancing out the window, he saw a rider speed past the inn and give a shout. He was the farmer's son from Brock Farm. "What's going on, Maggie?" And the two of them moved out into the taproom, where five of the village maids were clustered about the window and talking in quick whispers. Another rider burst beyond the low windows and a shouting up the street drew the young women out of the inn.

Ashwell joined them and watched as a yeoman struck a villager across his face with his riding whip and yelled at him never to return to the farm. The village man, obviously in his cups, caught the whip and almost toppled the young man from his horse. Rider and horse then wheeled about, heading toward the inn where the young ladies stood, aprons wafting in the breeze like the sails of a ship.

Ashwell called to him, "Ho! What is going forward?"

The rider, spurring his horse on and heading back to his farm, called out, "Rioting in Stinchfield! Better arm yourself!"

The young girls screamed and ran inside the inn, nearly knocking Ashwell over as they did so. Turning to Maggie, who had remained within but was now standing at the doorway, he said, "I think I know where Kate is. I suggest you stay here. Don't return to the manor. These riots have struck even in London and you'd not be safe at the manor."

Maggie pressed a hand against a now pale cheek and sank into a settle by the door. Ashwell was about to leave when he felt a pull on his coattail and Maggie, tears again coursing down her cheeks, said, "Please, find Thomas!"

Ashwell gave her a smile and reminded her to remain at the inn, then hurried toward the stables where the horses had been left unattended. Finding his own gear seemed to take forever, his heart racing along in a sudden fear of what might have befallen Kate. He knew she was at Leachwood, but why she had ventured forth on so foolhardy a mission he could not imagine. And knowing her, she would have discounted the value of taking her maid with her. He mounted the horse in a quick, smooth motion and within seconds was pounding out onto the cobbles of the High Street.

Kate could scarcely remain awake, the binds on her hands, which were wrapped behind the chair, though at first a mounting pain, having grown to a mere numbness in the last hour. The first shock of fear, when Sapperton had bound her feet and hands shortly after her arrival at Leachwood, had now robbed her of all energy. For the last hour she had dozed on and off.

She sat in a hard-backed chair in the conservatory, the warmth and humidity of the varied plantlife causing her to perspire.

He had ranted on and on about her stupidity and the whining villagers who were beneath his notice. She had at first argued with him but then he had threatened to gag her mouth, kissing her cheeks as he did so. She had never noticed his eyes before, how small and dark they were as though light found it impossible to penetrate them. And they were so sunk into his head that he was almost skeletal in appearance. And then she realized that he had passed beyond the brink of sanity, that he had slowly been doing so for some time, only she had never seen it before. Her earnest pleas changed to a silence that he appeared to find even more difficult to handle than her urgent cries that he reconsider his intention to remove all the grain from about Stinchfield.

Only once had she seen someone else—the housekeeper. Kate had seen her, and since Sapperton was in the room, she did not want to involve the elderly woman except to relay, if possible by her expression, her need for the woman's help.

Judging by the manner in which the housekeeper covered her mouth with her hand and by the startled, panicked expression in the woman's large brown eyes, Kate felt certain that help would soon arrive. But fifteen minutes passed and then twenty and then an hour and more.

At three o'clock, Sapperton brought in a bandbox full of scrolls that, to Kate, resembled the ones Rupert used for his poetry. With a strange high laugh, the earl withdrew a scroll and began reading. Kate listened to the words and cocked her head. Good Good, it was Rupert's poetry! What did Sapperton mean by it? He read for an hour without ceasing, and Kate began to think that she, too, would go mad.

When the clock had chimed four, the earl stood up and said, "I intend to torture you in just this manner, since you seem to be so fond of poets, until you relent and agree to marry me."

Kate, her senses worn down after so much madness, began laughing hysterically, at which time the earl left the room. Kate had not seen him since. Her mind fizzling down to sleep, she jerked her head awake once and, after only a minute or so, drifted off again. How long she had been asleep she didn't know, and she was not certain what woke her except that her head ached terribly. She felt pressure on her arm and found herself staring into Ashwell's concerned face. She watched his lips move but could not quite hear what he was saying, and she shook her head.

She felt the binds at her wrist loosening and when they were free, she could not move her arms at all. She felt George take her hands carefully, massaging her fingers, wrists, and arms slowly, bending each joint with great care and finally returning her hands to her lap. Kate stared at her fingers and tried to move them. But somehow they did not seem attached to her body. For several minutes, the viscount pressed and massaged her fingers, which were tingling almost unbearably. As the feeling returned, she began stretching her fingers and breathed a sigh of relief.

"Where is Sapperton?" she managed after a time as she flexed and balled up her hands, still staring at them.

"I don't know. Are you all right?" He tried to keep his voice steady and not to let the anger that burned in his breast overwhelm him.

He unbound her feet and was about to beg her to try to stand when the clinking of metal sounded at the doorway.

The earl's laughter, muffled by all the greenery, sounded like a flat note upon Ashwell's ears as he watched Sapperton set a branch of candles upon a small table by the door.

"You bastard!" the viscount cried.

Sapperton threw him a sword, hilt first, and Ashwell caught it neatly. He did not hesitate to attack the man who had pursued him through his nightmares.

Kate stood up from her chair, her legs nearly buckling at the knees as she heard Sapperton's laughter again, steel ringing against steel, the two men, transported somewhere out of time, engaged in a final battle. They danced among the oranges and heavy-scented jasmines, slicing through ferns and palm leaves, and all the while the earl's laughter, a shrill, tinny sound that gave the conservatory an unreal quality, echoed from window to window.

Kate cried, "No, Ashwell. Stop at once. You do not understand." But the viscount gave no indication that he heard her voice. His eyes were glinting in the failing light, the windows tinged with pink from the sunset, scattered clouds reflected in the glass, life falling to the brick floor in bits of green dashed with blood. Kate saw the blood and screamed for them to stop. "He is mad, I tell you!" she called to the

359

viscount. "Don't risk your life over him. He is mad, I tell you."

Both men wore black coats and she could not tell who had been hurt.

Ashwell appeared all flushed, his brow sweating, his eyes glowing with a fierce light. Sapperton paled and paled again, a strange unearthly smile pinned to his face, his crooked teeth a grey shadow. A cloud seemed to obscure the last bit of light, the two men dark images now as they thrust crossed swords and parried about the room. Sapperton took in great sucks of air, unable to catch his breath. His thrusts grew wild and undisciplined and Ashwell laughed at him, a sound that caused Kate to take a step backward, for it had the same mad quality of Sapperton's laugh.

"And now, my lord," Ashwell taunted the earl, circling his rapier in front of Sapperton, "I shall see you to your grave." He caught each wild thrust that the earl shoved at him.

Sapperton could scarcely breathe, his hand pressed against his chest. He slashed the air in front of Ashwell and the viscount caught his blade, slapping it harmlessly away as he would a child's sword.

Kate watched as the viscount's face became suddenly hard and cold and she knew he meant to kill him. "No," she cried in a long sound that seemed forever to travel to Ashwell's hearing.

Lord Ashwell heard the cry but saw only, in his mind's eye, the exact spot where he wished to send the sword through the earl's thin, diseased soul. He readied his sword, feeling the weight of it, and in that split second before action, he knew what the man's body would feel like before he sent the sword into the earl's flesh. But just as he acted, the earl, still clutching his chest, stumbled sideways, Ashwell's sword landing harmlessly into the trunk of palm.

Kate did not hesitate to intervene this time and she threw herself upon the viscount, who fought her off, knowing that his quarry had risen to his feet and was now escaping. Sapperton stumbled from the conservatory and Kate kept saying, "He is ill, he is ill. Let him go. He did not harm me. He has gone mad!"

Finally Ashwell ceased struggling with her and looked up into a broken fern frond, taking deep breaths and letting the heat of his blood, which seemed to have inflamed every nerve in his body, retreat slowly like soldiers called to battle but not permitted to rout the enemy.

"Why?" he asked, his deep voice held in check by the living things about them. "Why did you not let me finish him off?"

Kate rested her head on his arm. "He is mad, he is ill. Did you not see the way he clutched at his chest and how difficult it was for him to breathe? I think his heart has nearly failed him, even now perhaps he is dying."

Ashwell sat up, the sword falling by his side as he cried, "I was myself insane. To have found you in this condition—I could not account for my actions. What did he mean to do?"

Kate held her hand to her forehead as she sat next to the viscount. She could not refrain from laughing a little and, in a weak voice, said, "He—he meant to torture me by—" She began laughing in earnest, realizing how absurd the entire situation had become. "He spent nearly an hour reading Rupert's poetry to me."

Ashwell stared at her in disbelief. He had fought and nearly killed a man because of this?

Kate remembered that one of them had been hurt and she asked the poet if he had received a wound. But Ashwell shook his head in response and, in a voice of astonishment, said, "He had bound you to that chair for who knows how long, only to read poetry to you?"

When Kate nodded, he clasped his hands loosely between his knees and, staring at the brick path beneath his black boots, said, "You cannot know just how long I have waited for an opportunity to face him with a weapon more lethal than my fists."

Kate brushed a leaf from his hair and said, "He hurt the woman you loved, didn't he? The woman you spoke of on our journey back from Tewkesbury."

Ashwell thought of Amelia and, for the first time since her death, felt no disturbing ache tighten his chest. "Yes. He ruined her and she took her own life." No convulsive pain passed through him, only a vague sorrow that Amelia had lived so useless an existence.

Regarding Kate with a smile, he said, "How happy I am that he did not harm you." He saw a sudden reserve enter her brown eyes as she shifted away from him slightly. He could not resist leaning close to her and saying, "Of course, I suppose listening to Rupert's poetry for nigh on an hour may have done irreparable damage. Particularly when I know you to be so completely addicted to mine."

Kate, who had been prepared to make a long and appropriate speech of thanksgiving for his kind assistance in removing her bonds, took this remark as it was meant. Squaring her shoulders, she said, "Oh, the devil take you, Ashwell." And she rose quickly, only to find her legs still not perfectly useful, and was quite angry to have to accept his help as he supported her through the conservatory.

The housekeeper met them at the doorway, wringing her hands and saying, "Me lord, pray forgive me, but I canna find Lord Sapperton anywhere and two of his servants are in the kitchen, bloodied from head to foot with fighting. A riot has broken out in Stinchfield!"

But before the woman could turn away to lead them to the kitchens, Kate cried, "Mrs. Coln, why did you not call for someone to assist me?"

She pressed a hand against her white cheek, her eyes darting from side to side like a frightened rabbit, and cried, "Ye canna know what 'tis been like these last three weeks. He's been a madman, threatening to murder everyone in one breath, then apologizing in the next. When I saw ye in the early part o' the afternoon, I sent two men—his lordship's servants—for help, but they were beaten so badly!" She burst into tears. "And they returned a bit ago, but I had to send fer ta doctor. I dinnit know wat to do." And she burst into tears.

Kate placed her arm about the woman's shoulders and said, "I'm sorry. There, don't cry. All's well now. Pray, dry your tears and lead us to the kitchens at once."

Following the housekeeper, who kept pulling at the skirts of her black bombazine gown, Ashwell and Kate hurried toward the kitchens. Leachwood, a rambling estate of only two levels, but which had been added to by succeeding owners in a perfectly haphazard manner, seemed to stretch for miles as they twisted and turned here and there, finally reaching the kitchens. Once there, Kate thought her stomach would never cease reeling at the sight of both men, whose faces were swollen nearly beyond recognition as Doctor Adlestrop tended to them, working in his slow, steady manner and pressing linen cloths over sluggish wounds.

Looking at Kate over his spectacles, his white shirt stained with blood at the sleeves, the good doctor frowned. Turning his attention back to the man who sat before him in a limp fashion, his mouth open, blood and saliva draining from his swollen lips, he addressed the viscount, "Lord Ashwell, I hope you can find some means of stopping this terrible riot or a good many honest men will hang tomorrow when government troops arrive."

In a quiet voice, a hand pressed against her stomach, Kate said, "I would like to assist you if I may, Doctor."

Ashwell, who had been standing slightly in front of Kate, pulled her forward and placed a supporting arm about her waist. Before the doctor could speak, he looked down at her, his blue eyes serious, and said, "I know that you would wish to help Dr. Adlestrop but I firmly believe that you are needed in trying to stop this riot. The villagers respect you and, given Sapperton's condition, I've every reason to believe that Rupert will be happy to take his place and make those assurances that will end this riot."

Kate looked up into the poet's thoughtful blue eyes and heard his words, feeling a little numb about the edges of her spirit. When the doctor added that the suggestion had great merit, Kate nodded slowly and said, "I will do everything I can, of course."

Ashwell squeezed Kate's waist and the housekeeper, who felt she had borne all that she could for one evening, again burst into tears. But the doctor addressed her sharply, "Stubble it, Mrs. Coln. Since Miss Draycott cannot assist me, you will have to take her place." And the good woman, though sniffing once or twice, moved silently to empty a basin of pink-tinged water.

Lord Ashwell took Kate's hand and said, "Which way to the stables? Are you familiar with Leachwood?"

Kate, every thought now turned to the difficulties before them, nodded and led the way out of the kitchen to the stone buildings, separated by a few hundred yards from the main house. But halfway there, they both stopped at the glow of light coming from the direction of Quening and Ashwell cried, "Good God, they've torched at least a dozen hayricks."

Both Kate and the poet picked up their steps, nearly running to the stables where, with the help of a groom, they harnessed four of Sapperton's bays to a travelling chariot.

The stableboy, with his eyes sporting a fire nearly as bright as the burning hayricks, said, "I be 'appy to ride postillion, me lord."

Ashwell gestured for him to ascend the lead horse and climbed into the yellow coach. The doors were emblazoned with the earl's coat of arms, and he leaned out the window and yelled to the stableboy, "You'd best expect a great deal of mischief, my lad. If you're lacking a stout heart, you ought to dismount now, for I cannot be responsible for your safety." Turning to Kate, he asked, "Where will we find Rupert?"

Kate thought for a moment as she again rubbed her wrists. "Stinchfield. Sapperton said he had gone to the Bell Inn." Her memories of the earl's haunted face loomed up before her and she closed her eyes.

Leaning his head out the window, he cried, "To the Bell Inn and spring 'em!"

Chapter Nineteen

Even before they reached Stinchfield, they could hear the shouting of the mob and the firing of pistols and every manner of loud black-powder rifles.

Kate clenched her hands together in her lap and prayed that no one would perish from this evening's work. And all of it had been the fault of Lord Sapperton's demented mind, stealing food from people who had slaved the entire summer to bring in what little wheat the dry weather had produced.

Travelling at a sharp pace down the High Street, villagers began following the chariot with shouts of, "The earl's coach! Hang Lord Sapperton!"

Kate felt the coach rock as more than one projectile reached them. She started to raise the window-glass but Ashwell cried, "No, keep it down or some rock will shatter the window and cut us to ribbons." As the Bell Inn came into view, the rioters lining the street flowed in about them and they could no longer continue up the High Street.

Again, the mob immediately pulled the groom from the horse and Ashwell, opening the door and leaning his tall frame out into the street, cried, "Let him be! The earl has disappeared. We seek Rupert Westbourne, who can end this nightmare. He is an honest man and heir to Leachwood, as you know! He will not let the waggons leave Stinchfield. He will not let the people of this fair market town starve!"

The crowd seemed to quiet a little as shouts turned to mumbles, but a voice called out, "He lies! He'll protect his class and see all of us hang!"

The crowd raised their fists and jeered at Lord Ashwell. Kate thought for a moment that the horrors that had befallen some of the French aristocracy would soon befall them and could imagine a tumbril parting the crowd before them. The crowds did part, but instead of a tumbril Rupert emerged, poking his ivory-handled cane this way and that, and Kate let out a breath she did not even know she was holding.

Appearing at least seven feet tall, he called to Ashwell, "Pray, where is my miser of an uncle? Is he with you?"

Ashwell grinned. "No. He has disappeared."

"Then we shall have to put an end to this ridiculous farce." His authoritative voice seemed to silence a great portion of the mob about him. He was certainly a sight to behold, dressed in yellow satin knee breeches, a lavender coat, and a shocking emerald-green waistcoat.

Kate smiled, almost wanting to laugh, for in all the years she had known Rupert—his ridiculous costumes, his absurd poetry, his dreadful affectations—never had she really thought that he could command anything, and especially not a crowd half crazed with fear and drink. But the mob parted for him, backing away as he rapped and shoved his cane among them. And she remembered suddenly his grandfather, the late earl, and was put in mind of the old man who had been equally short of stature but certainly no fop, and who, when he desired to do so, could even command the House of Lords.

Ashwell answered, "I thought you might be able to finish this absurd business, and we've come only to fetch you back to Leachwood."

Most of the crowd quieted down considerably at these words exchanged between two men who had both saved a great many lives as a result of their involvement in the Luddite attack on the cloth mill. One drunken man, however, cried out, "Ye'll not take we fer a pack o' country rustics!" And he lunged at Rupert.

But in a quick piece of footwork, Rupert sidestepped the man's large paws, letting him fall harmlessly at his feet. And where the man had touched his lavender coat, Rupert dusted himself off in an affected manner and said to a rather burly man next to him, "See that this fellow is taken home, and I strongly suggest a cup of tea to revive him a little. He is quite off his feet!" And pulling a half crown from his pocket, he tossed it to the man.

Quening's smithy pocketed his largess and presented Rupert with a gap-toothed smile. "Ever since Edgecote, I thought ye were a right 'un!" And, addressing his compatriot, who still hadn't been able to gain his feet, he told him that he'd made nothing short of an arse of himself and would he like to go home now.

Rupert climbed into the travelling chariot and Kate could see that, while he held himself in the coolest pose ever, his forehead was beaded with sweat and his knuckles, folded about the head of his cane, were white.

Some of the crowd began dispersing but many followed them out toward Leachwood. Ashwell said, "You're full of pluck, Mr. Westbourne. I don't think I could have handled the crowd with such calm assurance."

Rupert held Ashwell's gaze and said, in a quiet voice, "I don't doubt for a second that had you not come along, I would now be hanging from the sign above the Bell Inn. I owe you a great debt, Lord Ashwell. You have but to ask anything of me and I shall do it."

Kate, never having known Rupert until this moment, tucked her arm about his and held it tightly. She could feel that he was trembling as he gave her a weak smile.

He said, "Where is my uncle?"

Kate looked at Ashwell, then back at Rupert. "We don't know. I was with him at Leachwood the entire afternoon, until but an hour ago."

Rupert regarded her with a startled expression and said, "I have known for some time that he wished to marry you and also that he had a certain instability in him. Did he—" he paused and took his lace kerchief from his coat pocket and, after wiping his brow in an unsteady manner, continued, "did he hurt you, Kate?"

Squeezing his arm, she said, "No. He did not. He kept me in the conservatory most of the afternoon, but he did not seem to wish to hurt me, only to keep me there."

Rupert said nothing for a moment, looking out at the countryside, at the blaze of the hayricks, and said, "But you don't know where he went?"

Ashwell said, "He and I fought with swords, and after some time he seemed to find breathing a great difficulty and he ran from the house. No one knows where he went."

"I think he is ill," Rupert said, and as they fell silent he looked about the countryside, passing villagers all heading toward the River Avenlode, and he cried, "Stop at once! There is no reason to go to Leachwood. No one will be there. I have just remembered that the waggons are at the mill by the river."

And with that, Ashwell leaned out the window and told the groom to ride posthaste to the flour mill just west of Stinchfield.

All along the road, villagers tried to stop them, Rupert kept his head out the window and shouted, "We'll keep the grain in Quening!" Over and over. And though the carriage was considerably jolted with clods of dirt and the groom took more than his share of abuse, they neared the river with more and more of the rioters following in their wake. Along the rutted road, which the earl never repaired, the travelling chariot bounded about and Kate thought she would have any number of bruises before the night was spent.

As the coach slowed, their progress halted by the mass of villagers that had congregated about the flour mill, Rupert leaned forward and, from a secret compartment in front of them, withdrew a pistol, a leather pouch containing several pistol balls, and a bag of powder. Without hesitation, he handed the weapon to Kate.

Holding the well-balanced pistol in hand, Kate hefted it several times and immediately packed the bore with powder, removing the rod from the underneath side of the pistol and sliding it into the bore. After retrieving a pistol ball from the pouch, she slid it into the pistol and tamped it firmly against the powder.

As they neared the mill where one of the waggons had been torched and was now lighting the night sky, Kate handed the pistol to Ashwell. Looking into his serious blue eyes, she frowned, "Pray, do not harm anyone. I have been so afraid that—"

He covered her hand with his own. "I promise you I won't." And with a grim set to his jaw, he said, "I shall only fire it if I cannot control this mob otherwise, and then only for effect."

Kate thought of Thomas, of his mother, of all the townspeople in Stinchfield who she had known since she was able to ride about the countryside, and she realized how easy it was for one man to jeopardize an entire community. Lord Sapperton had much to answer for.

A few hundred yards from the mill, where five waggons had been loaded with a vast quantity of wheat, readied for shipment to London where the earl could command as high a price as he desired, the crowd waved their fists and shouted at a number of the earl's labourers, who had been tied up and strapped to the grain sacks of the second waggon. Two of the men were crying pitifully and one of them just stared ahead, seeing nothing.

Ashwell said beneath his breath, "They mean to set them afire with the waggon." And in one swift movement, he threw open the door to the travelling chariot and leaped to the ground. Kate felt struck motionless by the horror of the mob's intention. Scanning the faces of the three men, she bit her hand to keep from screaming, for tied to the waggon was Jack Coates. Why? Even Mrs. Coates had believed he was involved with the rioters. Then why was he being held captive?

"George!" she cried. "They've got Thomas's father!" And she followed Ashwell into the crowd.

Kate felt her heart thundering in her ears and stayed doggedly at the viscount's heels. She heard his voice. "You there, and you. Make way for us! Stand aside! We must get to the waggons before they are set ablaze!"

Several men, who had followed the town coach from Stinchfield, helped to create a path. Men like Jack Coates, who wanted nothing to do with burning the wheat or murdering anyone. They just wanted food for their families.

The crowd seemed to roll in great waves as labourers and villagers demanded that the culprits be burned for their betrayal. Kate kept her eyes glued to Ashwell's back and, somewhere in her fogged mind, knew that Rupert was right on her own heels. They mustn't hurt Jack, her mind cried over and over.

Mrs. Coates found Kate and pulled on her arm, her face streaked with tears. "They be murderin' me Jack because he spoke against burnin' the wheat. Help us, Miss Kate!" But the crowd swarmed about Kate, the shouting a terrible din in her ears. The mob sucked Mrs. Coates in and she disappeared.

Kate was beyond fear, her feet in a plodding motion as she followed Ashwell. These desperate men mustn't harm anyone or the government would wreak so vicious a revenge that no family would be left untouched. Some would hang and others would find themselves transported to New South Wales, families torn apart, some destroyed forever.

A new shouting rose up as she heard the crowd recognize Rupert. "'Tis the heir to Leachwood. Bind him wi' the rest!"

Finally the crowd broke and Kate found herself thrust by dirty hands up onto one of the waggons, her feet slipping on the sacks of grain. Ashwell grabbed her hand and pulled her up. Two men seized her and, upon recognizing her, cried, "'Tis Miss Draycott!" And, as though they had just touched a burning coal, they backed away from her.

"Stop!" Kate cried as she looked out upon the crowd. "Stop this madness! You must listen to me!"

But too much ale had passed about the mob, and her pleas were drowned by men and women shouting that it was time to torch the waggons.

A pistol shot ripped through the air, and for a moment the crowd fell into a stunned silence. Ashwell tossed the now empty pistol, still smoking, to one of the men standing on the ground and wasted no time in addressing the crowd. "Good citizens of Quening and Stinchfield. None of this grain will leave your town. Mr. Westbourne has given his word as a gentleman and he promises to open the mill immediately, with no charge to any for this season's poor harvest, that all might have an honest share of the flour for the winter!"

A voice from the crowd cried out, "You've no say in the matter, my bonny poet!" And the crowd laughed and jeered at Ashwell. "Nobbut Sapperton can do sech a thing, an' he won't!"

Rupert, who was nearly sliding off the sacks himself, cried,

"But I can! As my uncle's heir, I will pledge my word that the mill shall be reopened and any as have need may use it. All of this grain"—he swept an arm about him, encompassing the four remaining waggons—"shall not leave this place and you may take what you like now! Only, don't burn any more of it." He cast his eyes toward the waggon where the men were tied and cried out, "And release these men, who have not harmed anyone!"

"They be traitors!" a woman's voice called out. "Them two worked fer Sapperton!"

Ashwell cried, "And which of you, given the choice, would not work even for Sapperton rather than starve yourselves? Don't punish them for seeing to their families as any of you would have, given the chance!"

A great mumbling accompanied this speech and Ashwell quickly slid from the waggon. Taking a hatchet from one of the men standing guard over the prisoners, he cut the ropes in a quick, deft motion as he ran from man to man. Kate, her heart still thudding, watched the crowd shift uneasily. She knew they were not certain whether to permit him to release the men or not. She saw one man and then another begin advancing toward him, and she cried, "Do not blame anyone, save the Earl of Sapperton, whose greed and twisted mind have brought our community to this dreadful state." Though she looked at the crowd in front of her, out of the corner of her eye she tried to see if the men were free yet. How slowly they all seemed to move from having been bound up, their joints stiff as they rubbed their wrists and tried to stand. Hurry, she thought. To the crowd, who seemed distracted by her words, she continued, "Sapperton alone is responsible and God will see that he is justly rewarded for his terrible crimes against all our villages. Even now, I have reason to believe that his heart is failing him, that he hasn't long to live. Is this not justice for the man?"

The crowd gasped at these words, uncertain what to think of this news, and a man's voice called out, "He ought to be hanged."

Rupert startled the crowd by saying, "Were there a true justice in this land, any man who treated his neighbours so cruelly would receive such a sentence. But the law ranges with the noblemen of the land, as you know only too well. And justice does not always prevail. But do not now take lives that are innocent and whose blood will surely stain your futures forever. Do not be deceived! The King will not let you remain unpunished! You will certainly feel the ropes about your own necks, or separation forever from your beloved England, in some far-off continent." The crowd seemed, word by word, to quiet down, and Kate could see that the men in the other waggon had been freed and were now standing near Ashwell, as though afraid to leave his protection. Jack Coates stood by his side and held the hatchet in his hand.

Rupert turned to one of the men that he knew to be sympathetic to ending the riot and, in a low voice, said, "You must fetch the miller immediately! Tell him, if he values his livelihood and his life, to open the mill tonight. Tell him I said so and will pay him handsomely! And be quick!"

From the crowd, a man's slurred voice called up to him, "Ye ain't more than a peacock with a man's body!" And the crowd laughed.

He struck an affected pose, for the sheer entertainment of the crowd, and said, "My good fellow! Do I detect a note of disbelief in your voice? Step forward!"

The man shoved his way to the front to stand just below Rupert. The dandy turned to one of the men behind him and cried, "Throw down a sack of grain to that man."

The crowd seemed stunned as a large, heavy sack of wheat hit the gravel in front of the man. Rupert asked, "Will this feed your family? Take it, then." And, waving his arm out over the crowd, he said, "Each of you take one for your families."

A great roar of approval filled the smoke-laden air about the waggons. Kate felt her own waggon begin to rock as several men mounted the sacks of grain and began handing them to the villagers waiting below. One by one, the sacks were hefted down and Kate now found her own balance jeopardized as the sacks began disappearing about her. Rupert climbed down nimbly, and Kate was quite peremptorily lifted off her feet and passed down a trail of villagers as though she, too, had been a sack of grain, and she started laughing. And the men laughed with her.

Within a half hour, not only was the grain distributed but the miller had arrived and the flour mill set in motion, the river diverted to the massive wheel that soon began humming and turning in its steady rhythm. The people about the banks of the river, torchlights reflected in the water, cheered as they hefted Rupert onto their shoulders and carried him about until the dandy said he might faint.

On the following morning, Kate lay on her side, her pillows bunched up under her head. With one hand tucked beneath her cheek, she thought over all the events of the day before. A nightmare of a day, as she recalled having been bound up in Sapperton's conservatory and later driving in his travelling chariot in search of Rupert, to finally confront the rioters. Her eyes burned and she felt as though she had been ridden over by a hundred horses. Her body ached and her eyes were swollen, the smoke from the fires of the night before having taken its toll.

Maggie opened the door slowly, bearing a large silver bed tray. Kate smelled the coffee and smiled as the aroma of a fresh-baked apricot tart permeated her bedchamber. She sat up, and Maggie placed the tray on her lap and plumped up her pillows. Kate looked at her maid and realized that Maggie wore an unusually solemn expression. "What is it? You look very unhappy, and I know for a fact that Thomas is safe."

Maggie placed both hands over her cheeks. "'Tis not Thomas, fer I seen him this morning afore he began his work. 'Tis someat dreadful and 'tis me own fault, miss. I be the one who done it. I wished him dead and now he is. The earl of Sapperton be dead!"

Kate felt her heart begin to pound. "He can't be! Did he not return to Leachwood?"

"No, they found him in the barn on ta squire's property."

Kate tilted her head back to look at Maggie, her voice full of shock. "Here? On our land?"

Maggie nodded. "Thomas found him this morning. Ta barn be full of grain. He'd used it to store more than a hundred sacks of wheat, and he were bent over them and smiling and cold as

373

the first frost." She lifted her apron and covered her face.

Kate shook her head and frowned. Why had she felt at all surprised? She had even said as much to the rioters the evening before. How odd it was to think of him dead. Gathered to his ancestors. Kate picked up her cup and, reclining against the pillows, sipped at the steaming black coffee.

She said, "Will you pull all the drapes back, Maggie? I wish to see the morning. And open all the windows! I want to smell the last of summer before autumn races through our little valley."

Maggie threw the curtains back and cried, "Do ye think 'tis me fault?" Her voice strained, her eyes pinched.

Kate smiled, fingering the rim of her cup. "I'm afraid you would have to share that blame with at least three hundred other persons today. You were not the only one that wished for his death." She too, had wished for it. How horrid! Yesterday he had been alive, such as his life was, and today he was gone. How quickly life could cease. Perhaps that was what Sir William meant. Life passed so quickly, and why had she accepted Mr. Cleeve's proposals, a man she had never met? Why had Ashwell teased her so?

And today Mr. Cleeve was to arrive.

Dressed in her finest morning gown of a delicate peach muslin, ruffles made up of the thin gauzy fabric circling the bottom of her gown, Kate kicked her skirts in front of her, watching the ruffles bounce. She was pacing the length of the drawing room, and Jaspar cried, "Sit down at once or I shall tie you to the sofa! I will not endure one more heavy sigh or languishing look! For heaven's sake, Kate, don't marry the fellow if you dislike it so much!"

Kate lifted her chin. That is precisely what everyone expected her to do—to leave poor Mr. Cleeve quite in the lurch after she had accepted his proposals. Well, she would not jilt him. Men were not permitted, according to society's rules, to do such a thing, and why a woman should be allowed to do so was the most abominable injustice ever! No, she would never jilt poor Mr. Cleeve.

But then, as she sat down on the sofa, her abrupt movement causing the little ruffles edging her low bodice to bounce, blue eyes that always seemed to her to be filled with summer's sharp, brilliant light would intrude on her mind and wreak havoc at the fringes of her guarded heart. Blast the man! Why had he so provoked her into accepting Cleeve's offer? A thousand times she had regretted her impulsive response to the rogue's clearly taunting words. It was Ashwell's fault. All of it from beginning to end. Had he only not been playing a masquerade—but that wouldn't fadge, for hadn't she given him every reason to play her for the perfectly scatterbrained idiot she was?

Lord, what was she to do? Her hands encased in delicate lace gloves, Kate twisted her pearl necklace around and around her fingers, chewing on the pearls and staring in a strange, obsessed fashion at the book lying on the table at her elbow. Good heavens, how had Ashwell's poetry come to be in the drawing room? Why, Mr. Cleeve would think she had a *tendre* for the poet!

She cocked her head. "Papa, who put this book here?" And as she glanced at her father, she noticed the particularly red appearance to his cheeks as he answered, in a bluff manner, "What book? Don't know what you're talking about! When did I ever bother with books?" And he picked up his most recent copy of a sporting magazine and Kate grimaced at him. For no reason at all, she then stood up in a quick, jerky manner and resumed pacing the floor.

When a carriage was heard on the drive, she knew that her heart had hit clear to the depths of her stomach and was only now, as she watched a large town coach lumber through the chestnut trees, returning to its normal position within her chest. Her feet felt frozen to the floor, and she could not move. She could only watch in doomed fascination as the coach pulled to a rocking stop in front of the manor. She felt faint, her ears buzzing a little, but when Thomas opened the door for Mr. Cleeve, her mind cleared instantly. And—oh, Lord in heaven, have mercy—he was bald and short and squat and how nervously he wiped his forehead!

"Oh, Papa," Kate cried, "What have I done?"

She felt her father suddenly beside her, his arm supporting her waist. "Good God, Kate! The man looks like a tradesman! Can this be pretty little Arabella's son? He even dresses like a merchant! What's this?"

Kate then had all the shock of seeing a very fashionable gentleman—tall, handsome, curling black locks, Ashwell in fact—descend from the same vehicle. She exclaimed, "What the devil is he doing here? Oh, I cannot greet them both at one and the same time! Oh, Lord, what shall I do? I cannot—" Then she grew angry and threw up her arms, nearly knocking Jaspar off balance. "Well, if this isn't just like that man! He's come to gloat over my—my choice of a husband. Well! We shall see who shall gloat over whom!"

Jaspar also threw up his hands. But in addition to this motion, he looked at the ceiling, not to admire the intricate scrollwork there but to cast an exasperated plea for heaven to help his daughter.

When the two men were escorted into the drawing room, Kate had recovered her spirits and was able to present a firm, tilted chin toward Ashwell and to smile in a sweet manner upon Mr. Cleeve.

Jaspar immediately came forward and bowed to Mr. Cleeve, saying, "You don't look a thing like either Arabella or Jack! And I won't believe for a moment that you were a sideslip, for Arabella would hardly have played fast and loose! She may have chosen the wrong man for all that, but she was a good girl." He nodded his head at these words that he felt were certainly the kindest things he could say to the offspring of two people for whom he still harboured a great deal of resentment.

Mr. Cleeve took the proffered hand, his face turning a brilliant shade of red as he then hastily wiped his beaded brow.

Jaspar bowed to Ashwell and stared at him hard, his eyes narrowing. "In fact, of the two of you, I'd say you look more like my cousin than this man." And then his eyes nearly popped from his head as he broke into a loud guffaw and slapped Ashwell on the shoulder. "Well, what a damned, rascally rogue you are!"

Kate scowled at her father and moved forward, extending her hand to Mr. Cleeve. The short man, casting an astonished glance toward the viscount, took her hand and, with a nervous laugh, said, "I am sorry to say there has been some little mistake."

Kate smiled at him and said, in an encouraging fashion, "Oh? And what is that, cousin?"

He laughed again. "I do beg your pardon, Miss Draycott, but you are under some great misapprehension. I am only Mr. Cleeve's solicitor. My name is Mr. Slad." He gestured to Lord Ashwell, bowing to his client, and continued, "May I present to you Mr. Cleeve. You, of course, know him by his title only— as Lord Ashwell."

Kate knew that somewhere from the time the two men had entered the room she had become quite deranged, and she blinked her eyes. Knowing that she could not have heard him correctly, she said, "I beg your pardon?"

Jaspar cried, as a smile overspread Ashwell's face, "By God, Arabella's minxish expression if ever I remember it. Now, why did I not see it before? Damme, what a great joke!" And he turned to his daughter. "You ought to marry Mr. Cleeve. I was greatly mistaken before. He is just the man for you." He promptly went to the table below Marianne's portrait and, pouring out four glasses of sherry, lifted the decanter in a salute to her. With a broad smile he brought each of them a glass of wine, saying that he should like to propose a toast.

Kate took the glass that Jaspar handed her, staring at the nut-coloured liquid as though it had just turned green and shaking her head. She glanced at the three men who were smiling at her, and her gaze fixed itself firmly upon Lord Ashwell. She could feel her own face harden and her eyes grow wide as she screamed, "You scoundrel! You lying, cheating, wretched excuse for a man! You tricked me! You made me write a letter that you knew—" She clenched the glass in her hand. "Will you never cease to torment me, you damned libertine!"

The solicitor, who had been taking a drink of his sherry, spit the drink all over himself as Kate's venomous words poured from her pretty lips. When he had entered the room, he had been struck with Miss Draycott's great beauty and perfectly ladylike demeanour. But this! Oh, what a fine story he would relate to his compatriots back at the firm. And he dabbed his handkerchief over the front of his plain black coat.

Jaspar said, "Now, Kate—"

Cutting her father off, Kate cried, "Do not, Papa! Do not 'Now, Kate' me! I will not have it!" And she stamped her foot.

In a quiet voice, Ashwell said, "We are to be married at three o'clock precisely. And I see by your clock that the hour is considerably advanced. I do apologize for our tardiness, but we lost track of the time, since I was telling everyone at the Swan and Goose of my good fortune and Mr. Beverstone insisted upon bringing out his very best brandy and toasting our forthcoming nuptials." He sighed with a deep sense of satisfaction and continued, "Of course, he did warn me that you were quite a termagant and that I ought to be prepared to whip you if necessary."

Kate listened to this speech with such a growing sense of outrage that her fury seemed to immobilize her tongue. After sputtering and spewing, she finally managed, "You, my Lord Ashwell, are quite the most insolent, arrogant, worthless creature of my acquaintance. And if you think for a moment that I will marry you, then you have bats in your belfry. I"— and she turned on her heel, setting her glass down on the table with a loud clink—"bid you good day." And she walked in a stately fashion toward the long windows that opened onto the rose garden. How well she had handled this perfectly disagreeable situation, and Kate decided that a walk among her flowers would calm her disturbed sensibilities.

But just as she was about to open the door to the garden, she felt herself scooped up bodily and flung, quite without ceremony, over Ashwell's solid shoulder.

"Set me down!" she cried. "At once!"

"Now, Kate," Jaspar began again. "You ought to marry him. You'll hardly get a better offer and I doubt that he'll ask a second time. What man would?"

Bouncing against Ashwell's shoulder and not finding it easy to speak, let alone breathe, she said, "He never asked me!"

Ashwell said, "But I did ask you, and you wrote me a very polite, though somewhat illegible letter saying that you would marry me. Or have you forgotten? I hope you don't mean to

378

jilt me, Kate. Why, I couldn't bear it! I should fall into a decline!"

"I hope you fall into a ditch, you useless scoundrel! Only such a fate would be too good for you." Every word hurt, since her stomach was settled into his shoulder, but she continued, "You ought to have your neck stretched, rats should chew off your fingers, the plague should swell up your face, the pox—oh, the pox on you!"

But his rich laughter, which always had a way of tearing at her soul, filled the entryway as he threw open the front door to the manor and breezed through. Kate had one last glimpse of Maggie crying and smiling at her, and Cook, with a large wooden ladle in her hand, slapping it against her other hand and smiling in a pleased fashion.

Halfway down the shady row of chestnut trees, with her father and Mr. Slad following discreetly behind, Kate begged Ashwell to put her down. Which he did, quite summarily. But before she could make good her intended escape, he had possessed himself of her hand and, hooking his arm through hers, held it so tightly that it was all she could do to keep from crying out at his strong grip. But she did not want to give him the satisfaction.

Instead, she pulled away from him and, under her breath, cried, "I will not marry you, I will not!"

He, on the other hand, seemed determined not to argue with her and, in response, said, "James and Mary are attending our nuptials. I have a special license from a bishop I am acquainted with, who happened to be staying in Cheltenham, and I know that your father approves of our marriage. All things considered, I think we have a fair chance at quite a happy future together. That is, of course, if you can learn to govern your tongue, my shrewish Kate."

The smile he cast her, his blue eyes full of summer, nearly undid her resolve, but she steeled her heart. After all, he could not actually force her to say her part in the ceremony. And with this thought, she relaxed a little until, as though reading her mind, he said, "I shall speak the bride's responses in our wedding, if necessary. I hope you understand that I simply cannot let you be so foolish as to ruin both of our lives."

They were just entering the village, and it seemed that word had spread of their forthcoming nuptials, since the little street was now lined with well-wishers. Kate grew quite pink at the sight of so many people, particularly when she had no intention of marrying the poet. But when many of the young girls began littering the cobbled street with yellow and pink rose petals, Kate knew a strong and sudden desire to bolt.

As they passed the Swan and Goose, the innkeeper cried, "That's the way, m'lord. Just drag her to the church! Though I doubt ye'll find much of heaven after." And the crowd about the inn broke into a great deal of laughter.

Lord Ashwell tipped his hat and said, "You are quite wrong. This woman shall be far more pleasant to me than the sweetest heaven I have ever heard described." At his fine words, the crowd cheered the viscount.

Kate wished that she might disappear or, at the very least, break from his stong grip and run into the hills above Chipping Fosseworth. This could not be happening to her!

She wished her mother were with her, to tell her what she must do. She saw the church tower appear, and a feeling of panic rose in her throat. To be married at all suddenly petrified her. She didn't want to marry anyone. And especially not this man beside her. Why, he was little more than a stranger! But he was not a stranger. He was Buckland, Ashwell, Cleeve. All one man, who had become so integral a part of her life, whose fate had been entwined with hers, just as he had said, so that she could not imagine her life without him. But, oh, that smug expression he wore! And her heart turned away from him.

Well! She would simply say to the vicar that she had been sorely used, that she did not wish to marry the rogue, that he had coerced her! She felt a hand grasp her free elbow and her father's voice penetrated into the tumult of her thoughts. "Don't be a fool, Kate." And then he released her arm and dropped back to resume his tracks with Mr. Slad. She looked back at him and saw that the entire village seemed to be following them. And as they neared the church, she heard the sweet strains of a very pretty harp flowing from the little stone building. The door was open, and as they crossed the threshold, the scent of jasmine and roses assailed her. The church was full of flowers and in front of the alter, dressed in a silk gown of light blue, stood Mary, bearing a large bouquet of late summer flowers that trailed a vast quantity of lavender, peach, and blue ribbons. James, a gentle smile on his lips, stood beside her.

"How very unfair of you, Ashwell!" Kate cried. "But if you think for a moment that I will submit to this scheme, simply because my dearest friend stands there"—she found tears biting her eyes and held them back—"you are greatly mistaken."

But he pulled her down the aisle where Mr. Dyrham, the vicar, stood in clerical robes, shifting uneasily upon his feet. He was a tall, thin man and had known Kate Draycott from the time she was born. He could not like the arrangements Lord Ashwell had made, but as he regarded Kate's rather impassioned countenance, he wondered how else a man would bring such a spirited female to the altar.

When they were halfway down the stone aisle, Ashwell stopped suddenly and turned to Kate, grasping her by the shoulders. In a low voice, so that no one could hear, he said, "I could have wooed you for the next year, but damnit, Kate, I did not want to wait that long for your pride to heal. I was wrong. I admit it, but you must forgive me."

Kate said in a quiet voice, her vision blurred with tears, "I can't forgive you, you blackguard."

And then he did the most wretched thing, dropping on his knee before her and kissing her gloved hand. He said, "I love you. I beg you to forgive me."

Kate bent slightly down to him, grabbing at his hands. She felt panicked again and cried, "Oh, do get up! What are you doing?"

And again he kissed her hand. "Will you do me the honour of becoming my wife?" And when she still did not speak, he quoted Shakespeare, *"Is not this well? Come, my sweet Kate. Better once than never, for never is too late."*

Kate turned to him and, in a desperate manner, as though she were a caged beast, looked wildly about the few assembled attendants—James, Mary, the vicar, her father, Mr. Slad. Her father's words came back to her, that Ashwell would not ask again. And then Sir William stepped through the door, his hat in hand, his face solemn. He did not try to approach them but gave her an encouraging, serious nod. He did not even smile. She remembered, as in a flood, everything he had said about her mother and her own stubbornness. She looked down at Ashwell, who had so wretchedly humbled himself on his knee—his knee! "Oh, George, I am such a stupid female. Are you certain you want to marry me?"

He rose slowly and gathered her in his arms, completing everyone's embarrassment by kissing her quite thoroughly even before the ceremony had actually begun. Only after the vicar had coughed a third time did he release her and gently lead her to the altar. In a whisper, he said, "*My sweet Kate, my bonny Kate, Kate the curst . . .*"

SURRENDER YOUR HEART
TO CONSTANCE O'BANYON!

MOONTIDE EMBRACE (2182, $3.95)

When Liberty Boudreaux's sister framed Judah Slaughter for murder, the notorious privateer swore revenge. But when he abducted the unsuspecting Liberty from a New Orleans masquerade ball, the brazen pirate had no idea he'd kidnapped the wrong Boudreaux—unaware who it really was writhing beneath him, first in protest, then in ecstasy.

GOLDEN PARADISE (2007, $3.95)

Beautiful Valentina Barrett knew she could never trust wealthy Marquis Vincente as a husband. But in the guise of "Jordanna", a veiled dancer at San Francisco's notorious Crystal Palace, Valentina couldn't resist making the handsome Marquis her lover!

SAVAGE SUMMER (1922, $3.95)

When Morgan Prescott saw Sky Dancer standing out on a balcony, his first thought was to climb up and carry the sultry vixen to his bed. But even as her violet eyes flashed defiance, repulsing his every advance, Morgan knew that nothing would stop him from branding the high-spirited beauty as his own!

SEPTEMBER MOON (1838;, $3.95)

Petite Cameron Madrid would never consent to allow arrogant Hunter Kingston to share her ranch's water supply. But the handsome landowner had decided to get his way through Cameron's weakness for romance—winning her with searing kisses and slow caresses, until she willingly gave in to anything Hunter wanted.

SAVAGE SPRING (1715, $3.95)

Being pursued for a murder she did not commit, Alexandria disguised herself as a boy, convincing handsome Taggert James to help her escape to Philadelphia. But even with danger dogging their every step, the young woman could not ignore the raging desire that her virile Indian protector ignited in her blood!

Available wherever paperbacks are sold, or order direct from the Publisher. Send cover price plus 50¢ per copy for mailing and handling to Zebra Books, Dept. 2625, 475 Park Avenue South, New York, N.Y. 10016. Residents of New York, New Jersey and Pennsylvania must include sales tax. DO NOT SEND CASH.

TURN TO CATHERINE CREEL—THE REAL THING—FOR THE FINEST IN HEART-SOARING ROMANCE!

CAPTIVE FLAME (2401, $3.95)

Meghan Kearney was grateful to American Devlin Montague for rescuing her from the gang of Bahamian cutthroats. But soon the handsome yet arrogant island planter insisted she serve his baser needs—and Meghan wondered if she'd merely traded one kind of imprisonment for another!

TEXAS SPITFIRE (2225, $3.95)

If fiery Dallas Brown failed to marry overbearing Ross Kincaid, she would lose her family inheritance. But though Dallas saw Kincaid as a low-down, shifty opportunist, the strong-willed beauty could not deny that he made her pulse race with an inexplicable flaming desire!

SCOUNDREL'S BRIDE (2062, $3.95)

Though filled with disgust for the seamen overrunning her island home, innocent Hillary Reynolds was overwhelmed by the tanned, masculine physique of dashing Ryan Gallagher. Until, in a moment of wild abandon, she offered herself like a purring tiger to his passionate, insistent caress!